SAFE SEX

William Edgar Boggan was born and
raised in the US Army, where his father
served for twenty-six years. As a child
he lived in Germany and throughout
the American South. He began writing
in high school and studied English and
American literature at Furman University. in South Carolina. After college
he worked as a carpenter and a mental
health attendant, then went into pub-
lishing. He has worked as an editor,
writer and designer on numerous print
and on-line publications, and now works
as a freelance writer and editorial con-
sultant. He lives in Atlanta.

SAFE SEX

William Edgar Boggan

FOURTH ESTATE • *London*

First published in Great Britain in 1996 by
Fourth Estate Limited
6 Salem Road
London W2 4BU

A catalogue record for this book is available from
the British Library.

ISBN 1–85702–506–7

Typeset by Palimpsest Book Production Limited,
Polmont, Stirlingshire
Printed in Great Britain by

This book is for Marian Young.

'Nothing is difficult to the one who has persistence.'

We are punished by our sins, not for them.
Dennis Murray, in conversation

ACKNOWLEDGEMENTS

The author would like to thank the following people, without whose assistance and support, *Safe Sex* would not have been possible:

Carol Lee Lorenzo; Mark Hodges; Wes Holden; Diana Margaret; Charlie Smith; David Shaw; Bill Sadler; Steve Thomas; Malcolm Kudra; Susan Andrews; Sean Hannity, Eric Stanger, and Mike Lawing of radio station WGST, Atlanta, Georgia; Gary Gaddy; Lee Weisbecker; Will Blythe; Stosh Ostrow, MD; Daniel J. DeNoon; Zenda Bowie of the American Lung Association of Georgia; Mary Ann Sumrall, MD, of the Fulton County Health Department; James Brawner, MD; Lee B. Reichman, MD, executive director, National Tuberculosis Center, University of Medicine and Dentistry of New Jersey, Newark, and the national tuberculosis hotline (1–800–4TB-DOCS); Thomas J. Warner; James Adams; Lt Col Edgar W. Boggan, USA (ret.); William Wilson, Robert Smith, MD, and our circle of mutual friends.

SAFE SEX

Chapter 1

I was living on the edge of Midtown then, and the apartment overlooked the big park and I slept on a pallet in the sun room. I would get up at dawn and have coffee watching the horse patrol take their morning constitutional, the white helmets bobbing side by side in twin lines through the morning fog. The fog would lift as the morning came on: the sun would burn it off the land and the park was green with spring and even the air seemed clean and nothing would ever die.

Then I would write for a couple of hours, and I would take a shower and go in to work on the magazine. The magazine paid for the writing that I did, it had bought the little computer that I worked on, and it paid the rent and the groceries. But mainly it bought the time to write.

I had wound up in Atlanta after I quit school in DC, after the accident. I had lived off my parents for a while, and I had tried to write at home, in a little studio I had set up like my father's, and I had liked it, it had been a dream. But I decided I needed to be someplace real, which meant a job doing something for my own money and a place of my own. I was scared of New York and DC was failure to me, but I knew some people in Atlanta; that is, I knew Corey Holland from school.

Corey Holland was a Young Republican headed for Harvard law school with whom I'd got drunk one night when I was supposed to be reading about the origins of the Vietnam War. He had knocked on my door with a bottle of bourbon and two glasses, looking for my roommate Kelsey to drink with, but Kelsey had been out and I had not wanted to read the book anyway.

'Fall's a crock of shit,' said Corey Holland, shaking his head at the book. 'He's nothing but an apologist for communism.' He would come back to this from time to time as we sat drinking in my room, it seemed important to him that I agree to his proposition about Fall, and it did not matter to me, I said I supposed he was right, and Corey Holland paused, and looked at me and said, 'You're an intelligent boy.'

What made me a boy and him a man I don't know, unless it was the Republicanism, or maybe, I remember thinking at the time, it was my name, *Willie*, like Willie Yeats and Willie Morris, my father always told me, but like some southern punk, I thought, *Willie Boy*,

Willie Stark, *Willie* hanging around the pool hall with the big boys. But, anyway, Corey Holland liked me and he was from Atlanta, so when I thought of running away there, I called him at school. He listened to me talk it all out, and I listened to the hollow, echoing sounds of the dorm behind him on the hall phone and I felt lost a little, like I should have been in school and couldn't be there, like a displaced person, and I felt the pressure of time, to hurry up and get somewhere and do something, before my time was all used up.

'Sure,' Corey Holland had said, and I could see him nodding and see his confident, young Republican face as he said the words, 'I can put you in touch with the right people.'

The right people had been a small publisher on the north side and a landlord in Midtown. I stayed at a motel outside of town on the interstate, and when I was registering I stopped, with the ballpoint in my hand, and I changed my name, from Willie to Wiley, like Wiley Post, the aviator who flew Will Rogers into oblivion in 1935. From childhood, I remembered pieces of a TV documentary on Rogers, with film clips of Post looking quite dashing with a black patch over one eye, a pilot in a time when flight was romantic, and standing there at the motel desk I decided I was Willie no longer, I would be Wiley now, and so I signed my name, *Wiley Jones*.

And I interviewed for a job at the publisher's. I had a résumé for William Jones that listed the journalism awards I had gotten as a freshman and a letter of introduction from Corey Holland's father, and I interviewed with the general manager, a woman named Patricia Patterson who wore her grey hair pulled back tightly into a bun and dressed in a grey pants suit with a white silk blouse.

She was having trouble with her computer when I got there, and a young man with a beard and longish hair parted down the middle bent over her shoulder and pecked at her keyboard and watched her screen and stroked his beard. He looked up at me as I came in and he smiled. Patricia Patterson frowned at him and said, 'Is it a virus?'

He looked down at her, and he said, 'You've got a circular reference in your worksheet, Patricia. It doesn't like it when you think in circles.'

She patted the desk beside her anxiously with an open hand, she said, 'Can you fix it?'

He smiled, he said, 'Sure. Let me get a copy of it, and I'll figure it out in my office.'

He got what he needed on to a floppy disk and left us; and Patricia

2

Patterson began to talk to me. She smoked cigarettes the whole time we talked, constantly, the way my mother smokes, in little white plastic filtered holders that were part of some plan to quit smoking by weaning herself off the nicotine. Her lipstick was deep red and it came off her lips on to the end of her cigarette holder.

She talked on and on about the company and the benefits and the job in Editorial, and I almost quit listening to her, gazing just to the left of her talking head and out her office window at the little airport where the office was located, at a row of small private planes lined up alongside the runway, and I thought of flying. I thought of Wiley Post and the old song *Some glad morning when this world is over, I'll fly away.* I felt my eyelids heavy after lunch in the warm afternoon, and I snapped back just as her red lips parted and closed on the white cigarette holder and she drew smoke and blew it out across the desk in a thin stream, and she said, 'Do you think Brackett Data sounds like your kind of place?' She smiled a little, meaningless smile, appropriately timed and insincere; you could tell that she did not smile much or easily.

'Yes, ma'am,' I said, and I smiled at her.

She set aside the Holland letter and picked up the résumé. She said, 'Well, you certainly sound like someone Brackett Data could use.'

'Thank you.'

Still looking at the résumé, she said, 'I didn't get into this sort of work until I was at least a junior.'

'I was in an accelerated program.'

'"For the gifted," it says here.' She lifted the résumé just off the surface of her desk.

I said, 'Yes, ma'am.' The gifted part was always difficult for me, I don't know why. I enjoyed being the smartest person in the room, but the feeling that I got whenever I talked about it with someone seemed to be that I shouldn't take such pleasure in it, I should want to be more average, and I didn't, I never wanted to be one of the boys.

She set the résumé aside and said, 'The position is associate editor. I didn't become an associate editor until I'd worked here over five years.'

I thought, *But you weren't gifted, were you?* But I said, 'It must be a position of some responsibility.'

'It is,' she said. 'Do you feel ready for it?'

I said immediately, 'I have always risen to the task before me.' I felt like we were playing chess and I was black, on the defence, and I wondered if it was just an interview style or if she was always playing with the people there.

She said, 'Yes,' and smiled her difficult smile again, and she said, 'Well, then, I don't see how we can say no to someone with your obvious qualifications.'

And I thought the gifted part had done it for me again, but I was wrong, I would find out later.

Then Patricia Patterson walked me through the office and showed me where everything was, introduced me to the other people who worked there. 'This is Wiley Jones,' she would say to them, and it felt strange to be called by the new name, it felt subversive. 'He's our new junior editor.' The women would smile as I sized them up, there was one good-looking blonde there, young, with moist soft pink dream lips that made me feel like kissing and sex, and the men in bright ties and white shirtsleeves would smile too and shake my hand strongly, and towards the back of the building, at the end of a long unlit hall and through a door marked CIRCULATION and into a dim room lined with boxes and stacks of magazines and books, was a young black man with his hair in dreadlocks in a T-shirt that said UHURU! who looked at me uncertainly yet not without a certain savvy feel to him, and I knew that he alone in all the company was sizing me up, and he said, 'Hey, bro.' I thought I was OK with him, he said, 'Welcome.' At last she took me to the publisher's office. We stood in the open doorway of a long room with a desk at one end and a small conference table at the other. A map of the United States covered the opposite wall. It was a quiet moment for Patricia Patterson, as if we were at a special place, like Kennedy's grave or the tomb of the Unknown Soldier, and we were supposed to be respectful here: no picnicking allowed in the cemetery.

There was no one inside. Patricia Patterson stood beside the open door with her hands together and she said, 'Mr Brackett is out of the office in the afternoons. He goes to the radio station, and after that, he works at the remote.'

I nodded, I had no idea what she was talking about, but I was obviously supposed to understand, so I made the moves of understanding.

'He'll see you the day after you start,' she said.

I said, 'When will that be?'

'We need you to start tomorrow if you can,' she said, with a look at me to confirm this. 'Sure,' I said.

I drove into town from Brackett's place, and managed to get lost

4

for a while in what they call the Morningside neighbourhood, and then I saw a woman gardening on her front lawn and asked her for directions and so found Midtown, Fourteenth and Piedmont, and met with the landlord, a little Sephardic Jew, Corey had told me, named Garcia, who owned several properties in the area.

We stood in the gravel parking lot behind the building and shook hands. 'This is going to be *the place* to live in a few years,' said Garcia, and he waved a hand at the building behind him. The back was a pale shade of landlord green and had metal fire stairs painted silver running up the corners to metal decks outside the back doors of the apartments. A red-haired woman walked out on one of the decks in a short, dark blue bathrobe that showed off her legs. I looked up and smiled at her: they were good legs, her hair hung down wet and red all around her white face and she drank coffee from a blue cup and I thought she looked back at me. The green and silver glowed around her under the grey March sky.

Garcia walked me inside one of the back doors and we stood at the bottom of a stairwell. 'We're going to fix this all up,' he said, and he gestured again, this time at the stairwell. Someone had painted a Day-Glo hand on the wall, pointing up the stairs beneath the word UP, and an empty whiskey bottle and some beer cans lay in one corner. The street doors were nailed shut. He pointed up and I followed his finger, UP, and saw the stairwell light, a single bulb hanging bare at the end of a line three floors up. 'We're going to put chandeliers in here,' he said.

I said, 'Have these always been apartments?' and I gestured at the Day-Glo hand.

He shook his head. 'It was a halfway house before we bought it. It just didn't work out that way. The neighbourhood's just too Midtown.'

Even though the neighbourhood was just too Midtown and because they had not put chandeliers in and because it would be a few years before this would be *the place* to live, I could afford the rent. Garcia showed me a place on the top floor on the Piedmont side of the building and I wrote him a checqoue. He walked me to his car and gave me a key that he took from a large ring in the glove compartment. In the back seat was a big sign that said REMODEL YOUR OWN APARTMENT.

'We're going to put that up next week,' said Garcia. 'As soon as we can get somebody to hang it.' He looked me up and down. 'Say,' he said, 'you don't know anything about building maintenance, do you?'

5

I shook my head. 'No, sir,' I said.

He said, 'Take it out of the rent, if you did.'

'Sorry,' I said and I smiled at him, 'I can't help you.'

He shrugged. 'I don't know anything about building maintenance, either,' he said. 'I just buy and sell the places. We'll fix this place up. Sell it. Buy another.'

I had next to nothing to move into the place, so I went to the Starvation Army and bought some furniture, an easy chair and a small desk, a student's desk, really, a desk for a kid, and a chair to go with it and an old floor lamp. I got a pallet to sleep on from an alternative design store, and the bathroom stuff at a K-Mart. I still wrote on a typewriter then, a second-hand Olympia portable that my father had brought back from Vietnam.

The first night at the place was difficult. I was alone in a way I hadn't been before, staying at the motel out on the interstate. They had room service there and people in the night, the night man on the desk, you could step outside your room in the dark and see bright blue neon and white fluorescence that said you were not alone, that said there was some kind of an American promise somewhere out there that if you did just the right thing, or did it often enough, you would never have to die, you would live for ever, like Mickey Mouse or dead Elvis or the assassins on the grassy knoll, suspended for ever and ageless, forever young in a history outside of history. That was what I thought of, lying in the little sun room with the stars shining through the phone lines out the window overhead, I thought of that kind of freedom.

If you want to know the truth, I was just freaked. I don't know how my father would say it if he were writing about it for the newspaper or one of his books, I don't know how to *put it into words*, but I was freaked. I had never been this alone before. I didn't have a phone to call home on, I was parentless and anonymous and living under an alias in a big city that I did not know, I had a job, I was supposed to show up tomorrow morning and do something, it wasn't a class in college, and the people only knew my job description, no one knew me, what I was really doing, writing the book, and I wondered if I had the nerve to tell them: that would make it real, to tell them, that would put it into time and out in the open where they might ask to see it or they might say, 'How's the writing going?' and then I would have to talk about it. Until I told them it could remain a dream of freedom, but once spoken of it became an earnest gamble, with a point and a result, and I would be real along with it, or else not real, and so the book had to work it had to make me Wiley Jones, not Willie but Wiley, and I was alone then, with the book, with the story, and without anyone who knew me, and I wished someone knew me, I wanted there to be someone somewhere who understood me and could explain me to myself and tell me I would be all right. And all I had was Corey Holland's father, who did not know me at all, bogus letters of introduction, addressed to people who knew me even less.

I rolled over on my pallet and lay with my head on my arms trying to sleep wide awake. After a while, I got up and put on my robe, and walked into the kitchen and poured myself a shot of vodka from the refrigerator and stepped outside on to the landing and drew a deep breath of the cool night air.

I heard people down below me, and I stepped softly, barefoot, to the edge of the landing and looked down towards the sounds and saw the red-haired woman at the door of her apartment, embracing a black guy in a suit, they were absorbed in each other under the dim light that shone from the fixture above her door. She lifted her leg up the side of his thigh and he slid his hand up her dress and lifted the hem above the top of her stockings, her skin was white as snow and she wore no panties, and he slipped his fingertips inside her and she moaned and reached down between his legs and stroked him up and down, and I got hard, watching his hand darkly stroking across her white ass, and, I looked at her red hair curling down around her shaking head and across her shoulders like fire, and I wanted to have her, too, I wanted to escape into her flesh, into some woman, and there was no woman there.

She reached out a hand and opened her door. It swung open slowly into the dark kitchen.

I turned away from them and drank all my vodka at once, it burned my throat and stomach, I wanted it to burn the desire out of me, and I went back inside to the sun room and turned on the light and sat down at my kid's desk and took the cover off the typewriter and put some paper in and began to write. I wrote about the light at the motel on the interstate and what it seemed to say to me. I could look out the window of the sun room and see the same kind of light shining from the street lamps, but here and now it seemed to say only lonesomeness and anonymity, over and over down the street. Everything was still in the shaded park. The traffic was light and listless and lonesome-sounding, so I did not look out the window, I looked inside and back instead and I tried to write about that promise that I had sensed, out there on the highway, I tried to write about that light.

7

Chapter 2

I didn't write on the typewriter much longer, I got the computer instead, I got it from Brackett, from the systems manager's supply of old equipment. His name was Stan, and he had been the man in Patricia Patterson's office the day I interviewed, he said, 'You write on a *typewriter?*' and he shook his head. He stroked his beard, thinking, and he said, 'No, man. We've got some stuff around here you can use,' and he took me from my office to the systems room, to a door in the back corner and into a deep closet lined with metal shelves. He turned on the single bulb in the closet. 'A lot of this is old CPM stuff,' he said, looking up and down the shelves, stroking his beard, putting the system together in his head, 'but we've got some DOS stuff in here, too.'

'Here!' he said, and he pointed to a machine sitting on the top shelf. 'Just the thing for a first novel,' he said. 'An 8088 the first PC.'

He reached up and hauled it all down on to the bottom shelf. He got the monitor from the shelf and set it beside the system unit. 'We've got some cables around here somewhere,' he said, then pointed to the back corner, 'in that box over there. We'll load it into your car.'

'Are you sure it will be all right?' I said.

'Sure,' he said. 'Just don't tell Matt I loaned it to you.' He looked at me then smiled and said, 'That's something you'll hear a lot around here: "just don't tell Matt",' and he stroked the ends of his moustache and smiled. He turned back to the shelves. 'There ought to be a printer back here, too,' he said, and he reached up to the top shelf again and got down another piece of equipment. 'This is only a nine-pin,' he said. He set the printer with the other stuff. 'But this ought to get you started.'

'Thanks,' I said.

'No problem,' he said. 'I just hate to see people working on *typewriters.*'

We carried the equipment down the hall together and out the back, running into Patricia Patterson in the main office. Stan smiled at her and said, 'Setting Wiley here up to work at home.' She nodded and said, 'Just don't tell Matt,' and Stan looked at me, *See?* his eyes smiled.

When I got back to my office, the pink dream from the day

before was waiting for me, leaning on the corner of my desk. She stood up as I came into the doorway, and she smiled. 'Hi,' she said, 'I'm Nickie. I'm Matt's secretary.'

'I'm Wiley,' I said, stepping into the office. 'It's good to meet you.'

'I'm sure,' she said, and she looked at the computer. 'Matt wanted me to show you a few things about the office system, since Grant's out of town with him today.'

'Grant?'

'Grant Cummings, the editor-in-chief. He'd show you this if he were here.'

'No one's here?'

'Just you in Editorial, today,' she said.

'That must be why Patricia wanted me to start today.'

Nickie smiled. 'Patricia's paranoid. She'd want somebody to be here if they could. She'd want somebody to pick up the phone and say "Editorial!" even if that's all they knew.'

I stepped closer and I could smell her, she wore oil of drakar. My senior year of high school I had obsessively dated a girl who bathed in the stuff. Anne Mathers. Anne Mathers would do everything but fuck me. She would always say, 'I can't *do it* with you,' just before she made me come, and I kept coming back to her, of course, enslaved to her play, because I could not believe there was not an implied promise that she would *do it*, eventually, and that *it* would be better than any other girl's, because all her foreplay was so masterful, because she was so good at making me helpless. But she never did *it*, she just talked about it while she masturbated me. So that smell meant sexual play to me, and helpless craving, and I began to wonder about Nickie, and what her tease was like and if she were teasing me now, in a pale pink suit with her ash blonde hair and pink lips and pink nails shining on the edge of the desk.

'I think I can handle answering the telephone,' I said, and I smiled back at her.

'I'm sure you can,' she said. 'But Matt wanted me to show you the office system, so you could read the magazines, and he wanted me to show you ProComm, too, so you could take a shot at some of the work.'

'Oky,' I said, and turned to the computer against the wall. 'Do I sit here?'

'That'll get us started.'

She typed for me, leaning over my shoulder and filling my head with her scent, and I looked up at her face in profile beside me and I thought we had definite possibilities, Nickie and I. '"Wiley Jones",' she said, 'that's your user name. And now we type Y to log on as a new user. Stan's already got you in the user data base.' She stood up. 'Now choose a password. I won't watch.' She turned away from the console.

I looked at the waiting prompt for a second, my mind full of sex and oil of drakar, I was very far from the office, and I typed REDHEAD. Nothing displayed when I entered the word, and the system asked me to confirm the selection by re-entering it. I typed REDHEAD again, and I thought about the black man's hand moving dark across the woman's smooth white ass. 'OK,' I said.

'Good,' said Nickie. 'Now you want P for ProComm.'

'What's Finder?' I said, and I pointed to the F selection on the menu.

'That's the search program. It's $150 per query.'

'That's a lot,' I said.

'It's Matt's profit centre,' she said. 'Matt likes his profit centre.'

'I can imagine.'

'Anyway, you get a package from PR Newswire once a week,' she said. 'For the news section. Have you used a modem before?'

'What's a modem?' I said.

She laughed a little. 'It's really simple,' she said. 'It's all automated, so you don't have to understand anything.'

'I like to understand things,' I said.

She gave me a curious look. 'Then you may not be very comfortable at Brackett Data,' she said. 'See where it says ProComm on the menu?' She pointed at the screen. 'That's what you want.'

I pressed P for ProComm, followed the instructions and the program loaded.

'Now press Alt-D,' said Nickie, 'to get the dialling directory.'

I pressed the keys and a screen of phone numbers appeared.

'See there, where it says CompuServe?' she said.

'Right,' I said, and I moved the screen highlight down to the CompuServe line and hit the enter key. The phone dialled, and the machine made noises, and then the program said **CONNECT** and began to beep at us.

'You're quick!' said Nickie, smiling.

'I'm Wiley,' I said, and I turned and smiled at her.

She smiled back, pleased, and I felt good. 'Hey, you're a fox! See?' she said, pointing at the screen again.

I read the message, `You have electronic mail waiting`. 'That's the copy from PR Newswire.'

'What is it?'

'Press releases.'

'About AIDS?'

'Right,' she said. 'You use them in the news section of *Survivor*. See the read option on the menu? Press that.'

More words scrolled on to the screen: `Message is binary`, they said, and another menu scrolled into view.

'There,' said Nickie, pointing. 'Download. That's what you want. You want to download the package.'

I pressed 7, to download, and a list scrolled up.

'CompuServe B-Plus,' she prompted me, and I pressed the corresponding number. Then the screen said, `Enter a filename for your computer`, and she said, 'It can be up to eight letters, followed by a period and a three-letter extension.'

So I called it `PR–AIDS.PKG`, and the download began, a little window opened and a bar graph grew rightward as the file was transferred.

Nickie said, 'You'll edit that. Matt said you're in charge of the news section.'

I said, 'I suppose I'll be doing a lot of reporting.'

She looked at me like I was a schoolkid. 'We don't do any original reporting here,' she said.

'What do we do, then?'

'We do PR Newswire,' she said, gesturing at the screen. 'We do press releases.'

I looked at her, and she smiled slyly very amused by my ignorance. I said, 'You like this, don't you?' smiling back at her.

'What?'

'Showing me the twisted ropes.'

She laughed. She said, 'You are wily.'

I liked her, I wanted to take her clothes off and see where else she was pink.

'Now do an Alt-F4,' she said, and I pressed the keys. The screen went black and the words appeared

      `Enter 'EXIT' to return to PROCOMM PLUS`
      `G:\PCPLUS>`

Nickie said, 'Now type *do* pr–aids. *pkg*.'

I did, and more words appeared.

```
copy pr-aids.pkg g:\wp\docs
1 file(s) copied.

g:
cd\wp\docs
pkunzip pr-aids.pkg
PKUNZIP (R) FAST! Extract Utility

Searching ZIP: PR-AIDS.PKG
Inflating: 05'04'91. DOC
```

I turned to her and said, 'What's PKUNZIP?'

She sighed; she'd explained this too many times before She said slowly, 'Zipping is a way of making a big file smaller.'

'OK,' I said.

'The people at PR Newswire zipped the file. That's like taking a big sheet of newspaper and folding it up until it fits in a number ten envelope.'

'I follow you,' I said.

'Now you're unzipping it.'

'Restoring it to the original size.'

'Right!' She smiled happily, I caught on fast.

I turned back to the computer screen.

```
                    exit
```

The screen went back to ProComm.

Nickie said, 'Now you can exit. Alt-X.' I pressed the keys and confirmed our exit. She went on. 'Now you edit that file 05'04'91.DOC in the word-processing document directory when you load Word Perfect. That's the W on the menu.'

'OK.'

'Right now you want L for Library.'

'I see how it works,' I said.

'It's intuitive,' she said, 'once you get past the front end.'

I watched the system work. 'So I can read back issues from the Library,' I said as a menu of magazine titles appeared.

'Yes,' she said. 'You want S for *Survivor*.' I pressed S. 'Of course,' she said, 'you miss the ads, reading the electronic version. They're the real meat of it.'

'The ads,' I said.

'Yes,' she said, and she looked at me. 'It's really all about the ads.'

'It's sure not about the writing,' I said.

She shook her head, and I liked the way her hair fell gently around

12

her face. 'It's advertising,' she said. 'Controlled circulation. Do you know what that is?'

I did, but I wanted her to stay longer, so I shook my head.

She said, 'That means Matt gives it away free, to people on mailing lists that he buys. And he can sell ad space on the basis of the number of readers he's got. See? They don't subscribe, so he controls the circulation.' She looked at me to see if I was following her, and I nodded. 'Actually,' she said, turning back to the computer, 'it's more complicated than that. He controls the circulation because he'll only give away *Survivor* to what they call "qualified" subscribers.'

'Who's qualified?' I said.

'Crazy people,' she said, and there was an edge in her voice. She was bothered by *Survivor*, she was bothered by being here.

'Why do you say that?' I said.

She sighed. 'It's hard to explain.' She held her hands up empty before her, full of an explanation she could not express; she let them drop and said, 'A qualified subscriber is a doctor, or a pharmacist, or an insurance company, or a stockbroker, or a drug company, or a researcher.' She looked at me again: did I understand? I looked back at her, waiting for the rest of it. Her delicate shoulders rose and fell a little sadly, the gesture touched me, all this hurt her, and she said quickly, in a rush, 'A qualified subscriber is anyone who makes money off AIDS.'

She was looking at me like I might think it was all her idea, personally, and I wanted to reassure her. I said, 'I think I see what you mean.' She relaxed a little, and I asked, 'How about people with AIDS? Are they qualified?'

She closed her eyes tightly, as if she felt a headache coming on, then opened them again, looked at me steadily and said 'No.'

My eyes fell to the floor as I thought about it. I said, 'I think I've got it.'

She said, 'We're all looking for other jobs.'

I looked at her, I wanted to get a job where she got one. 'It's not your fault,' I said.

'Thank you,' she said. She turned back to the computer screen that showed a listing of issue dates, she pointed at it and said, 'You pick a number and read it online.'

I looked at the numbers and nodded.

She said, 'But it's not about what it says. It's about the ads. That's why I brought you those hard copies.' She pointed to a stack of magazines on my desk, and I picked one up. The cover blurb said *You Need To Know: How To Spot the Carriers*, and I flipped the pages. I saw ads for home-test kits and drugs and blood treatments and disaster shelters and books about the millenaium. I closed it and put it back.

She said, 'We're just an advertising medium, really. Like the newspapers.'

'I like you,' I said suddenly.

That made her smile softly, I had told her she was OK. 'Why, thank you,' she said.

'You're welcome,' I said.

'You're all right, too,' she said. 'You're so innocent.'

I didn't know about that, I wanted to be hip. 'Is that good?' I asked.

She nodded. 'I don't trust guys who know everything.'

'I don't know everything,' I said.

'I know.' She laughed, and I laughed with her, I had made her laugh and I felt good.

'Well, you're set now,' she said, 'and I've got work to do.' She moved towards the door.

'Say,' I said, 'can I call you if I need you?' I smiled at her.

She looked pleased, but whether with herself, or me, or the two of us, I couldn't tell. She said, 'Sure.'

'*Survivor*,' I said. 'It's called *Survivor*. But there aren't any survivors, are there?'

She smiled at me softly, the way you might smile at talk about Santa Claus. 'As a matter of fact, there aren't.'

I said, 'Don't you think that's a little odd?'

'That's how Brackett Data looks at things,' she said, still smiling. 'And you might say Brackett Data is a little odd.' And then she left me.

Chapter 3

I met the redhead that evening. She parked next to me while I was unloading the computer equipment Stan had given me. She drove an old pink Mustang with a ragged convertible top, and she wore a pair of blue jeans and a yellow T-shirt that said *Venceremos!* in red script across her breasts, and I looked at her red red hair. She wore it up now, with strands hanging down here and there around her neck and ears, tiny green stone earrings nestled in her lobes and picked up the green of her eyes. She carried a briefcase, and I could smell her sweat faintly, a scent that made me think of her heat with the black man the night before, I wondered how she liked to be touched, and if she had any panties on today. I set the monitor on top of the computer beside the rear wheel of my car as she came walking around hers, and she stopped beside my tail-light, and smiled and said, 'Do you hack? Do you program?'

'No,' I said, smiling back quickly. 'I'm a writer.'

She said, 'Really?'

'Really.'

'What do you write?'

'I'm writing a novel. And I edit a magazine.'

'Really?' she said again.

'Really,' I said, and I smiled again. We stood there for a moment, like a couple of little kids, really, really, and I thought I liked her. 'I just moved in here,' I said.

'Yes,' she said. 'How do you like *the place*?'

I laughed. 'I can't wait for the chandeliers in the stairwells.'

She laughed with me. 'Really,' she said and she caught herself with the word again and laughed. She said, 'Garcia tells that to everybody who moves in here.'

'He's got a sign now,' I said.

'"Remodel Your Own Apartment,"' she said. 'He's had it up before.'

I said, 'My name is Wiley Jones.'

'I'm Alix Roberts,' and she held out a hand.

I shook it. Her skin was soft, but she was strong. I gestured at the computer and said, 'What about you, do you hack?'

'Yes,' she said. 'I'm sort of a writer too. Writing computer programs is a kind of writing, don't you think?'

'I couldn't say,' I said. 'I've never written one.'

'Then you wouldn't know.'

I tried it. 'I might like to find out, though.'

She smiled a little. 'Are you going to write your novel on this?' She gestured at the equipment.

'I'm going to try,' I said. 'You wouldn't want to help me set this up, would you?' I watched her hesitate, and I prompted her. 'I'll give you a cold beer.'

She smiled again, I liked her smile: her teeth were very white with her pale skin and her red red hair. She said, 'All right, let's do it.'

I carried the stuff upstairs and we set it up on one side of the sun room. She stood looking at the pallet under the other window, and I said, 'This is where I sleep,' and I felt suddenly risky, without knowing why, I had let her in close for a moment, and though I liked having Alix in my bedroom, I felt chancy and out there and unsure.

She said, 'It's cool in the sun rooms at night, they catch the breeze.' She stepped over to the computer on the desk and threw the red switch, and we watched it come on. She sat at the console and read the drive then said, 'It looks like you've got a word processor on here and a communications program.'

'We use that at work,' I said.

'A word processor?'

'A communications program.'

'Do you really?' She sounded interested by this.

'Yes,' I said. 'Can I do that sort of thing here?'

'If you've got a modem.'

'What's a modem?' I said.

She smiled at me over her shoulder.

She wasn't like Nickie, blonde and pink and delicate, and she wasn't like Anne Mathers, either; there was something real behind her tease. I liked her, her hair was red like fire and her skin was white like marble, she was these extremes and I wanted to travel into some extreme place with her. I wondered who the black man was and whether he would be back.

She settled herself at the console again and said, 'A modem is the hardware that physically connects you to the phone line.'

I said, 'Do I have a modem?'

'I don't know,' she said. 'Let's look inside.' She set the monitor to one side and opened the top of the machine with a little four-bladed screwdriver that she had on her key ring. I saw it and said, 'You're an engineer.'

'That's right.' She slid the cover off the unit and looked inside.

16

'There's your modem.' She pointed at a green-glass circuit board with something round on it that looked like a bell.

I said, 'Now if I only had a phone.'

'Aren't you getting one?'

'I've already got it, but they won't turn it on until tomorrow. My deposit's got to clear the bank.'

'It's hard to get them to extend you any credit when you live in the place here,' she said.

'But it's got atmosphere.'

She laughed and said, 'I knew something smelled around here.' She put the cover back on the machine, and tightened the screws, then set the monitor on top of it. She dusted it off with a yellow handkerchief from her hip pocket.

I didn't want her to go before I could find out about the black guy. I said, 'What about that beer?'

'Yes,' she said, 'what about that beer?'

I got two from the refrigerator and we sat in the sun room, looking at the park. She looked over her shoulder into the nearly empty living room behind us, and she said, 'You live simply.'

'Is that good?'

She sipped her beer. 'Engineers like simplicity.'

'Maybe I'm not simple,' I said. 'Maybe I'm just broke.' 'You're in the right place, either way.' She smiled.

'What about you?' I said. 'What's a bigtime engineer doing living at the place?'

She squinted at me a little then said, 'How old are you?'

'I'm twenty two,' I lied.

'And you edit a magazine.'

'OK,' I said, 'I'm the junior editor.' I shrugged.

She looked at me, she was measuring me. 'Were you trying to impress me?'

'Yes,' I said, I let her see some more of me, but I lost my breath a moment and covered myself with a drink of beer.

She sat back in the rocker, and held up her beer and picked at the corner of the label on the bottle. 'What's the magazine about?' she said.

'AIDS.'

'You're living in the right place, then,' she said.

'Why do you say that?'

'Didn't Garcia tell you?' She half-looked at me as she began to peel the label away from the bottle.

'Tell me what?' I said.

17

'What this place used to be.'

'He said it was a halfway house.'

'Halfway house,' she said, and she paused with her bottle. 'This was a hospice for people with AIDS.'

'A hospice?'

'You know.'

I said, 'A place to die.'

'Right.' She looked at me. 'Does that bother you?'

'I don't think so.'

'It's funny,' she said, returning to the bottle and peeling the label smoothly away from the sweating brown glass. 'They closed the hospice down, then two of the residents became tenants.'

'They moved in.'

'They never left.'

'That is funny,' I said. 'Are they still here?'

'They died a long time ago,' she said.

I saw the Day-Glo hand pointing up the stairwell, UP. I looked around the sun room: someone had died here.

Alix looked away, out the window. She watched something in the distance for a moment, and I followed her gaze to a flock of birds flying over the park. They circled together and roosted in a big oak tree. Then she turned to me again and asked 'What's wrong with college?'

'It's too academic,' I said.

She said, 'That's an answer to try on for size. What's really wrong?'

I nodded at the computer. 'I thought I'd see if I could really do it.'

'Write.'

'Yes,' I said. 'If I can do it, why waste the time in college?'

'That's more like it,' she said, 'but I still don't think that's quite the answer.'

I decided to tell her, but I wondered if she would understand. 'You want the answer?' I said.

'Sure.'

'I got scared.'

'Of what?'

'Dying,' I said.

'Are you dying?'

'No,' I said, 'not yet.'

'Not yet,' she said. 'But you're scared of it.'

'I have got to die some time,' I said.

'We all do.'

'But it's going to happen,' I said. She was like everybody else, it was just a word to her. 'It's going to happen to you personally.'

'You can't live thinking like that.'

'Why not?'

'You'd go crazy.'

'Maybe I've gone crazy,' I said.

She was looking at me closely now, she was interested, and I felt relieved to interest her. 'It's OK to be crazy,' she said and sat back in the rocker and rocked it once. 'What got you scared of dying?'

I drank some beer. 'I was in an accident about a year and a half ago.'

'You were hurt bad?'

'I broke my back.'

Her eyes widened a little. 'Jesus,' she said.

'And I broke broke both of my legs.'

'Jesus,' she said again. 'What hit you?'

'A car. A big white Ford Custom.'

She was looking at me again, waiting for me to go on.

I said, 'It was right before junior year was supposed to start. I was walking through Georgetown, on my way to see my faculty adviser. I was supposed to declare a major. It was a big deal.'

'Was it?'

'It was to my father. He wanted me to declare for journalism, like he had.'

'What did you want?' she said.

I smiled a little. 'English,' I said. 'If you let me, I'd just read all the time.'

'That's all right,' she said.

'We argued about it. He said you've got to make a living. And I hate that stuff, that practical kind of stuff.'

She laughed. 'Me too,' she said. 'Fuck it.' She drank her beer, smiling.

'So I was thinking about our argument, thinking about all that. I had a book of poetry with me, I took something to read in case I had to wait. I wasn't paying any attention, and I stepped out in the street against the light.'

'And it hit you?'

'Yes.'

'That's horrible,' she said. 'Were you conscious?'

'For a while,' I said. 'I lay on the ground and looked up at the grille of the car. It was huge over me and white, I remember noticing

19

that, the colour, or the lack of colour, and I looked beside me and I saw my book. It was open on the pavement, the pages turned back and forth in the air, slow, and I could see hundreds of tiny red spots across the printing, an accidental pattern like the background of a Japanese print, and then I realised that it was my own blood.'

She was fascinated. She said, 'How could you be conscious through all that pain?'

'I didn't feel the pain. Not right away. I felt a big numbness through my head, like I'd just been shot through with novocaine. I remember lying there and thinking that I couldn't feel anything and wondering if my spinal cord had been broken and trying to move my legs, and I couldn't move them, and I thought I was paralysed, and then the pain came, gradually at first, through the shock, and I knew I wasn't crippled, because I could feel all the broken things, and then I lost consciousness.'

I felt light through my guts as I told it, and my head felt dizzy, all floating on the cushion of the words of the horror, unreal it was now, as if it had happened to another body, not this one, to another me, it happened to Willie, not to Wiley, and yet it was there, too, immediate, as I told it, a frightening thing flooding over me. It was as if I had forgotten it, had let it slip out of immediacy with the healing and the passage of time, and now my words drew it back, and it left me breathless to talk about it.

She said, 'How long were you in the hospital?'

'A year.'

'A broken back.'

I drank some beer. I said, 'So after that it was hard to go back to school.'

'I can imagine it would be,' she said.

'I'd sit in classes, and I'd find myself thinking about lying in my hospital bed, I'd be thinking about my hospital room. It was a good room, it had a window with a tree outside. I couldn't listen any more. I started failing my classes, I couldn't listen, I was always checking my watch to see what time it was, to see if class was over yet, and it was never over soon enough.' I wondered how much she understood. Then I wondered how much I understood. I said, 'I had to have something real.' She was watching me closely, listening, I felt like I had her attention and I liked having her attention, and I saw the black man holding her, kissing her. 'How old are you?' I said.

'I'm thirty-two,' she said quietly. She set her beer on the floor, and lifted her hands to her head and undid her hair and let it down.

It fell around her face and shoulders, it shone like a cat's fur: she was beautiful, white and red. She shook her head and leaned and picked up the beer again and sat back and said, 'Is that too old for you?'

I said, 'Not at all. I can't wait to be thirty-two.'

'I'll bet you can't,' she said. She sipped the beer and looked at me. 'You're writing a novel,' she said. 'What's it about?'

I didn't know what it was about, but I wouldn't tell her that. 'It's a love story,' I said.

'You know about love,' she said.

I shrugged. 'Enough to write a novel.'

She nodded. She looked at me and said, 'You're precocious.'

'Is that good?'

She thought about it. 'Yes,' she said.

'You still haven't told me what you're doing here.'

'No, I haven't,' she said.

I smiled at her.

'I'm in jail,' she said and she stretched a little in her chair and sipped her beer. 'I landed on Park Place with four hotels and couldn't pay the rent. You know. Go to jail, go directly to jail, do not pass go, do not collect $200.'

'You're alone then,' I said. I didn't want the black man to be there. I didn't think he was or they wouldn't have been so hot in the doorway, they would have gone straight inside, but I didn't want him to be any sort of lover either, I wanted him to be someone casual that she had picked up for a quick fuck and forgotten already.

'You are precocious,' she said.

'You're right.'

'Your beer is making me sleepy.'

'It does that on an empty stomach.' I wanted her to stay for dinner.

She stood up. 'I need to be going.'

I stood up with her and held my beer in one hand. I wanted her back. I said, 'Come back when I get the phone.'

She looked at me, she knew I wanted her to stay.

'To show me how the communications program works,' I said.

'Oh, sure,' she said. 'Sure. I'll show you how it works.'

'How to communicate,' I said.

She smiled at this, she said, 'I don't know if we'll get that real.'

'Could be,' I said.

She shook her head wryly. 'You never can tell.'

So I thought she had left it open between us. I walked with her to the back door and out on to the landing. I said, 'Are you sure you wouldn't like another beer?'

She smiled again, she knew what I wanted. She said, 'You are precocious.'

'I'm a writer.'

'Well, you go write something,' she said, 'on your new computer. I'm going to take a shower now, and eat something, and when you get a phone, we'll communicate some.'

'All right.'

She turned and went down the stairs to her apartment. I stood at the top of the stairs watching her, watching her hips move inside her faded blue jeans, and they were tight enough so that I could just make out the panty lines, and as I listened to her loafers ringing on the metal stairs, I told myself that if she didn't look back it was because she was thinking of the black guy, leaving me to call him and see when they could get together and be hot again and as her right foot hit the landing, her head turned slightly and she glanced over her shoulder at me. She smiled the slightest smile, she liked me watching her, and the black guy was all over. I was glad, she was sexy and she enjoyed it and I enjoyed it with her.

I went back into the sun room and sat down at the console, looking at the sharp little amber letters `C:\WP` against the black screen. I opened the bottom drawer of the desk, and got my manuscript and I started the word processor and began to enter what I had written. I sipped the beer and decided I would get a bookcase tomorrow. I would set the printer on top of it, and keep my writing on it. So I was excited: there was Nickie to be excited about and there was Alix Roberts, without her panties and with them, too, and here was this machine to write on that made the words come like a river and then moved them around on the screen like mercury, and here I was writing, I was living, just like a real writer.

Chapter 4

Early the next morning, Patricia Patterson came to my office. I was arranging my desk and looking now and then at a picture on the opposite wall I hadn't noticed before a man in a blue suit with a red, white and blue striped necktie stood in front of some government building downtown, looking like the personification of a creed or conviction beneath a sky-blue sky. I knew I had seen him someplace before. Looking at it, I realised I had seen this same guy in Patricia Patterson's office, and hanging on the walls in the hallways, and I guessed it must be Matt Brackett, in the flesh, so to speak. I rolled my chair from side to side behind my desk and watched his eyes in the photograph, following me.

Just then, Patricia Patterson showed up. She leaned in my doorway with a cigarette going in one of her little plastic mouthpiece things and she puffed on it and said, 'Matt will see you now.' She led me out of editorial trailing smoke behind her and through the main office to Mr Brackett's door, where she paused for a moment and looked me up and down. I let her look: it reminded me of the way my mother used to look me over just before I went out of the house on a date, and it struck me as natural that she would want me to look good, because, after all, she had hired me. Nickie sat at her desk, outside Brackett's door, slicing open the morning mail, and I looked at her steadily while Patricia checked me out. Then she turned and knocked on the door to Brackett's office. I heard him say, 'Come in.'

She opened the door and Followed me in. We stood at the end of the office beside the conforence table and the wall map of the United States.

She said 'Matt, this is Wiley Jones.'

He looked up from his desk, preoccupied with something, he frowned and he said, 'Have you taken care of the Anna Louis matter?'

Patricia looked a little flustered, she said, 'Not yet.'

'Why not?' he said, curt and bothered.

'I wanted to discuss it with you again.'

'What is there to discuss?' he said. 'Fire her.'

And the thought came immediately, *I'm next, it's a trap.* My stomach was empty and I felt light-headed and full of fear, the way I did when my father lost it drunk and came out of his studio

23

slamming the door in the middle of the night, about to be gored, about to be fired on my second day at work.

'I agree,' said Patricia, 'but there may be room for a civil rights complaint here.'

'What?' he said, even more angry. 'She's too skinny. Fire her.'

'That's just it,' said Patricia. 'I'm not sure that skinny is a firing issue.'

'I've been over this before,' he said. 'I can fire anyone I want for any reason I can think of and Anna Louis is too damn skinny to work in member services. The members don't like skinny women. She's depressing, she looks like she has AIDS. Hell, for all we know, she does have AIDS. She's got to go. Do it now.'

Patricia's eyes dropped to the carpet. She said, 'Yes, Matt.'

He looked at me as if he had just noticed me. His face softened a bit with curiosity and he said, 'Who did you say this was?'

Patricia said, 'Wiley Jones. He started yesterday in Editorial.'

'Certainly,' he said. 'I knew that.' He stood up behind his desk and extended his hand to me. I walked the length of the room and took it, my knees were weak and my stomach turned, I remembered Anna Louis from Patricia's hiring tour: she had worn a severe black and white suit, her clothes hung on her with a loose anorexic look, and her skin was whiter than snow. Her deep shining dark eyes were round and moist and lined with dark shadow, Gothic girl, and now she would stand in the line at the Department of Labour, and a clerk would say, *Reason for termination?* and Anna would cry out, *I look like I have AIDS!* I saw the starved girl weeping. Matt Brackett's hand was cool and firm. He smiled with perfect teeth against a golfer's tan and his hair was clear white, combed back. His suit was blue and his tie a deep red with tiny silver stripes against a white shirt, just like in the pictures. He said, 'Good to meet you at last.'

'It's good to meet you too, sir.'

'Call me Matt,' he said. He gestured towards a chair and said, 'Have a seat.'

I sat. Behind me, Patricia Patterson said, 'I'll be with Anna if you need me,' and I heard the door close softly.

Matt sat and smiled at me. I smiled back. A computer on a typewriter stand at his elbow displayed some sort of data base: titles and keywords and text in fields across the screen, with **FINDER** in bold white letters on a purple band across the top. A clear pitcher of water stood on the desk between us, with two glasses. Matt poured some. 'Branch water?' he said.

24

'Thank you.'

He poured me a glass, too, still smiling, his teeth looked sharp.

'Pure water, the way God made it,' he said, and the water gurgled, filling the glass. 'The water of life.'

I took my glass and sipped. 'Quite refreshing,' I said.

A low, mahogany case to my right held about a thousand cassette tapes, and on top of it sat a black plastic deck and a walnut and aluminium reel-to-reel. I could see some titles printed in black capital letters on the spines of the cassettes: *The Wrong and the Right* and *Sex, Society, and Security* and *The Age of Impurity*. Most of the others had dates pencilled on them. Matt sat back and said, 'Did Nickie show you our system yesterday?'

'Yes, sir.'

'Call me Matt.'

'Sorry,' I shook my head at myself. 'Matt.'

'You're respectful,' he said. 'You were brought up right. I like that.'

'Thank you.'

'Patricia tells me you're taking some time off from school to see what the real world is like.'

'Yes, sir,' I said, 'I decided to test some of the theories.'

He laughed a little at this; it seemed to gratify something in him. 'That's good, that's very good. I like that. Put them to the acid test. Tell me, what year are you in?'

'I'm a sophomore,' I told him. 'A rising junior, actually.'

He sat back in his chair and thought a moment. 'When I was a sophomore,' he said, 'I campaigned for Richard Nixon. He was running against Kennedy then.' He smiled at this; he went back a long way. 'He should have won. He deserved to win. History would be very different had he won. But Kennedy's money bought the White House, that time. Never again, thank God.' He sat a little forward and his right hand formed into a fist on the desk.

'Yes,' I said.

'Matt,' he said.

I said, 'Yes, Matt.'

'That was a victory of appearance over reality, form over substance,' he said He expanded: 'Why, do you realise, that man used the highest office in this land to indulge in fornication with movie stars? Movie stars! Do you understand?'

I understood, I said, 'Yes, sir.'

'Matt,' he said shortly, and raised the glass of branch water and drained it. He folded his hands on the desk before him, and I noticed that the nails of two of his fingers were bitten down to the quick. He said, 'Disease is our subject here. Dis-ease,' he enunciated the two syllables distinctly. He went on: 'We minister to a mind and a body and a body politic all diseased, all dis-eased. Do you understand?'

I thought I was supposed to understand so I said, 'I think so.'

He said, 'I don't think you do.'

I said, 'No, sir,' and suddenly I just wanted to write the fucking novel, I didn't want to have to understand him. It felt warm in the office, close, then the air conditioning kicked on and I caught a whiff his aftershave, it mixed badly with the smell of my own, and I was hungry, I wanted to get out of there.

'Matt,' he smiled gently, and the finger went up again.

I felt slow, I said, 'Matt.'

He smiled bigger. He said, 'Modern life is a dis-ease. A continual unsettling. Whole peoples – our people – are given over in troops to dis-ease and death. Do you realise what is happening in Africa?'

'Sir?'

'Matt,' he smiled. 'Wholesale sexual suicide by the masculine members of a promiscuous culture that is too much like our own.' He looked at me as he paused to let the message sink in. Then he said, 'Like us: they can withstand neither their vices nor their remedies.'

I said, 'Yes, sir.' I remembered when my mother went through religion, sitting in church, waiting for the sermon to end. That had been just before she discovered Valium.

Matt smiled again, and leaned forward a bit and said softly, 'Did you know that in Africa they remove the woman's clitoris?'

'No, sir,' I said, and sweat broke out across my brow, my head lifted involuntarily, I was warm again and I tried to move my face further into the stream of cool air coming from the ceiling vent, but the air conditioning cut off and the room closed in snug around me.

He said slowly, 'The more to inhibit the wanton behaviour, you see. To soothe the dis-ease.'

I said, 'Does it work?'

'No,' he said quickly, and he slid his hands together again before him, the fingers tented together around each other, I noticed age spots on his well-tanned skin. He said, 'The black man is unfortunately limited by nature in his capacity to control himself, and it doesn't work.'

'I see,' I said. I was understanding things now.

'They are, however, the happiest people on earth,' he said, smiling at them over there in Africa, in Watts and Harlem; they sang the blues and danced. 'It's too bad we won't be able to save them from themselves.'

I said, 'I understand I'll be working on the news.'

He shook his head, 'Periodicals,' he said, and he turned and looked through a small stack of papers to his right, he pulled one from the middle and placed it before me to see. I leaned forward: it was an organisation chart, and his finger came out and pointed to a box near the bottom. *Wiley Jones*, it said, *Periodicals*. He said, 'I designed the chart myself.'

'I see,' I said, though I had no idea what doing periodicals meant.

He said, 'Periodicals expand our coverage while only marginally increasing costs.'

I knew this was supposed to interest me, I said, 'Really? How do you do that?'

'Libraries,' he said, 'instead of subscriptions.' He pointed at the data base and said, 'Finder here lists the articles, our circulation manager goes to Emory and photocopies them, you write them up. Let the alumni foot the bill.'

I said, 'Smart.'

'The circulation manager is our black staff,' he said.

'I remember meeting him,' I said.

'Fills orders, does errands,' he said. 'Quite capable, really.'

'I see.'

He smiled. 'I'm sure you do,' he said. 'You strike me as a bright young man.'

'Thank you,' I said, and I remembered it this time, 'Matt.'

He smiled bigger. 'That's it!' he said. 'What do you know about controlled circulation? Anything?'

'Sure,' I said,

'I did a study,' I said. 'It's covered in my résumé.'

'Yes,' he said, and he turned to the stack of papers again, found my résumé and read it over, he said again, to himself, 'Exceptional,' then looked up at me and said, 'Patricia tells me you're a friend of the Hollands.'

'I'm in school with their son,' I said.

'Intelligent bunch,' he said. 'They understand the nature of dis-ease. And they understand the importance of appearances and realities in treatment.'

I said, 'Treatment.'

The finger came up again. He said, "'Diseases desperate grown / by desperate appliance are relieved, / or not at all.' Hamlet said that.' He nodded, Hamlet was right again.

I said, 'Patricia didn't tell me you were a Shakespearean.'

'Found it in Bartlett's,' he said in a confidential tone. 'I use it on the radio show now and then. Intimidates the liberals, they never read anything written before 1960.' Sitting back in his chair, he said, 'Treatment. The liberals treat the disease with appearances of concern, but we will treat the soul dis-ease itself, soon. How will we treat it?'

He waited, and I realised I was supposed to answer, but I figured I wasn't supposed to answer correctly, and anyway, I did not know who *we* were. So I said, 'How?'

He pounded the desk once softly with his fist. 'With realism,' he said. 'That's real-ism,' he said, 'not liberalism or socialism or communism. Real-ism. Do you know what they're doing in Cuba?'

I said, 'I can't say I do.'

'Strict segregation,' he said. 'Private residences in private camps. None of this nonsense about rights. They take care of them there.'

'But they're socialists in Cuba, aren't they?'

'Yes!' he cried, and he pounded the desk again.

'Gives the lie to all their humanitarian claptrap, doesn't it? Why, they abort the foetuses of infected women. We can't allow that, of course.' He was the social scientist at work now, measuring out what could and couldn't be allowed. 'But Fidel has had a dose of real-ism: he knows his economy won't tolerate an epidemic of AIDS cases. There'd be revolution then, oh yes.' And he smiled, thinking of Fidel's impending revolt.

I sat there, wondering what the Cuban camps were like, waiting for the rest of it. I knew there was more.

'That's reality,' he said with a small wave of his hand, 'dollars and cents, dollars and *sense*.' He placed a finger aside his temple: 'that's the essence of real-ism, that's the *real* cost of AIDS. He italicised his words as he talked. 'Our investors column covers it,' he said.

'I saw that,' I said. 'I wasn't sure what it was.'

'Covers the standings of drug companies' stock,' he said. 'Important thing to know. You'll sometimes cross-reference a periodical review to the investors column. Clinical trials of vaccines and such. Brokers and financial analysts are among our qualified subscribers.'

'I see, sir,' and I did see, and he was *sir*, and I wondered if I wanted to stay at Brackett Data, I just wanted to pay the bills so I could write.

'Matt,' he said, in a low voice, as if it were a secret, he went on, 'There are people who would like to see operations like this one stopped.'

I said, 'Really?'

'The sort of people who voted for Jack Kennedy,' he said. 'Homosexuals, AIDS activists, leftists. The kind of people who voted for George McGovern.'

Now I knew who *we* were, and I wondered for an instant if I could pull it off here, he was Corey Holland writ large and I thought of my father, who had voted for George McGovern, I thought of what Matt might say or do if he knew about that.

'*Survivor* is read,' he said. '*Survivor* is one of the most widely read AIDS magazines in the country.'

'I had no idea,' I said; the idea repulsed me.

'A national distribution of 50,000, every month,' he said. 'And we don't pull punches like these other magazines, *AIDS* and *Behavioral Health*.' He frowned, *AIDS* and *Behavioral Health* incensed him. 'We call a victim a victim, by God. We label degenerates degenerate.'

I wondered if my name would be on the periodicals.

He sat back and looked at me, sizing me up. He said, 'I conduct many affairs from this central business – the radio show—' His hand rose into the air, the fingers spread apart, holding the many affairs gingerly – 'other things. If all works out well here for you, perhaps you'd care to aid me in some of those.'

'Whatever I can do to be of assistance.'

'I think you're going to be of great assistance, Wiley,' he said.

'I hope so,' I said, and I had no idea what I hoped, I recited my lines from the script I imagined in his head.

'Let's see what sort of job you do with periodicals,' he said, back to the business.

'When do I start?' I said. I thought periodicals would at least get me out of his office.

'Grant will show you,' he said. 'Have you met Grant Cummings?'

'No,' I said. 'Just Patricia, Stan and Nickie.'

'Grant is your supervisor, Grant Cummings, he heads up Editorial. He's been here a while. He understands our future potential.'

'Yes?'

29

He leaned forward and continued: 'I want you to think about the future at Brackett Data. I want you to think about us in terms of your future.'

'Mrs Patterson outlined the benefits.'

'But those are just the benefits,' he said, and he waved a hand at his computer. 'I want you to consider the future.'

'The computer,' I said, looking at the fields of data across his screen, wondering what reality they represented.

'Exactly,' he said, and he began to talk a little faster. 'In the future, everything will centre around it. Do you read *PC Magazine*? Print is dead. The book is over, finished, we live in cyberspace now. We're heading pell-mell towards the officeless office. Do you understand? Telecommuting. I do it. Eventually, you will, too.' He waved a hand again at his screen of data. 'The radio programme is an extension of that. The global village,' he said.

I said, 'I'll have to get Stan to show me more of our operation.'

'*Our* operation,' he said, and he smiled at me. 'I think you'll do fine here,' he said, and I thought the gifted part was seeing me through it.

I stood up with him and extended my hand. 'Thank you, Matt.'

'That's it!'

Outside the office, Nickie sat at the counter beside her desk, still opening mail. I leaned against the door and drew a deep breath and, with a will, relaxed my shoulders, I felt like I used to in the hospital when someone was examining me, like I was really having an out-of-body experience and couldn't feel the needles and the probes.

Nickie looked up at me and smiled. I smiled back as best I could and stepped over to her, I breathed in her scent and it carried me away from Matt.

'It's unnerving to talk to Matt,' she said, and cranked the lever down on the opener. 'Isn't it?'

'Yes, it is,' I said, and I laughed nervously.

'That's good, Wiley,' she said; 'to be able to laugh after an interview with Matt.'

I liked hearing my new name.

She said, 'Did he talk about telecommuting?'

'As a matter of fact, he did.'

'That'll be the day,' she said, and sliced open another letter, 'when he lets us work out of his sight.'

I looked at the door to his office. 'Can he hear you?' I said.

She shrugged. 'Who cares? I've been here too long.'

'How long is too long?' I said.

'Two years.' She pounded the letter-opener.

'That's not too long.'

'It is around here. 'Wait till you meet Cummings.'

'He's here today?'

'Baby,' she said and slipped another letter into the opener, 'he's been here for ever.' Her fist came down on the lever again.

'And how long is for ever?'

She stopped and looked at me. 'Long enough for Matt to trust him,' she said.

'He doesn't trust me?' I said.

She shook her head decisively.

'Why did he give me the job, then?' I asked.

She said, 'Because he had to.' She picked up the mail and began to sort it into piles. 'Because he can't do it all by himself. He would if he could, you know. He'd love that, hooked into some giant computer, all wired up with electrodes in his brain, cranking out this stuff month after month.' Her telephone rang, and she answered it. She looked at me and said, 'Yes, he's right here,' and she said, 'I'll tell him, yes,' and she hung up. 'That was Cummings,' she said. 'You're wanted in Editorial.'

I decided to try her. I said, 'Can I buy you lunch?'

She smiled. 'You are wily,' she said.

'You said it.'

'OK. Noon sharp, by the time clock,' she said with a slight smile, and I left her that way.

Chapter 5

When I got back to my office a guy in his middle forties with thick horn-rimmed glasses was waiting in my doorway. He smiled a kind smile and said softly, 'You must be Wiley.'

'Wiley Jones,' I said.

'Grant Cummings,' he said, he had one of the gentlest voices I'd ever heard. 'Editor-in-chief.'

He held out his right hand. It shook with fine tremors, the same way my father's did the morning after, and I took it, it was moist and warm. I wondered if he drank his coffee black, the way my father did, which jangled the nerves even worse, until finally he felt racked enough to take the first drink of the day. His hair was uncombed at the back and his pants were unpressed, and there was an old catsup stain on his blue and white tie. 'My office is right next door here,' he said, and he led me into it. He sat down at his desk, and produced a pack of little brown cigarettes from the clutter of papers and books and pulled a book of paper matches from his shirt pocket. He looked at me and asked, 'Do you smoke?'

'No, thank you,' I said.

'I shouldn't,' he said as he fumbled a cigarette from the pack and lit up. The flame trembled before the end of the cigarette. He waved the smoke away, then he looked at me again and said, 'Sorry I wasn't here to greet you yesterday.'

'That's all right,' I said. 'Nickie did a fine job of orienting me.'

'She's very efficient,' he said, 'and we were at an executive meeting of the Research Council.'

'What's that?'

'The AIDS Research Council,' he said. 'It's a group of AIDS businessmen Matt put together. What do you know about AIDS, anyway?'

I blinked. I said, 'I know how you get it.'

'Yes.' He nodded. 'And you know what to do about that.'

'Yes,' I said.

'Do you know where it comes from?'

'It came out of Africa, didn't it?'

'Out of Africa,' he said, and he turned and looked out the window of his office at the planes lined up for takeoff across the field. He said, 'Have you ever read that?'

'*Out of Africa?*'

He looked at me again. 'Then you *have* read it,' he said, his face brightening.

'No,' I said, 'but I've heard of it.'

'So few people read anything any more,' he said. 'Especially here.'

'I like to read,' I said. 'I'm writing a book.'

'Really?' he said, interested. 'About what?'

'It's a novel,' I said.

'I'll bet it's a love story,' he said.

'You're right.' I felt grateful for his approval, I wanted suddenly to write something he would like. 'I mean, I think it is.'

'A love story will sell,' he said. His right eyebrow rose significantly. 'You want to keep an eye to the dollar. All the great writers kept an eye to the dollar. James, Dickens.'

'Yes,' I said.

'You could say we keep an eye to the dollar here,' he said. 'We take a little different slant on things. Matt does. Have you met Matt?'

'I just came from his office.'

'I'll bet he talked to you about appearance and reality.'

'Yes,' I said, 'he did.'

'I had a professor in college who talked about that.' He turned and looked out the window again. 'He said it was Shakespeare's great theme. I can't really see Matt and Shakespeare together on anything, though.' He was talking out the window now, I felt like an eavesdropper. He faced me again. 'He didn't talk to you about the future, did he?'

'Why, yes, he did, there at the end,' I said.

'He did?' He sat up in his chair, surprised and obviously pleased. 'He got excited then. He must like you. That's a real plus. For us, I mean, for the editorial department. Of course, the editorial department is just me and you, but it's a plus, for once. He likes you. Matt likes you.'

'He talks about the future with people he likes?'

'It's a very good sign,' said Cummings. He sat gazing at me.

He took a puff on his cigarette, and said, 'How did you happen to apply for work here?'

'I was referred here by a friend.'

'A friend?'

'The Holland family.'

'Don't know them,' he said. 'I'm always curious about how people come to work here.'

'How did you come to work here?' I said.

His eyes betrayed surprise at the question. 'I was in upstate New York,' he said slowly. 'Working for a small publisher. It was a sudden thing. I had to leave suddenly, I had to arrange for employment quickly.' He took the cigarette from his mouth and smiled at me, there was something hopeful in the smile, some hope of understanding. 'I bought an Atlanta paper, because it was someplace far away.' He held his hands out palms up, empty, his fingers trembled slightly and his eyebrows rose. 'I saw this ad,' he said.

I felt responsible for him, I had asked the question that had got us here. I said, 'I see,' as if it were the only natural thing: he saw the ad, he got the job.

He put his hands together on the desk and he looked down at them. The cigarette smoke rose in a thin blue column, and he seemed to have strayed into some area of thought that held him. He coughed suddenly, his shoulders hunched and he coughed again and then he couldn't stop, he put his cigarette in the ashtray and he covered his face with his hands and coughed hard, with violence. With one hand over his mouth he reached to the bottom drawer of his desk and came up with a bottle of Vicks Day Care cough medicine. He opened the bottle of marmalade-coloured syrup and drank it like you would a Coke, great long swallows that you could watch take effect, easing him down from his fit and settling him. He set the bottle down and wiped his lips and said, 'Sorry. I've got a cold that just won't go away.'

I looked at the bottle of Day Care in his hand and wondered how much he went through in a week. It was one of the more ingenious drinking schemes I'd ever seen. He capped the bottle and put it to one side of his desk. Then he looked up at me again, his eyebrows rose, and he said, 'Yes, well. You were saying.'

'I was referred here.'

'By friends,' he said, and he smiled, he put the cigarette to his lips and drew on it.

I waited.

He looked away. He said, 'Did your friends tell you anything about Brackett Data?'

'No.'

He leaned toward me conspiratorially. 'Are you sure these people are your friends?'

This made me smile. I said, 'They're acquaintances, really.'

He sat back, his eyes closed for a moment, then said, 'I'm sorry.

34

That was out of line.' He opened his eyes, and they implored my understanding as he went on. 'It's just that Brackett Data takes a different slant on things.'

'Yes,' I said.

'You write,' he said. 'You think about the reader, surely.'

'Certainly.'

'Good,' he said. 'Good. We want the reader to like you.'

'Yes.'

He sat forward and looked at me; his eyes grew large and round. 'And who is the reader?' he said.

I shrugged. 'He's a hypothetical,' I said.

'Not here!' he said, and his eyebrows rose. 'Not at Brackett Data. Here he's The Reader.' He capitalised the letters with strokes of his cigarette. He said, 'He's Matt,' and he gave it another little touch with the cigarette.

'Matt?'

'That's right.'

I said 'What about your circulation?'

He sat back and waved his cigarette imperially. 'Leave it to the circulation department,' he said. 'This is Editorial.'

I said, 'Nickie showed me the Library yesterday.'

'You've seen the magazine, then,' he said, and he looked a little alarmed.

I said, 'I've read *Survivor*, yes.'

He swallwed and he looked at me and he said, 'Do you want to stay?'

'What do you mean?'

'You don't want to quit?'

I had been thinking about it, but I felt too lazy to go out and look for another job, and, then, sitting there, I thought that anywhere would be the same, doing something I didn't care about to finance something I did. So I said, 'Why would I want to quit?'

'A lot of people aren't too happy with the editorial slant around here.'

I shrugged again. I said, 'It's not my magazine.'

Grant Cummings smiled happily. 'That's the way to look at it.' He got up from his chair, and I rose with him, and he came around his desk and patted me on the back, he said, 'That's just the attitude to take.' We walked together back to my office.

'That was an interesting column about sex education in the latest issue,' I said.

Grant flushed and looked flustered, almost angry. 'Patricia Patterson made me write that,' he said.

'It said there's no such thing as safe sex,' I said.

We stepped into my office and Grant sat in the orange plastic chair across from my desk. He waved his cigarette in the air. 'Of course there's safe sex.'

'Well, of course,' I said. I leaned on the corner of the desk.

'But that's not the Brackett Data slant, you see?' His eyes narrowed and he looked at me closely. 'Here, there's no safe sex.'

'It usually is a risky proposition.' I thought I was being funny.

But he only shook his head. 'See,' he said, 'if there were safe sex, then it would be safe for the homosexuals, too. And we can't have that at Brackett Data. It's not like the movies here, let me tell you,' he said. He stopped suddenly and looked up at me, a little surprised. 'But I shouldn't be so negative,' he said, 'not when you're just starting.'

'It's all right,' I said. 'I like to know the score.'

'The score,' he said. He shook his head sadly and said, 'I wish I knew the score more often.'

'Maybe we can work on that.'

He brightened again. 'Yes,' he said, 'maybe we can.' He puffed on his cigarette, he said, '*We* – that has such a nice ring to it.'

'Yes, it does.'

'It's lonely here, sometimes,' he said.

'In the editorial department?'

'It's because we're not a profit centre,' he said.

I said, 'Nickie talked about that. Matt likes profit centres.'

He nodded, he said, 'Editorial isn't one, of course.' He leaned forward in a confidential pose. 'It could be one,' he said. 'I mean, I could make it a sort of personal profit centre, if I lacked principle.' He sat back. 'The way Matt does,' he said.

He made me curious. 'What could we do?' I said.

'We could trade editorial coverage for ad space,' he said quietly, in a tone I thought Matt might have reserved for a venereal disease.

'Oh,' I said. I'd heard a lot about this from my father, of course, and I was a little surprised at Grant, I thought everybody did it as a matter of course. I said, 'We wouldn't want to do that.'

'I should say not,' he said.

'What is a profit centre here?' I said.

'Oh, Finder!' he said.

'He mentioned Finder, and so did Nickie,' I said. 'What is it?'

36

'The data base,' he said. 'It's a search service for AIDS information. One hundred and fifty dollars per query. It's *the* profit centre.'

'I'll bet,' I said.

'Actually,' he said, 'Finder finances everything we do.'

'The magazines?'

'And the books, and the radio show,' he said. 'Only Finder makes real money. Without it, Matt would go broke.'

'Does he know that?' I said.

He frowned sadly and he said, 'It's difficult to say exactly what Matt knows. It raises all sorts of questions about the nature of knowledge. What is it, after all? What do any of us know, for a certainty?'

I said, 'Is it one of those things Stan mentioned, that you just don't tell Matt?'

Grant said, 'It's more in the nature of the madwoman in the attic. Matt knows about it, but he won't discuss it.'

I laughed at this, and Grant smiled, then he said, 'They want me to do it.'

'Who?' I said. 'Do what?'

'Sales,' he said. 'Trade editiorial for ads.'

'Oh,' I said, 'don't do it. Put your foot down.'

He looked at me a moment, searching for my understanding again, his eyes were big and brown and wet behind the thick lenses of his glasses and rimmed with red. He said, 'I try to be a good editor. I am a good editor, ordinarily.'

'I'm sure you are.'

'I worked for Little, Brown once. I edited law textbooks. Now that was a job. I had an office with oak bookshelves and a view of the Boston Common.' He looked around him, as if he had actually been in Boston and had to reorient himself now. 'I can edit anything, I've always said that. You don't have to believe the copy to edit it, and I certainly don't believe what goes on at Brackett Data, editorially speaking, I mean, but they make it so hard here, they make it so hard.'

'What do they do?' I said.

He frowned. He talked into the air, as if to an imaginary journalism class. 'There are only two acceptable AIDS victims: transfusion cases and kids. Everybody else got it sexing around, so they deserve it. All right. That's a point of view. This is a democracy, there's room for all points of view.' He put his hands on his knees and his face became pained. He said, 'But we get calls from these people, you know? ACT UP calls here, and who has to deal with them? Matt? Patricia Patterson? No!' He shook his head. 'Me, that's who.' He tapped his chest with a finger, and his voice became tinged with self-pity. 'Grant Cummings. I'm the only person in this whole company who's actually talked to an AIDS patient. I'm the only person here who understands the functioning of the virus. Everybody else is too busy. Everybody else is upholding morality or selling ads.' He lost his breath and looked at me. 'You'll find out,' he said, with a little undercurrent of resentful anger, 'if you stay.'

I looked at him.

Then he said, 'You will stay, won't you?' There was a faint pleading edge to his voice.

'I don't see why not,' I said.

'You're different from the others,' he said, relieved.

'What others?'

'The other junior editors they've had in here.'

'What were they like?'

'Journalism majors,' he said, and he shrugged tiredly. 'All out to climb the ladder, all ambition and salt.'

'Salt?' I said.

He looked at me again, as if he were weighing his words. 'There's no place to go at Brackett Data. There's no up from here.'

I thought of the hand painted on the stairwell wall at the place.

'You could get *my* job, of course,' he said, 'if you wanted it. But no one wants it. This is not the place for a young man on the move.'

'No,' I said, 'apparently not.'

'But you're different,' he said.

'I'm not on the move,' I said.

'Well, you're writing your novel,' he said.

'Yes,' I said.

'You're just here to —'

I picked it up from him. 'I'm just here to survive,' I said.

He looked at me and nodded slowly. 'That's the reason I'm here, too,' he said, 'if you really want to know. In fact, I'd say that's why we're all here, all of us.' He seemed pleased by his realisation. He looked at me he said, 'We're just trying to survive.'

He drew on his cigarette, and then began to cough badly. I crossed to him and patted him on the back, but it did no good. Then I remembered his medicine and got it from his desk. When I returned Grant was standing by the desk, bent over and coughing.

I gave him the Day Care and steered him back into the orange chair. He sat down, coughing, but managed to lift the bottle to his lips and drink it. It worked like honey, he stopped coughing almost immediately.

'That's a bad cough,' I said.

'Summer colds are the worst,' he said, sitting there with the bottle in one hand and the butt of his cigarette in the other. He took one last drag on it, and then made a wretched face at it, and looked at me and said, 'I hate it when I smoke the filter.'

Chapter 6

Nickie directed me to a Chinese place down the road from the little airport, and we split a beer in two glasses while we read the menu. Her warm scent filled my car and my head. She was plain today, dressed a pale pink and white striped blouse and a short black skirt that rose well above her knees as she sat in the car, and very little makeup, but she still looked good that way. When she crossed her legs I heard the soft sound of her stockings rubbing against each other, thigh to thingh, and I imagined the warmth, I imagined her moist heat, I wanted to feel my hand there. I glanced at her as I drove and I thought she looked fine, I looked at the line of her breasts, small and delicate looking, and I suddenly wanted to take the rest of the day off with her and take her to some green spring field and take off her clothes very beautifully and slowly and fuck her even slower than that.

I downshifted the car turning into the parking lot and said, 'I really like the way you smell.'

The restaurant was one of those places in a shopping centre, phoney with plastic lanterns, but run by real Chinese who spoke their own language among themselves. Nickie sat across from me and said, 'I'm having lunch special number four, what about you?' When the door of the restaurant opened, the slightest breeze carried her smell across the table to me. I didn't want anything to eat.

She closed her menu and set it on her empty plate. She lit a cigarette and sipped her beer and looked at me, smiling. 'I'll have my usual,' I said.

'What's that?'

'Sweet and sour.'

She pointed a finger at me and said, 'Now, you're up to something here, and I want to find out what it is.'

'What do you mean?'

'I mean, what are you doing at Brackett Data *really*?'

I wondered how she knew I was doing more than making a living. I rested my elbows on the table and folded my hands together above my plate. 'Really,' I said, 'I'm writing a novel.'

She smiled, satisfied with her acumen. 'I thought you had something cooking besides this job. What's it about?'

She looked delicious, and I wondered what Wiley Post would do. 'It's a love story,' I said.

40

She smiled at me again, she suspected something. 'You're making this up,' she said.

'It's a novel,' I said. 'I make it up as I go along.'

She laughed at this, and I liked her laugh, it connected with her deep insides, and I wondered if she laughed when she came.

She studied me for a moment and then said, 'Don't tell Matt you're writing a book.'

'Why not?' I said.

'It would make him very nervous,' she said, 'since the shooting.'

'The shooting?' I said.

She nodded. 'Patricia didn't tell you that, did she?'

'The shooting?' I said again.

'One of Matt's lesser accomplishments,' she said. 'He shot a man last year.'

'How?' I said. 'I mean, why?'

'The guy came after him,' she said, and she sipped her beer. 'Didn't you notice the gun when you talked to him?'

'The gun?'

'He carries a gun.' She looked at me, to see how the news was affecting me.

'Jesus,' I said.

'People threaten him all the time,' she said. 'And one guy came after him in the parking lot at the radio station.'

'He mentioned a radio show,' I said. 'Is he on the radio, too?'

She smiled almost cruelly, cynically, enjoying my astonishment. She said, 'He's everywhere, baby.'

'Christ,' I said, trying to imagine all that *dis-ease* on the radio.

She said, 'He can't help you now. He used to be here, but he left when Matt took over.'

I saw Jesus, then, leaving the room, I shook my head a little to clear it, I said, 'Who did he shoot?'

'A black man,' she said.

'That figures.'

'He was the father of this guy the police killed downtown. The witnesses said it was murder, but they were all black, too. So Matt talked about blacks and lawlessness on the radio, and this guy came after him.'

'Was he armed?'

'A 9 millimetre,' she said.

'What's Matt carry?'

'A 38,' she said. 'Police special. Of course.'

'And he just shot him.'

'Right there in the parking lot at the station. Two times, in the stomach.'

'Was Matt hit?'

'Flesh wound in the side,' she said. 'Boy, that was a million-dollar wound. He broadcast the very next day from his hospital bed. Charged three times the going rate for the air time.'

I stared down at the table in front of me, I reached to her pack of cigarettes and lit one, I couldn't absorb it all – dis-ease, dead Negroes, cops murdering people. I saw Nickie looking at me, she looked wise to something, and I knew she was trying to freak me out. I decided that I wasn't going to let her, I was going to show her I could handle it, and when she saw that I could she would let me fuck her, I thought madly, I lifted my face to hers and blew smoke up into the air above us. She smiled grimly and said, 'How did you wind up here, anyway?'

'Grant asked me that too,' I said. 'Why is everyone so curious about how I got this job?'

She lifted her menu and looked around for the waitress. 'Everyone expects you to resign.'

'Why?'

'Why not?' she said. 'Why would anybody work for a place as weird as Brackett Data?'

'I just want to write,' I said.

Now she blew smoke, she said, 'For *Brackett Data*?' I could hear the italics.

'My novel,' I said. 'I quit school to write.'

'You're from Atlanta?'

'DC.'

'Why'd you come here?' she said. 'Why not write at home?'

'I did,' I said. 'My father's a writer.'

'Really?'

I said, 'My father's Nathaniel Jones,' and I waited for her reaction.

But she shook her head a little and said, 'I'm sorry, should I know who that is?'

I laughed, I thought it was wonderful she'd never heard of him. 'Congratulations,' I said. 'Nathaniel Jones won the Pulitzer Prize for journalism in 1968. He covered the war in Vietnam.'

'Wow,' she said. 'And you're working for Brackett Data.'

'Don't tell them,' I said. 'I don't want it to make a difference.'

'I understand,' she said, but she looked at me differently now.

42

I drank some more beer. 'So he set me up a little studio off the back of the house.'

'Neat.'

'Yes, it was. It was sort of a small version of his own study.'

'Oh, I'll bet that was no good,' she said.

'No, it was all right,' I said, 'but it wasn't real. Do you know what I mean?'

She said, 'What was it like?'

I said, 'Growing up, I spent a lot of time taking care of my mother.'

'Your mother?'

'My dad is away a lot. He's always been away a lot.'

'So you took care of your mother,' she said. 'How did you do that?'

'Oh.' I lifted my eyes, recalling it. 'I never went anywhere when I was a kid.'

'That took care of her?'

'Yes. If I didn't go anywhere, she never had to worry about me.'

'I get it,' she said.

'Sure,' I said. 'So there I was, writing at home. But my mother was always asking me how I felt, if everything was all right, whether I wanted to have friends over. That's one of the ways I would take care of her – I'd have friends over so she would quit worrying about it.'

She said, 'You took care of her by letting her take care of you.'

'When I didn't need any care,' I said.

She said, 'What about your father?'

'Oh, he was in and out on business. He's always been in and out on business.' I didn't really want to get into the business with her.

'He's off winning Pulitzer Prizes while you take care of his wife.'

'I kept the boyfriends away, didn't I?'

She lit another cigarette and the waitress brought the food. She put it out and said, 'It never fails.'

As we began to eat, I said, 'You still haven't told me how you wound up at Brackett Data.'

'I was a temp,' she said. 'I went to work for an agency right after I moved here, and I came to Brackett Data on an assignment. They offered me the job.'

'And you took it.'

'Low self-esteem,' she said, and I smiled at her.

'You're sharp,' I said. 'I like you.'

'I know,' she said, suddenly pleased with herself. Her hand strayed absently to the top button on her blouse, and I felt strong for her, I wanted her badly and I wanted her to like me. 'You told me yesterday,' she said.

'I meant it,' I said. 'Do you like me?' I smiled back at her softly.

But she said, 'I don't know yet.'

'You must like me a little,' I said. 'You came to lunch with me.'

She said, 'You're pretty sharp yourself. What year of school were you in when you dropped out for the big world?'

'I was a sophomore,' I said. 'Rising junior, really.'

She nodded at this and looked at me thoughtfully.

I said, 'Now you know how old I am without asking directly.'

'Do you want to know how old I am?' she said. 'Would you like to see if I still have all my teeth?'

I laughed.

'I'll be twenty-two in September,' she said.

'I'll remember.'

She smiled suddenly and said, 'I know what you're up to.'

'What am I up to?'

'You're writing a book all right,' she went along, 'but it's not a love story. You're writing an exposé of American small business.'

I laughed again, hard this time, but I could see the black man bleeding on the black asphalt of the parking lot.

'That's Matt,' she said. 'Keeping the *small* in small business for twenty years. That's what you're doing here. Field work. Research.'

I was enjoying her. 'Found out,' I said.

'I'm sharp,' she said. 'You said so.'

I leaned across to her and spoke in a low tone. 'Is my secret safe with you?'

I could smell oil of drakar above the sweet and sour, her lips looked so soft, and I heard her whisper, 'I'm on your side.'

Chapter 7

I read back issues of *Survivor* to see what the periodicals section was like and it was dry, I figured I could be dry, but it was full of intricate scientific detail, and that worried me. I saw some more ads, I saw an enormous machine of stainless steel and brown and orange tubing that recirculated blood during surgery so the patient wouldn't need a transfusion. I supposed this patient was a survivor.

Grant came into my office carrying a stack of photocopies and a thick, green, thumb-indexed book that looked like a dictionary. He smoked one of his little cigars and set the stuff down on top of my out-box. He said, 'Here's the material for periodicals.'

I looked at him. I said, 'This is fairly technical, isn't it?'

He shrugged. 'Technical is as technical does, I suppose. I brought you a medical dictionary.' He gestured at the green book, then squinted and looked thoughtful. 'It's a kind of music, really. You'll develop a sense for it.'

'Do you think I'll be good at it?' I said.

He puffed on his cigar and wagged his head from side to side, escaping the cloud of smoke. 'Matt wants you to do it. He says mine are too specialised, too concerned with medical minutiae. So I'd like to see you give it a shot, too,' he said. 'The Reader, you know.' He smiled, but the smile vanished suddenly and he said, 'Unless you really mind.'

'Oh, I don't mind.'

'Just quote them a lot,' he said. 'Scientists like that.'

I began writing reviews of the research that I thought I understood, mostly social studies, AIDS in Amsterdam drug addicts and Veneotian prostitutes, 'HIV Infection as Leading Cause of Death Among Young Adults in US Cities and States', and I saw what Grant meant about it being like music. I would start with the abstract and look at the last sentence or maybe the last two to see what the research had proven, and if it had proven anything, I could use that for the lead. If it hadn't it made sounds like *Further research is necessary*, and there was nothing to write about so I skipped it. Next, I paraphrased the section on patients and methods, where they outlined what they'd done and whom they'd done it to. Past that, I couldn't understand a lot of what they said, but here and there certain passages would give me a definite feeling of significance, and I thought that must be the music part that Grant meant, so I'd quote them there. Then, according to the company style, I'd end the review with the name and address of the corresponding author and leave it to him to deal with the consequences of a mention in *Survivor*.

I got up to speed with it pretty quickly and soon I was turning them out like sausages, little word-processed turds. Then Grant came back to see how I was making out.

'Not bad,' he said, sitting at my console and scrolling through the document while he sipped his Day Care and chewed on the butt of his cigar. 'You've got it down,' he said. He was happy, he turned in the seat and smiled back at me. 'You've really got it.'

I stood behind him, leaning on my desk. 'It was easy,' I said.

'Matt'll love you,' he said. 'He thinks this scientific bullshit really enhances the magazine's prestige. Which is his prestige, of course.' He was happy, he took a long drink of the Day Care and smiled up at me.

Later I was still working on the periodicals when the speaker on my telephone came on. I started at the sudden sound and sat back at my desk looking at the phone. An announcer was introducing Matt, 'Matt Brackett,' he said, 'and the Voice of Reason.' Music played, soul music. I thought of my light out on the interstate, and then Matt's voice came on, calm, assured, reasonable, the same voice with which he had begun his interview with me, he was talking about nature: 'They go against Nature, and Nature strikes back. That's simple enough, isn't it?'

I tapped the phone, I thought it was picking up radio reception, but the voices continued.

'That's only your idea of Nature,' said a man who sounded like he was talking over a phone line. 'That's only what you think.'

Matt laughed, like the guy had just walked into something, and I felt creepy suddenly, like I was back in high school with bullies and rules closing in on me. Matt said, 'We're on 138 radio stations throughtout the south and west, my friend. That represents the thinking of a lot of people.'

'But reality isn't up for a vote,' said the man.

'Reality is up for a vote every day, according to your deviant friends,' said Matt. 'They're the ones who say everything is relative, not me.'

'But you can't —'

'Can't what?' said Matt. 'Listen, I'm just a businessman. I've got a corporation, I'm just a CEO. I deal in reality every day. Dollars and cents, that's reality, my friend, and there's nothing relative about it. Profit and loss, that's reality. Now your friends talk up something about diversity. I know about diversity. I've diversified my business with this radio show, so I know about diversity. But they don't know about diversity. I'm diverse. People like me are diverse. We're heterosexual, that's diverse, isn't it? Two sexes, not just one. But your friends aren't diverse, then, are they? No, they're just deviant, and they just use diversity as some kind of Orwellian code word. It's Newspeak, my friend, you're a victim of doublethink.'

I reached for the phone, as if to hang it up, and I saw my hand was shaking a little, the way Grant Cummings shook, and my mouth was dry. I was afraid.

I heard Matt talking in Grant's office, too, and I stepped inside, and there was Matt on the speaker phone, but Grant wasn't around. One of his brown cigarettes sat smoking slowly in the ashtray, next to a pile of papers.

I left Grant's office and walked over to the systems department. Stan sat at his desk, gazing into his console screen and tweaking his moustache. Matt would say something – 'The blacks and the feminazis are all in this together, you know, they always have been' – and Stan would twirl the end of the moustache. His other hand lay lightly on the corner of the keyboard, the way a pianist rests his hands above the keys just before starting into the music. Matt talked about the incompetent blacks and the feminazis who got all the good jobs. Stan saw me in the doorway and smiled, 'Hi,' he said.

I said, 'What's that?'

'What's what?'

'That,' I said, pointing. 'On the telephones.'

'That's Matt's radio show,' he said, glancing down at his deskset.

'Do we have to listen to it?'

He reached to his phone and twisted a round knob at the base of the set. Matt went away. 'Now, you can't do that,' he said. 'You can't turn yours all the way off. Only systems people can turn him all the way off. He likes computers.' He smiled at this. 'But you can turn him down,' he said.

'That's good to know,' I said. 'How long does the show last?'

'Till five,' said Stan, and he tweaked his moustache. *See?* his eyes said.

I went back to my office and listened to Matt talk a while. He said, 'The blacks don't even amount to 15 per cent of the population. Why do we have to listen to them anyway?' Then he started taking phone calls. The callers were both types, Matt's fans, and blacks and feminazis. The blacks always lost the conversation, and they were conversations that were either won or lost. Most of the non-fans were women as well as black, feminazis, and it hurt to listen to them walk into Matt's setups, he was slick, a master of the syllogism. But most of the callers were fans, who called to agree with him because he agreed with them. They called to be outrageous, as outrageous as the show would let them be. After a while, I turned him down as low as I could, and it was barely tolerable. I could still hear him and the callers, like white noise or the vitreous floating in your field of vision, and periodically some bit of the dialogue would infect my consciousness, Matt would say, 'The liberals have resorted to this because they simply can't compete, and that's the truth,' or a caller would cry out, 'Bracket those jerks, Matt!'

About 4.30, Grant came back.

'About to wind it up?' he said. His eyes shone, and he smoked a cigarette, and he was carrying the open bottle of Day Care.

'I've killed about ten pages,' I said.

'Kill space, that's the idea,' he said. He leaned forward and looked over the hard copy on my desk. He said, 'I guess you figured out how to turn down the radio show.'

'Stan showed me.'

He was plainly embarrassed. To help him out, I said, 'Matt certainly seems to inspire strong feelings.'

'He does that,' he said, agreeing quickly. 'He does that right here in the office, as a matter of fact. You'll see that after you've been here a while.'

I suddenly felt depressed, not by Grant, but by the whole situation, all I wanted to do was write a novel and here I was reading and writing about lymph nodes and core proteins and troops of hookers in Vienna and Prague. I said, 'Do you think I'll be here a while?'

He started in his seat and he said, 'You're not quitting, are you?'

I said, 'Oh, why not? Everyone seems to expect it.'

'Don't quit,' he said beseechingly. 'Please. It's just that everyone else has quit. 'you're the third junior editor we've had this month.'

'The other two quit?'

'After a couple of days.' He smoked his cigarette and sat back in the chair, he flicked ashes into the trash can. 'They had journalism degrees. I told Patricia not to hire anyone with a journalism degree, but she never listens to me.'

I said, 'So I was hired because I have no degree?'

'You were hired because you're a dropout. They thought you might not care so much.'

I sat there and thought about it, Matt talked to someone on the telephone. I thought about the gifted part, I never realised if it was this insignificant, and I knew then that I was not in school any more. I thought about the book, too, and the writing, I thought about sitting in the sun room and watching the park: I saw the people walking through the evening and children playing on the big swings. And I thought about the light in the night at the motel out on the interstate and the promise, that freedom, that immortality. That was all real to me, but I was an American worker now, with reality sandwiched in between the office hours. Grant waited anxiously across the desk, and I shook my head and said, 'I don't care what goes on at Brackett Data.'

He brightened and smiled at me. 'You want to write your book,' he said.

I said, 'I don't know all that I want.'

He looked a little sad, as if I reminded him of something sad from years before. His free hand wandered to the bottle of Day Care, caressing the glass.

'I don't know,' I said.

'I understand,' he said.

I said, 'I'll do whatever you want.'

'I'd like to read your book some time.'

'Great,' I said, and I felt a twinge of the same freaked-out fear I had the first night in the apartment, now I *had* to write the thing, to have something to show to Grant.

He lifted the bottle of Day Care absently and took a sip. I nearly asked him if I could have a drink, too.

Chapter 8

The next morning I met with Grant in his office. I stood in his doorway, I said, 'I'm curious about our circulation.'

'Free to the trade,' said Grant, shrugging, there was nothing to be curious about.

'Oh, I know we mail it out to all these lists,' I said, 'but who really reads it?'

'As far as I'm concerned, we've got one reader,' Grant said. He poured some Day Care into a coffee cup, he lifted it with both hands and put it to his lips. He said, 'You could get a circulation audit from Simon.'

'Who's that?'

'Simon English, the circulation manager.'

I remembered him because he was the only black in the company, I recalled the long dark hall that ended in a shadowy back room behind a door labelled CIRCULATION. I said, 'I think I remember where his office is.'

'He's got the biggest office in the company,' Grant said. 'It's full of Matt's books.'

'Matt's books?' He had said something about books the day before.

Oh, 'he's written a ton of books, on all kinds of subjects.'

'You're kidding.'

'We kid a lot around here,' he said, and he lit cigarette. The match flame shone steadily in his hand, the cough medicine worked.

I said, 'I'm going to go see that audit now.'

Simon English's office was at the end of the building, past the sales and the art departments. I knocked on the door.

'Come in,' said a young man's voice.

The room was full of rows of grey metal shelving, stacked with magazines and books. Index cards taped to the ends of the shelves announced their contents, RIGHT ABOUT THE COMET, said one near the door. The air was heavy with the smell of stale smoke, and I couldn't see English anywhere. I said, 'Hello?'

'Close the door,' said the voice.

I closed the door and followed the voice through the rows of shelves to the far corner of the room, where Simon English sat at a high-backed desk, French inhaling a long, thin, pastel green cigarette. He held his head back, and smoke rolled out his mouth and sucked up into his flared nostrils as he watched me through seriously bloodshot eyes. 'Have a seat,' he said. I sat across from him in an orange plastic chair like the one in my office. On the wall behind him a black Venus stripped off a red raincoat across a triptych poster. By the third panel, she stood proudly in a yellow bikini, yellow triangles barely covering her nipples and pubis, nearly naked Africa. I stared at her. Simon said, 'Yes, she is.'

I turned from her and said, 'I'm Wiley Jones, I'm a new editor.'

'I remember,' he said, and he extended a hand around the computer on his desk. 'How do you like it so far?'

'It's all right,' I said.

'It's like Vietnam,' he said.' As long as you do what you're told, you can do whatever you want.' He smiled, he had perfect white teeth.

But he did not look old enough. I said, 'Were you in Vietnam?'

'My old man was,' he said. 'Vietnam was the white man's last war.'

'What about the Gulf?' I said.

'Gas war,' he said. 'The white man is all used up.'

'I know,' I said.

He took a long slow drag on his cigarette, the smoke snaked up through his nostrils sensuously as he savoured it. 'How'd you find out?' he said.

I smiled back at him. 'I am a white man.'

He laughed, deep and satisfied, He enjoyed my bankruptcy.

He put his cigarette out and reached into the desk drawer and got another, a short, fat unfiltered job, which he put to his lips and lit with a chrome-plated Zippo. He inhaled deeply and passed it across the desk to me, and I realised it was a joint. I took it as he said, through his held breath, 'You can draw easy on it, because it's so big.'

I took an easy toke, it smoked mild, and I felt it working on me immediately. Simon got good stuff.

I passed it back to him. 'Who here smokes?' I said.

'Nickie. Everybody in the art department. And Margaret.'

'Who's Margaret?' The joint came back to me.

'You haven't met Margaret?' he said. 'The Divine Margaret. She's head of member services for the AIDS Research Council.' He drew deep on the cigarette and brushed the ashes off gently into an ashtray beside his computer. He stared steadily at the end of the burning joint. He was very stoned.

51

He blinked and he sat up and said, 'Do you want any more of this?'

'No, thanks,' I said. 'I'm fine.'

'You bet you're fine,' he said, and he smiled easily. He tamped out the burning joint and put it back in the drawer and lit one of his green cigarettes.

I said, 'This is very good dope.'

'Yes, she is,' he said.

I said, 'I was wondering about our circulation.'

'Sure,' he said. 'You want to see an audit?'

'Yes.'

'*Survivor*, right?' He opened another drawer and pulled out a file full of copies of the last circulation audit for *Survivor*. He slid one out and handed it to me.

I examined it. There was a box on the form labelled 'Direct Request,' and the figure in the box read 7 per cent. I pointed at it, and I said to Simon, 'Does this mean what I think it means?'

His eyes followed my pointing finger. 'Those are the DRs, the direct requests. They're 7 per cent. That means that 7 per cent of the people on the list actually asked to get the magazine. The rest are forced subscriptions, from off the lists we buy.' He watched me as I examined the audit and then turned back to him. His eyes smiled like Stan's. *See?* they said.

I looked back at the audit. The number seven hung framed in a serious black box before me, seven, seven, seven.

'This is very good dope,' I said,

'She must be,' he said. 'That's the second time you've said so.'

'I don't want to go back to work.'

'Don't,' he said. 'I won't.'

I stood up. 'I'd better.'

Simon English nodded solemnly, he said, 'Work is a very serious thing. Are you OK?'

I said, 'I'm too OK,' I laughed a little.

'If you get into a problem, come back. This office is an excellent place to hide.'

'I'll remember that,' I said.

He sat up. 'Don't forget your audit,' he said.

'Thanks.'

I drifted out of the office with the audit in my hand. Seven, seven, seven, it was printed on green paper, the colour of surgery walls, and I looked down at it, checking out the list of reader categories: *MD, Researcher, Chief Executive Officer* – and I bumped into the wall when I should have turned. I looked up suddenly, embarrassed and relieved that no one had seen me, and I wandered down the hall, past the salesmen's offices, they were selling on the phone, I heard their pitches as I passed. I came out in the main office and saw Matt stepping out of his office with some papers in his hand just as Nickie sliced open the morning mail. He saw me, and I was heavily stoned, and he raised the papers high into the air and called to me, 'Superlative work!'

I didn't know what he was talking about. I raised a hand and waved at him weakly.

'Come here,' he called, and I crossed the office to him, Nickie stopped work and looked up at me with a wry smile.

Matt reached a hand to my shoulder and said, 'Come into my office.' He steered me towards the door and I looked back at Nickie, she smiled cruelly and waved at me. The door closed on her smiling face.

'You've got it!' said Matt, he held me by the shoulder, and I looked into his face: I could see all the pores of his skin, he said, 'This is just what the magazine has needed for years!' He waved the papers in my face, and I recognised them at last, they were a printout of my periodicals. 'Not a bunch of scientific rubbish, but the social meaning of the dis-ease.' I remembered the lead article, on HIV infection spread by prostitution. I had been uncertain whether The Reader would like it, since it said that not much infection was spread this way. 'The dis-ease that these parasites infect us with. Come in, have a seat, we have a lot to discuss.'

He marched to his desk, and I stumbled after him, hoping I wouldn't have to talk much. I sat in one of the chairs and said, 'May I have a glass of water, please?'

He said, 'You can have anything you want.' He held up the pitcher of branch water and a glass and poured as he talked. 'Anyone who can take dry-as-dust periodicals and turn them into editorial with this kind of pop can have whatever he desires.' He passed the glass to me and I drank from it.

'Thank you,' I said.

'Thank *you*,' he smiled. 'I swear, you're just what I've been looking for.' He picked up the printout and scanned it, then read aloud from the drug addict article: '"A shortcoming of the study design was its failure to examine the effect of syringe distribution on rates of addiction in Amsterdam.' On target! That's the kind of irresponsible pseudo-science we want to highlight. I knew we would find the right man.'

I thought about the two junior editors who had resigned. I wondered what their periodicals had been like.

'The social angle, that's what it's needed all along,' Matt said, and he thumped the desk with his fist. He leaned forward and spoke softly. 'That's what scares the piss out of everybody. Fornicate with these whores and you run the risk of this virus. *Die* for your concupiscence, what do you think of that?'

I couldn't think, the office was warm, I wanted to go back to Circulation, I wanted Simon to tell me what to do, I said, 'Serves them right.'

He hit the desk hard this time. 'Absolutely!' he cried. 'The wages of Babylon will be visited upon them.'

I lifted my glass and drank, the water was alive in my mouth, it slid down my throat like an eel.

A crafty look stole across his face, and he stood up and said, 'Come with me over here.'

We walked to the other end of the office. A computer sat on the conference table, one from the art department with a big monitor and a picture displayed on it, a man and woman from the waist up, both naked the man stood behind the woman and kissed her on the neck, she laid her head aside for him, and held her eyes closed and a red oval covered her breasts. The copy inside it said, 'Reliable protection for today's enlightened lovers'. I didn't like the oval, she was pretty and I wanted to see her breasts.

Matt stood to one side, looking at me as I gazed at the graphic, and he said slowly, 'What do you think?'

I shrugged, I said, 'Are we selling condoms now?'

'Precisely,' he smiled. 'You're so quick.' He sounded pleased. He reached down to the keyboard and scrolled the rest of the ad on to the screen, some copy I was too stoned to read and two boxes of condoms, green and blue, one with ribs and one without. He said, 'Now both of these contain a spermicide that also kills HIV. That's why they're qualified to run in *Survivor*.'

Otherwise, they'd be about fucking, I thought. 'I see,' I said.

'There's a lot of money in these products,' he said, 'and we're going after it. But we have to preserve our integrity. That's where you come in.'

'Me?' I looked at him.

'I want you to test them,' he said.

I saw myself with a roomful of Viennese whores and boxes and boxes of condoms, and if I got HIV, we wouldn't run the ad. So there. Then it clicked. I pointed at the screen. 'The ads,' I said.

'Precisely,' he said again. 'I want everything to be within the bounds of good taste and in keeping with our editorial position.'

Somewhere to the right of Hitler, I thought. 'OK,' I said.

He smiled big. He said, 'You'd be amazed what some magazines publish.'

I looked at him again, I said, 'I'm sure.'

He hesitated for just an instant, then he said, tentatively, 'Have you seen them?'

I had no idea what he meant so I said, 'I don't think so.'

He looked towards his desk and seemed to think about something for a moment, then he said, 'Here, I'll show you.'

He crossed to a bookcase in the corner behind his desk. He knelt down, and got a box of magazines from the bottom shelf and brought it to the table. It was one of those storage things that hold a year's worth and have a spine like a book. He slid it open and pulled the magazines from it and placed them on the table.

They were men's magazines, thick and expensive with women peering seductively from the covers in dramatic colours. Matt reached into his coat pocket and put on a pair of reading glasses, and picked the top magazine off the stack and thumbed through it, turning towards the back. 'Here,' he said. He pointed to a column at the edge of the page. A bare-breasted woman held a condom in its wrapper up to her chin like a wrapped piece of candy and looked into the camera lewdly. Her body was airbrushed away just at the edge of her nipples. 'Lascivious,' said Matt. Some publishers will do anything for money.'

I didn't know where we were going, but I had to hold on in the stone, I said, 'It's sad.'

'We can't have anything like this in *Survivor*,' he said.

'We won't.'

He picked up the magazine and flipped the pages for a moment, looking, then he turned to the centre. He placed it on the table before me. A woman sat naked on a bed with her legs spread wide apart and her hands on her thighs. She wore athletic shoes and driving gloves. She had red hair, red, red pubic hair curling round and round her cunt. Matt said, 'Have you ever seen anything like that?'

I swallowed, 'No, sir,' I said. I wondered what her name was, probably one of those men's magazines' names, Tara or Serena or Kimberley.

'Here,' he said, and he took another magazine from the stack, 'look at this one.' He laid another woman on the table in front of me. This one was blonde, like Nickie, blonde and pink, doing tricks with an aluminium exercise bar mounted on a mirrored wall. Matt said, 'It's disgusting.'

I said, 'Yes, sir.' I thought of Simon's girl, I thought we were all perverts here, I looked at the blonde in the picture and felt horny, I felt good looking at her, I felt safe from Matt with her.

He put a hand on my shoulder. 'Matt,' he reminded me. The reading glasses made him look grandfatherly. He sat down at the conference table. He took a third magazine and turned through it slowly. He said, 'We've all seen things like this before.'

'Yes,' I said.

'But where do you suppose they find these women, Wiley?' He turned to another picture. This woman showed her ass and did things with her tongue over her shoulder. He put his finger on her face. He said, 'Where would you find a woman like that?'

I'd wanted to find a woman like that since puberty, I thought. I looked at her, I liked the way she looked. 'I suppose I would look in bars,' I said.

'Bars,' he said.

'Yes, sir.'

'Matt.'

'I'm sorry. Matt.'

'I don't drink alcohol,' he said. 'But I would like to find a woman like this.' He looked up at me steadily now, over the top of his reading glasses.

·'Yes.'

He said, 'Could you find a woman like this for me?'

I thought, If I could find this woman, I'd tell her all about you. I said, 'I don't know. I've never found women for somebody else before.'

He smiled. He said, 'You've never been a procurer?'

'No, sir.'

'Matt.'

'Matt.' I couldn't believe he did not know I was stoned.

'You wouldn't be one now,' he said. 'I find women like this and save them.'

'Yes?'

'I have a personal ministry.'

'Yes?'

He sat back from the table, he expanded. 'Not everyone knows about it. Not everyone in the company.'

I said, 'Yes.'

56

'I believe you can help me with this.'

I swallowed again. I said, 'What can I do?' and my voice cracked.

'Have some more water,' he said, and I went to the desk and refilled my glass.

He smiled at me again. 'You're a young man,' he said. 'You have appetites. Let me harness those appetites. You can find a woman like this much easier than I can.'

I looked at the blonde at the exercise bar and said, 'I suppose.' I have never liked exercise.

'When you find one of these women, give her this and tell her to use it.' He reached into his shirt pocket and drew out a business card. He handed it to me, and I took a second to focus on it. It said:

The Gospel According to Matthew
404 302–4000

He said, 'That's a dedicated line,' and reached back into his pocket and came out with a handful of the cards. 'Here,' he said, 'take several.' I took them and looked down at them in my hand, and I was stoned, I'd never seen anything so black and white. He waited, then said, 'Better put them away.' He whispered it, and I understood: the cards were our secret thing.

He turned quickly through the magazine, pausing over the pictures. He said, 'I've saved a number of these women.' He looked down through his reading glasses at the women. 'Would you like to meet some of the women I have saved?'

I swallowed some water. I said, 'Yes?'

The woman in the magazine before him held her breasts up to the camera and stuck out her tongue. I'd never seen a tongue so long, it snaked down from her mouth and licked her left nipple. He said, 'Some other time, perhaps.'

He closed the magazines and put them back into their box, and he said, 'The insertions and mechanicals for the condom advertisements will be sent to you first, rather than the art department. I'm sure you'll do the right thing.'

I stood up. The stack of cards in my shirt pocket, had real weight. Matt gestured at the computer then put a hand on my shoulder and gently pressed me towards the door. He said, 'And I'm sure you'll do the right thing with the other matter, too.'

I glanced over at the bookcase behind his desk. It was full of the magazine boxes, and I wondered if anyone else knew, I thought of Patricia Patterson, I could see her: she fit a cigarette into one of her filters and kissed it with her bright red lipstick.

Matt opened the door for me, he smiled the whole time, he showed his white-capped teeth, and he pushed me gently along and out, he said. 'Thank you very much, Wiley,' and he closed the door softly behind me.

Nickie looked up from her desk. Her hair was mussed, it fell over her forehead a little, and her mouth was open, lips in a soft pink O, and she said, 'Oh, Wiley, have you had enough?'

Chapter 9

I saw Alix that Saturday morning, after I finished writing. I got out of my bathrobe and slipped into pair of cutoffs and carried a cup of coffee out on to the back landing and, looking down, saw her outside her door lying on a beach lounger, sunbathing in a red bikini. Her red hair lay across the head of the green and white lounger, she was red on red. I called to her, 'Hello, down there.'

She opened her eyes and, shielding them from the sun with her hand, looked up at me. She said, 'Oh, hello, Wiley.'

She remembered my name, then. I said, 'They turned on my phone yesterday.'

She continued to look at me. 'Good,' she said. 'We'll get into that communications program.'

'Today?'

'Sure.' She sat up, and reached down for her sunglasses and put them on. They were mirrored and the light sparkled off them. She got up and pulled on a blue chambray workshirt she had been lying on and she came slowly up the stairs. She stood in front of me with her hard aluminium eyes shining, and she rested her weight on her right hip, she looked good. She said, 'Have you been writing today?'

'Yes,' I said. 'I wrote 246 words today.'

'Your word processor counts words?'

'Yes.' She shone with a thin film of tanning oil, I could smell it, and I thought of Nickie's smell, the way her legs had rubbed against each other in the car and the way I wanted to fuck her, and I wanted to fuck Alix, too, then, standing there, I wanted to have them both.

'That's what computers are really good at,' she said; 'counting things.'

'How do they communicate, then?'

'By counting things to each other.'

'So everything they do is counting.'

'They count from zero to one, and then they count from one to zero.'

'Come and show me,' I said, and I opened the back door for her.

Inside, she looked at the back of the computer and she looked at the phone. She kept her sunglasses on. She said, 'Do you have another length of line cord?'

'What's line cord?' I said.

She held up the phone. 'It's what hooks this to the jack.'

'No,' I said.

'No problem,' she said. 'I've got some downstairs.'

We went down to her place, through the back door and the kitchen and into her living room. *This is where she lives*, I thought, and I looked for any traces of a man, a regular. One wall was lined with crates stacked up for shelves, filled with paperbacks and computer equipment. *Steal This Book*, said one of the books, and *Lady Chatterley's Lover*, and *Structured Analysis and System Specification*, and their spines were creased and worn, they had been read. In the centre of the wall was a desk, with an office chair and a big colour computer, turned on, the screen glowing softly with different colours in different windows. I saw a splash of flesh in a small window in the lower right-hand corner, and Alix crossed quickly to the machine, stepping between me and the screen, and clicked on this window with the mouse and closed it. Across the room sat a big soft sofa, all cushions and round corners. She bent to a cardboard box beside the desk and came up with a short piece of line cord. 'OK,' she said.

I noticed the age of the paint job. 'You've been living here a while,' I said.

'That's right,' she said.

As we passed back through the kitchen, I glanced behind me and caught a glimpse into her bedroom, the walls were blue and pictureless, and the bed was unmade. She stopped at the refrigerator and got a Pabst Blue Ribbon beer. 'Do you want one?' she asked.

I said, 'Why not?' and she passed me one. She took hers and ran it over her forehead; she was still hot from the sun.

We went back to my place and into the sun room. Alix unplugged the line cord from the phone and plugged in the shorter piece. Then she set the phone beside the computer and plugged the phone into the machine. Then she plugged the line cord that ran from the wall jack into the machine as well. She sat back in the desk chair and said, 'That completes the circuit, see?'

I leaned closer to watch over her shoulder, I breathed in the strong smell of her sweat and the tanning oil.

'Now we start the communications program.' She typed in the commands at the console and Pro Comm came up. Then she loaded the dialling directory and the listing of names and numbers appeared. The second name on the list was **Brackett Data**. 'Try that,' I said, and pointed at it. 'Try Brackett Data.'

She highlighted **Brackett Data** on the screen and pressed the return key. Through the computer's speaker I heard the dial tone, followed by the punching of the phone number.

A few seconds passed and the ringing started, and then the phone picked up at the other end and a high-pitched tone came out of the speaker. The tone rose in pitch then broke into a rasping noise that ended with a clicking sound. Everything fell silent and the screen cleared. In the upper left-hand corner it said

CONNECT 9400

and we were connected.

Type began to scroll by on the screen. I said, 'What's it doing?'

She sipped her beer and said, 'It's running a script.'

'What's that?'

'That's a set of responses it's programmed to run when it connects with this number.'

The screen cleared again and a line of type appeared:

Enter your name, please>

and the response came automatically:

Matt Brackett

I said, 'That's the owner of the company.'

'Yeah?' She looked at me over her shoulder, smiling. 'Hey, this must have been his computer.'

A menu scrolled up, it was similar to the menu on the network at the office, but it had more options, some I hadn't seen before. At the head of the list it said Personal Menu. I said 'What do we do now?'

Alix slid her chair back. She said, 'If you're the owner of the company, you can probably do anything you want.'

I looked at the menu, I looked at Alix, I tried to decide what I wanted to do, and I went a little dreamy, standing there, with the smell of tanning oil and sweat and the memory of Nickie, and the morning beer forsting everything over. I said, 'You decide.'

She said, 'Let's try Mail. Let's read his mail.' She typed *m*. The screen cleared in a second and a line of type appeared:

Scanning main board

Then:

Messages for you: 255184, 255187. Read now? (y/n)

Alix leaned back in the chair and looked up at me over her shoulder. She said, 'Let's read his mail. I'll bet it's something sexual.'

I looked down at her, her thighs glistened with oil and sweat, her breasts rested heavily inside her bikini top. I said, 'Let's read it.'

She smiled and tapped *y* on the keyboard. The system said

Read message command?>

and she typed 255184, 255187. There were several lines of computer babble, network addresses and hieroglyphics, and then the messages appeared, one at a time:

Fr: MB

To: MB

In the future, the HIV/AIDS cases strictly segregated. Bar code tattoos on the forehead.

Fr: MB

To: MB

In the future, all the testing updated into one central data base. Who will control it? No one controls it now. Part of the problem. In the future, no such problem.

Alix stared at the screen for a long time. She was very quiet, and I thought something was wrong. I said, 'He publishes a magazine about AIDS, you know,' and she came out of it. She said slowly, 'From MB to MB. He writes notes to himself.' She sat up quickly and typed something I couldn't see. She laughed harshly, she was replying to his message. The screen prompted her for a *From* and she typed MB. She laughed again and typed the message:

In the future, everything will be round.

'What did you do that for?' I said. 'Now he'll know someone's been on.'

She looked at me over her shoulder. 'Don't you want him to know? If he's such a control freak, it ought to really fuck with his head.'

I thought about it, I looked at the message on the screen, I looked at her. 'You like that, to fuck with his head?' I smiled at her.

'Sure,' she said and she smiled back. 'I like to mind-fuck these mothers.'

'Fuck the system,' I said.

'Right on,' she cried, smiling brightly. '*Venceremos!*' She hoisted her beer and drank long from it.

'This excites you,' I said.

She nodded, she smiled, and she spoke loudly, she said, 'It's exciting to violate my probation.'

'Your probation?'

She turned in her seat to face me. Her nipples showed hard through the bikini top and she breathed quickly, she said, 'I'm on probation.' She drank some more beer, and shrugged, a delicious little movement of her body.

'What for?' I said.

'Hacking. Five years. This is the last year.'

'You broke into computer systems.'

She took another long pull on the beer. 'And stole things, yes.'

I sat down. 'What did you steal?'

'Credit records, mostly.'

'What did you do with them?'

'Sold them to private investigators, mostly.' She drank some more of her beer, she was drinking it fast, and she smiled excitedly at me. She stretched like a cat, and her body looked very good to me. She said, 'This feels really good. This is what it's all about.'

'What?'

'Hacking,' she said. She pointed at the console with her beer bottle. 'Fucking. Computers.'

'They're about breaking and entering?'

'They're about subversive activity.' She leaned closer to me, and I looked at her face, her metallic eyes, and her soft round breasts breathing, she excited me, an older woman, a mistress of secret arts. 'They're about fucking people like Matt Brackett.'

'You don't even know Matt Brackett,' I said, 'do you?'

'You know him,' she said. 'Isn't he worth fucking with?'

I looked at her, she looked good, excited all red red hair and sleek gleaming sunglasses and blue chambray shirt and red bikini and well-oiled white skin and sweat, and I wanted to fuck with her. I could feel the difference in our ages as something sexual; I wanted her to teach me things sexual, I wanted to show her how I could learn. I nodded, I said, 'He makes money off fear.'

'There you are, then,' she said. 'He's a parasite, isn't he?'

'I guess so.'

'Well, then,' she said, 'let's fuck up his Monday morning.' She gestured at the computer behind her and turned to it again. She tapped a key and sent the message. 'Anyway,' she said, 'if he'd had something sexual in his mail, I'd have left him alone.'

I laughed.

'It would have been something human,' she said. 'Instead you get all this bullshit about Controlling the future.'

'You're great,' I said, and I touched her on the shoulder. She looked up at me from behind her sunglasses.

'Thanks,' she said. 'I haven't had this much fun in years.'

'Any time,' I said.

She took us back to the main menu. 'Anyway,' she said, 'as Matt Brackett, this is probably what will turn you on the most.' She pointed to a line on the menu:

S System

'As the owner of the company, you would have superuser privileges.'

'Superuser,' I said.

'Yeah,' she laughed a little. 'I always thought that was the right name for some of these fucks.' Her sunglasses caught the light in a brilliant smile. She stood up.

I said, 'You're leaving?' I pointed at **S System**. 'Don't you want to get turned on the most?'

She laughed, but she looked at me steadily 'Sure,' she said slowly, 'but I need to watch it. I don't need any more trouble now. I've only got ten months to go.' She stepped around her chair and out of the sun room. I stood up, following her moves.

I didn't want her to go, I said suddenly, 'Would you take off your sunglasses?'

She paused, turning to me and thinking. She reached up and took them off. I felt like she had undressed for me. I said, 'Your eyes are green.'

'Yes,' she said, and she smiled slightly.

'I remembered,' I said. 'I just wanted to see them.'

She looked at me and put the sunglasses back on, I hoped I had fucked with her, I knew she had fucked with me. I said, 'Thank you.'

'Any time.'

Chapter 10

I called Nickie that evening. 'Is this Nickie?' I said when the other end answered.

'No,' said a voice that sounded like Nickie, 'this is Brenda, Nickie's roommate. Hold on and I'll get her.'

I sat in my Starvation Army rocking chair watching the park in the early evening. The day was long and you could still see people out walking as the sun went down. I saw a father out with his little boy.

Nickie said, 'Hello.'

'Hello, yourself,' I said. 'This is Wiley. I got a phone yesterday.'

'Good for you. Am I your first call?'

'I couldn't imagine a more auspicious start.'

'Neither can I. What else are you doing tonight?'

'What are you doing?' I said. 'It's Saturday night.'

'I was going to rent some videos and make popcorn.'

'Do you use real butter?'

'Does that make a difference?'

'Of course.'

'Then I use real butter.'

I said, 'I'd be delighted to come.'

'Boy,' she said, 'talk about sure of yourself.'

I laughed. 'If I don't invite myself, who will?'

'I might,' she said, 'if you'd give me a chance.'

'I'm sorry.'

'All right,' she said, and she paused for a moment, then said, 'Say, would you like to come over and watch a video with me?'

In the park, the little boy was running from his father; they were playing tag, they chased into the playground towards the southern end of the park, the father held back and pretended to let the little boy get away.

'Sure,' I said. 'And maybe we can go out afterwards.'

'Sure,' she said, 'have a drink.'

'Or something.'

'Or something.'

'What time should I come over?' I said.

'Say about 7.30.'

'And where do you live?'

'Coming from Midtown?' she said, and she began to give me directions.

The father surged ahead through the swings and almost caught the little boy, but the boy was too quick for him, and the father stopped and called to him to stop, and the boy laughed, full of himself, and the father lost his temper and quickly came after him, he caught his son running and jerked him off his feet, and I could hear him distantly and harsh. 'You come when I call you,' he barked, and he spun the boy around and the boy began to cry, and then the father's hands were empty, tripped up by his anger, and the two of them stood there, helpless together in their ruined evening.

Nickie lived in a duplex on a circle of duplexes. I parked and climbed the steep steps to her front door, the door was open, and first I looked through the screen door into the living room. Then I rang the bell.

She came in from what I assumed was the kitchen and motioned me in, and I opened the door and stepped inside. She wore a pair of khaki shorts that showed off her legs and a red knit halter top that clung to her form. Her form was *lissom*, I thought suddenly, I had discovered the word 'lissom' that morning, using the thesaurus on the word processor, and I liked it, I had been looking for a use for it all day, and now I had found one, and a use for all its synonyms, too: *agile, limber, lithe,* and *supple*.

I said, 'It's good to see you.'

'It's been so long,' she smiled.

I was smiling too. 'You know what I mean,' I said.

'Yes,' she said, 'well, do you like *la bizarrerie?*'

'I'm writing a novel, remember?'

'Well, *la bizarrerie* is what I got: *Blue Velvet.*'

'That's fine,' I said. A kernel popped loudly in the kitchen.

'Real butter is melting on the stove,' she said.

I smiled bigger. I said, 'That's fine, too.'

'Everything is fine with you,' she said. 'Have you ever noticed that?'

I got two Budweisers from the refrigerator and Nickie served up the popcorn and poured butter on to it from a small black skillet. 'Do you like it salty?' she said.

'Well —'

'I like it salty,' she said.

'That's fine.'

'There you go again,' she said, and she set the skillet down on the stove and picked up a big salt shaker and began to pour it on the corn. 'That sort of thing will get you in trouble at Brackett Data.'

'How?'

'Matt will say something to you some day, and you'll say "fine," and he'll stick you with a project, and then where will you be?'

'Maybe I'd do all right with the project.'

'Nobody does all right with Matt's projects.'

'Why not?'

'Because that's what they are – Matt's. He never really delegates. He gives you something to do, and then he's in your face until it's ruined.'

'I see.'

'And you stand around saying everything's fine.' Her little breasts shook sweetly as she sprinkled the salt and her hair shook around her face, she was like a little girl, cooking like her mother. 'You shouldn't do that with Matt,' she said.

'What about with you?'

She picked up the bowl of popcorn. 'Come on,' she said, 'and bring that beer.'

We watched *Blue Velvet* twice and ate popcorn and drank a few beers until around midnight. We started out sitting on the sofa with the popcorn on the coffee table in front of us, and we wound up with pillows on the floor. Nickie's hair came a little undone, and she looked good that way, just a little undone around the edges, and I began to think about undoing her a little more. When the movie ended for the second time, she rolled off her pillow and on to the floor facing me and she said, 'What do you want to do now, Ollie?'

I rolled off my pillow to be with her and I turned an empty beer bottle on its side. I said, 'Well, Stanley, could play spin the bottle.'

'OK,' she said. 'I've never played that.'

'Neither have I.'

'I know how it works, though.'

'Do you?'

'Yes,' she said, and she rolled over and kissed me very lightly, very quickly. Then she rolled back and said, 'Now you spin the bottle. Right?'

'That's fine,' I said, and I reached for her. She let me find her, and I kissed her for a long moment, deep, I was hungrier than I realised, and she kissed me back, it had been a long time for her too,

67

she excited me with her tongue probing greedily into my mouth and her hands moving across my body. She lay back, pulling me after her. I slid my hand inside her top and up on to one of her small breasts, I felt the nipple hard between my fingers, and I could feel her breathing, sharp and sudden and excited. She broke the kiss, and pushed herself away from me, with her hands against my shoulders, and she lay looking down at my hand beneath her top, on her breast, and she sighed and rolled away.

I looked at her body curled away from me, and I wanted to fuck her very much, she looked so vulnerable and round everywhere, through her shoulders and across her bottom, I was helpless with her and I could smell oil of drakar on my hands, on my clothes. 'What's the matter?' I said.

She rolled on to her back, and looked up at the ceiling and sighed. She looked good. She said, 'What do we do Monday morning for a follow-up?'

'Who cares?' I said.

'What?' she said, and she looked at me. 'Are you in love with me?'

I looked at her. Her eyes were a cool grey, her look was cool, she was thinking herself through this, and her lips were pink without lipstick, I wanted to touch them. I said it: 'Yes,' I said, and I meant it, I would have said anything to be what she wanted. What did she want?

She said, 'Things happen fast for you.'

I said, 'I can't help it. I want you.'

'I want you too,' she said, and she laid a finger against my cheek, she was thinking, she was weighing it.

'Doesn't it matter that I love you?' I said.

'How could you love me?' she said. 'You just met me the other day.'

'I know you, though,' I said. 'I really do.' *Really, really.*

'Tell me about myself, if you know me.'

I looked at her while I thought. I said, 'You want to be free, like I do. You want it almost more than you want to make love to me.'

She said, 'Almost?'

'Maybe more, then,' I said, 'tonight. But that's because you don't know yet that you can love me and still be free.'

She looked coolly back at me. When she spoke her voice had a slight edge in it that it hadn't had before. She said, 'I fucked another editor once.'

'You like editors.'

'He was in love with me,' she said. 'But I wasn't in love with him. I just wanted to fuck one night.'

I looked at her. I reached over and smoothed a lock of hair back behind her ear.

She said, 'He was like a puppy dog.'

I nodded.

She said, 'Are you like a puppy dog when you're in love?'

'I'm a machine,' I said.

'A love machine?'

'A sex machine,' I promised her.

'You're just talking.' And she looked faintly bitter, she wanted to fuck me, she wanted me to fuck her, and, at the same time, she wanted something guaranteed, too. Something safe and ensured.

'You would like a sex machine,' I said.

'I want to fuck you,' she said. 'I know that.'

'I want you to.'

'I'm not going to,' she said, and she rolled a little away from me and sat up and began running her hands through her ash yellow hair, pushing it back behind her ears. 'Not tonight,' she said.

I sat up with her. 'Why not?' I said.

'Too fast,' she said. 'You'd think I'm easy. Anyway, I'd just get it all twisted up, and we'd still have to work together, and it would be hell.'

'How do you twist it up?'

'I either fall in love with you, or else I don't.'

'That covers it,' I said.

'If I fall in love with you, I lose it.'

'What do you lose?'

'Myself,' she said. 'I become like a slave.'

'And if you just want to fuck?'

'I don't know what I want until it's too late.'

'Do you always get it all twisted up?'

'Always,' she said. 'I'm a twister.' She sat up on her knees, and put her hands on her hips and looked at me.

'You look good,' I said, 'for a twister.'

She smiled at me, she looked a little sad. She said, 'Go home, Wiley, before we fuck and have to go to work anyway.'

It was over. I knew she was telling the truth, and I stood up, I was still hard, in my pants, and I felt the little animal of my anger with her curling up in my breast. But I knew that if I let it out, there would be no tomorrow with her, and I wanted a tomorrow with her.

Her eyes followed me as I stood up, and she said, 'You're writing a love story. Aren't there things in it like this?'

'I don't know yet,' I said. 'I haven't got that far.'

She said, 'There ought to be.'

I wanted to let her know that it was all right not to fuck me. 'There will be,' I said. I reached down to her. She took my hand and pulled herself up and stood looking at me for a moment, holding on to my hand by her fingertips, and I looked back, I wanted her to change her mind and I thought she might, there, at that moment.

But she did not.

Chapter 11

Monday morning Nickie brought a new batch of periodicals and a fat joint from Simon. She wore black slacks and a white blouse and her lips were painted pink; she made me think of Good 'n' Plenty candy. I said, 'Watch out for those black and white outfits. You know what happened to Anna Louis?'

She said, 'I'm too fat,' and gave her hips a little wiggle that made me laugh. 'Matt's in a meeting with Patricia Patterson and the head of the AIDS Research Council all morning. Let's get off.'

'With you?' I said. 'Any time.'

We got two large coffees from the break room and got high while I looked through Simon's stack of new research. Nickie sat in the orange chair and smiled, toking on the green cigarette, and said, 'I like Simon English, don't you? He adds a Caribbean touch to the office.'

'Vietnam,' I said. 'Smoking behind the lieutenant's back.'

She passed the joint to me, I took it and drew on it and it hit me all at once smoothly and clearly. I looked down at the photocopy in front of me: 'Hong Kong Masseuses as a Vector for HIV,' it said. There was a note taped to it from Simon: 'Matt said to be on the lookout for stuff like this – enjoy!'

'Whatever,' she said, she waved her hand and reached for the joint. I handed it to her.

I spread my hands flat on the desk and gazed down at them. I counted my fingers, from one to ten.

Nickie said, 'You like this stuff, I take it.'

'Very good stuff,' I nodded. I looked at her, she looked good, stoned, crisp black and white. I reached across the desk and brushed her cheek with my fingertips. She smiled big, she liked it, but she said, 'Watch it, now.'

I sat back and sighed, I saw the black Venus on Simon's wall and I wanted her, I looked at Nickie and wanted her, I felt like I needed a woman badly, this minute, and so I changed the subject. 'I've got Matt's old computer at home,' I said.

'I'll bet that's interesting.'

'It is,' I said, and I debated for a moment telling the rest of it. But I was too stoned to do anything but tell her the truth. 'It's got his communications program on it.'

'So?'

'So that means I can log on to the company data base as if I were Matt Brackett.'

'You should be wary of anything that makes you resemble Matt Brackett.'

'I'm serious.'

'So am I. What are you going to do, as if you were Matt Brackett?'

I looked at her. 'I haven't thought yet.'

'Ah-ha,' she said, holding up a finger. 'And when you think, you'll realise that there is *nothing* to be done, as if you were Matt Brackett.'

'Tell me about it,' I said, I was thinking about the Gospel According to Matthew. I put the joint to my lips and drew on it and looked at her. Her face looked sweet to me.

She said, 'Matt's got a thing about women.'

'Me, too.'

'No, he's very particular about women. That was Anna's problem.'

'I thought she looked like she had AIDS.'

Her eyebrows rose. She said, 'Haven't you seen Cassandra?'

'Who's Cassandra?'

'Mrs Brackett.'

I shook my head. 'What's she look like?'

'Like she had AIDS.'

'You're kidding.'

She stood up and came around the desk to the shelves behind me. I turned my chair, watching her, she browsed through some back issues of *Survivor*. 'Here,' she said and she held one up for me to see.

Matt stood before a convention crowd with a tall, very thin, well-dressed woman. She looked famished, when she was naked you would have been able to see her ribs, her high cheekbones stood out, severe, she wore heavy lipstick, and rouge and eyeshadow, I said, 'Anorexia?'

Nickie shook her head. 'Ex-model.'

'How'd she meet Matt?'

'Matt used to collect models.'

'Really?' I remembered the women spread across the pages of Matt's magazines.

'Really,' she smiled. 'That was Anna's problem. She looked too much like Cassandra.'

'He doesn't like her?'

'Not since she left him for the president of the AIDS Research Council.'

'Wow,' I said.

'He collects models, too, I guess,' she smiled.

'And he's in a meeting with the guy right now?'

She shook her head. 'It was last year's president.'

'What happened to him?'

'Well,' her smile grew bigger, 'he missed re-election.'

I laughed.

She said, 'I'd have voted for him, though.'

'So they divorced.'

'Real ugly,' she said. 'Matt had to buy her off or she threatened to tell everything.'

'What's everything?'

'Nobody knows,' she said. 'Matt bought her off.'

I thought about it. I said, 'I wonder what the hell it was.'

She said, 'I bet it was money.'

'No,' I said.

She nodded. 'Money and taxes and stuff like that.'

'I bet it was something kinkier than that. He's into some weird shit.'

'Sure,' she said. 'But Cassandra knows heavier stuff than that. Stuff that could land him in prison, I'll bet.'

'You really think so?'

'Matt's a crook,' she said. 'He's said it on the radio show: "I am not a crook." That's how you know he is one.'

We both laughed. I said, 'What are you doing for lunch?'

'That's why I wanted to get high,' she said. 'They're having an Executive Committee meeting. I love taking notes when I'm stoned. Matt says I make serendipitous jumps.'

'What's the Executive Committee?'

'Oh, you know,' she said, 'like the Politburo.'

'They don't have a Politburo any more,' I said.

'They do here,' she said. 'They call it the Executive Committee.' Over the rim of her coffee cup, her eyes were smiling.

I wanted her, I whispered, 'Don't you want me to away from all this squalor? Isn't it time yet?'

'I still don't know what I want.'

'Yes, you do. You want to be free.'

She smiled. 'Yes,' she said.

'And you want a sex machine.'

She smiled bigger. 'Maybe.'

'Maybe?' I said. 'Be my lover.'

She laughed. She said, 'This is good stuff.' And I laughed with her then, to stay even, but she kept making me feel like she would fuck me, if I could just please her enough, if I could just charm her. She stayed while I talked about it, didn't she? She enjoyed listening to me, she enjoyed my desire. But she didn't want me badly enough, not the way I wanted her, and I went limp, my heart was suddenly bitter and I felt tense and sore across the back of my neck.

She said, 'I need to be like Margaret.'

'Who's Margaret?' I said, sitting back in my chair.

'She's head of member services.'

'Simon talked about her. The Divine Margaret.'

'That's her.'

'Why do you need to be like Margaret?'

'She doesn't twist it up.'

'What do you mean?'

She looked at the door. She opened it, and looked out and shut it again. Then she looked at me and said, 'Margaret's fucking Jim Neill.'

'Who's Jim Neill?'

'He's vice-president of Sales.'

'Lucky Jim,' I said.

'They always take off for a week after the conferences.'

'What conferences?'

'The AIDS Research Council conferences. They go to Cancún, places like that.'

'You want to go to Cancún? Let's go to Cancún.'

She shook her head, there was something serious about this Margaret business. 'The point is Margaret doesn't get it all twisted up. She's found something that works for her.'

'I would work for you.' I crossed my hands and rested my chin on them.

'I don't know,' she said.

My neck ached dully. 'You like me to make love to you,' I said. 'You like this. I'm making love to you right now and you like it.'

'I'm scared,' she said. 'Haven't you ever been scared?'

'I'm scared of dying,' I said.

'Aren't you scared of anything else?'

'Alongside dying, what is there to be scared of?'

She said, 'Sex, baby,' and she drank some coffee. She shook her head at me and lit a cigarette.

'Maybe you should talk to Margaret,' I said.

74

'There's an idea,' she said and she blew smoke. 'I'll say, "Margaret, how can you fuck them and work with them at the same time?"'

'That should get her attention.'

She looked at me levelly and said, 'Have you ever done it with anyone you had to work with?'

I thought a lie would be coming up. I said, 'I've done it with women I had classes with,' which was true.

'How many?'

'What?' I had heard her, but I was thinking about the lie.

'How many women?'

I said, 'Enough.'

'You're lying.' She turned her head away from me, she was a little angry and, I thought, a little hurt.

I said quickly, 'There was Laura Petty and there was Deanna Farris. Two. There were two.' I hadn't lied yet, not really.

She turned back to me. She said, 'And you can handle it?'

'I can handle it.'

'I don't know if I can handle it,' she said. She looked down at her lap, thinking. 'Maybe if I smoked a lot more dope.'

'We could do that,' I said, 'if that's what makes you feel free.'

She said, 'Look, you having a good time?'

I said, 'I enjoy you.'

'Enjoy me some more, then.'

I needed another drug. 'Give me one of your cigarettes,' I said, and she passed me the pack and her lighter.

She said, 'Whatever are you going to do around here now that you're high?'

I gave up, I said, 'What do you do?'

'I file things and read the magazines.'

'I'll file things and read the magazines.'

'You don't have anything to file.'

'I'll get something,' I said. 'Bring me some mail, and I'll file it.'

She said, 'You do get interesting mail, the AIDS mail. There's a book for you in it this morning. A review copy. *Sex for One*, it's called.'

I looked at her. I reached back and rubbed my neck. I said, 'I suppose that's the safest there is.'

Chapter 12

I was sitting at my desk around 11.30, gazing at condom ads on my computer, when the phone rang. It was Marian, the receptionist, and she apologised for buzzing me. 'No one else seems to be available,' she said.

'That's all right,' I said. 'What is it?'

'It's a person with AIDS, on 79.'

'Oh shit,' I said, and I sat back in my chair. The button for 79 was lit and blinking. 'What does he want?'

'He's sick,' she said, 'and he wants help.'

'He called here for help?'

'He's desperate.'

Everything moved before me in time, slowly and gracefully, a ballet of disease. I said, 'OK.' I pushed the button for 79 and said, 'This is Wiley Jones. Can I help you?'

'I hope so,' said a young man's voice on the other end. 'My name is Dick Cunningham and I've got AIDS.'

'Yes.'

'I've got CMV,' he said. 'Do you know what that is?'

I cleared my throat. I said, 'I just started working here.'

'Oh, great.' His voice was edged with tears and he had to stop for a moment. Then he spoke slowly and deliberately. 'CMV is *cytomegalovirus*. It's an opportunistic infection that people with AIDS get. And I've got it. I've got CMV retinitis.'

'Yes.'

'CMV retinitis affects the eyes,' he said and his voice broke just a little. 'It makes you blind.'

'Yes.'

'It's making me blind in my right eye, right now.' I said again, 'Yes.'

'And a friend of mine saw a show on television about it, where they talked about CMV retinitis, and he said they said they had a treatment for it, but I didn't see the show, so I don't know who they are, and I'm trying to find out what this treatment is before I go blind, do you see?'

I could see the blindness circling around him blackly, closing on him like a little death, I could see him turning in the closing circle. I could feel his aloneness, I remembered my hospital bed in the night, and wanting to leave it and not being able to. I said, 'Yes.'

He said, 'Can you help me? I've called everywhere else, believe me, I wouldn't call except you're the only one left.'

I said, 'I'll try.' I picked up a pencil and pulled a notepad over in front of me. I wrote on it, CMV TV, and I said, 'Your friend doesn't remember what he was watching?'

'He doesn't have AIDS.'

I had been rushing along with him, and now I stopped, with all the other people who didn't have AIDS. Then I said, 'When did he see it?'

'Some time last week.'

I wrote down the date. I said, 'Do you know, was it cable or network?'

'I don't know,' he said, 'I don't know.' And his voice cracked and he began to cry, softly, on the other end of the line.

I sat back in my chair and listened and waited until he was done. He said, 'I'm sorry.'

'It's all right,' I said. 'Where are you? You and your friend.'

'We're in San Francisco.'

'What's your phone number?'

He gave it to me, but he said it quickly and I lost track of it, stoned, and I had to stop him. I said, 'Could you repeat that, a little slower?' and he did. I sat back in my chair, looking at the notes across the yellow legal pad before me, and I said, 'I'll have to call you back.'

'When can you call me?'

I didn't know. I looked at my watch. I said, 'I'll call you before I go home today.'

'You will?' he said. 'That would be wonderful.' His whole tone had changed: he had been carrying CMV retinitis by himself all week and now he had given some of it to someone else to carry.

Stoned, I could see CMV retinitis: it was like a permanent broken back in a hospital ward for ever, it was a little piece of eternity, and eternity was blackness and aloneness and uncertainty and death. I looked at the paper in my hands and went next door to Grant's office.

Grant was on the phone, he must have been on it for a while or Marian would have given him the AIDS call. He looked up and motioned me inside, and I took a seat. He had a little cigar going and his bottle of medicine sat open on his desk beside a large white styrofoam cup full of black coffee. I reached across the desk to his pack of Kents, and took one and lit it, and sat back waiting.

He was talking to a woman, I could tell from the tone in his voice, and she knew him pretty well. He was defensive, sitting hunched over the phone and, I saw, sweating just a little bit, he said, 'I was only late with it that one time before, Julia, and all I'm asking for now is a little extension. Surely —'

And the woman cut him off. She wouldn't give him any time, I guessed. I sat in the chair, smoked the Kent and looked at the paper in my hands, *CMV TV, San Francisco*, and the phone number, written once and crossed out and written again.

When he hung up, he said 'Bitch', and you could tell he wanted to be able to say that to her face. He took a long swig on the Day Care, and his features smoothed out, it was all right now for Julia to be a bitch. 'And what's up with Wiley Jones?' he said.

I said, 'I just talked to a guy with AIDS.'

'Oh, my,' he said, and he looked serious. 'How did it go?'

'I don't know,' I said. 'I told him I'd call him back today.'

'What's he want?'

'He's got CMV retinitis, and he's trying to trace down something a friend saw on television about it.'

'Oh, Jesus, that could take for ever.'

'Yeah.' I looked at him. 'What should I do?'

He looked blank for a second, then he said, 'What should you do? What should you do? You should try Finder, that's what you should do. Come on,' and he turned his chair to face his computer and he bit down on his little cigar and pulled up Finder.

'How's it work?' I said, standing behind him and looking at the screen.

'You've got two search methods, straight and Boolean.'

'What's Boolean?'

'That's where you search for more than one thing at a time, like *CMV* and *retinitis*, or *HIV* or *blood test*.' He turned to me 'See?'

'I've got it.'

'Yes,' he said, 'and you can limit the search by dates as well.'

'His friend saw the TV show last week.'

Grant nodded and entered a date two weeks old. We searched for *CMV* and *retinitis*, and we got about twenty hits. Grant sat back in his chair. 'That's good,' he said, browsing over the list of finds returned by the program. He pointed to a line on the lower half of the screen. 'There it is,' he said, and I read the entry:

Cable Health Network, 05/06/91 EST2030, 'The Eyes Have It: Current Care for Your Vision,' 30 min., rbrdcst 05/08/91 PST1930.

'That's it?' I said. 'That's the show his friend saw?'

Grant tapped the screen with his finger. 'The most current collection of AIDS data in the world,' he said and he turned to me. 'And it all belongs to Matt.'

'How does it work?'

'That?' he pointed over his shoulder at the screen behind him. 'That snippet probably came from one of the clipping services. Little moles out there clipping stories with the words *AIDS* and *HIV* in them. The transcription and data entry is all done overnight by a company out on Jimmy Carter Boulevard. One of Matt's former editors runs it. Used to be a pretty good writer.'

'Well, I can call this guy right now, then.'

'Sure.'

It made me feel good, it made me feel like we had done something about AIDS, AIDS was out there blinding people in San Francisco, and Grant and I had done something about it. I picked up his phone and dialled the number and got the guy on the line again. I said, 'This is Wiley Jones again with *AIDS Survivor*.'

'Yes,' he said, he sounded excited. 'Have you found something already?'

'Yes,' I said, 'we just ran a search against our data base.'

I looked at Grant and I saw his face change expression. Something was in the doorway, watching us. I turned and saw Matt. I smiled at him, but he just stood there, watching. I covered the mouthpiece with my hand and said, 'This guy's got AIDS,' and I was stoned, and Matt was red, white, and blue framed in the doorway, the live version of the photograph screwed to Grant's office wall. He stepped into the office and held out his hand. It was smooth and steady and well manicured, and I didn't understand, but I gave him the phone.

He took it and spoke into it clearly. He said, 'This is Matt Brackett, I'm the CEO here, may I have your name?'

The guy told Matt his name.

Matt said, 'Yes, Mr Cunningham, you need to understand there is a charge of $150 an hour for searches of our data. If you'd like, you can put that on your credit card.'

The guy said something.

Matt said, 'Then I'm sorry we can't do business with you today. Good luck to you.' And he stepped past me to Grant's desk and hung up the phone.

He turned to me and said, 'Wiley, you're new here, so it's not your fault, but Grant and I have been over this ground before, and the charge for Finder's services is $150 an hour.' He shook his head. 'We're not doing this for anyone's health.' He looked at me. 'Is that clear?'

I looked at him and felt all the blood drain to my feet, I felt cold, I said, 'Yes, sir.'

'Call me Matt, please,' he said, pointing at me. He looked over my shoulder. 'Grant, I have several editorial matters I want to discuss with you. If you could join me in my office?'

I went back to my office. I dialled Nickie and told her about it.

'That's Matt,' was all she said.

'But you can't help these people at $150 an hour.'

'That's true, too,' she said. 'But it isn't supposed to help people.'

'What's it supposed to do, then?'

'It's supposed to make Matt feel like a captain of data.'

'A what?'

'A captain of data. That's like a captain of industry, only even more meaningless.'

'A captain of data.'

'Sure. That's what the magazines are for. They make Matt feel like a little William Randolph Hearst.'

'So the whole thing is about how Matt feels?'

'That's right.'

'What about how I feel?'

'Matt has the money,' she said. 'He gets to have the feelings. You want feelings, go get yourself some money.'

'And what are all these feelings of his?' I said. 'They don't seem to connect him with other people.'

'No, they don't,' she said. 'But that's not why Matt has feelings.'

'Why does Matt have feelings?'

'To make a soft human surface for his self-centredness,' she said. 'The same reason Matt does everything he does.'

I looked at the picture of Matt on the wall. I noticed how smug he looked in all his pictures, like he had told you so and now, here he was, right again. Listening to Nickie, I saw he looked like a fortress of emotions, real human feeling, just like you and I have, all wrapped tightly and secured against influence within the confines of a bulletproof tailored blue suit, with a little flair there in the tie, a little wild colour, some red, white and blue.

I got off the phone and I sighed.

Then I called Dick Cunningham in San Francisco, and I told him about his television show.

Chapter 13

I spent the rest of the morning doing the mail, reading *Sex for One* and coasting slowly down from the stone. I read back issues. I was still circling down around lunch time when Grant came into my office and sat down. He was smoking a pipe now and he looked amused. He said, 'What do you know about hackers?'

I looked at him. It was very strong and subtle dope, so that just when I thought I was straight again, something stoned would happen inside me. It happened now. 'What I read in the papers,' I said. 'They break into computer systems, don't they?'

'Yes,' he said and he sucked on his pipe. 'Matt thinks we've got a hacker.'

'Somebody breaking into our system?'

He nodded. 'Somebody logged on to the system this weekend and read Matt's e-mail and left him a message.'

I stayed calm, but it registered: Alix had fucked us up and now we would be caught, we would be in trouble, she would blow her probation and I would lose the job and have to quit writing until I could start again somewhere else, all of the imponding doom swooping above me in a stoned second. But through the little clinch of fear I did notice that I was thinking in terms of *us*, not just *me*. 'You're kidding,' I said.

'No. Apparently somebody really bored out there decided to give us a try and took a peek at Matt's electronic correspondence.'

'How does he know?'

'Whoever did it left Matt a sarcastic note.'

'Really?' *Really, really.* 'What did it say?'

'"In the future, everything will be round."' He laughed a little. 'Sort of clever. Matt's always writing things about the future.'

'What is he going to do about it?'

'He's changed his password. To "Orlando".' He sat back in the chair and puffed on his pipe. With a faraway look in his eyes, he said, 'Have you ever read *Orlando*?'

I shook my head.

He said, 'Virginia Woolf, now there was a woman.'

I was curious. I said, 'If Matt's changed his password, how do you know it?'

'I saw it on a note on Stan's desk. It was in Matt's handwriting. That wretched little scrawl.' He accented his words with a small wave of his pipe, tipping the stem into the air. He said, 'That's what hackers call *social engineering*. I socially engineered it.'

I said, 'Orlando.'

'Great book.'

I went to Systems to see the extent of Alix's damage, and there wasn't any. Stan was alone at his terminal, writing a computer program. He gazed into the screen and tweaked his moustache.

I noticed a vacant terminal behind him, working by itself. The command **123** appeared by itself at the prompt, and the program executed: a spreadsheet was loaded and figures were entered and the worksheet recalculated, all at a vacant keyboard. I said to Stan, 'What's that? Is it haunted?'

He looked over his shoulder and saw what I was talking about. 'That's Matt,' he said, 'telecommuting.'

'Matt?'

'Yeah,' said Stan, 'he's at home, working.'

'How does he do that?'

Stan pointed across the Systems office at a tall, grey metal bookcase full of software. 'Carbon Copy,' he said.

'What's that?'

'It's a communications program. You run it on two computers connected by modem, and it lets you use the remote system.'

The possibilities for this program opened up wide and instantly. 'That's fantastic,' I said, smiling despite myself.

'Yeah, it's keen,' said Stan. 'All you need is a phone.'

'I've got a phone.'

He laughed, looking at me curiously. 'I've got one too,' he said. On Matt's spreadsheet, a cell was zeroed out, and then the worksheet was recalculated again. 'In fact, I use this same program sometimes, on the weekends.'

'That's really fantastic,' I said again, and I wondered idly if Stan knew Simon English, really knew him, I meant, *really, really*.

'Sure,' he said. 'It's Matt's kind of program, lets him be in two places at once.'

Carbon Copy made me feel very happy. I said, 'Do you think I could borrow this program?'

'*Borrow?*' he said, and his eyes smiled.

'Steal?'

'The word is *pirate*.'

'Then could I pirate that program?'

'Sure,' he said. He crossed the room to the shelf of software, and opened one of the disk files and thumbed through it. He found a diskette and brought it to me.

'Isn't there a manual?'

'Matt pirated it,' he said, and his eyes smiled, *See?* 'All we've got are the two zips.'

'A zip,' I said, 'Nickie showed me what that was. There's a program to unzip it, right?'

'That's right,' he said. 'PKUNZIP. The disk has two zips of Carbon Copy, one for the local station and one for the remote. You need two, because each one has a serial number, and when they connect over the phone line, the first thing they do is exchange serial numbers. If the number's the same, they disconnect.'

'OK,' I said. 'So, to telecommute, I unzip one here and one at home.'

'Right,' said Stan. 'And you set the one here to answer the phone and use the one at home to call.'

'I think I understand it.'

He took the diskette from me. 'I'll make you a copy.'

'That's everything I need?'

'That's everything.' He slid the diskette and a blank into the drives of his machine. 'PKUNZIP is on the disk, too,' he said, and the drive light came on as the copy started. He sat back in his chair and put his feet on the desk. 'Knock yourself out,' he said.

Chapter 14

I unzipped Carbon Copy in a directory on my machine when I got home that night. There was a box with a menu in the lower right-hand corner of the screen, and I pressed function keys to see what was what. A screen called Data Link Maintenance held the system parameters, and I wasn't sure they were set right, so I loaded the communications program and checked the settings there, then corrected the ones in Carbon Copy to match. Then I pulled up what it called the call table, and I read a list of names and phone numbers. There was a list of passwords, too, and I added one to it: *Redhead*. I smiled to myself, satisfied.

When I thought I had done everything I could with Carbon Copy, I started the communications program again and tried to log on to Brackett Data as Matt. Now the system would not admit me. I broke off and called up the screen of phone numbers and looked at it. Alix had said the computer ran a script, and the last column on the screen was headed **Script**. Under this heading, alongside **Brackett Data**, it said **Matt**. There was a file on this computer named *Matt*, and it played Matt's log-on routine every time you called Brackett Data. But I didn't know how to fix it with *Orlando*.

I got two beers from the refrigerator and went down to Alix's apartment. She answered the door, wearing a business suit. Her hair was up. I said, 'Join me in a beer?' I handed her a bottle and she took it. She unscrewed the bottle cap with her bare hand and drank a little.

She said, 'What do you really want?'

She sounded pleasant enough about it, she enjoyed me, I thought, so I went ahead. 'Really, I want you to show me how to change a script in the communications program.'

'You're into communication, aren't you?' she said, and she unbuttoned the collar of her blouse.

'Yes,' I said, 'I'm a writer, remember?'

'I keep forgetting.' She stepped away from the door. 'Come on in.'

I followed her to her living room. The computer screen glowed in windowed colours on her desk, in the middle of the crowded wall. She sat on the big sofa and looked through a pile of mail on her coffee table. I sat in an easy chair and sipped my beer.

She stood up, she said, 'Give me a minute to change', and left the room.

I went over to her desk and sat before the big screen of her computer. It was more than a foot across, and the resolution was very fine. One of the windows was labelled **Alix**, and I saw a graphics program there. I knew it from school, where an astronomy professor my freshman year had had computer graphics of the solar system. I clicked on the icon and loaded the program.

A window opened and filled with a listing of graphics files. They all had names like MWS05998.JPG. I highlighted one at random and hit the return key. A second passed, then the window filled with a full-colour image of a young man, naked and erect and beckoning the user. His cock was huge. I felt myself flushing, and I clicked on the exit button and hurried back to the easy chair with my beer and sat down. I drank the beer and I thought about my cock and the guy's in the picture, and I wondered how Alix felt about it.

She had changed into a red-and-white striped T-shirt and cutoff blue jeans. Her hair was still up, but it was mussed where she had squeezed it through the neck of the T-shirt. She said, 'You should switch to Pabst. It's sweeter.'

'You like sweet beer?'

'I like sweet things,' she said. She took a long drink from the Budweiser and said, 'So what do you want to do with the communications program?'

'Matt's changed his password.'

'And you know the new one already?'

'It's "Orlando".'

'Pretty good social engineering,' she said, and she smiled. 'You realise, you have to buy me dinner for doing this.'

'Of course,' I said, and I stood up. 'Are we ready to start?'

She got a diskette and we went back up to my place. She sat before the computer and inserted her diskette in it. I watched over her shoulder. 'This program is an editor,' she said. 'It's like a programmer's word processor. It'll save the file in a format the computer can read.'

I said, 'The script file is called *Matt*.'

She glanced at me. 'You learn fast.' She copied the editor on to my computer and loaded the *Matt* file. 'There it is,' she said, and she pointed to a line in the script that said.

```
WAITFOR 'password>'
TRANSMIT 'Paper/Tiger'
```

'Here's his old password,' she said, pointing at the words

Paper/Tiger, 'and we'll insert the new one.' She typed **Orlando** and deleted the old password. Then she saved the file and quit the program. She said, 'Now let's see if it works.'

She started the communications program and chose Brackett Data from the menu. This time it logged on with no problem. She turned and smiled up at me. I looked down at her, I wanted to muss her red hair. I toasted her with my beer and sipped it instead.

She looked pleased with herself, with the hacking, and she said, 'Let's do something.' She typed S for System and waited while a new menu appeared.

'What do you want to do?' I said.

'Wreak havoc,' she said, and then she laughed.

I didn't know whether she was serious, and I was afraid for a moment. I was noticing that she always made me feel like a kid, inexperienced and inadequate, and this made me risky, wanting to do something to impress her. 'What do you really want to do?' I said.

'I don't know yet. Let's look around. Pull up a chair.'

I moved the rocker over beside her and sat down. The menu had a number of items on it, including Accounting and ARC.

'Try ARC,' I said. 'I'll bet that's the AIDS Research Council.'

'What's that?'

'Some group of AIDS businessmen.'

'AIDS *businessmen?*'

I shrugged. 'I guess at Brackett Data,' I said, 'AIDS is a business.'

She turned back to the screen and looked at it for a second, then selected ARC from the menu. ARC led us to another menu, and we poked around in it for a while. We ran some spreadsheets which meant nothing to us, and we read some letters in Matt's word processor, which meant next to nothing. I sat back in the rocker. 'This is boring,' I said.

Alix looked at me. 'You've got to persevere if you're going to hack. You've got to wade through tons of this shit to get to the good stuff.'

'What's the good stuff?'

She shrugged. 'You tell me. You work there.'

I said, 'Matt is having an affair with patricia Patterson. That would be good stuff.'

'See,' she said. 'You're like me, looking for the sexual stuff.' She turned back to the console, and we exited the ARC menu. She read the System menu again. 'Here,' she said, pointing, 'let's try this.'

'What?'

'Communications.'

The Communications menu was fairly long, too. 'Here!' she said and pointed at the screen. I followed her finger to the word **Users**.

'What's that?' I said.

'I'll bet that's a list of the users.'

'So?'

'So it might have everyone's password in it. It would be like a master key to the insides of the whole company. Let's look.'

She tapped U for Users, and in a minute a screen came up with a user's record. She said, 'Who's Ralph Abel?'

'He's one of the salesmen.'

'Look,' she said. 'His password is Ticonderoga. It does, it has everyone's password.'

'How can we get it?' I said.

She thought for a second. She pointed to the bottom of the screen, where a small menu of commands was listed. 'We'll edit the file, then drop to the operating system and find it by date. Once we know the name, we'll just download it.'

'Download it?'

'Copy it over the phone line from their system to ours.'

I heard her say that word, *ours*. I said, 'Won't there be a record of the download?'

'If there is, it'll be Matt's record,' she said. 'No problems.'

She pressed a key to add a new user, and typed in *George Herbert Bush* and a DC phone number. She set dates for membership on the board and made up a password, then saved the record.

'OK,' I said, 'how do we get out of this and into the operating system?'

'That's on the System menu,' she said, 'option D for DOS.'

She quit the Communications menu, and called up the System again. When we picked D for DOS the screen cleared and said

Microsoft(R) MS-DOS(R) Version 4.01

(C) Copyright Microsoft Corp 1981–1990

She typed **set** and the screen filled with strings of computer babble. She said, 'I'll bet that's where it is,' and she pointed to a long list of directories.

I said, 'What are you doing?'

'I'll bet the users file is in the same directory with the bulletin board software. It almost always is. And that's this directory.'

I looked at the screen. She was paging through the file list, looking at the dates and times of the files. 'There it is,' she said.

'Where?'

'There.' She pointed to a file name in the listing. 'Write it down. How original. "Users.Log."'

She typed **exit**, and we were back at the System menu. She backed out of this menu and worked her way over to a download menu. She requested a download of C:\BBS\USERS.LOG, and after a second, the system told her to proceed. She said, 'Ha!' loudly and she tapped some keys too fast for me to see and entered the file name again. Then she sat back in her chair and took a long pull on her beer, finishing it.

'You look like you're enjoying yourself,' I said.

'I am.'

'Are you sure you won't get in trouble?'

She relaxed a little, and she looked good, relaxed. 'Only if you turn me in. Are you going to turn me in?'

'Of course not.'

'I didn't think so.' She smiled at me. 'Why turn me on just to turn me in, right?' One eyebrow rose slightly.

'Pointless,' I said.

She turned back to the computer. After she got the file, she logged off the system, and then she loaded what she called a debugger, which allowed her to look at the users' log. The display filled with rows of numbers and letters, but it all meant something to her, she said, 'Shit, this thing isn't even encrypted.' She reached for her beer again, but it was empty. She looked at me, she said, 'Get me another one, will you?'

I got two more beers, and while I was opening them, the phone rang. On the second ring, Alix called, 'Do you want me to get that?'

I thought it must be Nickie, and I thought it would pique her interest, so I called back, 'Sure.' I heard Alix saying, 'Hello.'

When I got to the sun room, she was sitting before the computer holding the phone in her hand, smiling. I said, 'Who is it?'

She smiled, 'Some woman wants to talk to *Willie.*'

I took the phone from Alix and said, 'Hello, Mother.'

My mother said, 'Hello, Willie. Have you been trying to call me?'

'No, ma'am,' I said, and Alix smiled bigger, 'I'm sorry, but I haven't. I just got the phone.'

'Oh,' she said. 'Well, I just wondered how you were doing down there.'

She was smoking, I could hear her blowing smoke, I thought of all the times I had crushed her packs of cigarettes when I was little, trying to get her to stop. I said, 'I'm doing fine.'

'You must be,' she said. 'Who was that who answered the phone?'

'That was Alix,' I said. 'She's a friend of mine.' Alix was looking at me now.

'Alix,' she said. 'You've got a girlfriend,' and now she was smiling, too, I could hear the smile in her voice.

'Not exactly.'

'Not exactly,' she said. 'What does that mean?'

'I guess that means it's nothing serious.'

Alix laughed silently, rocking in her seat, and she whispered, 'It's nothing serious, Willie!'

I said, 'We're just friends. That's what they say, isn't it?'

My mother said, 'Well, where do you live down there? You haven't written or anything.'

'I was going to call you,' I said.

'You were? When?' She had a different kind of smile in her voice now, hurt that I hadn't called her already, and scolding me for making excuses, but perversely satisfied that I hadn't, since my neglect confirmed all her most secretly gratifying suspicions of lovelessness and abandonment, and I hated her for just a second, I wished she were dead and not embarrassing me in front of Alix, I wished my father would be her husband and take care of her so I could go after my own women.

'I don't know,' I sighed. 'It hardly matters now, does it?'

She paused. 'I suppose not,' she said. 'But let me get your address.'

I gave it to her and she wrote it down. 'Really, Willie,' she said, 'you've got to stay in better touch than this. I had to call information to get your number.'

'I'll try to do better about it.'

'You promise, now.'

'I promise.' Alix rocked back in her seat and laughed hard, silently.

'Good,' she said. 'Now, tell me everything, so I can tell Nathaniel when he comes home.'

'I'm fine,' I said. 'I've got a job.'

'Doing what?'

'Editing for a small publisher.'

'Anyone we would know?'

'I doubt it,' I said. 'It's controlled circulation.'

'Controlled circulation?' she said. She did not like them giving it away for free. 'Willie, surely you could get on with a real magazine.'

'It doesn't matter,' I said.

'What do you mean, it doesn't matter?'

'I mean, it's just something to keep things together while I write this book.'

'What book?'

'My book. That's the real part.'

The book made her pause. I knew she wouldn't say anything about it. I said, 'How's business?'

'Oh, he's gone a lot,' said my mother. 'Like always, you know.'

'Yes, I do.'

'You do, don't you?' she said, and her voice changed again, filled with soft emotion for her Willie. I took a long, hard drink of beer that stuck in my throat, I felt it going all the way down to my stomach, I felt like she was talking to her lover.

Alix crossed her legs and crossed her arms and sat forward watching me. I held up my free hand empty, what could I do?

'It's lonesome here without you,' she said.

'I'll write you,' I said, I hurried, I wanted off the phone, I wanted to hit my father in his face, I wanted to show him, I wanted to take off Alix's clothes and feel her breasts and her cunt and make her lose control, see her come.

She said, 'Are you taking good care of yourself, Willie?'

'Yes, ma'am.' I turned away from Alix and looked out the window at the park a solitary figure in a long coat moved across it. Everyone else was at home now, everyone was someplace having dinner, and this one was homeless, carried everything he owned on his back in a long coat, had no place to go. 'Are you?'

'Are you exercising?' she said. 'Remember what Dr Hutchens said, it's important that you exercise.'

'I walk every day,' I said. 'I live across the street from a big park.' I watched my walker in the park, he walked steadily away, but he looked over his shoulder from time to time, as if he heard something following him.

My mother said, 'Well, then.'

'Yes,' I said. We were always, at the end, in a place where I said, simply, *Yes*.

'You be sure to get your rest, too.'

'Yes, ma'am,' I said. 'So should you.'

She laughed. 'Well,' she said, 'when you get to be my age, you don't need as much sleep.'

This made me smile, for some reason. My walker disappeared under a clump of trees. I said, 'Yes, ma'am,' and turned back to Alix, who sat watching me.

'You promise you'll write,' said my mother.

'I promise.'

'All right.'

'We'll talk again soon,' I said. I hung up the phone.

Alix said, 'Really, Willie', and she shook her head.

'Wiley,' I said, 'please.'

She looked at me and smiled and drank her beer. She said, 'We're just friends, though? And here I thought you were serious, but the truth comes out when you talk to your mother, doesn't it?'

'All right,' I said.

She laughed then turned back to the computer and pointed at the display. 'I can write you a viewer for this in a couple of hours,' she said.

I looked at her back, her shoulders looked delicate but she seemed very strong, and I liked that, it made me feel free. I looked at the computer screen and said, 'What will that do?'

'It will allow you to read the file. Let's go down to my place.'

She copied the file to a disk and we went downstairs. At the console of the big computer in the middle of her living-room wall she opened a window onscreen and began typing in computer code that I couldn't understand. She said, 'There's some dope in the tin on the coffee table. Roll us one and put some music on.'

In a saltine tin on the coffee table was a baggie full of marijuana and a package of JB cigarette papers. I rolled a joint carefully. I said, 'Where's a light?'

Matches on the stove,' she said over her shoulder.

I got the matches from the kitchen and lit up and carried it back to her. She sat back in her chair and drew hard on it. She spoke through the smoke while she stared hard at her computer code: 'Put some music on, honey.' Then she passed the joint back to me and went on coding.

I heard that one word, *honey*, and it was *our* computer system, and it all excited me, and I looked at her red hair in the evening shadows and the white skin of her legs, and everything glowed blue and white from the screen of the computer. I thought about her

91

graphics program and I wondered what she did with it, I wondered if she would let me watch, I wanted to watch her being sexual. I went to the stereo in the corner of the living room, I was smoking the joint, and I picked out some jazz and put it on, and Cedar Walton strummed the piano like it was a guitar, and I carried the joint back to her at the computer and she took it and inhaled. She sat back in her chair, her eyelids heavy, and she stared into the screen of the computer. I looked at her, she was excited, her nipples were hard beneath the T-shirt and she stroked her thighs with her open hands before she returned to her typing, the machine was what did it for her, the dope just iced it, she was on a long, long head trip and she smoked the dope to fuck with herself while she did it.

She typed several short lines of the computer language fast, and she handed the joint back to me. The piano made a roof over us and a wall around us, and I wandered into her sun room and looked out at the park.

Behind me, Alix said, 'Let's try this.'

'Is it ready?'

'Maybe. It's quick and dirty, but it might work.'

She started it up and a listing from the users' log appeared on her screen. It was a crude listing, one item to a line, but you could read the file. Alix said, 'Now you can log on as whoever you like. It's perfect cover.'

I smiled at the melodramatic word. I said, 'Are we spying?'

'You bet,' she said. 'We're spying on Brackett Data.'

'What do you suppose is there to spy?'

She shrugged. 'Brackett Data stuff. You work there.'

'There're back issues of the magazines.'

'What about Brackett's personal stuff?'

'Maybe,' I said. 'Or it could be just more notes about the future.'

She stood up. 'I say we log on again and look.' She gestured at her console. 'I'll get a printout of this later. Let's go.'

She led me back to my own apartment and we logged on to Brackett Data again. She sat at the console and grazed through the system, using Matt's menu. It struck me that I was thinking of him now simply as Matt, the way he wanted everyone to. I lay on my pallet and read my manuscript, stoned, for about an hour. I was drowsy from all the beer, so I got up and made a pot of coffee. I brought two cups back to the sun room, gave one to Alix and said, 'I thought I was going to have to buy you dinner.'

She looked up from the computer. For a moment, it looked like she did not know who I was. Then it seemed to register and she relaxed, she had been tensed over the console and intent on the system. 'That's right,' she said. She sipped the coffee.

'Where do you want to eat?'

She drank a little more coffee and thought. 'Let's go to Pop's.'

'Where's that?'

'Right next door. It's an old neighbourhood bar.'

'How old?'

'Old,' she said. 'It's been going out of business ever since I moved in here.'

'Bar fare?' I said. 'Beer and sandwiches?'

'Beer and sandwiches and alcoholism.'

'Really?'

'Some of the regulars are pretty sad,' she said. 'But he's got colour TV and darts.'

'Pop's then,' I said. 'Let's go.'

Chapter 15

Pop's fronted the park, next door to the apartments. Through the big windows I could see the people out for the evening, I could see the big swing set and children rising and falling. The food seemed to bring Alix down a little, she did not seem so wired after we ate. The alcoholics sat solitary at the bar in business suits and nursed their drinks alone. The television showed soundless wrestling, while an old jukebox played softly sad cowboy music, and a pair of college guys played darts and looked at Alix. I said, 'You're the only woman here.'

She smiled at me and drank her beer from the bottle. 'It's that kind of bar, Wiley. Does that make you nervous?'

'Not if it doesn't bother you,' I said. I toasted her with my mug.

'I'll bet,' she said. 'You're still so young.'

'I'm twenty-two,' I lied again, I was getting good at it. 'You know, free, white, and twenty-two. Only you're not supposed to equate free and white any more.'

She leaned forward with the bottle of beer in both her hands and said, 'Well, I'm free, white, and thirty-two, and I haven't had this good a time since before I got arrested.'

'I'd almost forgotten about that,' I said. 'Tell me, are you a felon?'

'You bet,' she said, and she looked around us, she stretched in her chair. 'I like Pop's,' she said, she was happy. 'It's down and out.'

'You like things down and out.'

She shrugged, as if to excuse herself for some weakness. 'I like broken things.'

'I thought you liked simplicity.'

'Being broken makes you simple,' she said. She nodded privately towards the dart players. 'They don't belong here. Couple of Tech students. They're slumming.'

'We're not.'

'We're broken,' she said.

'I'm broken?' I didn't feel broken. I felt used up, but I didn't feel broken.

'If you weren't broken, you'd be back there in school. Like all the schoolboys.' She glanced at the dart players.

'I'm not a schoolboy,' I said.

94

And she looked happy, she said, 'You're a hacker.'

I laid my hands open on the table before her, I said, 'I'm whatever you'll have me be.'

She looked at me and she said, 'Proteus.'

'Who's that?'

'A sea god. The Greeks. He could change his shape at will.'

I lifted my hands empty over the table, I nodded. 'Proteus, then,' I said.

'You are Proteus, and I am Confusion.'

'Confusion?'

'That was my handle, back when I hacked.'

'Confusion.'

She said, 'You know something about me, but I don't know much about you.'

'What do you want to know? I told you about my accident.'

'That was in the papers. Tell me something secret.'

'OK,' I said. 'I don't know how to write a novel.'

'That's no secret.'

'It's not?'

'How could you know anything about it? You haven't done it yet. Tell me something real secret.'

'I don't know anything about love.'

'Not anything?'

'How could I know anything about it? I haven't done it yet.'

She smiled, she shook her head. 'Are you telling me secrets, Proteus, or are you just playing with the words?'

'I'm telling you secrets, Confusion,' I said.

'How can you do love?'

'I need someone to show me how.'

'Whoever could that be?'

I said, 'Is that a secret too?'

'I don't think so,' she said. She sat looking at me, softly. With her head on one side, she said, 'You've got to tell me a real secret, Proteus, if you want me to teach you things. You've got to tell me something you're afraid to tell.'

I said, 'Were you afraid to tell me about your probation?'

'That interested you, didn't it?'

'Were you afraid to tell me about it?'

She tore at the corner of the label on her beer bottle and began to peel it away. 'It scares some guys off. Felony. That's a lot of power for a woman.'

'That doesn't bother me.'

95

'I have my weaknesses, too.'

'Will you tell me about them?'

'Maybe. Some day. If you tell me about yours.'

I took a sip of beer, and I felt afraid and I thought about it: I thought that because I felt afraid, it must be the right thing to do. So I told her, I said, 'I masturbate over you.' In the park, a boy rode high into the air on the big swing. I felt weightless.

She looked at me, surprised and trying to contain it, and then she looked around the room, to see if someone had overheard me. I thought the guy on her computer had the biggest cock I'd ever seen, and I had the sudden wild idea that she had actually taken the photograph. The Tech boys put the darts away and finished their beers and went outside. They got into an old dark green MG with a shattered headlight and drove away into the evening. The alcoholics nursed their drinks silently at the bar.

She turned back to me and smiled a little. She said, 'Really?'

I said, 'Really.' I drank some more beer, waiting to see which way she would go.

She said, 'You've changed shape on me, Proteus.'

'It's what you wanted,' I said. 'I always try to give you what you want.'

'Do you know what I want, Proteus?'

I shook my head.

'I want to go upstairs,' she said.

Chapter 16

We made love on the big sofa across the living room from the blue computer. This was after we found out I did not have any condoms and I drove down to the drug store in the shopping centre on the corner where Morningside began and I got some. She absolutely refused to do it without the protection. She went along with me to the drug store and when I told the pharmacist I wanted a box of Fourex, she said, 'No, Ramses Extras', and we both turned to her, and an old woman with grey hair and a blue raincoat sitting on a bench waiting for a prescription looked up at all of us.

Alix said, 'The lambskins aren't as safe.'

The pharmacist was a black man with a shaved head and a pair of aviator glasses tinted brown. He turned from Alix to me, and his eyebrows rose in a question.

I said, 'A box of Ramses Extras.'

'Ribbed,' she said.

The pharmacist looked at her closely: he'd never seen a woman this particular, and he turned to me again, and the old lady laughed softly, and I said, 'Ribbed.'

He said, 'Box of twelve or twenty-four?'

I said, 'Twelve.'

Alix said, 'Twenty-four.' She said, 'I've got the money if you don't.'

And the old lady laughed again, she lifted her hands from her lap into the air, it was so wonderful.

In the parking lot, I stood beside the car with the keys in my hand and left the door locked while Alix waited. I said, 'You had to do that, didn't you?'

She smiled at me. 'I do it right, Proteus.'

'Does this have anything to do with Confusion?'

'This has everything to do with Confusion,' she said. 'This is pure Confusion, isn't it, honey? What's the matter, were you embarrassed?'

I said nothing.

'Oh, you were embarrassed by Confusion,' she said, and her voice was singsongy like a parody of Miss Alix on *Romper Room*, but she moved close to me and put an arm around my shoulders and put her other hand between my legs. She squeezed me softly, and kissed me on the neck and whispered in my ear, 'I think you're sweet when you're all excited.'

And now I took my turn and looked around to see if anyone was watching. Night had fallen, and the lights of the mall were bright, bold colours in the fresh darkness. She took her hand away and said, 'Let them watch. It's OK.' She rubbed the back of my neck with her other hand. She said, 'It's OK, what I do.'

I said, 'I've never been with anyone like you before.'

'Do you want me to stop?'

I spoke immediately, I said, 'No.'

She laughed a little. 'You like it, this way?'

'You're exciting.'

'You like to be excited.'

'Yes,' I said. 'I do.'

'Let's go, then,' she said, and she gestured for me to unlock her door. 'It's time for me to be exciting.'

I had thought everything would have been spoiled by then, the moment interrupted and so broken. But Alix laughed at me and took me back to her place and took off her clothes while I took off mine, and she sat me on the big soft sofa, and she put some music on, rap music, and she rolled another joint and we smoked it while the Negroes rapped to us, *some foreign power, some group of terrorists, there is something changing in the climate of consciousness on this planet today.* The words were hot, with a rapid beat, and we caught the heat in the close apartment in the warm spring night, and we sat facing each other on the soft cushions of the sofa and she reached up and took her hair down and it fell long and red over her white shoulders and her white breasts and she looked into my eyes and licked her lips and spit into her open palm and reached across and took me into her hand and rubbed me sleekly up and down, licking her lips and looking into my eyes to see my insides coming out for her. She bent low now and then to gaze at my cock and fondle it with her hands and eyes, to kiss it and tease me with her tongue, until I had to stop her or come all over her, and when she stopped she sat back and smiled at me and said 'Yes' very softly. Her breath came quickly, she was excited, she was tense and her nipples were stiff and she wanted to fuck, and I lay there getting my breath back and I thought of Nickie for one moment, I thought of Anne Mathers and then I didn't think of either of them again. I sat up and reached for Alix and stroked her cunt, and she quickly took my hands and held them before her and caressed them, examining them thoroughly, lovingly, kissing them and licking them and sucking on my fingers in a way that made me very hard, and then she let me touch her again. I watched her eyes while I made her come, I watched her green eyes open and close in wonder and ecstasy, I watched her body whip around on the fingers of my hand, in the blue light from the machine with the Negroes rapping, and she came, she thrust her hips at me, coming to me for more and more, she came across the sofa and on to me and took me in her mouth and sucked hard and almost hurt me. She found the condoms and tore one open with her fingernails, and took her mouth slowly off me and slid the wet latex on to me and pushed it down around me and she rose up over me and came down smoothly and I went into her and she said, 'Yes, honey, oh yes, yes', and put her breasts into my face to be kissed and said 'Yes' again as I kissed her. And she rocked above me up and down and I came inside her and she was over me in the blue light and she was blue electricity riding on the end of me and we were outside of time for a moment, for a moment of time, nothing was real but the coming with each other, nothing could touch me but her, and no one could touch her but me.

When we were through, we lay together in our sweat among the big soft cushions, and she ran a finger down my temple. She said, 'I do not love you, Proteus.'

I said, 'I know.'

'I want to keep that straight,' she said. 'I'm not in love.'

'That's a song,' I said, and I sang a little of it to her. *'Out of love, not in love with nobody.'*

She stroked my face again. 'You have a good voice,' she said. 'Tell me another secret.'

'I'm not in love with you, either,' I said.

'Good,' she said. 'Then we'll probably enjoy this, while it lasts.'

'Maybe we'll even enjoy it after it's over.'

'You are an optimist.'

'How many men have you made love to?'

'That's none of your business.'

'It isn't? Somebody asked me that just today.'

'Somebody asked you how many men you've made love to?' She smiled at me.

'This woman wanted to know how many times I've gone to bed with women I had to work with.'

'I take it this is somebody you work with.'

'Yes.'

'Did you tell them it was none of their business?'

'No. I said I'd done it twice.'

'Is that true?'

'It's mostly true.'

'You only told her part of the truth.'

'I told her I fucked these two girls in the same English class. But really I was fucking these two girls in the English class at the same time.'

'You cheat, Proteus.'

'Sometimes.' And I wondered if I shouldn't have told her.

'How can I trust you?' she said.

'You can trust me because I'm not in love with you.'

She laughed, she said, 'Good, I like your cheating. It'll keep me from being in love with you, too. Are you in love with this woman you work with?'

I rolled over on to my side and let my head rest on her breast. I held her other breast in my hand and held the nipple between thumb and forefinger. 'I might be,' I said. 'I'm in lust with her.'

She yanked my hair. 'You take yourself too seriously,' she said, and frowned slightly.

I rubbed my scalp. 'Sorry,' I said.

'Are you in lust with me?'

I wondered what was going on inside her. I said, 'Very much.'

'But this other woman won't do you because you have to work together.'

'Exactly.'

'She thinks, Proteus. You don't.'

'You've fucked people you work with?'

'We weren't talking about fucking, we were talking about love and lust.'

'What if love is really fucking?'

'I've often suspected that,' she said.

I laughed at her.

She said, 'Anyway, you're not concerned about fucking. You just fucked me, but you're talking all about this other woman.'

'Sorry.'

'Fucking's for me,' she said, and she placed her index finger between her breasts, I looked there and I saw a bead of sweat making its way down her chest: she was hot, and I liked her that way. 'Fucking's got nothing to do with her.'

'No?'

100

'No,' she said. 'Maybe you're in love with her because she won't fuck you. Maybe if she fucked you it would all go away.'

'Maybe.'

'Would you like to pretend that I'm her? I could dress up like her and put on her makeup and dye my hair and you could pretend to fuck her.'

'Like Jimmy Stewart does Kim Novak in *Vertigo*.'

'Sure. We could do it. I'm into multiple personalities.'

'Like *Three Faces of Eve*.'

'No, like *Sybil*. I said *multiple*. You know, *lots*.'

'How many personalities do you have?'

'Right now, just three.'

'What are they?'

'There's me, and there's my bitch, and now Confusion is back. But I had more than that back when I hacked.'

'How many?'

She shrugged, under me. 'Lots. I never counted.'

'Count.'

'I had a Confusion personality, that was me when I was online, and I had a Sheri the secretary personality sometimes, when I was doing social engineering, and a Cathleen the phone company supervisor personality, for when I had to phreak. And I had an Alix Roberts personality, of course, I used that for job applications and with people I fucked.'

'That must be a special personality. It has a complete name.'

'Yes, Alix Roberts is rather special. Not everyone gets to see her.'

'Have I seen her?'

'I fucked you, didn't I?'

'What's she good at?'

'Job interviews and fucking.'

'She makes pretty good conversation, too.'

'That's Confusion doing the talking.'

'Oh.'

'And there's my bitch personality, I've always got that to fall back into from any personality I happen to be in.'

'Have I seen that one?'

'Not yet,' she said. 'Do you want to?'

'I don't know,' I said. 'Sometimes bitchery can be very sexual.'

'My bitchery is very sexual, Proteus.'

I sat up on the sofa, looking at her. I said, 'Then you'll have to show it to me some time.'

She lay back looking at me. She said, 'I think I have to love somebody to really bitch with them. It's like Norman Mailer and the knife, you know.'

'Norman Mailer and the knife?'

'He stabbed his wife once. One of his wives. With a penknife, I think it was.'

'Really?'

'Really. Anyway, he wrote a poem about it. And he said, *So long as you use a knife, there's some love left.*'

'And that's what your bitch is like?'

'I think so.'

'Love me, then,' I said.

'Oh, Proteus,' she said, and she frowned sourly. 'We were doing so well just fucking each other.'

'OK,' I said, 'fuck me.'

'I already have.' She sat up and stretched. I turned to watch her.

'Fuck me some more,' I said.

She looked back at me. 'What's this woman's name?'

'Who?'

'The one you're in love with.'

'Nickie.'

'I'll be Nickie right now, then,' she said. She squeezed her legs together and covered her breasts with her crossed arms. She looked at me over her shoulder. 'Do you want me to Nickie fuck you?'

I looked at her. I thought about it. 'No.'

'See? It's got nothing to do with fucking.'

'Be Alix Roberts and I'll fuck you.'

'Alix Roberts doesn't feel like fucking any more tonight,' she said. 'See?' She smiled at me.

'You're not being Alix Roberts, you're being Confusion.'

She laughed and stretched again and got up from the sofa.

'I'm going to get one of your sweet beers,' I said. 'Do you want one?'

She shook her head, and I went to the kitchen to get the beer. When I came back, she was sitting before the computer, naked, typing something into the program she had written to read the users' log. The apartment was hot, we both glistened with sweat in the blue light from the computer, and I went into the sun room and threw open the windows all around, one at a time, from left to right. It caught a spring breeze and I sat in a lounger, drank my beer and watched the lights of the traffic go by below us. Alix left the computer alone to put some more rap music on, and when I finished the beer, I went into the living room and got dressed.

Alix said over her shoulder, 'Leaving?' A black man talked to other black men on the stereo, he said, *we do whatever we do to survive.*

'It's late,' I said, 'and it's only Monday night.'

She still sat naked in front of the computer, coding. She said, 'I'll have this something nice for you tomorrow. It'll have a better interface.'

I looked at the black letters across the white window in the blue screen and nodded. I said, 'I like interfacing with you, Confusion.'

She looked at me, her eyelids heavy and dreamy looking, she laughed at me softly and said, 'You fuck real good, too, honey.'

I closed my eyes. A black preacher spoke out earnestly on the stereo: *Mary McLeod Bethune said the true worth of a race must be measured by the character of its woman,* and I looked at her, crossed the room and bent down and kissed her goodnight, kissing her deeply, and she kissed me back, and I caressed her breasts as softly as I could, I wanted it to be good for her, I wanted to be special for her. And then I left her.

Chapter 17

I overslept the next morning, I got no writing done and was twenty minutes late to the office. I did not feel too bad about missing the writing, because I had plans for that, but I did not want to get caught late. I didn't want to blow the job, it was turning into a perfect setup. I slipped past the time clock and saw Nickie watching me from her desk outside Matt's office. I stood in the entrance foyer with my briefcase and made a motion for her to tell me if the coast was clear. I felt like Grant Cummings. Nickie looked at me, her face said, *Who, me?* like she wouldn't dream of helping someone subvert the office routine, then she looked away suddenly and turned back to me and shook her head urgently. I ducked behind the time-clock door and waited. I heard nothing for what seemed like a long time, then looked out again, and she sat at her desk laughing at me silently.

I stepped out, looking around cautiously. The main office was absolutely empty, and I walked over to her desk and said, 'You liked doing that to me, didn't you?' I couldn't help smiling, her little breasts shook like leaves as she laughed at me, but I said, 'I'll get you for this.'

'Oh,' she said. Her lips formed a sweet O and I wanted to kiss her. 'You're all right,' she said. 'You've delivered your body, just like the rest of us.'

After I got squared away in my office, and had messed up the desk to look officious, I got a cup of coffee and unzipped Carbon Copy on my terminal. I had left the machine turned on at my apartment, with Carbon Copy loaded and waiting to answer the phone. Now I entered my phone number and called myself up.

The modem went through its high-pitched fuzzy sound and connected, and a window opened on my screen and prompted me for the password. I typed *Redhead* and two windows opened, one labelled **Your Dialogue** and the other **Remote Operator's Dialogue**. I sipped my coffee and read the directory of the machine in my apartment. I switched directories to get to my novel, and loaded Word Perfect and pulled up the manuscript. I reread the first paragraph and made a change in the second sentence.

I smiled at myself as I sipped my coffee and began to work. I wrote, *Her nipples were as red as her hair*, writing there in my officeless office, telecommuting to my homeless home.

Chapter 18

When I got home Alix's car was sitting in the same place it had been in that morning, it hadn't been moved. I wondered what she had done all day long; rested, I thought, looking up the steps to her door and thinking about fucking her, feeling my cock good between my legs and strong, knowing suddenly that I was better for her than the guy on her computer, wondering if she wanted me again, hoping she did. I stopped by her apartment on my way up.

She came to the door in her blue bathrobe, sipping a glass of orange juice, and she looked through the blinds, checking me out first before she opened the door. Her hair was down around her face. She said, 'Hello, Wiley.'

I leaned against the green-painted brick of the wall and smiled at her and said, 'You mean Proteus, don't you?'

She smiled back a little, but she seemed tired. 'Proteus,' she said.

'How are you?' I said. 'Are you sick?'

'I'm a little tired today. I didn't go to work.'

'I saw your car,' I said. 'Let me fix you some supper.'

She studied me for a moment; she seemed to be thinking something through carefully. She said, 'I do not love you, Proteus.'

'I don't want anything,' I said. 'I just want to do you a favour.'

'All right.'

'I'll be back.' I went upstairs, and pulled off my tie and changed into a pair of cutoffs. Then I went back down to her place. She had a lot of vegetables and a wok, so I made some stir-fry while she watched a ghost story on her VCR in the living room. I found two bottles of wine laid down under the kitchen sink, a red one and a white, and I chilled the white and opened it for supper.

We ate on the coffee table in the living room and drank wine from juice glasses. She sat on the sofa and I sat on the floor and the ghost story played: Julie Harris fell in love with Hill House and died there. The computer screen glowed blue in the middle of the wall.

'This is good,' she said, eating.

I said, 'Thank you.' A breeze blew through the open windows of the sun room, but it was a warm breeze, without any cool to it. It was a warm evening; she laid her bathrobe open at the neck and brushed her hair back over her shoulders and I unbuttoned my shirt.

While the video rewound, she sipped at her wine and set it on the coffee table and she said to me, 'I have something I should tell you, Wiley.'

'What's that?'

'I should have told you last night.'

'Yes?'

'I was afraid to.'

'I can't imagine you afraid,' I said. 'What is it?'

She bit her lower lip and looked at me, I watched her eyes going over me.

I said, 'You're measuring me.'

'Yes,' she said.

I said, 'Do I measure up?'

She said, 'I'm HIV positive.'

I didn't hear her, I didn't want to. I said, 'You're what?'

She said, 'I'm HIV positive.' Her hands lay open in her lap, and she sat still, looking at me.

It was still between us in the heat. I felt myself suspended crazy around her words, afraid and my balls shrinking in the fear like it was cold, and it was hot, and I could feel everything, I felt a drop of sweat slide down my right side from my armpit, and I saw her face, still and shining brightly with a thin film of perspiration in the early evening light that flooded slowly in through the sun-room windows. Out in the park, a young man in khakis walked with a woman in a pink dress. Her shoulders were bare except for two straps of pink and her skin was white as Alix's and her hair was jet black and cut short, framing her round face. She held a rose in one hand, she held it out to him and he bent forward amd smelled it. A small girl ran by them pulling a yellow balloon. The traffic murmured on the avenue outside, white noise, pausing for the light.

I swallowed some wine, it was fruity and thick in my mouth. I said, 'Who's this talking now? Is this Confusion talking?'

She said, 'This is Alix.' She looked down at her empty hands.

It felt hot. I wiped my mouth with my napkin and I drank the rest of my wine. It was warm. I said, 'Are you sure this isn't just the bitch?'

She looked away, out the sun-room windows. She said, 'This is Alix.'

'Or maybe this is someone else altogether,' I said. 'Is that it?'

She said nothing.

I said, 'That's it. This is not Confusion, this is Cunning. Cunning, come to scare me away.'

She turned to face me, and she shook her head hard, angry and irritated. 'This isn't hacker bullshit,' she said. 'This is Alix talking to Wiley.'

This was Alix.

I looked into her face. Her green eyes looked back into me. Her hair was darker red at her scalpline where the sweat dampened it. I felt the sweat on the back of my neck, I felt the heat cross my brow. I said, 'You should have told me last night.'

'What would you have done?'

I said nothing, I looked at her.

She said, 'Would you have fucked me?'

'Yes.'

She laughed once, shortly, and looked away. She said, 'Oh, Wiley, really.'

'All right,' I said. 'I don't know.'

'Don't you?' she said, turning to me again. 'I think you do.'

'I don't know,' I said.

'Do you want to fuck me now?'

'Right now?'

'Now that you know.'

And I realised that I wanted to impress her, and that I did not know how to. She was thirty-two, and I thought of all the men she must have fucked, I thought of the guy in the picture. I said, 'I don't want to lose you.'

She said, 'You haven't got me.'

'You know what I mean.'

'You don't want to stop now?'

I said, 'I don't want to stop.' I remembered the feeling of her taking me in her mouth the night before, like a woman in a magazine, and I wanted her to do it again and again, and now she would not. I wanted to take back the last ten minutes and unsay all the words and fuck with her just one more time, just once more, I wanted to step back and undo it, take it all back and look both ways before I crossed this time. I lost my breath and I was floating, adrift – did I have it? had I caught it? how could I have caught it? I tried to recall the night before, I tried to think it through calmly. I remembered the careful way she had handled my hands and cock the night before, making love to them, she had examined me, and I thought we were safe, I insisted we were safe, it did not spread in the saliva, it could not penetrate the latex membrane, there had been no exchange of fluids, her cunt on my hand. I looked down at my right hand, empty, she had come in my hand, flowing freely across my fingertips and palm, and I wondered if I should have washed it, was there any danger there? was it too late now? If it was too late now, it was too late. It was too late, wasn't it? Some way. I looked at her and I said again, 'I don't want to stop.'

She sighed. 'I wish you would just get angry.'

'Maybe I don't get angry.'

'Do you get scared?'

Dick Cunningham cried softly into the phone, all alone with CMV retinitis, and the softest breeze swept through the apartment, but it did not cool either of us. 'Yes,' I said, 'I'm scared.'

'You needn't be,' she said. 'We were safe. But you need to be angry.'

I said, 'Do you want to stop?'

She sat still, watching me, I wondered what she saw. She said, 'I don't usually tell people this.'

'You don't want to stop,' I said.

'Usually, I go to bars, and I get picked up, and nothing comes of it.'

'Do you use a condom, then, too?'

'Yes,' she said. 'I insist on it.'

'Does anybody ever guess why?'

'No,' she said. 'They never have.'

I said again, 'Do you want to stop?'

She looked hard at me. She said, 'No, I don't.' She looked away. Outside the sun-room windows the young man in khaki was kissing the woman in pink, they kissed lightly and then smiled at each other. He had his hands on her bare shoulders. Alix turned back to me, her face shiny with sweat. She said, 'Do you want to get tested?'

'Yes.'

'I know a place where you can get tested for free. Or almost free. But you'll test negative. We were safe.'

'All right.' I still wanted to be tested.

'It's always better to be sure,' she said. 'That's why I got tested. It's always better to know.'

'How did you get it?' I said.

'I was in love,' she said. She looked at something in the air before her, her lover, something.

'And he had it.'

'Yes.'

'What was his name?'

108

'Stephen.'

'Is he still alive?'

She shook her head. 'He got pneumocystis pneumonia.'

'Do you know how he got it?'

'He used to do injection drugs.' She closed her eyes and sighed, then opened then again and looked at me. 'No mysteries. He was clean when he died. He was clean seven years.'

'That's a long time.'

She was looking at me hard, measuring me again. Her hands were in tight little fists in her lap. She opened them and smoothed down the fabric of her robe across her thighs. She pulled her robe open at her throat and she breathed deeply. She said, 'Will you still fuck me?'

Her robe had parted over her knees and I could just see the soft white flesh of her inner thigh. Her skin was smooth and soft and the colour of ivory, I could feel her tongue against the head of my cock the night before, I looked at her lips now, the colour of blood, her mouth was open a little, she was waiting for my answer. I said, 'Yes.'

Her mouth closed, and she wet her lips with her tongue. She said, 'You don't have to.'

I stood up and moved to the sofa, her eyes following me. I reached inside her robe and put my hand between her legs, I held her cunt. She was hot, the air was warm around us, close. She leaned near and kissed me lightly on the lips, just a brush of flesh, she took my hand away from her and stood up and drew me after her.

We went into her bedroom. It was blue, like a robin's egg, and the dying sunlight filtered into the room through thin brown rattan blinds. The bed was blue, dark blue sheets, unmade all day, I could see where she had lain, the windings in the fabric in the shape of her body. The windows were open and the warm breeze blew through the blinds, through the room, and the soft sounds of traffic stirring came up from the street. She dropped her robe to the floor as I followed her and I bent to pick it up. She sat on the edge of the bed, turned towards me, and spread her legs wide for me to see. Her green eyes burned. She was Confusion. She was strong, and I wanted to show her all my weaknesses. I let loose the robe. I crossed the room to her and she reached and undid my cutoffs and drew out my cock and bent forward over it and began to kiss me there. I rose hard to meet her lips, and she took me in her mouth, and my knees buckled and she held my hips tightly in her hands and sucked. I said her name. I put my hands through her red hair, I put my cock deeper into her mouth. At the head of the bed I saw the box of Extras from the night before and a colour Polaroid of a blond-haired young man in a frame from the drug store. He sat at her kitchen table and smiled and waved at the camera. Stephen, I thought, Stephen watches here, this is her secret place, this is where she is Alix Roberts, this is where she is HIV positive.

I took her head in my hands and raised her up and kissed her deeply and long, and I moved my hand between her legs and began to caress her there and she made a long low sound that sounded like fucking, and I laid her back across the bed and kissed her breasts and caressed her until she came in my hand, curling into a ball around my fingers and saying 'Don't stop.' We were wet with sweat, we stained the sheets a darker blue, we burned like a fever together. She kissed me and she kissed my hand, she stretched and reached to the box of condoms and she took one and opened it one-handed and slid it on to me and slid herself on to me and began to fuck me and I came very quickly inside the condom inside of her, and then we lay still, joined together. I held her lightly and let my hands wander over her, and she lay on top of me, holding my cock inside her and whispering in my ear, 'Oh, Wiley, you make me come so good, do I make you come so good when you fuck me?' and I lay there with her, I was sailing, easily, I was Wiley, and I said, 'Yes, Alix,' I said, 'Yes.'

Chapter 19

My father called me the next night. I was in the sun room of my apartment, reading over my manuscript, or I probably would have missed him, which would have been all right with me.

The first thing he said was, 'Marie tells me you're working for a controlled circulation magazine.' He didn't like it any better than my mother had.

I reached for my beer and took a long drink. I hadn't expected the call, and I wondered what he wanted. 'That's right,' I said. I saved the manuscript and exited the word-processing program. I didn't want it loaded, I had a history of destroying things after I talked with him, smashing ashtrays and breaking bottles, and I didn't want to destroy the novel.

'Come on,' he said, 'you can do better than that. You can find somebody with enough self-esteem to charge actual money for their magazine.'

I stood up from the desk, with my beer in one hand and the phone in the other. It would be a fight about work tonight, I thought, and I thought I could win that one. I said, 'I don't care about any of that. I just want something to support me while I write this novel.'

He waited a moment then I heard him sigh, he was so patient, wasn't he? I heard the ice clinking in his glass as he drank his bourbon, and he said, 'Well, what's this novel about?'

'It's a love story,' I said.

'Well,' he said, 'at least love stories sell.'

'Yes, they do,' I said, 'some of them.'

He said, 'It's a romance?'

I laughed out loud at him. I saw pink book covers among the paperbacks at the grocery store, low-cut bosoms and long, flowing hair. 'No,' I said, 'it's not a romance, it's a love story.'

'Look,' he said, 'if you want, I know some people at the *Constitution* down there, I could set you up, get you on to something real.'

The novel was not real, of course, and I knew exactly how he felt and more. Sitting there in the early mornings stalled and not knowing what to write, my heart would sink and then Brackett Data would become real and I would be trapped in it: massaging periodicals and downloading packages. I drew a deep breath and said, 'The novel is real', and I felt a little tremor of doubt and fear. Maybe he was right after all.

I could see him. He would be shaking his head now, full of experience, a lifetime in journalism. 'I'm not saying your novel isn't serious to you, but surely you can see the advantages of a real job with a real paper. Controlled circulation only prepares you for more controlled circulation. It's a dead end. What is it, anyway, trade press?'

'It's about AIDS.'

'AIDS,' he repeated. It surprised him, he had expected something industrial, like *World of Refuse* or *International Plastic*. 'Well, that's different.'

'Yes,' I said. 'It's got a different slant on things. I'll have the circulation manager put you on the complimentary list.'

'That's all right,' he said. 'I get enough to read already. But what about the *Constitution*?'

'A newspaper job will only prepare me for more newspaper work,' I said. 'It's a dead end, too, see?'

'It's a real job.'

I sighed, I felt tired, arguing for it more on faith. 'So is writing the novel,' I said.

He was silent. I said nothing. When he spoke again at last, he said, 'I'm going to send you a credit card, an American Express.'

'What for?'

'Emergencies,' he said. 'You can't tell. You might find yourself in a jam for cash some time, you might need it.'

'Is that what you had in Saigon?' I said. 'Your father's American Express card?'

I could see him shake his head again, the head-shake always preceded the expression of misunderstanding, I didn't understand him, that was the problem. He sighed again, and waited for the sigh to sink in. I had hurt his feelings, I was supposed to be surprised.

There was a long silence between us, and I watched the people moving randomly across the park, through the shadows of the trees long with evening across the dry grass. I decided to push him a little. 'How's Sarah?' I said. And I wondered what he would say, we weren't supposed to talk about Sarah, she was his steady mistress, he'd been fucking her for years in between the others, and all of it was all right with my mother, which somehow made it none of my business.

'Why do you ask?'

'I just asked,' I said. 'I was just making conversation.'

'Our conversation about Sarah usually isn't very pleasant,' he said.

'Well, then, how are *you* doing?' I said. He couldn't risk anything with me, he had to be in charge, he had to have his Pulitzer Prize sitting on his desk so you'd know who he was and act accordingly. I ran my hand through my hair and ground my teeth together. Then I went ahead and said it. 'Have *you* started any novels lately?'

He was silent. He had started one a long time ago, a big one about Vietnam that he had never been able to finish. It sat in a banker's box in a corner of his study, where he drank, it was something he would talk about on hot summer nights. When the weather got muggy like Saigon, he would sweat and drink his bourbon and water and talk about getting back to it, getting a second Pulitzer.

Finally, he said, 'Not lately', and he paused again before he changed the subject. 'Marie tells me you have a girlfriend.'

'Yes.'

'Well, what's she like?'

I took a deep breath, and I thought about it a moment. 'She's thirty-two,' I said.

He laughed. He said, 'Well, you're not slow.'

And I decided to tell him, I thought it would fuck with his head, and so I said it, I said, 'She has AIDS.'

'What?'

'I said, she has AIDS.'

'Christ.'

Got you, motherfucker.

He said, 'Well, do you—' and he let it hang there, and I said, 'I fuck her, yes.'

He said, 'Well, I mean—' and it hung again, and I picked it up, I said, 'I protect myself.'

'Well, you're that smart,' he said. 'Where did you meet her? Does she work on the magazine?'

I laughed again. 'This company would never hire anybody with AIDS,' I said. 'She lives in the building here, she's a neighbour.'

'Christ,' he said again. 'Well, you must be in love with her.'

'What else could explain it?' I said.

'But, really, Willie,' he said, 'you ought to think about this.'

'When did you ever think about it?' I said. 'Unless it was after it was done and it was too late.'

'Willie,' he said, 'you can talk about me all you want, you know it doesn't matter, but AIDS, I mean, really, I've never run that kind of risk.'

'How do you know?' I said.

And he was silent.

I said, 'Maybe you ought to get tested. For Sarah's sake, at least.'

He was still silent and I waited. He said, 'I'll have American Express send the card directly to you.'

And I thought, *Confusion would take the fucking card.* I said, 'All right' but I knew what that would mean, I knew it, and it came out immediately: we were together now, with the credit card, we were father and son, and I would do things to please my father, wouldn't I? I wouldn't finish the novel, would I? He said, 'Sarah will be in Atlanta soon. She's got a commission down there.'

I knew then why he had called and I played my end of it, I said, 'Tell her to call me. I'll take her out to dinner on your American Express card.' That's what it was for, wasn't it? So Daddy with his friends at the *Constitution* could pay for dinner for his mistress Sarah with his son Willie, Sarah who would probably, then, talk to Willie about his future, Sarah who was so beautiful but poverty-stricken because she had spent her future on painting and art, the way Willie wanted to, Willie who might just come around to the newspaper office if he'd only listen to his father's cunt, and he knew me that much, he knew I'd listen to her. Because he knew he would.

'I'd like that,' he said.

'I like Sarah,' I said, 'really I do. She's always been good to me.'

'I'll give her your number, then,' he said.

'Give her this one, too,' I said, and gave him Alix's number. 'In case I'm out.'

'I'm sure she'll look you up,' he said.

I said, 'How's Mother? She called once.'

'She appreciated your letter,' he said. I had sent her a note.

'Is she getting out at all?' I said. 'She never goes anywhere unless you take her.'

'You exaggerate.'

'She depends on you for everything, you know that.'

'She's a grown woman.'

'Why do you think she puts up with Sarah and all the others?' I said. 'She's afraid to be alone.'

He sighed and again there was a long silence. 'Haven't we been over this before?' he said at last. And then, slowly, 'What doesn't bother your mother shouldn't bother you. We agreed to that, I thought.'

114

'Yes,' I said. 'I guess I forgot for a minute.' I took a long drink of the beer.

'That's all right,' he said. 'Your mother can look after herself.'

So it was useless, everything with him was useless, and you took the American Express card. I remembered when I had been a boy and had read about syphilis for the first time. I had thought of my mother crying in the night alone in their room down the hall from mine, where I lay awake with a flashlight under the covers reading about social diseases in a family medical encyclopaedia, and I hoped my father would get syphilis, I hoped that it would stop him. Now I sighed, and I reflected that, at least, I didn't feel like smashing anything, and I said, 'I suppose she had better.'

Chapter 20

Two weeks later I got two boxes of condoms from an ad agency. The boxes were red, white and blue. I took one home and showed it to Alix. She said, 'Three colours never found together in nature', and she popped one of the condoms open and slid it on to a bottle of beer she was drinking. We were sitting in my sun room. She had been hacking when I got home, tuned into Brackett Data after hours and reading everyone's mail. She sat at the computer in blue-jean cutoffs and a red T-shirt that said BATTERIES INCLUDED. I sat down on the pallet and pulled off my tie. She had her hair up and played with the condom and that made me want to take it down, to muss her. She pulled the condom down hard over the mouth of the bottle, trying to break it. She said, 'These are good.' She slipped the condom off the bottle and drank some beer.

I said, 'Did you take the day off?'

'Yes,' she said. 'I took a mental health day.' She took the condom, and drew it back like a rubber band and let it fly at me. I batted it away, the lubrication came off on my hand.

She said, 'I've been checking out Brackett Data for you.'

'Yes?'

'Your Nickie.'

'What about her?'

'There's a salesman wants to fuck her.'

'Who?'

'Someone named Jim Neill.'

'He fucks Margaret.'

'I know. They're going to the Bahamas after the summer conference.'

'And he wants to fuck Nickie.'

'He's always asking her to do him special favours.'

'Like what?'

She shrugged. 'Type letters, prepare reports. The other salesmen use this Marian who answers the phone.'

'How do you know Marian answers the phone?'

'I read all the job descriptions.'

I said, 'You've been busy.'

'I've been hacking the old man, too,' she said.' I checked his credit record this morning. He's solid, but we could fix it otherwise.'

'Why would I want to do that?'

'Because you can.' She nodded at the screen. 'Same reason he does things.'

I thought about it. 'I suppose so,' I said, 'but let's not do it today.'

'All right,' she said. 'We won't, but we will, OK?'

I shrugged.

She said, 'Did you know he has three phones into his house?'

'Really?'

She nodded. 'He's got one for him and one for his business.'

'What was his last phone bill?'

'$156,73 for the residence, $313.10 for the business,' she said. 'He's got call forwarding, three-way, call waiting, the works.'

'Pretty good,' I said.

'I thought so,' she smiled, proud of her hacking. 'Then he's got this third line that's secret.'

'If it's secret how do you know about it?'

'No one has secrets from Confusion,' she said.

I took the beer from her and took a long sip. I gave it back to her and slipped off my loafers and started to unbutton my shirt. 'So what's this third number all about?' I said.

'That's what I'd like to know. It's unlisted, and it's not in his real name.'

'What name is it in?'

'B&D Ministries.'

'Bondage and domination.'

She smiled. 'I thought of that, too.'

'You would,' I said. I pulled off my shirt and slipped out of my khakis. Alix slid down from the chair on to the pallet beside me. The sun was bright through the windows, the sky was a ceiling of white clouds broken through here and there by patches of blue. I picked up a pair of cutoffs from the corner and pulled them on. I peeled off my socks and slipped into a pair of thongs. Alix wiped her forehead with the beer bottle.

She said, 'What's B&D Ministries, really?'

'How would I know?' I said.

'You've got these cards in your desk,' she said. She took one of Matt's cards from her hip pocket. 'They've got the third phone number on them.'

'You went through my desk?'

'I was looking for your manuscript. I wanted to read it.'

'Don't you ever ask?'

'It's no fun if you ask.' She shrugged, she was becoming Confusion.

I went to the kitchen to get another beer. When I came back she was lying on the pallet with her arms folded behind her head. She said, 'You never said what B&D Ministries is.'

'No, I didn't,' I said. I drank some beer.

'Well?'

'I don't like you going through my desk.'

'I suppose you've never done anything like that.'

I said, 'Why do you have pictures of naked men on your computer?'

She said, 'I like to look at them while I masturbate.' She said it quickly, I couldn't surprise her, I couldn't stop her.

'You masturbate?' I said.

'Yes,' she said. 'I like to.'

I let it pass. I said, 'You really want to know, don't you?'

'You should tell me,' she said. 'You shouldn't keep secrets from me.'

'All right,' I said, and I sat in the chair beside the desk. 'Matt's got a personal ministry.'

'What's that mean?'

'He helps young women in distress.'

She said, 'He runs a home for wayward girls.'

I nodded. 'Something like that.'

She sat up and looked at me, she didn't believe me. 'What is it really? Why do you have the cards?'

I took a deep breath and closed my eyes. 'It's crazy,' I said.

'I thought so.'

'He's got these magazines in his office.'

'Skin magazines. Stroke books.'

'Yes.'

'He wants you to procure women for him.'

I shrugged. 'Yes.'

She smiled, she was a good detective, a true hacker. She said, 'What's the Gospel According to Matthew?'

'I don't know. He saves that up for the women.'

She smiled bigger. 'I want to find out,' she said.

I felt suddenly tense through my stomach and the back of my neck. I said, 'What do you mean, exactly?'

'Procure me for him,' she said.

'You?'

'Not *me*,' she said. 'Confusion.'

118

'What would Confusion do with Matt Brackett?'

'Confuse him.'

I shook my head. I didn't like this, I had to stop it. 'He's already confused enough.'

'Well, if not me, who, then?'

'Nobody, then.'

'You're going to let Matt down?'

'That's right.'

She frowned. She pulled the card from her pocket again and looked at it. 'Let's call him, at least.'

'Why do you want to do this? It's crazy.'

'That's why I want to do it,' she smiled and shook her head at me, I was a drag, I didn't want to do crazy stuff.

I said, 'You've got the number.'

'Good,' she said, and she stood up and stepped over to the desk, and picked up the phone and dialled. She was grinning, she was happy, beyond anyone's control. I put my hands on her hips and drew her closer to me, I thought I could distract her. She swayed towards me while she listened. She said, 'It's a recording.' I pulled her T-shirt up and kissed her bare midriff. She ran her free hand through my hair. She spoke into the phone in a voice she put on, 'Hello, Matthew, this is Connie Phone. I got one of your cards last night at Rupert's, and I wanted to find out what the Gospel is according to you. I know that means *good news*, and I want to hear some of that, all right. I don't have a phone of my own, or I'd leave you a number, but I'll call you back, and we'll see about getting together in person. Ciao, now.'

She hung up. I hadn't distracted her, but I was hot now, I unbuttoned her cutoffs and nuzzled her. She said, 'You'll help me, won't you, honey?'

I held her ass in my hands and pulled her closer to me. I said, 'I'll help you. What do you want?'

She said, 'I want to hack Matt Brackett.'

'Is he a computer?' I licked her and unzipped the cutoffs.

'He's a system, honey.' She put her hands through my hair and drew me nearer, I kissed the soft skin of her smooth white belly. She lifted my head. She said, 'Let's try out one of these patriotic ones.'

119

Chapter 21

That evening, Alix and I lay together drinking cold duck with the lights out and watching the moon and the summer stars above the big park. The night was warm and a little humid, we were naked, it was easy to be naked with Alix. My phone rang, and Alix rolled off the pallet and crawled across the sun room and stood up on her knees beside the desk, answering it. She said, 'Sure,' and turned to me. 'It's for Willie,' she said, she held the phone out to me, her hair down around her shoulders.

'My mother?'

She shook her head. 'Some other woman,' she said and she offered the phone to me again. 'You make out, don't you?'

I got up and took the receiver from her and sat down at the desk. She lay back on the pallet, drinking the duck with her feet resting on the windowsill, lifting her head off the pillow to meet the glass halfway. I said, 'This is Wiley.'

'Hello, *Wiley*,' said Sarah, and she sounded pleased to find me at home. I looked at Alix in the shadows: she was staring out the window, pretending not to listen while she listened. I said, 'Hello. How are you? Where are you?'

'I'm fine,' she said. 'I'm in Atlanta. I've got a commission down here. A bank. *Lots* of money.'

'Good. You deserve it.'

'You're sweet to say so.'

'It's true,' I said. 'You're a good artist.'

'Oh, I remember now why I love you so much.' She was smiling, happy.

'Sure you do,' I said. 'I'll say whatever you want.'

Alix sat up and drank her wine and began to pull on her cutoffs. Her left foot caught up in the ragged denim and she kicked her way through it, tearing it with a sharp sound. I wondered where we were going. My neck felt stiff, and I heard her whisper 'Fuck'. heard the zipper of the cutoffs close.

'Where are you staying?' I asked.

'I'm in a hotel at someplace called Lenox Square.'

'That's up in Buckhead.'

'What's Buckhead?'

'That's where the rich people live,' I said. 'It's nightclub land. And the governor lives in Buckhead.'

'Where are you?'

'I'm in Midtown.'

'Is that better than Buckhead?'

'Sure,' I said. 'All the gay people live in Midtown.'

Alix put a hand on my shoulder and I turned to her. She had on her T-shirt, she held a fresh glass of the cold duck in one hand and she reached down between my legs with the other and took hold of my cock and balls and squeezed them quick and hard, smiling tightly, showing her teeth. She whispered, 'I'm going downstairs, Proteus.' She released me and left.

I lost my breath. I turned back to the phone as Sarah said, 'Where's Midtown from here? I can get a rental car tomorrow.'

I could still feel Alix's hand, I had seen a challenge in her eyes, she wanted me to do something, *do something, Proteus*, and Sarah said, 'Wiley?' and I drew a deep breath and said, 'I'm south of you.'

'Want to have lunch?'

'I'm not an artist,' I said. 'I've got to be at The Office.'

'You are an artist,' she said, and I liked her saying it. 'Nathaniel told me you're writing a book.'

'That's true,' I said. 'But isn't?'

'Yours is different, I'm sure It's good,' she said. 'I'll bet it's very good. What's it about?'

'It's a love story.'

'Oh,' she said. 'You're writing a love story? I want to read it. Can you show it to me?'

'Sure,' I said.

'We'll have to get together soon, then.'

'Where's your bank?' I said.

'Someplace called Colony Square.'

'That's just up the street from where I live. All the homeless people wear ties there.'

She laughed. 'Do you wear a tie to your office?' she said.

'Yes,' I said.

'I'll bet you just hate that, don't you?'

'It's a very square place.'

'Well, that's not you.'

'I do a good square imitation, though.'

'All good artists do.'

'I saw a picture of Picasso wearing a tie.'

'That's how I got this commission.'

'You wore a tie?'

'I imitated a square.'

121

'You're smart,' I said.

'You too,' she said.

'But we already knew all this,' I said. 'Let's talk about something new.'

She laughed. Then she said, 'I've really missed you', and the words came out slowly. 'I've missed our walks, and I miss talking with you.'

Towards the end of my convalescence, we used to go for walks together through the District, sometimes we would share a matinée or a cheap early dinner. She usually spent the evenings with my father, she would smile and touch my hand and leave me.

I said, 'I've missed you too, Sarah.'

'Have you really?' she said.

'Yes,' I said. 'I've never been alone like this before.'

'You can't be that lonely,' she said. 'Nathaniel said you had a girlfriend.'

'Yes,' I said, 'now.'

'Oh, I see,' she smiled. 'You were alone before your girlfriend.'

I flushed with embarrassment. I always felt like such a boy with Sarah: she was not just a woman, she was the *other* woman, she was the *mistress*. Now she did what a mistress does, I suppose, she covered my embarrassment with grace. 'Alone in a city. I know how that feels,' she said.

And I imagined her, alone in Buckhead, and alone in Washington with Nathaniel Jones, sitting alone with the great man in some low-lit colonial bar in Georgetown, drinking colonial bourbon with him, her long blonde hair spread gracefully across her shoulders and her breasts. I thought of how many men she could have had, if she had wanted them, instead of him.

She said, 'What's your girlfriend's name?'

'Alix Roberts.'

'Is she an artist?'

'She's an artist with a computer.' I said. 'She's a programmer. She's really sharp.'

'You wouldn't have anything to do with anybody else,' she said. 'Is it love? Or can you tell me?'

I laughed. 'I can tell you anything, can't I, Sarah?'

'I hope so,' she said. She paused a moment, and I finished my wine. Then she nudged, she said, 'So, tell me.'

Outside, a breeze picked up a little, and I felt it fresh across my face. In the unlit room I let the cool air kiss me everywhere, and I did not know if it was love or not. I wondered when I would ever know what love was. 'I suppose it could be,' I said.

'"Suppose,"' she said. 'You're Nathaniel's son, all right. If you say you love this girl, you might miss a different one tomorrow.' And I did not want to be his son, but I could hear the shrewdness in her voice and see her intelligent blue eyes. She knew how this worked, there was no real fencing with Sarah, not for long, she kept up with the Joneses. I set the empty wine glass on my desk and ran my fingertip around its lip, I smiled at her and I said, 'Yes, I suppose.'

And she laughed; she made it seem very light to be his son. She said, 'Well, since work is so important you can't have lunch with me tomorrow, when can we see each other?'

'How about tomorrow night?' I said. 'We could go to dinner.'

'I'm on an expense account.'

'An artist with funding!'

'Daddy Warbucks, sweetheart,' she said, and she laughed hard. The money was her revenge on all the squares, the years. 'I get $65 a day *to eat*. Can you imagine?'

'That's real decadence, Sarah.'

'You said it. I mean, these people spend $70,000 on just a car. Do you know?'

'Sounds like my boss.'

'Ooh,' she said. 'Let's eat up their money tomorrow night.'

'Sounds good to me,' I said. 'I'll drive. What hotel are you in?'

'A Ritz-Carlton,' she said. 'I've got this great view of the biggest shopping mall I've ever seen. There's a Macy's and a Neiman-Marcus.'

'And tall buildings, too, a skyline,' I smiled. 'Why are you in Buckhead when the job is here in Midtown?'

'I've got to meet with the interior designer,' she said. 'She's up here. And the bankers, they're in the Financial Centre. That's here in – what is it?'

'Buckhead.'

'What a strange name,' she said. 'Why do they call it that?'

'The Virginians had already used Williamsburg.'

She laughed, she said, 'I love you, Wiley,' and she said again, '*Wiley*. I like it. When did you change it?'

'Right after I moved down here.'

'I like it,' she said again. I was glad she liked it. I stood naked in the sun room with the stars above the park and the breezes blew

123

cool around me. I said, '*Willie* is a boy's name,' and she said, quick and soft, 'Oh, you're not a boy.'

'No,' I said, and I felt that she believed me, I felt that I believed me.

Chapter 22

Nickie came by my office the next morning at 9.30. She brought two styrofoam cups of coffee on a stack of mail and closed the door and sat down in the plastic chair. The red, white and blue box of condoms still sat on my desk between us, and she put the coffee on it. She settled herself and said, 'I'm going to get you a more comfortable chair.'

'Are you?' I sipped the hot coffee.

'I'd visit you more often that way.'

'Really?'

'Really.'

'You're looking good,' I said. She was in pink again, a pink suit with grey trim, all sharp and pink and blonde.

She held up a finger for me to wait, then she picked up her cigarettes and dug around in the pack. She came out with a short one, it looked like a Lucky Strike, and I thought of Simon English, she had been to see Simon English. She held it up and said, 'Matt's out sick today.'

'All right,' I smiled, and she lit it up.

We passed it back and forth several times. It was good, it was smooth, it was Simon English.

Nickie said, 'What have you been up to? You haven't come by much lately.'

I shrugged. I didn't want to tell her about Alix, and then again I did. 'I've been writing a lot,' I said.

'Your love story?' she said. 'Tell me your love story.'

I'd made a mistake, I didn't want to talk about my writing. I said, 'Tell me yours.'

She drank some coffee and took a long drag on the cigarette. 'I miss you coming around,' she said.

This made me feel good, and I reached across my desk for the cigarette. She handed it back to me. 'I'll come around, then.'

'Do,' she said. 'Brenda's out of town.'

'Where'd she go?'

'Savannah. She knows a yacht in Savannah.'

'Lucky Brenda.'

'You ought to come over,' she said. 'We could play spin the bottle again.'

'You want to play?'

She turned her head to one side. She said, 'I like you, Wiley.'

'And you want to play?'

'I miss you coming around.'

'Have you had your talk with Margaret?' I asked.

'The Divine Margaret,' she said. She was stoned, she was staring at me, and she said softly, 'Do you love me?'

I thought about it, I thought about Alix, Alix was so real, but I couldn't say *no*. I said, 'Maybe.'

She said, 'Only maybe?'

'I don't get much encouragement.' I took a drag on the cigarette and held it out for her. She stared at it, and I said, 'Do you want any more?'

She nodded and took the cigarette. She said, 'I can talk to you like this.' She held it burning before her. She took a short puff then set it across the edge of the box of condoms to burn itself out.

I said, 'You can't talk to me otherwise?'

'It scares me.' She sat back and stretched a little, she looked like a pink cat stretching.

I took a short puff and it came back to life. 'Smoke some more,' I said.

She shook her head. 'I've still got to work.'

'You're so conscientious,' I said.

'I haven't got an office to hide in, like you do.'

I looked at the office around me, the bookshelves, the picture of Matt on the wall above her head. 'We all need someplace we can hide.'

She said, 'That's really true, Wiley.'

'You can hide here any time you want.'

She said, 'Are you hiding back here? 'What are you hiding from?'

'I'm not hiding, I'm running.'

She smiled lazily. She said, 'What are you running from, then?'

'From dying.'

'You'll have to run a long way.'

I said, 'What do you want to be, Nickie?'

She closed her eyes and swung her head back, she was stoned, she was into it. She opened her eyes, and looked at me and said, 'I want to be up there.'

'Up where?' I said.

'I like what you do for me when you make love to me, Wiley.'

'You're *not* scared,' I said.

She smiled and shook her head again. She said, 'Come see me tonight. Come see me and see what I want to play.'

I could remember the feel of her in my hands. I could call Sarah and change dinner to Saturday night. 'All right,' I said. After work.'

'Yes,' she said. 'Let's not wait.' She looked at her watch.

I said, 'Time to read magazines and file things.'

She smiled slightly, pink lips in a soft curl. 'What are you going to do?' she said.

'I think I'll write something.'

'What?'

'Something subversive.'

'Safe sex.'

'Yes. There is safe sex.'

'You mustn't say so.'

'There is.'

'Just don't tell Matt.'

Chapter 23

I met the Divine Margaret later that morning. 'Wiley Jones,' Grant said, standing in my office doorway, 'Margaret Divine.'

She smiled pleasantly and shook my hand lightly, then sat down. She was compact and cunning as a doll, with a perfectly proportioned little body and creamy white skin like painted china. She wore red, a red silk blouse and a red skirt, with red shoes and a black suede belt, and her hair was raven black, black on black, and I wondered if she coloured it, if she had any grey that she rinsed out. She had a small white rosebud pinned to her bluse, and she smelled delicately of roses. The box of condoms sat on the edge of the desk and Nickie's joint was still there. I took it and put it in my desk drawer, simply, without any display, but Margaret watched me do it, and I watched her watching me.

Grant stood over us and said, 'Margaret has an idea for a new magazine.'

'Great,' I said, and I smiled. She smiled the same way automatically.

'Margaret is head of member services,' said Grant.

'I know,' I said.

'You've heard of me,' she said.

'The Divine Margaret,' I said.

She laughed. It was a pleasant laugh, full of her, and her little teeth were white like perfect pearls. I looked at her closely. She was around forty, I guessed, and she still looked good, she had always looked good, you could tell that, and she would look good even as she grew older. I thought of Jim Neill fucking her, I tried to imagine her fucking as she laughed and showed her shining white teeth.

Grant held his hands out and fine tremors ran through them ever so slightly, 'I've got to talk with Stan about the page makeup program.'

I said, 'OK. I'm sure Margaret can fill me in.'

He left us, and Margaret drew her chair closer to my desk. I smelled the roses a bit stronger. She said, 'I want a magazine for the members.'

'A professional journal?'

'You read minds.'

'Sometimes.'

She said, 'Well, sometimes I read minds too.' She sat back and looked at me. She was like a flawlessly painted toy, and I wanted to play with her.

She said, 'Do you know Simon English?'

'Oh, yes.'

'He's another mind-reader,' she said.

'There are quite a number of us around here.'

'You'd be surprised,' she said.

I decided to risk it. I took the joint from my desk drawer and set it back on the box of condoms, and I thought she had an effect like Alix on me: she brought out the risk-taking, the breathlessness. I trembled inwardly, uncertain until she laughed softly. She drew her head back and looked at me, smiling. She stood up and closed the door and said, 'Do you have a light?'

After we had smoked the rest of it, she told me about the magazine she wanted, for the members of the AIDS Research Council, with articles based on the talks they gave to each other at their quarterly meetings. 'Pictures of the members,' she said, leaning forward and framing a picture with her hands, 'They'll want that.'

We looked at each other through the frame. Her hands were perfect manicured, and I thought of her feeling up Jim Neill with those soft-looking hands, I thought of her caress, and I wondered what she would feel like. She said slowly, 'And, of course, we can charge more for the ads, since the market is so highly targeted. It's *the* market for AIDS.'

She sat back, tilted her head a bit to one side and said, 'So who do you smoke with around here?'

'Is it safe to say?'

She smiled and showed her teeth. 'I know all the company secrets.'

I wondered if she did. I said, 'Nickie was by earlier.'

'Nickie,' she said, surprised. 'I didn't know. I'll have to talk with her.'

'Do that,' I said. 'She thinks a lot of you.'

'Does she really?' More and more surprises.

'Really,' I said.

Margaret nodded slowly. 'We'll have to talk to Matt,' she said.

'About Nickie?'

'About the new magazine,' she smiled. 'You're stoned.'

'So are you,' I said.

'I think about it,' she said. 'We'll talk to Matt about the magazine. We'll talk to Nickie about something else.'

I liked her cleverness. 'Something else?' I asked.

'How to succeed,' she said.

'How do you do that?'

'You're pretty good at it,' she said. She picked up the box of condoms. 'You're Matt's guardian of morals, that's quite a success at Brackett Data.' She set the condoms down.

'I don't understand how it works, though.'

'That's because it comes naturally to you.'

'How does it work?'

'Watch me,' she said.

'With pleasure,' I said. My heart beat a little faster.

She paused and looked at me, she had heard me right, and she smiled, satisfied with herself, then went on, 'You must let everything be Matt's idea.'

'Yes.'

'You do that already,' she said. 'You just do it naturally, so you don't notice it.'

'You don't do it naturally?'

She paused, then said, 'I do it naturally, but I've taken the time to think about it.'

'I need time.'

'Yes, you do,' she said, gazing into my stoned face. 'But not a great deal of it.'

Her lips were red as her rose, and they shone with the paint, as red as Alix's lips and just as hard. I thought about smearing the paint, I thought of kissing Alix hard, the red smeared around her mouth, and I wondered again how Margaret fucked. I looked at the redness of her cheeks and took the clothes off her little body in my mind: she was the Divine Margaret, she did it naturally and took the time to think about it. That must be safe sex.

Someone knocked on my door, and it was Grant. He dragged a chair in from his office and sat down in the corner near the doorway. I looked at him, mildly amazed. He was not stoned, he was not in on the joke. Grant would never be in on the joke, I realised. He sat smiling at us, looking from me to Margaret and back again, and he put his trembling hands together in his lap and he said, 'Well, and do we have a name for it yet?'

130

Chapter 24

Nickie said, 'Margaret took me out to lunch today.'

We were sitting at her kitchen table, drinking gin and tonics on empty stomachs. She had a half-gallon of gin, a bottle with a handle and a pourer built into the mouth. The tonic was running low, but we weren't using much of it anyway. It was her idea; I supposed she wanted to get drunk first. I thought about Alix and I wanted to get drunk first, too. And I needed to call Sarah, but the moment was wrong to bring it up.

I said, 'Yes?' I saw the time on the kitchen clock. There was still time to catch Sarah and explain, but I didn't think I could explain Sarah to Nickie.

'She asked me out,' she said, and she drank some gin. She had pulled off her pink jacket, she wore a white blouse, and she had loosened the sleeves and unbuttoned it from the collar to just above her breasts. I could see a thin golden chain hanging around her neck and the lacey edge of the top of her brassière.

'How was it?'

She thought about it. She drank some. 'Margaret's different,' she said.

'Did you talk with her?'

She nodded.

I said, 'What did she say?'

'She said to fuck you and forget about it.'

'Can you do that?'

'If I can get high enough.'

I thought about Alix, I thought about her white body out in the sun and never tanning and the way my own flesh looked so dark alongside hers. I wondered what she would say to me right now, if she knew what I was doing. And I wondered what I was doing. I was hacking Nickie, I was doing social engineering, and I wondered if I could do it, I wondered why I wanted to.

Nickie said, 'I go to Rupert's.'

Rupert's was a nightclub in Buckhead. I said, 'Do you?'

She drank some gin. She said, 'I get all dressed up, sexy, and I go to Rupert's.'

'That's a good way to get AIDS.'

'No,' she said, 'I take condoms with me.'

'Does anybody ever argue with you?' I said. 'About the condoms, I mean.'

'The last one did.'

'What was his name?'

'Rodger. With a D.'

'Did Rodger with a D have a last name?'

'None of them do,' she said. Her blue eyes closed heavily, then opened again. 'Neither do I.'

I drank my gin and tonic. I poured some more gin and passed on the tonic. I had never drunk straight gin before, and it burned everything, I liked the burning, the smell of it burned my nostrils and it burned my tongue, and it tasted cheap and greasy, like the gin that Winston Smith drinks in *Nineteen Eighty-Four*, and I thought of Winston's dream where he shoots Julia full of arrows. The gin was hard to drink and I liked it because it was hard, I looked at the glass and thought of all the good hard things in life – writing, blues, cunt. I reached across the table and got one of Nickie's cigarettes and lit it. The menthol filled my head, and the gin burned, and I liked it all, I could feel it.

She said, 'What do you do?'

'About what?' I said.

She looked annoyed, then drank some more. 'You know,' she said, waving her hand in a circle in the air above the table. 'I go to Rupert's. What do you do?'

'Oh,' I said. I thought about it. I wanted to see her all dressed up, sexy, and I wanted to fuck her, but I wanted to tell her about Alix, too, I wanted to see what it would do to her, what she would do with it. 'I have a neighbour.'

She looked a little surprised, she said, 'You fuck one of your neighbours?'

'That's right.'

She drank some gin, thinking about it. 'What's her name?'

'Alix,' I said, 'with an I.'

'That's a man's name,' she said.

'So is Nickie,' I said.

She smiled, she said, 'Do you like women with men's names?'

I shook my head. I thought: *Sarah is not a man's name.* 'What *do* you like, then?'

'I like you,' I said.

She held her drink in both hands. She said, 'Are you really in love with me?' It took a lot for her to ask, I knew. I felt like she had taken off some most private piece of clothing, I felt like I could fuck her now, if I wanted to, and I felt like I had to take care of her now, too.

I drank some gin, and it was hard to do, I said, 'I don't think so, any more.'

'Because of Alix.'

'Probably.'

'But you still want to fuck me.'

'Yes.'

'You can do that, two at once.'

'I did it once before.'

She sat with her eyes on me and her head turned a little to one side. She said, 'Do you want to do that again?'

I said, 'What do you want, Nickie?' I lifted the gin to my lips and the smell of it was good now, like oil of drakar, gin would always smell like Nickie, now, it was all right, I was drunk on it, on her.

She held her drink in both hands and looked into it. 'I guess I want you to love me,' she said.

Smiling slightly, she was thinking, I could tell. She said, 'I don't want to fuck you if you're fucking this Alix person. I don't want to be seconds.'

I was tense, waiting on what she wanted.

'But I still want you to make love to me,' she said. She sat looking at me, her eyelids were heavy with the gin, and my head was light from it.

I thought about it. I said, 'I think I understand.'

She smiled slightly. 'Do you?' she said. She got up from the table and came around to my side, she stood beside me for a moment, and I looked up at her, she laid a hand alongside my face and caressed it, and then turned and walked out of the kitchen.

I left the gin and followed her out, and she was waiting at the turn of the stairs, looking for me with one foot on the stair above the other and her fingers on the buttons of her blouse. When she saw me she undid it and dropped it behind her as she rose, she stopped and unhooked her brassière and did the same. I followed behind her, picking up her clothes.

At the door to her bedroom, she unzipped her skirt and let it fall to the floor. She stepped out of it and went in. I picked up the skirt and carried her things inside and dropped them into a chair before a vanity. She turned and did not look at me, but sat down on the edge of her bed and rolled off her panty hose. She

133

lay back across the bed and spread her legs a little apart and she reached down between them and felt herself, and ever so slightly parted the lips of her cunt.

I knelt at her feet, between her legs, and my head was heavy and my tongue was thick, I was dry, I was thirsty. I stroked her inner thighs with my hands, I squeezed her flesh and gently pushed her legs apart. I bent my head into her cunt and kissed her there, and she sighed 'Put me up there', and I kissed her again, and I licked her this time, I was thirsty, and the taste mixed with the gin and then obliterated it and I liked it, it made me hard for her and I wanted to do it for Alix, I wanted to taste her the way I was tasting Nickie, and it stunned me that I could not, I would never be able to love Alix this way, and I wanted to. I lifted my head suddenly, shocked with wanting Alix. Nickie lay back on the bed and sighed and made sounds of pleasure, and I bent into her again, and she sat up and held my head in her hands between her legs, she whispered my name.

I fucked her with my tongue and I sucked her and she came, sitting up above me with her hands on my neck, and I sucked and she fell back across the bed and twisted her legs around my neck and pulled me into her cunt with them. She said my name again and sat up and released me and took my head in her hands and pulled me up and kissed me deeply, she tasted of gin and menthol cigarettes, and she reached her hand down between my legs and felt me there, hard, and she unbuckled my belt and unzipped my pants. She was drunk and clumsy and couldn't get the zipper to work and I had to help her with it and she reached inside and took me in her hand and I came as she touched me, hot white soft spurts filling her hand, and she kissed me and she said my name and she held me and lay back, taking me with her, and I laid my head on her breast and I loved her with my hand until she came again. She came quickly and hard the second time, wrapping her arms around my neck and squeezing me close and kissing me deeply just after the climax, and then we lay there together, arms around each other, and we were drunk together. She lay back in my arms with her mouth open and her eyes heavy and she passed out then, looking at me, a light flickered in her eyes and they went blank, unfocused, and her eyelids fluttered down and she was gone, and I lay above her looking into her face and I thought of Alix, I thought of her red red hair, and I wondered if I would tell her, and I knew that I would, and then I wondered what she would say and do. I wondered if I had hurt her, and I realised that I did not

134

believe she could be hurt. Through Nickie's bedroom window I could see the sunlight fading, and after a while, I released myself from her sleeping hold and I got up and pulled my pants on and left her there, careful to lock the doors behind me.

Chapter 25

As I came in the back door, I heard Alix in the sun room hacking, I heard the little keys going hack, hack, hack. None of the lights were on, everything was dark. I closed the back door behind me and called out to her, 'Hello, what are you doing?' as I got a beer from the refrigerator.

She called back, 'Writing a suicide note.'

I heard the sounds of traffic from the avenue, a semi shifted down through the gears and creaked to a stop at the light. I needed to wash Nickie off my face, I needed to call Sarah, but something was wrong. I went out to see Alix instead.

She sat at the console, typing. She was leaning over it, hair crowded down around her face, and the console lit her in amber. Street light flooded through the windows from outside. I drank some beer and said, 'Are you killing yourself?'

'She said over her shoulder, 'I killed myself a long time ago.'

I looked at what she was writing. She had started a new paragraph with the words *I killed myself with my cunt*. She turned and looked up at me. She said, 'Did you fuck your Nickie tonight?'

She was daring me. I wanted to see what she would do. I said, 'What do you think?'

She said, 'I can smell her on you.'

I drank some beer. She had a beer of her own, sitting at one end of the keyboard, and she drank from it now and said, 'Was it good?'

I said, 'You want me to tell you?'

'I would tell you,' she said. 'You'd want to know, wouldn't you?'

'It was pretty good,' I said.

She drank some beer and turned to me again. She said, 'But not as good as me.'

I looked at her levelly, I would not look away. 'No,' I said, 'not as good as you.'

She laughed. She turned to the console again and set the beer down. 'That's pretty good for me,' she said, 'considering you fucked her without any protection.'

'How do you know that?'

'You have no secrets from Confusion.'

'Are you Confusion now?' I said.

She said, 'Aren't you confused?' And she started another paragraph and typed *You better protect yourself from my cunt, you fucker.*

I said, 'That's a poem, not a suicide note.'

'Poem, then,' she said. 'Confusion is a poet, too.'

'Along with everything else.'

'Everything else.'

'When will you be Alix again?'

She picked up her beer and lifted it to her lips and tilted her head back and chugged it. I watched the muscles in her throat move. She set the empty bottle down with violence, she stood up and turned to me and took me by the neck and kissed me hard, she ran her hands over my face while she kissed me and she moved her body against mine. Then she drew away from me, with my head in her hands, and she said, 'Do you want Alix?'

I said, 'Aren't you upset?'

She said, 'Would it upset you?'

'Yes,' I said, and I turned away from her and looked out the windows. 'Yes, I think it would.'

She said, 'Why? Are you in love?'

Out the window, darkness had fallen over the park. The stoplight changed from red to green and traffic moved around the corner. I said, 'No.'

She smiled, she said, 'You are. You're in love.'

'No,' I said.

'Not with me,' she said. 'With yourself.'

I turned to her. 'What's that mean?'

'You're going to help me, right?' she said. 'Help the poor victim of AIDS. That's what you're in love with.'

'I shouldn't help you?'

'You can't help me,' she laughed. 'No one can help me.'

'What do you want?' I said. I was a little angry.

She said, 'I want to die of old age.'

'No,' I said slowly, shaking my head, 'I wasn't talking about your fucking disease. What do you want from me?'

'I want you to fuck me.'

'That's Confusion talking,' I said. 'What does Alix want?'

She turned from me to the computer. Her words ran across the screen in broken lines. She turned it off without saving them. I was shocked, I would never do something like that. She said, 'I don't know what Alix wants.'

I said, 'Who doesn't know what Alix wants? Confusion?'

She looked at the dead machine, she said, 'Alix doesn't know.'

'I think she does,' I said. 'I think Confusion just doesn't want to admit it.'

'You're so smart,' she said and she turned to me. 'College boy. What does Alix want?'

I said, 'I would give a lot to hear you say it.'

She laughed at me again.

I said, 'You're so goddamn tough. Does that ever let up?'

'I change skin when it wears out.'

'If Alix is feeling thin, you just put on Confusion.'

'That's right.'

'Why didn't you save what you wrote?' I pointed at the machine behind her. 'Didn't you want me to read it?'

'I write a lot,' she said. 'I throw a lot away.'

'You said it was a suicide note. Why did you say that?'

'Because dying gets your attention.'

'You want my attention? You want it?'

She stared at me. Her jaw was set. 'Fuck you.'

'You wish,' I said.

She said, 'I'll get you for this. I'll get you tonight.' And she turned and left the apartment.

I stood there, watching her go, watching her sweet round ass move across the living room and out the door, and I felt like she had taken my balls with her, and I said, 'Fuck!' and I made a fist and hit the door jamb. My hand hurt and I winced and set the beer down and nursed it. I sat in the chair at the desk and felt sorry for myself over all these women.

I sat up and got the phone and dialled information and got the number for the Ritz-Carlton in Buckhead. But the woman on the desk said that Sarah Dresden didn't answer. I sighed and hung up, I couldn't remember ever having been this drunk before, there in the sun room with Old Mr Boston cheap gin and Nickie's cunt on my breath. I decided to fuck it.

So I got pretty far drunk by the time she got back. It was about 12.30. I was sitting on the back landing waiting for her and drinking beer, and I saw her car pull into the lot followed by a white Jaguar. She got out of her car and pointed at the driver of the Jag and laughed and a guy got out of the Jag and came over to her and took her in his arms and kissed her, and she kissed him back. She was dressed for a club, all leather and slits and heels and her hair up for someone to take it down. The guy was in a suit. They laughed together, and she took him by the hand and led him up the stairs to

138

her apartment. She fumbled in her purse for her keys and laughed, then looked up the stairs at me, and she said, 'Oh, hey, Wiley,' and she waved. The guy looked up, too. His hair was blond, I couldn't see his face. He said, 'Hey, Wiley.'

I got up and took my chair inside and got another beer. In the sun room I sat looking out the windows over the empty avenue and the darkened park. I thought about calling Nickie, I thought about trying the Ritz-Carlton again, but I didn't do either. I didn't do anything. I sat there quietly drunk and thought about Alix fucking the blond, sucking his cock, and everything she would do. I thought she must be pretty badly in love with me to do this.

Chapter 26

Her fucking the blond guy didn't bother me until the next day. It was Saturday, and I felt pretty sick from all the beer on top of all the gin. I wasn't so sure any more that she had fucked him because she loved me. I wasn't so sure about anything, but nothing could bother me through the detritus left by the gin and Budweiser. I tried everything I could think of: I took a cool shower and a bunch of aspirin and drank a tall glass of milk and sat in the sun room drinking black coffee until about 10.30. Then I got dressed in a pair of cutoffs and went out on the landing, and I saw that the guy's Jag was still there, and that's when it bothered me. I thought of them sitting together over breakfast, and I felt impatient for him to leave so I could talk with her, I felt like I had things to say she needed to hear, and I felt like she was eleven years older than I was and I wondered how old the white Jag was, and I put on my wristwatch to better clock the time.

I got a book of Yeats and sat in the rocker reading, but I would pace periodically from the sun room to the back landing and look out into the parking lot to see if the Jag was gone yet, and it was never gone. I imagined the two of them talking over coffee and laughing together, I wondered if she would show him her computer, and what she would show him. Then, around noon, I walked out the back door and looked down and both their cars were gone. Wonderful, I thought, they're going to make a day of it.

I went back inside and turned on the computer and tried to write, but I only wound up writing about Alix, there she was all over my love story, everywhere I looked. So I wrote a description of the way she lay out back in her impenetrable shades and red bikini, not tanning. The picture made me horny and I tried to masturbate, but it only made me feel worse, like I would never fuck anybody again. Finally, I got a beer from the refrigerator, and I thought it was all finished with Alix and I wondered what it had been, with her, with Confusion. I finished the beer and got another one and stepped out back and there she was, lying there on her landing in her red bikini with her hair up and not tanning on her green and white plastic folding chaise. She had her mirror shades on, but I felt she was watching me. She had to be. I got her a beer and carried it down the stairs to her. The door to her apartment stood open behind her and music drifted out, a hot beat, piano riffs and trumpet cool glissandos, black men rapping, I caught some words about freedom.

I held out the beer and she paused a moment, then took it. She said, 'When are you going to get some Pabst?'

I drank some beer. 'I'll pick up some today. What's his name?' I said.

'Rodger,' she said, 'with a D.'

'Did you go to Rupert's?'

She turned her head to look at me better. 'How did you know?' she said.

'Did he argue with you about the condoms?'

She said, 'You're psychic this morning.'

'But you won the argument,' I said.

She said nothing.

I said, 'Your cunt won the argument. It wins all the arguments.'

She almost smiled.

I said, 'Was he good?'

She said, 'You want me to tell you?'

'I told you.'

'He was good,' she said.

I tried it, I said, 'But not as good as me.' I sat down on the foot of the chaise, I noticed she moved her feet aside to make room for me. She looked at me from behind the sunglasses and she said, 'I do not love you, Proteus.'

'What do you do?' I said. 'Instead of love.'

'I hack.'

'Do you hack me?'

'You bet.' She spit the words.

I said, 'And I just hacked Nickie.'

'That's right.'

'But it bothered you.'

'It shouldn't.'

'What should it do?'

She said nothing.

I said, 'It bothered me that you let him stay over. Rodger with a D.'

She turned her head a little.

I said, 'I guess it shouldn't bother me, though, like Nickie shouldn't bother you.' I laughed at myself a little. 'The fucking part didn't bother me. It was you two sitting and talking afterwards that bothered me.'

'The personal part.'

141

For a second I wondered if she realised what she had said, but then I remembered that this was Confusion talking, and she always realised what she had said. 'Yes,' I said. 'The personal part.'

She said, 'I thought Nickie was afraid of you.'

'Nickie is afraid of Nickie.'

'What changed it?'

'I hacked her,' I said. 'I gave her the password.'

'What was it?'

'Alix Roberts.'

'Really?'

'Really. She wanted to know what I did for sex, so I told her.'

'And that turned her on.'

'She forgot herself for a while.'

'Pretty good social engineering.' The sunlight glinted off her sunglasses in little stars. She lifted the bottle of beer to her lips and drank.

'How about you?' I said. 'How did you hack Rodger with a D?'

She rolled over on to her stomach. 'He was easy,' she said over her shoulder.

I set down my beer and picked up her bottle of tanning oil, poured some out in my hand and began to rub it on to her back. Her skin was hot under the sun. 'What did you do?' I said.

'I Confused him. He liked her.'

'That's different.'

'You like her, too.'

'Do I?' I was rubbing the tanning oil under the strap of her top and I stopped rubbing and untied it. She turned her head to see what I was doing. I poured more oil on to her back and began to rub it in.

'She excites you,' she said. 'Confusion will do anything. You like it, and it scares you, too.'

'Is that good?'

'There's a part to sex that should be scary,' she said.

I rubbed her back with both hands, it worked the kinks out of my shoulders and my upper back. 'Was it scary with Rodger with a D?'

She sighed. 'Of course not. Was it scary with Nickie?'

'No,' I said. 'It was like giving away candy.'

She said, 'Is it scary with me?'

'Yes,' I said, and I could feel the fear and the lust and the desire all welling through me at once. 'Sex with you is fucking with death.'

142

I stopped rubbing the oil in and let my hands rest in the centre of her back. She lay still, and I wondered for a moment if it were possible to go too far with her.

She rolled over. Her hands were crossed over her breasts and the strings of her top trailed loose down her sides. I looked into her face and, in shadow under a green sky with the sun a white star in each of her lenses, I saw my own face staring back at me. She said, 'It's scary with you too.'

I said, 'What's so scary about it?'

She sat up, her face was close to mine, my face was huge and distorted across her lenses, and then she turned aside and put her feet down on the landing. She said, 'I don't know.' She seemed to be thinking. She looked away across the parking lot and over the outbuildings to the skyline of Midtown and the city beyond it. She held her hands over her breasts. 'You're not supposed to feel that good when you're dying,' she said.

She stood up and went inside. After a moment, I followed her.

She was standing in the bathroom, and when I looked close I saw that she was crying. She was trying to retie the top of her bikini, and she was crying. She was calm, the tears flowed calmly down her face from behind the mirror shades, and she did not make any sound. Music came in from the living room, changed now, white man's music, exhausted, luxurious, the singer sang, *we can make believe that Kennedy is still alive.* Looking in the bathroom mirror, she brushed her hand across her face beneath the shades, and she sniffled, and she drew a long, tired breath and said softly, 'Fuck it,' and dropped the bikini top to the floor. Slowly she took off her sunglasses and put them down. She sighed, and then she turned to me. The fingertips of her left hand rested on the edge of the bathroom sink, and it was cool in the shadows of the apartment. We stood looking at each other for a moment, and the music played; and she reached up and with one move of her fingers she let her hair down. She shook her head and it fell out across her shoulders. She said, 'I love you. I don't want you to fuck anybody but me. And I won't fuck anybody but you. I'll love you better than God.'

I was quiet, and we both stood still, and she looked straight into my eyes, and her eyes shone green like tourmaline, like a cat's eyes, and her lips parted and she waited. The lines of the tears shone down her face, and her face was calm, composed, and her red red hair fell down across her breasts, her nipples hard and erect, and I felt like fucking, my cock heavy and light and swelling, and I did not breathe, and when I

143

spoke the words came softly and slow. I said, 'Is this Alix talking?'

She closed her eyes, and her hand on the sink made a small fist, and she sighed and she opened her eyes again, and she opened her hand. She said, 'This is Alix talking to Wiley.'

I reached to her through the bathroom door, my fingertips alongside her face, and she turned her head a little, into my hand, her lips brushing my fingers, then she turned her head the other way, she rubbed her face against my hand like a cat. I said, 'I'm in love with Alix.'

She stepped forward, and I took her in my arms, and we held each other, we touched each other's bare flesh and kissed again and again, I knelt before her and buried my face between her legs while I slipped her bikini down from her hips, her hair curled up beneath my lips and I kissed her there and she held my head in her hands and she said 'Be careful' in a whisper, she had never said *Be careful*, Confusion would never say *Be careful*. I put both my hands between her legs and caressed her with my fingertips and she was wet and I wanted to kiss her, but she said *Be careful* and I was afraid. I stood up and she undid my cutoffs for me and they slid down to my knees and I stepped out of them and she took my cock in her hand, it was hard and she kissed me lightly on the mouth and bent to kiss it and she licked it long and she took it into her mouth and sucked hard and I wanted to come in her mouth, I wanted to come *for her*, I wanted her to have my cock, I wanted her to have my insides and see what I wanted, I wanted to give her everything I wanted, and she stood and took my head in her hands and kissed me a long time with her tongue moving deeply in my mouth, and I kissed her back, and we moved into the bedroom. She went ahead of me, crawling on to the bed covered now with red and yellow sheets and pillows, torn apart from fucking Roger with a D, and looking at me over her shoulder, she reached the head of the bed and looked back at me and spread her legs for me to see and she was pink and wet and I remember the shape of her breasts hanging down heavy, her nipples swollen and hard, and she reached into the box of condoms at the head of the bed and tossed one backwards to me. Stephen sat at the kitchen table and smiled on us in Polacolor, and I took the condom out of its white plastic and rolled it on and followed her on to the bed, and she laid her head down on the pillow looking back at me and I held her by the hips and she thrust gently back on to me as I went into her from behind, and we began to fuck, we began to *make love*, we made it right there on the bed, and she made the sounds of fucking and she said, 'Wiley', and looked back at me over her shoulder and she opened her mouth wide and loved me back, she let me be an animal, and she was an animal, and I let her be an animal, and at some time the music stopped and there was no sound any more but us, and it was hot and we were wet with sweat, and she let me be the centre, she was my centre, her cunt around me with me at the centre, she let me be, she wanted it that way, she loved it that way, and the seed did not stop coming inside her, I felt it fill the condom, warm and wet around the head of my cock, and I fell on her, I took her breasts in my hands and squeezed them hard as I came, and she twisted beneath me and squeezed my cock with her cunt and she said, 'Wiley', smiling long and slow.

We lay together for a while, and then I came out of her. She sat up and over me and took the condom off me, and she bent and licked the come away, and it made me hard again, and she took me in her mouth and sucked, and I wanted to be inside her again, without the protection this time, I wanted to feel her on my cock, I wanted nothing between us, and I sat up and drew her up towards me and put my cock between her legs, and she pushed against me and said, 'No! It's too dangerous', and she pulled away from me and rolled into a ball on the other side of the bed and lay looking at me, her lips parted and her eyes watchful. I lay on my side looking back at her. I said, 'I want you.'

She said, 'Do you want to die? Get another condom.'

I shrugged. 'It's not the same.'

She lay looking at me. She took my cock in her hand and stroked it once. She made a ring of her thumb and forefinger and slid it slowly up and down me. She said, 'I can make my mouth like a cunt.'

I said, 'I wanted you to teach me love.'

She said, 'Do you want to fuck my face?'

I was very hard and I was in her hand. I whispered, 'Yes.'

She bent down and took me into her mouth. I lay back and felt her mouth around me, wet flesh on my flesh and her tongue stroking me as she sucked and breathed, she looked up at me with her green eyes and put her hands on my face, her fingers outstretched and caressing my cheeks, trembling as she strained to reach me, and she drew them down my chest and down my belly to my cock, her nails just scraping my skin as they moved over me. She held my balls in her hands and she sucked and nodded, her head rising up and down on me, riding, and I could not come again but

145

I could feel it, and I felt it. I cried out and I sat up and drew her to me and I kissed her long and deep and reached with my hand down between her legs and petted her there and she coiled her legs up around me, spread and open for me, for my hands, and I stroked her with my fingers and she shook, she trembled for my touch and it made my cock hurt with wanting her. I had never fucked before, I would not know what it was without her, and when she came, I cried out for her, she said, *Yes o yes yes*, and she said, *Wiley, Wiley*, and I said *I love you*, and she came in my hands, trembling and gripping me by the shoulders, and I said *Alix*, and she kissed me. I laid her down and rose up above her and I held her body in my arms and I looked at her, her sweet face in its passion, her green eyes and her lips the colour of blood and her red hair and her nipples brown as berries and hard and her tender cunt, the red hair there dark wet with come and electric beneath my incredible hands, and I bent and I kissed her there, softly, the way you would kiss a wound, and she took my head in her hands and she said, *Will you please be careful I love you so much*, and I kissed her there softly and I rested my head on her and closed my eyes and felt the love for her inside me and she held me softly in her hands and we lay together, still.

Chapter 27

I woke up first, and I looked at her sleeping, she had turned away from me in the heat and she had her back to me now, I touched her, with my fingertips, I traced along her side from her hip to her arm, and I got a little hard just looking at her, I was in love with her. I thought the words, *I am in love with you*, looking at her lying there, and I had never been in love before, I had only thought it had been love. I had never known anyone like her, I had told her that, and I would tell her everything, I would tell her anything she wanted, I loved her. I moved closer to her and put my arm around her and nestled in the back of her neck and began to kiss her softly through her red hair, began to work it away from her face and towards me, began to move my hand across her breasts, asleep, began to wake her.

She rolled back into my arm and kissed me around my mouth, just waking up and she said, 'I love you, Wiley. You, Wiley.' She tapped on my chest with her finger. I had never seen her like this, I had never seen her waking up before, I had never seen her in love.

I said the words. 'I love you,' I said.

She looked at me with eyes wide, blinking away the sleep. She said, 'You do?'

She moved close to me on the bed, she held her hands before her and spread them across my chest and she curled up close to me and she said, 'You do?'

'I love you,' I said, and I held her. I said, 'I love you, sleepy.'

'Who's sleepy?' she said.

'You are.'

'No, I'm ready.'

'What are you ready for?'

'I'm ready to rock,' she said, and she straightened out and rolled back from me and made her hands into fists and began to play at punching on me. 'Let's rock,' she said.

'We need music.' I smiled at her and blocked her punches with my open hands.

She rolled away from me and over to the bedside table and turned on the clock radio. She said, 'Let's rock,' and she shimmied her hips from side to side and made the bed shake. She switched the dial around listening for something, pausing for a moment on the stations so that stray lyrics sang out through the air with guitar riffs and drumbeats. Then she stopped, and she sat up on her elbows listening. I heard Matt's voice, and she said, 'Hey, it's him.' She looked over her shoulder at me. 'It's the Gospel According to Matthew.'

'No,' I said, 'this is the Voice of Reason.'

'What's the difference?'

'The Federal Communications Commission says this is OK for you,' I said.

She turned back to the radio and listened. 'There are ways to make love that are normal,' said Matt, 'and there are ways to make what some persons call love that are perverse. That's all.'

The caller spoke, he sounded gay. 'So you judge people by how they make love,' he said.

'That's one way,' said Matt.

'But the point is,' said the caller, 'you judge people.'

'Certainly I do.'

'Who are you to judge people?'

'I'm an American,' said Matt, 'and I'm a businessman. Are you trying to tell me you don't judge people? You judge me, don't you?'

'I may judge you, but I don't judge your expressions of love.'

'You make implicit judgements of that. You call us names. You call us *straights*. That's an implicit judgement. That seems to me to say something about our *expressions of love*.'

'What do you dislike about that, about being called straight?'

'I don't dislike anything about it,' said Matt. 'I *am* straight! But hold up a minute, here, fellow, who told you that profane acts of lust that are explicitly condemned not only in the Christian Bible but in every document of major religion in the world – who told you that buggery, that's what it is, after all, who told you that buggery is an *expression of love*? Who told you that these kinds of *abnormal* sexual *appetites* have *anything to do* with *love*?'

He spoke in italics, and I could see him with the headset on, talking fast into the microphone. 'It's Matt,' I said.

Alix listened intently. I moved across the bed and lay beside her. She turned to me, smiling like Confusion, and she ran a hand through her hair, her eyes shone with mischief and her nipples swelled up hard, and she said, 'Can we call him?'

'Do you want to?'

'Hell,' she said, and an eyebrow arched over a green eye, 'I want to fuck him.' I thought of the gun, I saw a man bleeding on a parking lot.

When Matt broke for a commercial, the announcer gave out a number. Alix picked up her phone from the bedside table, turned it on and dialled. She sat up in bed and crossed her legs, and I could tell when they answered, because she changed, she changed so fast I couldn't stop her, her face changed and her eyes got subtly bigger, wider, and she breathed through her open mouth and she said, 'Hi. My name's Connie Phone, and I'm calling on my cellular from Norcross.'

She was talking to the screener, I figured, because Matt was on the radio again, talking to another caller, another guy, but this time one of his fans. Matt had fans, I realised, people who listened to him and believed what he said, not so much believed what he said but believed what he believed: he spoke for them, people who could not speak for themselves, and they, in return, bought what he advertised.

'Norcross, that's right here in town,' said Connie, and she listened for a moment. 'Oh, sure, I get it.' Alix pushed the mute button on the phone and said, 'I've got to get past this complete asshole,' and then she was Connie again, it was some social engineering to watch.

'Well, I want to talk to Matt,' said Connie. 'Why do I have to talk to you? When do I get to talk to Matt?'

She listened again. Alix crossed her eyes and stuck out her tongue.

Connie said, 'Well, I just want to tell him he's right on, is all,' and then she listened again. 'Well, of course I've got a subject, do you think I'd call if I didn't have a subject? I want to talk about what Matt's talking about.' She stuck out her tongue at the phone, and I didn't know who this was, Connie or Alix, or maybe, I thought, it was Confusion, calling all the shots for everybody. Then she said, 'Well, I want to talk about my expressions of love.'

She looked at me. She pushed the mute button again and said, 'That put me on hold.'

The screener came back in a minute. Connie listened and said, 'Sure, I've got a question. I mean, I know the answer, but I'll bet there're lots of people who don't. My question is, what's the difference between an appetite and an expression of love? Is that a question for you? Is that one OK?'

She listened to the guy for a moment, then she licked her lips

149

and winked at me. I sat cross-legged at her feet and bowed my head in admiration.

The screener came back. 'What?' said Connie. 'Oh, yeah, sure,' she said, and she turned the radio off and spoke into the phone again. 'Is that better? All right.'

She waited for Matt, then, and while she waited she moved down the bed to me and stood up on her knees before me and took hold of my cock and held it. I said, 'What are you doing?' and Connie said, 'I'm waiting for Matt, honey.'

I grew hard in her hand and she stroked it once and lifted it up and bent and kissed it on the very tip, lingering there, then she sat up quickly and said, 'Yeah, hey,' into the phone.

She gripped me tightly in her hand, 'Hey,' she said again, 'that's right, you're right, I mean, you're right on, Matt, that's not how I express love, I can tell you', and she stroked my cock while she talked, she was free now, I could see it, she was a wild animal running reckless and free, she would do anything she wanted to, and I felt it come over me, the ease and the wildness, it did not matter any more what I did, what anyone thought, I felt the pavement hard beneath my head and heard a ringing in my ears and people running, gathering around, and saw the blood across the pages of poetry in the morning breeze, and I squeezed my hand between her legs and reached her cunt and slid my index finger inside her, and she made an O with her mouth and rocked her hips around my hand and squeezed her cunt around it, and she said, 'Well, last week, I was in this place in Buckhead, I guess I better not say the name, should I?

'No, I didn't think so. But anyway this guy gave me this card that said "*The Gospel According to Matthew*", and I thought, now, this is about love, you know, the gospel and all, this has got to be about love, real love, I mean, don't you think?'

I stroked her long with my hand, in and out, and she bit her lip while she listened to Matt talk back to her, and I saw him, sweating out the moment, I wanted to see the old man sweat, and she rocked her hips a little and nodded her head at me, yes, O yes.

And she said, 'Well, I mean, love is important to me, you know, and how you make love is important to me, too. I was with this man once, he was a taxicab mechanic, and I was with him, oh, I mean, we weren't married or anything, but we were serious.

'I mean, I thought we were serious.

'I was serious anyway. But I found out he expected me to sodomise him, and, well, I was shocked, you know? I mean, that's sodomy, like in the Bible, like Sodom and the Sodomites and Lot's wife and all that, and I'd never done anything like that, I mean that's *gross*, when you think about it.

'And when I think about two men doing that to each other, I mean, you're right, Matt, that's not love, that couldn't be love.'

She fell silent and listened and I stroked her cunt and she shook her head and pushed me away and I lay back on the bed and she bent over me and took the head of my cock into her mouth and I could hear Matt talking through the receiver as she bit down on me a little and looked up at me with her wild smiling green eyes. She teased me with her teeth while Matt talked to her, and she laid her head against my thigh and said, 'Yeah, well, I called this gospel fellow and he had a tape and I left a message, but I didn't leave my number, you know, because I just wouldn't do that. Not until I know it's safe.

'I don't want any freak stuff, you know, I mean I want to talk about love, you know. I think I know about love, and I think you know about love.'

She stuck her tongue out and licked my cock from the base to the tip, and she let go of me and sat up on her knees and passed the phone from one hand to the other and put it to her ear and said, 'Don't you?' and I heard silence on the other end.

'Sure you do,' she said and she smiled. She sat down on the bed and said, 'But sometimes I have appetites, you know, that I don't understand, and I wondered if you could talk some more about these appetites, and if the other callers could talk some about their appetites. I mean, what do you *do* with them, you know?

'Because I have them, but I'm not always sure they're right, you know? That's what I want to ask this gospel fellow, if I call him again.

'But what do *you* think? Do you think I ought to call the Gospel again?'

I put my hands on her things and pushed to spread them apart, and she parted them for me, and I put my hands on her cunt, I slipped two fingers inside her as she said, 'I mean, I'm tired, you know, I mean, I'm twenty-eight and I'm still single and I'm tired of these clubs, you know?

'Like, this card, 'The Gospel According to Matthew,' I've got a special feeling about it, like it was intended, you know what I mean? Like I was supposed to get it.'

I stroked her clitoris and she sat up straight, she spread her legs wider and she made a great O with her mouth, pausing in her talk for a surprised second, and then she said, 'And I need to know soon, if I should call him back, because I haven't got much time.

'I mean, I don't feel like I've got a whole lot of time. If you look at the magazines the men look at, all the girls are eighteen, you know, and that really makes me feel awful, because I'm twenty-eight, and I wonder if this Matthew could help me, you know?'

I stroked her harder and she stood up on her knees and bit her lip, she said, 'What do you think, Matt, what do you think I ought to do?'

I stroked her fast and she closed her eyes and her open mouth went slack and I heard Matt talking and she held the phone out before her and pressed the mute button and held it and she came, she cried out as she lost it and fell across the bed and on to me, writhing and twisting with it while Matt talked on and on and I caressed her, and she held the phone tight in her hand and rolled away from my hand on to her back and bit her lower lip and drew a deep breath and put the phone to her ear and released the mute and said, 'Thank you.'

Matt said something more and she looked up at me, sitting above her, and she reached up with her free hand and caressed my cheek and she said, 'You know, I'm all talked out.' Matt said something, and she looked at me and her eyes were soft now and she said, 'But, you know, I just want to say I think you're just a terrible wonderful man. I really do.'

Her fingers traced around my lips, and she said, 'Ciao, now', and turned off the phone.

Chapter 28

She called the Gospel According to Matthew again after we had supper that night, and this time she got through to him. She sat on the sofa in the living room in an extra-large T-shirt with a picture of a skateboarder flying across it and the words SOCIAL DETOURS on a scroll above him. She sat up on her knees and talked into the phone, she said, 'Matt Brackett said I should call you back.'

She paused to listen to Matt.

She said, 'I was on the Voice of Reason show today, talking about you. Was that all right?'

I walked over to the computer and pulled up the graphics program. I set it for slide show and it began to display her pictures. Some of them showed couples fucking, and I liked these, I wished she had a picture of us fucking, I would like to see us. The others showed guys with their cocks erect, and I measured myself against them: some of them were smaller than me and some of them were bigger, and I looked at Alix, at Connie, talking to the Gospel According to Matthew, and I wondered about the difference it made, I decided I could ask her because Alix would tell me the truth.

'I won't do it again,' she said, 'I promise. Can you forgive me?'

She listened, she looked up at the computer while Matt talked. A particularly big guy came onscreen and she pointed at him with her eyes wide and licked her lips.

'Well, sure, I've got a phone,' she said, and she turned inward, concentrating on the social engineering, 'but I've been around, you know? I mean, I don't know you, I mean, I didn't. I feel like I know you now, isn't that funny? We've just been talking a couple of minutes and already I feel safe with you.'

I went into the kitchen and picked up the extension. Matt was saying, 'So I want you to tell me that.'

'Well, I go to Rupert's a lot,' said Connie, 'and other places. And I meet a lot of different guys.'

'Yes,' said Matt, speaking softly.

'And we go out, you know.'

'But I don't know,' said Matt.

'You want me to tell you?' she said. 'What do you want me to tell you?'

'I want you to confess,' said Matt. 'That's why you feel so

153

strongly about calling me, really, that's why you feel safe with me. Because at last you can confess, and, secretly, you know that, and, secretly, you want to do it. And I want you to.'

She said, 'Well, where do I start?'

There was a pause at the other end, then Matt said, 'What do you most like to do with these men you go out with?'

There was another pause, as Connie thought, or Alix or Confusion, and then she began to speak, slowly, softly, hesitantly, talking to him about fucking. I listened closely and I thought I could hear him breathing, listening on the other end. And I listened to her, she was good at this too. She said, 'And there's sodomy, too. How do you feel about sodomy?'

Matt said, 'What do you mean by that, exactly?' He spoke softly, and his voice had an edge of anticipation to it.

'I mean,' she said, and she paused for a moment and then she went ahead, 'I suck cock.'

I heard Matt draw a deep breath. He said nothing.

She said, 'I lied to Matt Brackett about that. I told him I don't do sodomy. But I like it.'

'You do?'

'I like it a lot. What do you think about that?'

Matt said, 'Do you swallow the bodily fluid?'

'Yes,' she said, she spoke very softly, she sounded like a child, she was Connie Phone. 'Men seem to like that the best. Can you tell me why that is?'

'Yes, I can,' he said. 'But the bodily fluid must be pure.'

'Pure.'

'You may contract grave illness if the fluid is not pure.'

'Illness,' she said. 'What illness?'

'You need to be tested.'

'What do you mean?'

'The Ministry has a medical function. It will test you. The Ministry is total in its aspect,' he said.

'Total as in all?'

'All.'

She said, 'Well, I guess so.'

'Yes,' he said.

'Where do I go to be tested?'

'You know Wiley,' he said.

'The guy who gave me the card?' she said, and I thought I could hear a smile. 'Yeah, I know him.'

'Then Wiley can take you to the test.'

'When?' she said.

'Meet Wiley Monday night at Rupert's,' he said. 'Can you?'

'Oh yes,' she said, and now I was sure I heard a smile, 'I'll be there.'

'Be there,' he echoed her, 'and you will be tested.'

'I don't do so good on tests.'

'It is a simple test,' he said; 'a test of the bodily fluids.'

She said, 'I'm good with bodily fluids.'

'Do you wish to confess more?'

'Do you want me to?'

'Confession is good for you,' he said, 'after so long without an unburdening.'

She said, 'Well, all right', and she began to talk again, about sucking cock now, and he listened, and I listened to him breathing, and I set the phone softly down on the kitchen table and went back into the living room and sat beside her on the sofa while she talked in hushed tones into the phone. She said in a whisper, 'I can make my face like a cunt', and she sat up on her knees and curled around the phone, concentrating on it. On the computer screen a redhead held a huge cock in her mouth and looked out at the camera, and I got up and wandered into the sun room while she talked on and on to Matt. In the Saturday night park across the street I picked up a young couple, two teenagers out for the evening, walking past the big swings swinging with children and under the trees, they did not seem at that moment to care anything about AIDS or HIV or the Gospel According to Matthew or arguments on the radio or social engineering or any of it, and I thought of Anne Mathers and I smiled at them, at her, wherever she was, and Alix whispered on the phone behind me as the sun climbed down.

Chapter 29

Sarah called Sunday morning while I was writing in my sun room. I picked up the phone before the second ring and said hello, and she said, 'You stood me up, sweetheart. What's the matter?'

'I'm really sorry,' I said, and I sat back in my chair, limp and deflated by my embarrassment. I looked at the amber words across the computer screen, I thought I was through writing for the day. 'I was going to call you later today.'

'It's OK,' she said. 'What happened?'

I took a breath, I looked out the window. I could tell Sarah anything, couldn't I? I said, 'It's all right?'

'Sure.'

'You're really not angry?'

'All right, she said,' maybe a little angry, Friday night. But more worried than angry.'

'Worried?' I said, surprised.

She said, 'I worry about you, Wiley.'

'What did you worry?'

'I worried—' she said, and paused. A smile crept into her words as she went on, 'I worried that you had fallen into the arms of some siren.' And she laughed hard, a laughter sweet-sounding and full of pleasure, it made me feel good.

I smiled with her, and I said, 'Then maybe I'd better not tell you.'

'Oh!' she said, her voice full of exasperation. 'It was another woman,' she said. 'I knew it was another woman.' But it was a joke she could not sustain, and she laughed again.

'Actually, it was two women,' I said.

'Impressive,' she said. 'Was Alix one of them?'

'Yes.'

'That's good.' She sounded like a schoolteacher encouraging a child. 'Are you two breaking up?'

'No,' I said quickly. 'She said she loved me.'

'Which one?'

'Alix.'

'Oh,' she said. 'What did the other one say?'

'She said she liked it when I told her I was in love with her.'

'You told her you were in love with her, too?'

'That was before Alix,' I said.

'All right. So, what did you do?'

'Well, I made love to her, sort of.'

'Sort of?' she said. 'Did you make her kind of pregnant?'

'You don't understand,' I said.

'Make me understand,' she said, and she was smiling at me. 'I want to. How did you *sort of* make love to her?'

I swallowed, I said, 'Think a minute.'

A moment of silence passed. Finally, she said, I think I follow you.'

'Sure you do.'

'You gave her an orgasm,' she said. She sighed, they went on, 'You know, you fascinate me, Wiley.'

'Really?'

'This is a side of you I've always wondered about.'

I tried to imagine Sarah wondering about me, thinking about me *fucking*. Did she picture me in her mind? how did she picture me? how did the picture make her feel? I had thought about what it would be like to fuck Sarah, what she must feel like, and sitting there telling her about these other women, I had begun to feel a little cocky, I began to understand the meaning of the word. *He's cocky*, I thought. *Cock Robin, Cock Wiley, here comes the wily cock.* I felt pleasant in my cock, and I saw her on the other end of the line, I was in my robe and I wondered what she was wearing, I wanted to ask her, I said, 'Well, what would you like me to tell you?'

'Everything,' she said.

I swallowed again, I didn't know where we were going.

She said, and I heard the edge of a smile in her voice, 'Can you, Wiley?'

'You're not going to tell Nathaniel, are you?'

'Do you think I'd betray you?'

I felt badly for having asked. I said, 'Not really.'

'Well, then.'

I sat back in my chair and looked at the computer screen again, I felt a sudden exhilaration with this woman listening to me talk about my sex life, my women, I wondered if I felt a little like my father, with my mother and Sarah, too, plus all his whores. I did not want that, and I knew I was not drunk on it the way he was all the time, and I thought I might write some more after all, I thought I needed to. I said softly, 'I just love women, Sarah.'

She said, 'That's all right.'

'I can't help it.'

'Poor Wiley,' she said. 'I'm so glad I'm not your age.'

I said, 'What did you do then?'

She sighed, and she began to talk. 'I was apprenticed to a master muralist in Paris, and I was in love with him secretly.'

I pictured it in my mind, I saw her mixing colours in the master's studio. I said, 'Did you keep it secret?'

She said, 'I kept secrets about as well as you do.'

I said, 'I keep the important ones.'

'With two women,' she said, 'I guess you do.'

'Who was the muralist?'

She sighed again, with pleasure in the memory. 'His name was Paul. Paul Coudreau. He was the most beautiful man I'd ever seen.'

Something in her voice made me say, 'I bet that's still true.'

'Yes,' she said, with surprise. 'Yes, it is.'

'What became of him?'

'He died in a fall down a flight of stairs.' Her voice was flat and matter-of-fact, history intruding on memory, and she paused a moment, then went on. 'We were drinking in the Quarter, and he broke his back,' she said. 'But he didn't survive, the way you did.'

'I'm sorry.'

She was silent for a moment, and then she said, 'Do you want to know what I really think?'

'Sure.'

'I think you survived to make up for him.'

I felt strange, Paul Coudreau reincarnate, I said, 'Thank you, Sarah.'

She said, 'You're important to me, Wiley. You always have been.'

I heard the back door open, I said, 'I think Alix is coming.'

'I'll let you go then,' she said.

Alix came through the back of the apartment in a new pair of cutoffs and a yellow T-shirt with the single word BRAT stencilled across her chest in red letters. She carried a tray with a coffee pot, two cups and two tall glasses of tomato juice, and she had to turn at an odd angle, sideways and a little backwards, to get through the narrow door from the kitchen into the empty living room. I held the phone and watched her, and she saw me and smiled. I had left her sleeping downstairs but she knew where to find me, and this knowledge pleased her, was a way of possessing me and loving me, and I smiled back at her, I loved her and I knew that the writing was over for the morning after all. I said to Sarah, 'I'll call you.'

'Do,' she said.

158

Chapter 30

Matt said, 'Wiley, will you please see me in my office after the meeting?' Everyone in the conference room turned and looked at me for a second, a room full of faces all focused on me, and I took them all in and looked back at Matt. He stood at the podium at the head of the table, looking at me, too, between Patricia and Nickie. I looked at Nickie all in powder blue, and when my eyes met hers she smiled slightly, and I knew then that I would never fuck her. I said, 'Yes, sir. I mean, yes, Matt,' and everyone laughed.

I stopped at Nickie's desk and said, 'How was your weekend?'

She sat back in her chair and stretched. 'I went to Rupert's Saturday night.'

I leaned closer. I said, 'Rodger with a D?' and I envied Rodger, for having her when I would never have her again.

Her eyebrows rose and she smiled slightly. She pointed at Matt's door. 'He's ready to see you,' she said.

Matt stood up as I came in. He was smiling broadly and held his hand extended for me to shake. I approached the desk and took it. He said, 'You're doing a bang-up job.'

I said, 'Thank you, sir.'

He released my hand, and held up a finger and said, 'Matt!'

I sat facing him.

His voice dropped. 'You've done a really bang-up job with Miss Phone.'

'Thank you.'

'Wherever did you find her?'

'In a club.'

'At Rupert's? She mentioned Rupert's.'

'Rupert's, yes.'

'I've never been there,' he said. He held his hands together on his desk, and leaned forward and said softly, 'Have you fornicated with her?'

I thought fast. I spoke softly. 'I let her sodomise me.'

He sat back and nodded seriously. 'I knew you were a thinking man,' he said. 'So many aren't.'

I said, 'She seemed to want to do it.'

'That's a good sign,' he said. 'A very good sign.'

I said, 'I take it you've talked with her.'

'She's a verbally facile young woman,' he said. 'But you're right to avoid fornication, until we know for sure.'

'Know?' *We* were going to know something.

'She needs to be tested. That's what I wanted to see you about.'

'Yes.'

'I want you to meet her tonight at Rupert's and take her for the testing.'

'Where do I take her?'

He wrote an address on a small pad on his desk and passed the sheet to me. 'Do you know where that is?' he asked

It was a Cobb County address, far out in the suburbs where the buses did not run. I said, 'I can find it.'

'You take her there for the testing. The door will be locked but ring the bell and tell them the Ministry sent you and they'll buzz you in.'

'Testing for what?' I said, and he looked at me. I was supposed to understand, and I thought I did, so I went ahead and said it: 'HIV?'

'Of course,' he said. 'HIV. And syphilis, gonorrhoea, hepatitis.' He tapped his desk with the tip of his forefinger as he named each disease.

I said, 'That's prudent.'

'It's restraint,' he said and he tapped the blotter again, 'that's all it is. The average man simply does not restrain himself. And the average man is diseased, dis-eased.' He held his hands out open to encompass the two of us. 'We can restrain ourselves. I knew you could when we first met. I knew you would be the one for the job. Those others, they wouldn't have been reliable, they wouldn't have been discreet enough.'

'Others?' I said.

'The other junior editors, the ones we let Grant pick out,' he said, and he waved a hand over his desk, brushing the others away. 'I knew the moment I saw you that you were the one.'

I thought about the gifted part.

He beamed at me for a moment. Then he said, 'Well, you understand everything, as usual. Now I need you back at the magazines.'

'Right,' I said.

He raised a finger and said, 'Have you ever thought about the radio show? Think about writing for it. We need good copy for my commentaries,' he said, and he stood up. 'So far I've done all the writing myself, but I've seen the job you're doing on the periodicals and I think you might have just the right touch.'

I was standing now.

'Do it!' he smiled. 'Think it up.'

Outside, Nickie looked up from her desk. I leaned over to her and said, 'Can we talk?'

'Sure.'

'In my office.'

Five minutes later, she came into my office with two cups of coffee. She pushed the door closed behind her with her foot and smiled at me. I sat at my desk, thinking. She set the coffees down and sat across from me. She picked up one of the coffees and sipped from it, then lit a cigarette, her eyes watching me the whole time. I lit up too and we both sat there a moment, drinking coffee and smoking her thin women's menthol cigarettes.

I said, 'How was Rodger with a D the second time around?'

She laughed a little. 'Not as good as you,' she said, and then she blushed, and my heart broke for her, she looked so sweet and vulnerable and fuckable. She hid it all behind her cup of coffee, drinking deep, and I lifted mine to my lips, it was hot and black, and I did not look at her again until she had collected herself.

'I need you to do something,' I said.

'What is it?'

'I need you to pretend to be Alix.'

'What do you mean?'

'Alix needs to pass an HIV test.'

She stared at me, and I let it sink in. I drew hard on the cigarette, I thought I might take up smoking.

Nickie said, 'Alix can't pass an HIV test?'

'No,' I said, 'she can't.'

Her eyes widened and she watched me with a look of faint worry and hurt. She said, 'Is this the same Alix you told me about Friday night?'

'Yes.'

Her mouth was open a little, and the tip of her tongue slid once around her lips. 'You went down on me and you're fucking somebody who's HIV positive?' Her voice was tight and tense.

I measured her, I remembered the look on Alix's face when she told me about the HIV, the way she measured me. I said, 'Don't worry, you're safe.'

'I'll worry if I fucking want to,' she said, her voice rising. 'You went down on me and you might be HIV positive.' She was loud,

161

and I looked at the closed door, I hoped the room could contain the secret.

'I'm not,' I said. 'Alix is very careful.'

'Bully for fucking Alix,' she said. 'Do you mind if I'm a little concerned about what you did to me?'

I sat back and stared at her. I drew a deep breath and she glowed with anger, she looked very hot. Friday night I had put her up there, but now I had done something to her, and I thought of her all dressed up sexy at Rupert's, I thought the words *tight little bitch*, and I said, 'Your Rodger with a D fucked Alix himself Friday night. So I didn't do anything to you that you weren't already doing to yourself.'

She sat still with her mouth open, her eyes helpless and terrified, the smoke rising in a thread from her cigarette, the ash growing unattended. She said, 'Rodger?' The ash fell on to the carpet.

I said, 'He hangs out at Rupert's and fucks like a bunny. But he's not as good as me. Two women have told me so.' I leaned forward across my desk and said, 'I need you, Nickie. I need you to get at Matt. Don't you want to get at Matt?'

She said, 'What's this got to do with Matt?'

I reached into my wallet and got one of the ministry cards. I slid it across the desk to her and she picked it up and read it. She said, 'This is Matt?'

'Matt's got a ministry for young women,' I told her.

'What does he do?'

'He saves them.'

'From what?'

'From themselves, I guess,' I said. 'But they've got to pass an HIV test before he'll save them.'

She set the card down on the edge of the desk and said, 'Shit. You're just pimping for Matt.'

'He thinks so.'

She picked up the card again, she put it together. 'Alix called him.'

'We're hacking Matt Brackett,' I said.

'Hacking him?'

'Why not?' I said. 'He's just a system, like a computer is a system. He can be hacked.'

'You want me to help.'

'Don't you want to?' I said. 'Don't you want to get even?'

She seemed to think about it. 'Even?' she said.

A copy of *Survivor* lay open on my desk, and Matt looked back at me from the head of the editorial page, a column denouncing needle exchanges for drug addicts. I looked at Nickie and said, 'Yes. I want to get even.'

She set the card down beside the box of condoms. She bit her lip. She said, 'I made Rodger use a condom.'

'Good.'

'He didn't want to,' she said, 'but I told him I wouldn't fuck him otherwise. I wouldn't fuck anybody otherwise.'

I said, 'Alix is the same way.'

'Is she?'

'I always wear one.'

'Do you know if she made him wear one?'

'She said she did.'

She thought a moment, her eyes softened. She said, 'Are you in love with Alix, Wiley?'

I measured her again, she looked ready for it. I said, 'Yes.'

She sat very still, very quiet, just looking at me, the way you look at someone you have lost, the way I looked at her earlier, sitting in the conference room, and I looked steadily back at her, I didn't want to break her gaze. She said very softly, 'Were you really in love with me?'

I said, 'Yes.' I said it to hurt her, I said it to make her feel like she had missed something good.

She turned her head to one side and sat looking at me for several moments, she looked like a question mark. She put her cigarette to her lips and drew on it and blew smoke. She said, 'What do we have to do?'

'We go to this place out in Cobb and you tell them that you're Connie Phone, and you get tested.'

'Who's Connie Phone?'

'That's who Alix is with Matt.'

She drank a little coffee and said, 'What's Alix going to do once she passes this test?'

'I don't know.'

She sat and thought about it. 'I might be afraid to ask,' she said.

I closed the magazine and said, 'Will you do it? We're fucked if you won't do it.'

The smoke was rising in a thin column from the cigarette in her hand, along with the steam coming off her coffee into the air. She shrugged. 'All right,' she said. 'I'll do it.'

I sat back. We were silent for a moment, and then I said, 'I'll put you up there for this. If you want.'

'I don't want to confuse things with you and your Alix.'

I thought, *my* Alix. I thought, *confuse* things. I could see her red red hair, her hard red lips, her mirror shades.

Nickie stood up. 'When do we go to Cobb?' she said.

'I'll pick you up around six, if that's OK.'

'That's OK,' she said. She picked up the gospel card and looked at it again. 'Whatever you do to him, I don't know if I want to know.' She handed me the card. 'You don't want to leave this lying around loose.'

She was almost out the door when she turned and said, 'You really were in love with me, weren't you?'

I looked back at her, all in powder blue, and I said, 'Yes, I think I was.'

Chapter 31

I picked her up at six. I grabbed a burger for supper and didn't go home, so I hadn't seen Alix to tell her about the testing. Nickie had changed into blue jeans and a red and white checked blouse, red, white and blue, and I said, 'Three colours never found together in nature', and she smiled a little, and put on a pair of sunglasses. We stood for a moment, looking at each other in our sunglasses.

She sat beside me while I drove and she said, 'Do you know how long this is going to take?'

'Forty-five minutes to get out to Cobb, forty-five to get back, ten minutes for the test, a couple of hours altogether,' I said. 'It's just a blood test.'

'Like when you get married?'

'I suppose,' I said. 'Does it feel like getting married?'

'It feels big,' she said. 'I've never done anything like this.'

'What is this,' I said, 'that we're doing?'

'We're fucking Matt.'

I smiled. 'You've never fucked Matt before.'

She laughed. 'Never this big,' she said. 'I throw away his mail sometimes.'

'Do you really?'

She nodded. 'The stuff that looks too sick.'

'Such as?'

'All the stuff from the Republican Party,' she said. 'He got a letter from a California survivalist group the other day. I threw that one away.'

'What did they want?'

'A false sense of security,' she said. 'They wanted information about how to spot people with AIDS, what to do to them.'

'What to do to them,' I echoed.

'Right,' she said. 'That's what they all want to know. How to fix the people with AIDS.'

I thought about Alix. I said, 'It's not enough that we just let them die.'

Nickie nodded.

I said, 'I think I'm going to enjoy fucking Matt.'

She said, 'I am. I've thought about it all day. Matt needs to be fucked. 'What all these people are afraid of is fucking around. They all say we're not supposed to fuck around, you know?'

'I know.'

'They must be fucking around somehow,' she said, 'even though they say we're not supposed to.'

'*We're* not supposed to.'

'Right,' she said, 'it's us that's not supposed to. It's you and me.'

I said, 'Well, it was a fucking beautiful day, fucking sun fucking shining away, I was fucking walking down this fucking country lane, and I fucking saw the fucking farmer's daughter, and we got into a converfuckingsation, and one fucking thing led to another, and the first fucking thing you know, we were having sexual intercourse.'

She laughed. I smiled at her.

Cobb County was white people *en masse*, it was housing developments with *pointe* in the names and supermalls and lots of traffic and heat waving up from broad black pavements edged with flowering fruit trees, and black faces who had enough money for cars, they didn't let the city buses come to Cobb. In March I had read a story in the paper about a high-school kid who got killed out there when he showed up at the wrong party, beaten to death by kids from the rival high school, the paper said they urinated on him while he lay unconscious in the back yard by the swimming pool. Matt lived out here somewhere. I stopped at an Amoco station with a sign that said GAS/FOOD MART to get directions. I bought a pack of cigarettes for Nickie and showed the cashier Matt's note.

'That's the mall,' she said. She wore a yellow smile-face button that changed to a frown as she moved.

'That figures,' I said. 'How do I get there?'

'You go back up to the light and take a right on to the access road. It'll take you up to the next exit, and that's the mall.'

The mall was a place about the size of Disneyland with enormous mansard roofs coloured blue and shining plastic in the sun. I parked and we walked across the lot to the closest entrance.

Inside it was a summer Monday night at the mall, nothing much doing but the American people out walking in the air conditioning and kids with skateboards being pursued by mall security who made me think of Alix's SOCIAL DETOURS T-shirt. I wondered what she was doing right then, as we stood before a backlit map of the mall and tried to find Health Labs, Inc., and there it was, a small pink box with the number 157 in a white circle inside it, on the mezzanine just beyond the food court.

And walking through the mall with Nickie beside me I saw AIDS. It trickled in, slowly, out of Africa, like Zinjanthropus. Africa stood

166

behind the counter of the corner cookie store, her deep black girl's face turned up suddenly with a question in her brown eyes, a little open-mouthed and looking into the softly smiling face of her manager looking down at her as he caressed her ass inside the shorts of her golden cookie-coloured uniform. I just glimpsed his hand behind the counter as we passed, the surreptitious gesture of the secret desire: there was the white man, all used up, and I saw her body, her legs long and well formed and her breasts round and high, and I could see why he wanted her the way he did, the way one animal needs another, the hunger in the thighs. And what if she had AIDS? I thought, passing by the people in line for their cookies and milk before the yellow and blue front of the little store, would she tell him? why? Then he had it, too, and he took it home in suburbia here and gave it to his wife, or his white girlfriend, or both, and it waited, secretly, for years, HIV, curled into the genome and working in the lymph nodes, waiting, and while it waited in him, in her, in the wife and the girlfriend, they fucked. That was all. A boy and a girl rolled past us on skateboards, both in extra-large T-shirts that flapped around them and hid the shapes of their indestructible bodies, and they fucked too, I thought, without any protection, without any knowledge or instruction, just blind fucking, just blind fucking need, spreading a virus in a painfully slow but ever-widening circle, spending their energy to feed the relentness need, and all these people thought they were immune, because they were white people, because they were straight people, as if you could be immune to need, to fucking, to love.

Health Labs, Inc. was a black door and a front window covered with closed narrow blinds. The place was locked up, as Matt had said it would be, but they had a speaker phone, and I rang them inside and in a moment a man's voice said 'Yes?'

I said, 'I'm from the Ministry.'

'Are you with Miss Phone?'

'That's right.'

'Come right in,' he said, and the door buzzed as the lock slipped free.

Inside, we stood in a waiting area. There were serigraphs on the three walls, abstract patterns in earth colours, and a vacant receptionist's desk, and a square wood and glass table covered with *People* and *Time* before two empty earth-coloured couches. The door to the back opened and a young guy came out in blue jeans and a green hospital smock with a blue badge that said CLAYTON in white letters. Looking at me, he said, 'You're here for the Ministry testing?'

167

'That's right,' I said, and I nodded at Nickie. 'This is Miss Phone.'

Clayton said, 'Right this way.' He held open a door and we went along with him.

In the back there was a collection room, like you would see in any hospital or clinic, jars of gauze and cotton, boxes of disposable syringes, everything white and sterile and shining aluminium and sharp and vaguely pointed at you. On a white desk sat a box with a half-eaten cheeseburger and some fries. A book lay next to it, open and face down, and I read the title upside down on the dustjacket: *For the First Time the Original Uncut 'Stranger in a Strange Land.'*

'I was just having supper,' said Clayton.

'Sorry to interrupt.'

'That's OK,' he said. 'The evenings are long out here.'

I said, 'Well, you can catch up on your reading.'

His face flickered with interest, he thought he heard a fan. 'Do you read Heinlein?' he said.

'I'm in the magazine business,' I said. 'I never read books.' Nickie snickered.

'Oh,' he said. He'd never heard that one before.

He had Nickie sit in a chair beside the desk and he sat in front of her on a brown revolving stool, while I stood behind him and watched. He reached to an open box on the desk and he put on a pair of latex gloves. He got a syringe ready, and he said, 'If you ever change your mind about the books, you might want to give Heinlein a try.' Then he pulled Nickie's left arm out straight along the desk top and applied a tourniquet and felt for a vein. 'Maybe I will,' I said.

Nickie watched him as he worked, and I watched him too. He found the vein and then he lost it and had to start over.

Finally he told her to make a fist. She made one and bit her lip. He felt for the vein, and rolled it around and slid the needle in smoothly and missed it. 'Ouch,' she said softly, and he said, 'You have rolling veins,' and he tried it again and missed again and then again and finally got it.

He released the tourniquet from her upper arm, and I watched the deep red blood flow into the tube. Nickie bit her lower lip and looked away, and in that move she looked so vulnerable and soft that I felt the old feeling for her for a moment and I wanted her again. Clayton sat back and said, 'That book is one of Heinlein's masterpieces.' Nickie said to him, 'When will we know the results?'

He looked surprised that she could speak, and annoyed that she had changed the subject. 'Twenty-four hours,' he said.

'It takes longer than that, doesn't it?' she said.

'Well,' he said, 'the Ministry pays for it.'

'I'll bet,' she said. 'How do you get it together so fast?'

'This is PCR,' he said, nodding at the needle in her arm, and warming up to her, this was his other area of expertise, along with science fiction, and he liked showing off to the pretty blonde. 'This is the best there is.'

'PCR.' She stared at the wall, not looking at either of us.

'Polymerase chain reaction,' he said. 'It exponentially multiplies proviral DNA.'

Big words, I thought.

'That's called *amplifying* the DNA,' he said. 'Do you know what DNA is? You'd be surprised how many people don't.' He was Mr Science, he underlined the keywords as he talked. 'You see, HIV can exist within the host cell DNA as what we call provirus. That's the precursor of the animal virus that causes AIDS.' The syringe filled with blood.

'We take your blood, and we separate the white cells from it and break them open and extract your DNA. Then we *denature* the DNA, we break it down from double strands to single strands, and we add something called *oligonucleotide* primers and an enzyme called *Taq 1*.'

He withdrew the tube full of blood from the syringe and inserted another one. She looked down to see what he was doing, and the blood flowed freely into the new collector, and her expression sickened. She looked away again. He said, 'We heat and cool the sample because that promotes amplification. Then we add *probes*, little DNA probes that act to detect the proviral DNA if it's there. If it's there, see, the probes can *label* it and then we can see it and then we know you're HIV-positive.' He smiled.

'What do you do then?' she said.

He looked at her blankly.

She nodded at her arm. 'This hurts. Is it done yet?'

He started and looked down and then withdrew the second tube from the syringe and smoothly withdrew the needle from the vein. He reached into a jar full of cotton swabs soaking in alcohol and rubbed the site of the puncture. She took it from him and sat rubbing her arm.

'It's all state of the art,' he went on talking to her as he bundled the two tubes of blood together with a rubber band. 'It's the most

169

sensitive assay there is. PCR can detect one molecule of viral DNA in ten microlitres of blood.'

'That's sensitive,' she said.

'PCR can find a needle in a haystack. And we run an additional test for p24,' he said. 'This is all state of the art.' He waved a hand at the room.

He glanced at me over his shoulder then, and he seemed to me for a second to be looking frightened at someone following him. He said to me, 'p24 is an HIV core protein that's present in the bloodstream for the first six weeks or so following an exposure. A long time before antibodies to the virus appear. The p stands for protein, and the 24 is the molecular weight in kilodaltons.'

'This certainly is sensitive, isn't it?' said Nickie, and she looked at me with smiling eyes.

'Is that what you do here?' I said. 'Test people for HIV?'

'We do a lot of lab work,' he said and he turned to me on his revolving stool. 'But we're in the mall to test for HIV, yes.'

'Do you get much business?'

'We give out HIV-free cards, see?' he said, and he reached for his wallet and got out a sort of ID card and passed it to me. It was printed in blue and green ink with intricate scrollwork like money and laminated in heavy plastic like a credit card, an American Express, and it said that George Clayton had tested clear of antibodies to HIV on 1 June 1991. I smiled and handed the card back to him.

I said, 'How much does one of those cost?'

'Two hundred and fifty dollars,' he said.

'That's very sensitive,' I said.

'What?' he said.

I said, 'Do you sell a lot of them?'

'We do all right,' he said. 'Would you like to get one?'

'Sure,' I said.

'They can come in handy,' he said, nodding. 'For insurance and social purposes too.'

'Social purposes?' I said.

'You're single, I suppose?' he said.

'Yes,' I said.

'Then proof of clear health can make a difference for you in today's society. That's what I call it,' he said. 'A bloodstream clear of virus.'

I said, 'Can you put it on the Ministry's tab?'

Sale closed, he winked at me. 'Sure thing,' he said.

After he changed gloves and drew my blood, I took care of the paperwork for myself and Connie Phone. Clayton looked at the forms and said, 'You're neighbours.' I had given Connie Alix's address.

'It's a small world,' I said. 'You'll mail us the cards, right?'

He looked at me. 'We Fedex them,' he said, 'if there's no problem.'

'What if there's a problem?'

'Then we have post-test counselling.'

'Who does that?'

He stood up. 'We have a part-time social worker,' he said.

'Really?' I said. 'Part-time?'

'She's here on Mondays and Thursdays. We have post-test counselling on Mondays and Thursdays.'

'How much does that cost?' I said.

'Oh, that's included in the two-fifty.'

'That's a deal,' said Nickie.

George turned to her. He said, 'We provide full service.'

'Like the gas stations used to do,' she said.

George stood looking at her with the paperwork in his hand.

Chapter 32

When I got home, Alix was hacking Brackett Data in my sun room. The apartment was hot, and she sat at the terminal in her bikini, with her top hung across the back of the chair. Her hair was piled up on top of her head and held together with bobby pins and coming undone down around her ears and neck. I walked in behind her and put my hands on her shoulders and massaged them. She was wet with sweat. She said, 'It's too hot' and I bent and kissed her lightly on the neck.

'What have you got there?' I said, and I took off my tie and draped it over the back of the rocking chair.

'Just the mail.'

'Any good stuff in there?' I smiled at her back.

She said, 'This Margaret Divine has dumped that salesman.'

'Jim Neill.'

'Yeah.'

'What does she say?'

'Nothing. She just dropped him cold.'

'Snow queen.'

'Didn't even say goodbye.'

'What's he doing?'

She turned in her chair and watched me undress. I slipped out of my khakis and pulled off my shirt. The shirt was wet, I was wet with sweat. She said, 'He's pretty pathetic about it.' She made a mock sad face. '"Must see you," he says. "Be reasonable."'

The windows were all open and I stood still a moment, letting the evening air cool my body, I looked out at the golden sun resting on the horizon, just above the treetops. 'I guess he thinks it's not reasonable that she should drop him,' I said.

'Right,' she said. 'I bet he never asked her to be reasonable when she was going down on him.'

I laughed and turned to her. I said, 'I never ask you to be reasonable, do I?'

She smiled and reached for me and caressed me between the legs and I got a little hard. 'I thought it was too hot,' I said.

'Where've you been, anyway?' she said.

'Getting an HIV test for Connie Phone.'

'Really?'

'Really. The Ministry wanted one.'

'Is Connie going to pass?'

'Yes.'

'How does she manage that?'

'I got Nickie to take it for her.'

'Nickie.' She said the name flatly, and her voice had a little edge to it. Her face looked serious – Nickie was out of the picture, wasn't she?

'Yes,' I said. 'She doesn't like him any better than the rest of us.'

She looked at me for a moment, then she brushed her fingers down my leg, and I took a step closer to her. She said, 'What does Nickie know about us?'

'She knows about us.'

'What does she know?'

'She knows I love you.'

'You told her that?'

'Yes.'

'Good.'

'You're jealous.'

'Alix may be jealous,' she said. 'Confusion wants Nickie in her place.'

'Where's that?'

'A history book.'

I laughed. I said, 'Tell Confusion not to worry.'

She looked at me a moment, measuring me again. Finally she said, 'Who was that that called the other night?'

'When?' I said.

'The woman who wanted to talk to Willie,' she said. 'Not your mother.'

'That was Sarah,' I said.

'All right,' she made a hard face and closed her eyes with patience. 'Who is Sarah?'

'She's my father's mistress.'

Her eyes opened and she looked at me with a curiosity I hadn't seen in her before. She said, 'Your father has a mistress?'

'That's my dad,' I said, and I slipped my briefs down my legs and kicked them off. I turned to the pallet and reached for my robe. 'He's got a newspaper column, and a wife, and a son, and a mistress, and a Pulitzer, and a Jaguar, and a house in Georgetown, and everything. He needs a big box to put it all in.'

Alix sighed a small sigh and said, 'What's your father's mistress call you about?'

173

'We're old friends,' I said, standing and slipping the robe on, tying the belt and turning to her. 'A boy's best friend is his father's mistress.'

'Have you ever fucked her?'

I laughed out loud. I said, 'For Christ's sake, Alix, she's not a whore.'

She said, 'Well —'

I cut her off, 'She's my father's mistress, OK?' I looked at her hard, and she looked back at me levelly. I said, 'She's an artist. She's a friend of mine. We talk about my writing, she says it's OK for me to write, my father says I need to get a real job, and my mother takes Valium and smokes too much. Of the three, I prefer listening to Sarah. All right?'

I stepped to her and caressed her face, her eyes quickened with my touch, and she said softly, 'Do you really love me, Wiley?'

'Yes,' I said.

'Why?' she said, and I wondered if I didn't hear Confusion talking again.

'Why do you love me?' I said.

'Because you know I'm positive and you fuck me anyway.'

I studied her face. Her eyes shone brightly with unshed tears, she was earnest, Confusion was being honest. I said, 'What's that mean?'

She turned her head, thinking of another way to say it. At last she said, 'You keep up with me.' She looked at me and I returned the look, smiling slightly, pleased I could keep up. She said, 'No one's been able to keep up with me since Stephen.'

I looked steadily into her face. A car radio played outside in the evening traffic, a kid Stevie Winwood sang the blues out in front of his blue piano, and she blushed, suddenly, and surprised me. She looked down into her lap to hide it from me, Confusion could not blush, Confusion could not be baffled, but Confusion had just given away something serious and real, and I wanted suddenly to fuck her gently and beautifully. I put my hand under her chin and nudged her head up mildly, she lifted her green eyes to mine and said, 'Nothing stops you.'

My heart swelled and my throat closed and I swallowed, I said, 'I love you, Alix.'

She shook her head, she blinked and I felt a tear on my hand, she said, 'I just can't get over you.'

'Do you want to?'

174

She lifted her face to me again, she said, 'Confusion wants to. Confusion is hard. She's a hard woman.'

'I love her, too,' I said.

She drew me to her and held me close by the waist and said, 'You would.' I ran my hands across her bare back; her skin was smooth and white, and after a moment she released me and sat back. Her breasts were bare and lovely, and she folded her hands between her knees and leaned towards me a little, looking up, and said, 'Now why do you love me, Wiley?'

I stepped away from her and sat down on the pallet. 'It's hard to put it into words,' I said.

'I know.'

I looked at her to get focused on the love. Then I started, I said, 'I told you about my accident.'

She said, 'That's why I thought you might understand me.'

I nodded. 'I think I can.'

She smiled slightly. 'I think you do, honey.'

'And I think you understand me.'

'Yes.'

'Dying changes things.'

'Yes.'

'You understand that. You understand that change.'

She breathed deep, she looked good to me, and I could tell she was feeling better and better as I spoke, and I wanted to speak for a long gentle time and tell her things over and over about how beautiful she was in her understanding, to make her feel what I felt down in my cock, sleek and beautiful and full of come. I said, 'Everybody acts as if they're going to live for ever.'

'They sure do,' she said, and her head shook a little from side to side.

'You don't.'

'No.'

'That makes you dangerous.'

And she betrayed a slight smile, she tried not to show it, but she liked what I was saying, telling her what I loved.

'I love your danger,' I said. 'It excites me.'

'Confusion.'

'Alix,' I shook my head. 'Alix is dangerous because she knows she's not going to live for ever. You know there's only death waiting for us, and when you know that, really know it, there's nothing left to be afraid of.'

'Nothing but dying,' she said.

175

I thought there was a little more, I said, 'And being alone.'

'Are you alone, Wiley? I'm here with you.'

'We're alone together,' I said.

She leaned back against the desk, her breasts looked sweet to me, she said, 'You die alone. That's what you're thinking. That's what you're afraid of, isn't it?'

I said, 'Stephen died alone, didn't he? I mean, you couldn't go with him.'

The light of the late sun cast wonderfully across her bare skin. She said, 'I went with him as far as I could.' She stood up and stepped towards me. She knelt on the floor before me, her knees together on the hardwood and her hands down on her thighs. 'We're all going to die,' she said. 'That's why what you do makes a difference. If you lived for ever, it wouldn't matter what you did.'

'Matt Brackett thinks he's going to live for ever,' I said.

She said, 'So do most people. That's why what they do makes no impression.' She placed her hands on my shoulders and squeezed them pleasurably. 'Matt Brackett is alone,' she said.

I put my hands on her arms, I said, 'I love you because you're not afraid.'

She said, 'I get afraid.'

'Of what?'

'I don't want to die.'

'But you're going to,' I said, 'and you know it. It makes a difference. It doesn't make any difference with Matt.'

'You want it to make a difference with him,' she said.

'It ought to make a difference.'

She took my hands and lifted them and kissed my fingertips. 'Then it will,' she said.

'What do you mean?'

'We're hacking him, right?'

'Right.'

'Then, it'll make a difference,' she said. 'That'll be part of the hack.' She bent again and licked my fingertips, she made me hard with her tongue, and she said, 'It'll be like my present to you.' She stood back and looked at me with my hands in hers and she said, 'I love you, Wiley.'

I said, 'It's not too hot.'

She kissed my hands again and drew them to her breast.

176

Chapter 33

We made love for a while in the sun room while the city gave up heat into the cooling evening air, we were like a long slow train disappearing into the night. Then we took a cold shower together and bathed each other. She fixed a big salad and we ate at her place, and, before we went to bed, Confusion called the Gospel According to Matthew. She talked into the portable phone while she opened a cold bottle of white wine in the kitchen and I listened on the living-room extension.

'I'm just fixing myself a little wine cooler,' Connie said. 'Is that OK? I mean, is that in the Gospel According to Matthew?'

Matt said, 'That's perfectly all right, Connie. In moderation.'

'Oh, I moderate it,' she said, and I heard the cork slide free of the bottleneck with a tiny pop of compressed air. 'I never drink more than one bottle at a time,' she said. ''Cause I like my wine cooler, it helps me to unlax, like the Kingfish used to say.'

Matt laughed. 'It's a shame they can't show those old programmes any more,' he said.

'Isn't it, though?' I heard her pick up the bottle and the glasses. She carried it all into the living room, cradling the portable against her shoulder. Her hair was down around her shoulders, and she had on a pale green silk dressing gown that I could see through, I looked at the curling red hair of her pubis and I thought about the way she fucked me. I sat on the sofa in a pair of cutoffs and no shirt. As she passed in front of me I reached and took the glasses from her and she sat with the bottle on the floor on the other side of the coffee table. She said, 'That test was scary.'

'Really?' said Matt. I wondered if he had ever been tested.

'I don't like needles and pointy things,' she said.

'It's for your own good,' said Matt. 'I'm sure everything will turn out fine, with a careful girl like you.'

'I'm careful,' she said. 'You noticed that, didn't you?'

'Yes, I did,' he said, and I could hear him smiling, satisfied, he had noticed her.

'So what's next?' she said. 'I mean, after I get my card.'

I poured the wine, and she took hers and had a sip.

Matt said, 'Well, then, I should think, it would be time for us to meet.'

'In person.'

'In person.' You could hear the slick smile in his voice.

'Gee, I like talking with you,' she said.

'And I like talking with you,' said Matt, smiling and smiling.

'I mean, I *really* like it.'

'That's good,' said Matt. 'It's good for you.'

'I liked confessing to you.'

'Honest confession is good for the soul,' he said.

'Did you like it?' she said. 'Did you like my confession?'

He paused. He was getting Confused now, and I wondered what he would say.

He said, 'I like the trust you put in me.'

'I trust you,' she said, and she took a long drink of her wine and poured some more. 'I want to confess some more.'

'Yes?'

'It excites me to confess.'

'Yes.'

She spoke very softly now. She said, 'Does it excite you?'

He paused again, Confused. He said, 'It inspires me in my work.'

She said softly, 'I made love to Wiley after the test tonight. Would you like me to confess to that?'

He paused a moment, and then he said, 'Do you feel the need to?'

'I like to get excited,' she said. 'Don't you like to get excited?'

She had him thoroughly Confused, I thought, but he said, 'My desires are totally secondary to your needs to confess.'

'My needs,' she said, and she went on: 'Well, then, I'll tell you, I took Wiley home with me, we live in the same building, you know, and the test had scared me and when I get scared I like a man around, you know, but Wiley wouldn't let me, I mean, make love, to him, you know, because we don't know if I passed the test yet, but he did let me sodomise him, that's what he called it, and then he made me with his hands, he put on some latex gloves he had and he made me come.'

Matt cleared his throat. 'Yes?' he said.

She said, 'I like taking Wiley in my mouth,' and she looked up at me across the coffee table, and I grew a little hard, listening to her, and she said, 'He's so hard and straight, the way I like, and I like to hold his balls while I suck him, he always tastes salty, and I just love to do it for him.' She sat up suddenly, and she said, 'Is that shameful? Is that an appetite or is it an expression of love?'

He cleared his throat again. 'That all depends,' he said.

178

'On what?' she said quickly.

He had to think a moment. Then he said, 'On your motive.'

She said, 'Well, my motive was to turn Wiley on, you know, to make him come.'

He said nothing, he was Confused. Then he said, 'That's a good motive, then, I think. That's not self-seeking, is it?'

'No!' she said.

He said, 'What does Wiley do to you?'

'Oh,' she said long, and she sat up and talked earnestly into the phone. 'He does me with his hands so good, and he says he'll do me all the way once I get my card, I don't think anybody has ever done me as good as Wiley does. He takes his time. So many guys just have no time to do me right, you know what I mean? Like you, I bet you just take all the time in the world.'

There was silence on the other end.

'I can tell from the way you listen,' she said, 'any guy who listens like you do must be real patient, and you listen to a lot of women, don't you?'

'Not as many as you might think,' he said.

'Sure,' she said, 'I know I'm not the only one. Say, the man at the test said they'd know by tomorrow if I passed, then Wiley will do me all the way, and I'll have something to confess to you. Yeah, I'll tell you all about it. I like to tell you all about it.' She sipped some wine, and I could hear him breathing, waiting and listening. She said, 'Would you like to know what I have on right now?'

'Yes,' he said, the word came quickly, but then he caught himself, he added, 'I mean, if you feel the need to confess something about how you dress.'

'Oh, I don't have anything on,' she said.

'You don't,' he said.

'No,' she said, and she winked at me. Then she said, 'I don't wear anything when I talk to you.'

He said, 'Oh.'

'It's bad, I know,' she made the word *bad* sound delicious. 'I'm so bad, but I just can't help it when I'm with you.'

He was silent, he was baffled, she had put him exactly where he wanted to be and he couldn't allow it.

'When do you think I'll get my card?' she said.

'What?' he said, suddenly diverted. 'Oh, you should have that the day after tomorrow.'

'I'll call you then,' she said.

'You're going?'

'Yes,' she said. 'I'm tired from all that testing, and I want to go to bed.' She poured some more wine and drank some. She said, 'Would you like me to tell you about my bedroom?'

He said, weakly, 'Do you feel the need?'

'I'm so tired now,' she said, 'I'll call you in the morning. Will you be there?'

'Yes,' he said.

'I'll call you early, before I go to work, and I'll be in bed when I call, OK?'

'All right.'

'You're so patient.'

'Yes.'

'And when you get impatient with me, you just remember, we've got all the time in the world, you and me.'

I heard him breathe deeply.

'Ciao,' she said.

Chapter 34

A courier delivered an envelope to Alix's on Wednesday morning before we left for work. Then he carried another envelope up the stairs to my door and knocked. I called to him from Alix's doorway, 'I'm down here', and he brought my package back.

Alix sat at the kitchen table in her bathrobe, opening the heavy red, white and blue envelope. 'Oh, look,' she said, spilling it out on to the table, 'it's my get-out-of-jail-free card.'

I opened mine, and it was the card, like Clayton's. It said that Wiley Jones had tested clear of antibodies to HIV on 17 June 1991.

Alix held the card up before her and looked at it. I watched her, and I wished that it were true, I wished that Connie Phone was clear of antibodies, and for a moment her face had a faraway look on it. Then she waved it back and forth and said, 'This means Wiley gets to do me all the way, and I get to tell Matt about it.'

I said, 'You should be a writer.'

'You're the writer, honey, not me,' she said. 'I could make lots of trouble with this.'

'Confusion could,' I said. 'Better watch Confusion when she's got her hands on that.'

She laughed. 'I know what I'll do,' she said. 'I'll make a bracelet out of it and wear it to Rupert's.'

'Like a little advertisement,' I said.

'Don't leave home without it,' she said. 'You can wear yours, too. We'll go together, we can get a foursome going.'

'You should loan it to Nickie some time. After all,' I said.

She said, 'I may let Nickie watch, honey.'

'She might like to watch,' I said. 'She's just the littlest bit kinky.'

'Oh,' she cried out loud suddenly, excited, and she looked at her watch. 'There's time to call him,' she said, and she picked up the portable from the table and dialled the Gospel. But Matt had already left and she got the answering machine. She slumped a little in her chair, disappointed, then perked up again and said, 'Hello, Gospel, this is Connie, and I got the good news this morning. Just thought you'd want to know.' She sat forward around the phone, and her voice softened as she said, 'I'm going to call Wiley now, so we'll have something to talk about tonight. Ciao.' She set the phone down on the table and looked at me. I was standing beside the refrigerator with my card in one hand and the empty courier envelope in the other. Her eyes lit up with mischief, and she said, 'Do you have time to do me all the way before you go to work, honey?'

I laughed, and she laughed with me. I said, 'You'll make me late.'

She said, 'Oh, that would be terrible, wouldn't it?' She got up from the table and came across the kitchen to me, put her arm around me and reached down between my legs. I grew hard at her touch.

'It wouldn't be that terrible,' I said.

'I didn't think so,' she said, and she began to nuzzle my neck, while I reached inside her robe and felt her breasts.

I said, 'Are you going to tell Matt about this?' and I moved my hand down to her cunt.

'Not right away,' she said. 'I'm not going to call him for a while.'

'Make him wait.'

'That's right.'

'You're a tease,' I said, and I kissed her on the neck, near her ear. 'I didn't know you were a tease.'

She drew a little away from me and put her arms around my neck and said, 'Yes, you did.'

Chapter 35

That Sunday I took a break from the writing and called Sarah. I knew she would be up, even though it was early. Sarah always got up early to catch the morning light and paint, she said that it fed her, that it broke the fast of darkness.

She answered on the second ring, and said, 'I thought it was you.'

'How could you tell?'

'Only you or Nathaniel would call this early on a Sunday morning, and I talked to him last night.'

I let it pass, I imagined him momentarily, drunk on Saturday night and calling his mistress far away. I said, 'What are you doing today?'

'Seducing a banker.'

'Really?'

She laughed. 'I've made a hit with the bankers, and they're all vying to take me to lunch and dinner.'

I laughed with her. I said, 'I'll be that makes a picture.'

She said, 'I get to play the artiste while these yuppies fall all over themselves.'

I said, 'Who's the quarry today?'

'The executive vice-president of marketing,' she said. 'We're having lunch at someplace called Bacchanalia.'

'What will you wear?'

'I haven't decided yet. Either something clinging and gauzy and teasing or else some old blue jeans and my new Lou Reed T-shirt.'

I laughed again.

'I'm serious,' she said. 'I'm the artiste. They indulge me.' I heard an enormous sarcastic smile in her voice. 'They've never been with an artiste before.'

'Neither have I,' I said.

'Neither have I!' she laughed. '*Artiste*,' she said contemptuously. 'This banker actually called me that in a meeting one day. Can you imagine?'

'He thought he was complimenting you, Sarah.'

'Christ,' she said. 'It makes me wonder what I'd be going through if I was a man.' She sighed. 'Anyway, that's the content of today's happy hour. What are you doing?'

'Right now,' I said, 'I'm taking a break from writing.'

'Oh – you were going to show me your manuscript.'

'I will.'

'When?' she said. 'When can I see you?'

I felt a familiar, boyish thrill. It used to excite me to be with her in the afternoons in DC, we would go to a movie, she liked French films in the original French, with subtitles for me, and I would sit beside her in the dark and smell her perfume and feel very manly and adult to be with her, the *mistress*, and I just knew that the other men wondered if we were mother and son or sister and brother or lover and lover, and I would try to imagine her lover, to be like a man who had possessed her, to sit like him and hold myself the way he would and look at her and talk to her his way, so they would believe I was a man like them and better, because I had Sarah.

I said, 'How about tomorrow night?'

'Can't,' she said. 'Bankers. Bankers all week.'

'Friday, too?'

'Friday?' she said. 'I've got lunch free. How about that?'

'I've got to work.'

'I've got a rental,' she said. 'A Lincoln Towncar. Red with a brown leather interior.'

'Classy.'

'I picked it myself,' she said. 'So I'll come to your office and treat you.'

'On your expense account,' I said.

'*Les frais de représentation, c'est moi,*' she said, and she broke into a laugh that sounded mischievous and playful, full of art and a sweet guile that you had to forgive. 'Oh,' she said with real earnestness in her voice, 'I just love decadence.'

'So do I,' I smiled.

'Good!' she said. 'Now you have to bring me up to date. How's your love life?'

'She's fine.'

'*She?* Is that singular?'

'Yes.'

'As in Alix?'

'Yes.'

'Good for you,' she said. 'Or is it? Does it make you happy?'

'I think so.'

'The grass is always greener, you know,' she said. 'You may find yourself missing all that greener grass.'

'I might,' I admitted.

184

'What will you do then?' she teased.

For a moment it was real, it could happen, it probably would, and I had no feeling for what I might do then, and I was afraid, afraid of myself, afraid of hurting Alix. I didn't know if I could watch her die, I didn't know I wouldn't run from it. I said, 'I suppose I'll find out, won't I?'

She laughed and said, 'Oh, yes.

We all find out, whether we want to or not.'

I was curious, I said, 'Do you think I'll cheat on her?' It mattered to me what Sarah thought.

She paused. I could feel her weighing me in her mind; she said, 'Yes.' I heard the word like a heavy bell distantly ringing, I felt empty and hungry for breakfast, and my coffee was cold and I needed a cigarette. She went ahead quickly, as if to soften it: 'But she'll let you come back. Cheaters are awfully attractive.' When I said nothing she said, 'You don't know that, do you?'

'What?'

'How attractive you are.'

I could feel the mistress making things all right now, after she had let the truth come in. I smiled at her thankfully, and said, 'Now there's a subject I could write about.'

She said, 'You are attractive, Wiley, you're one of the most attractive men I know. I don't know when you got to be so attractive.'

'Neither of us was watching,' I said.

She said, 'Do you want me to tell you or not?'

'Of course,' I laughed.

'Well,' she began, with a sly tone, 'you're dangerous.'

'Me?' I did not think of myself as dangerous, Confusion was dangerous, or Margaret Divine, or even Sarah.

She said, 'In all your innocence.'

'Now that's me,' I said, a little ruefully. I remembered Nickie calling me *innocent* that first day in the office, and I remembered that she would not fuck me.

'Oh, you'll do something very bad some day,' she said. 'And it will be something very clever. Because you think, the way a storm gathers.'

'I think too much,' I said. 'It screws up the writing, it stays too much in the head.'

'Maybe,' she said, 'but it's attractive to a certain kind of woman.' She paused and then said, 'To me, anyway.'

185

She let the words hang there between us. She said, 'You could be evil, you know.'

I said, 'I thought I was innocent.'

'That's What's dangerous,' she said. 'Experience is limited. But innocence is capable of anything.'

'I don't want to be innocent,' I said, and I felt urgent to lose it.

She said softly, 'I'm glad. You're not yet real when you're still innocent.'

I looked out the windows up the boulevard and across the park. The brown land was absolutely empty under a pale blue, cloudless summer sky, a Sunday morning before church, the heat just beginning to build for the day. 'I want that,' I said. 'I want something real.'

'That's attractive too. Do you know how many men don't want anything real?'

I thought of Matt Brackett, I thought of *Survivor* and HIV tests, and I said, 'Yes.'

She said, 'Then you know what I mean.'

'Yes.'

'So you mustn't be innocent any more.'

'How do you lose it?' I said.

She said, 'That's different for all of us.'

'How did you lose it?'

'Oh!' she said suddenly, 'my breakfast date will be here in twenty minutes.'

'You have a date for Sunday breakfast?'

She laughed. 'A banker who hasn't lost his innocence yet.'

'Is he going to lose it today?' I smiled.

'He might,' she smiled. 'Or he may never.'

I felt a sudden rush of love for her 'Will you tell me about it?' I asked

'Friday,' she said, 'at lunch.' And she hung up.

Chapter 36

I had Production work up a dummy of the member services magazine and I sent it to Margaret Divine early the next week. She brought it back by my office just before lunch on Tuesday. She was a bright burning dot of yellow and red: bright yellow cotton knit blouse clinging to her body with a small v at the neckline and a small red rosebud above her right breast. A darker yellow handkerchief skirt teased you with glimpses of her legs among the flames, and bright red smiling lips and red fingernails. She had the dummy with her. 'You do read minds,' she said. 'This is exactly what I wanted.' She tapped the book with a finger.

'Really,' I said.

'Yes,' she smiled, cute red lips and white pearls of teeth. And she sat there, waiting for me.

I said, 'When does the first issue go to press?'

'I've talked to Matt about it,' she said, 'and I'm writing a letter to the members announcing it. The presentations from the last five years are in directories on drive G. You pick out the ones you want to use and, baby, we can fly any time you want.'

'Fly,' I said.

'Absolutely soar,' she said, and she waved her hand through the air between us like a wing.

I couldn't help smiling, she seemed so happy with the book.

She looked down suddenly at her watch. 'You're late,' she said.

'I am?'

'I didn't think you were ever late,' she said. 'But it's five minutes past noon. You were supposed to take me to lunch five minutes ago.'

'I'm late,' I said. I stood up and grabbed my sunglasses, and we left for lunch.

Outside, the June sun was bright and hot and the leaves hung down listlessly from the flowering fruit trees that decorated the islands in the parking lot.

'Let's take my car,' said Margaret, and she held out her keys and pointed to a burgundy red BMW with very darkly tinted windows sitting in one of the reserved spots close to the back door.

I looked down at the keys, and I wondered which one was the key to her house, and if she had a house, she looked more like a condo to me. Then I looked at the car. 'With pleasure,' I said.

Inside the car, she got out a black pair of sunglasses from a case clipped to the window shade, and I slipped mine on, too, genuine green-glass Wiley Post aviator shades, so we were both cool, and close in the car I could smell her perfume strongly, a strong scent of musk, a live, wrestling warm animal smell mixed with the scent of the rosebud. She was a little animal, all packed into her clothes with a tight hot sexual scent, and I breathed her in deep and said, 'Is that Chinese place good for you?'

She said, 'Let's just drive around for a while.'

I looked at her, and she looked hot, in the summer day, and she looked cool, in the black shades. She looked like an offer of something, and I imagined her fucking again, I saw her perfect little body naked in a snow white bed with red lips kissing and red nails grasping, and Alix was there beside her; in my mind, Alix said *I can make my face like a cunt* and I felt twin tendrils of guilt and desire curl up inside my chest, and I drew a breath and said, 'Drive around?'

She pulled one of Simon English's smooth, fat joints from her purse and held it up for me to see.

I said, 'Drive around', and I started the engine, and the radio and the air conditioner started up with it, and the music was loud, the radio was tuned to Georgia Tech, I could tell from the music, a jazz violin, Sugarcane Harris with Frank Zappa, like my father liked to listen to while he drank alone talking to himself in his study, and Margaret sat back in her seat and lit the joint and got it going and passed it over to me. I drew lightly on it while I backed the car out of the parking space, and we tooled around the airport for a while, past the hangars and the flight school, smoking, and she said, 'Do you like driving my car?'

I looked at her, watching me sideways with a slight smile on her face.

'It's a good car,' she said.

'How fast does it go?'

'Very fast.'

'Can I take it out on the highway some time and see?'

'Oh, you really should,' she said. 'It handles best at high speeds.'

I drove out to the parking lot nearest the main runway, at the end of the observation deck that ran from the foot of the control tower down the side of the field, and we sat with the motor running and the air conditioning going and the Georgia Tech music playing and we watched the little planes land and take off. She smoked the joint hard, she sighed and said, 'Oh, I love to get fucked up', and she waved it burning in the air with a flourish and handed it to me. 'You finish it,' she said. I took a long drag and parked it in the ashtray. She sat beside me with her head laid back on the headrest. A yellow airplane took off in front of us and the music got bluesy.

'How is the Legion of Decency today?' she asked

The little gag failed to make me smile. I said, 'I'm doing fine naturally, like the last time we talked.'

'How fortunate for you. You are the fortunate one.'

'I'm grateful for it.'

'What we are not grateful for, we soon lose,' she said. 'I had lunch with your Nickie girlfriend last week.'

'She told me.'

She lifted her head from the headrest and said, 'Did she tell you what I told her?'

'She did.'

She rested her head again. 'Then she's indiscreet.'

'She doesn't have the knack that you and I have.'

'Precisely,' she said. 'We are the gifted ones.'

I wondered if she had checked out my résumé, and then I began to wonder what she knew, and I noticed that she said *we*: the two of us were together in something, then, and I looked at the lines of her tight little body inside the knit blouse and I had a sudden impulse to reach across the car and touch her, the way I would have touched some perfect doll in a display, just to see if I could get away with it. I wanted to know what we were into, and she excited me, things began to come in a rush in my head and I had to catch my breath. I felt her between my legs, I felt drawn between her and Confusion, Confusion smiled, riot sparkling, Confusion would do anything, and Alix bent her head standing before the mirror in the shadows and tears came down her cheeks and she said *Fuck it* softly and gave in and said she loved me. And now Margaret Divine wanted me to drive her car, and she had not even said goodbye to Jim Neill, and this made me feel her stronger, with that old Anne Mathers lust for someone you can't have, made me want to fuck her, and Alix said, *I don't want you to fuck anybody but me*, and Margaret Divine had come after me for something and wanted me to drive her car and was not dying. I looked at her perfect profile against the deepened blue of the sky through the tinted window, I looked at the roundness of her precise red lips, and I said, 'You said you know all the company secrets.'

'Every one worth knowing.'

'Tell me one,' I said.

She turned and looked at me. The pink tip of her tongue slipped out between her red lips and she licked them, the violin was wailing and the Mothers were flying with it, building to a big push just before the end. 'No,' she said. 'You tell me a secret first, and then I'll tell you one.'

I looked across the car seat at her, I saw myself in my Wiley Post shades reflected back at me in her black ones. I thought about it and I went ahead, I said, 'You've dropped Jim Neill.' The words came suddenly and I was into something with her, fucked up with her in her fast car, and I was suddenly anxious: she might say *no* to me, or she might say *yes*.

She sat still and looked at me levelly. I could not see her eyes through the black of her sunglasses, and I wanted to, I thought they might have told me something about her. She said, 'You are the gifted one.'

'You've read my résumé.'

Her eyebrows rose a little, and she continued to look at me, and the violin ended. I looked out the windshield as a blue plane with an overhead wing sped up the runway and passed us into the air, the engine roaring high and loud and then fading away into space.

I turned back to her. She was watching the blue plane disappear into the sky. I said to her, 'It's your turn.'

'What?' she said, and she turned to me.

'It's your turn to tell me a secret.'

'Do I have one you don't know?' she said, and she threw her head back. She was all black sunglasses and red lips and white teeth and clear white skin, she had spent some money on her teeth, she had spent some on her skin.

I said, 'There's a lot you could tell me.'

She sat back in her seat, looking at me sideways. She said, 'I have my own company. Did you know that?'

'No, I didn't.'

'I do.'

'What does it do?'

'Nothing, yet.'

'That's my kind of company,' I said. 'Can I work for you?'

'Actually, I was rather counting on it,' she said. The music started up again, a Bahamian number. A lone singer sang out a faintly bluegrass tune, *I had a great dream from Heaven last night.*

I said, 'Well, as long as you're doing nothing, I'm all yours. What's the company called?'

'You'll like this part,' she said, and she held up a finger like the Buddha teaching.

'Yes?'

'Divine Intelligence,' she said.

'That is good,' I said. 'When do you figure out what it does?'

'When I get some intelligence.'

I looked her up and down, and I tried to see her naked. I saw Confusion, I held the one in my mind and the other in my eye, and I weighed myself. 'You've already got the divine part,' I said.

'You noticed,' she said.

I said, 'Where are you going to get the intelligence?'

'I don't know yet,' she said. 'I thought maybe you could help me with that.'

'Me?'

'You're pretty good at intelligence,' she said. 'How did you know about Jim Neill?'

The air conditioning was very cold and her nipples were erect, pressing faintly through the knit yellow fabric of her blouse. I said, 'I know as much as Matt, I think.'

She laughed. 'Matt doesn't know about Jim Neill.'

'He doesn't?'

'Matt doesn't know much at all. Haven't you heard the company chorus? "Just don't tell Matt." You know more than Matt,' she said. 'We all do.'

'Then how come he's the boss?'

'The boss never knows,' she said. 'The boss cannot know. I learned that in the revolution.'

'What revolution?'

'The University of Wisconsin, class of 1971,' she said, and she looked out the windshield across the runways. 'I was in the SDS. You didn't know that, did you? Weathermen out lost in the storm. That's something else Matt doesn't know.' She turned to me. 'I was into free love.'

'Really?'

'Really.' We sat looking at each other for a moment.

'What kind of love are you into now?' I said. The radio sang, *I know some day I'll be singing above.*

The black lenses hid everything about her. She said, 'The real kind.'

'That ought to be free,' I said.

'Yes,' she said, 'it ought to be.'

'It's not free with Jim Neill.'

'No,' she said, 'not with Jim Neill.' She had spent some time on Jim Neill, I wondered how much time she would spend on me.

'Who then?' I said.

She smiled at some secret, turned away and looked at the airport, then turned back and looked steadily at me. She said, 'Did you enjoy Nickie?'

I didn't want to tell her about Nickie. I said, 'I enjoyed pleasing her.'

'I enjoyed giving her to you.'

'You enjoy being the Divine Margaret.'

She laughed, her head rocked back, she enjoyed it. 'Oh, yes,' she said, 'yes, I do.'

'What does the Divine Margaret do, really?'

'Really?'

'Really.'

She said, 'The Divine Margaret *knows* people.' Her voice was a whisper, this was a secret.

'How do you know them?'

'Carnally.'

'Like a vampire.'

'Just like that,' she said. Her perfect teeth showed through her red lips, and I looked down frankly at her breasts. I wanted to touch them, I thought about Jim Neill touching them and how he must want them now that he could not touch them any more, and I wondered how she liked that, that being wanted impossibly, and I wondered if it were impossible for me. The singer on the radio sang out, *Glory to Jesus, who save us from sin.*

'How did you wind up at Brackett Data?' I asked

She looked at me a moment, then she said, 'You come to a place like this when you're afraid. What were you afraid of?'

'Dying.'

'Were you dying?'

'I almost did.'

'And you came to Brackett Data?'

'I began to do absurd things.'

'What's an absurdity?'

I said, 'I make love.'

'To Nickie.'

'To Alix,' I said.

Her head rose slightly. 'Who's Alix?'

I looked out the window. 'Alix is dying.' I turned back to her

192

and looked into the black sunglasses. I wanted to see her reaction, and I could not.

She looked away from my gaze. She said, 'Does Alix love you?'

'Yes,' I said, and I thought of her, I saw her sitting in her blue bathrobe and telling me she was HIV positive, she bit her lip and measured me against the truth, and I finally wondered why she had told me. I thought it must have been hard to decide to tell the truth to a kid, of all people, to a Wiley Jones from a magazine. I wondered what it was about me that let her show some of her real insides, what it was that drew her out of Confusion and Rupert's and Rodger with a D. And I felt sad and tired and disappointed with myself and very old and responsible for her love, as if it were something she trusted me with, and, right now, I didn't want the trust, I didn't want the dying, I was too young to be trusted and I didn't deserve it. I was a kid being led through life by his cock, and I wanted this hot yellow and red easy talking little doll, Margaret Divine, with her roses and her colours and her not dying, I wanted to escape into her body, from Alix, from dying, and from the feeling that wanting her gave me of guilt and betrayal; and then too, quietly and calmly turning and looking at her now across the air-conditioned space of the car seat with a singer singing about the love of God, I wanted also to know what she could tell me, I wanted to see what she could show me.

'I imagine she's grateful,' said Margaret. She turned her head and looked at me. 'Was Nickie grateful?'

'I pleased her,' I said.

Her lands lay flat upon her thighs. She said calmly, 'Why don't you make me grateful, too?'

'What?'

'Please me,' she said, nodding with the words. 'Why don't you please me, too?'

Please me, I thought, *will it please me if I please you?* and Nickie lay back and whispered, 'Put me up there', and Alix sat on the edge of the bed and spread her legs for me to see, and now here was Margaret, too, and I thought that she could show me things, the way Alix showed me things, and I wanted to see what she could show me, I wanted to go with her. And I thought of Alix and I was guilty and I was looking for some way to go with Margaret and stay with Alix and there was no way, you could go with her or you could stay, and I wanted to do both and I could not, and I could not let her get away, never let them get away. I reached across the car seat and took her right breast in my hand. Her mouth opened and she drew a sharp breath and I felt it through her breast and she looked at me, and I wanted to see her eyes. I reached with my other hand and took her sunglasses from her face, and her eyes were nothing, they were little blank black discs staring flatly at me, and her lips came together and she moved toward me, taking my jaw in her hand, and I kissed her then, and she kissed me back. I dropped her glasses and I reached to the edge of her skirt and lifted it up, felt the nylon stretched tight across her thigh and the soft cotton of panty at her centre, and she kissed me hard and held my swelling cock and closed her legs tightly around my hand, then broke free, suddenly, and sat back, open mouthed, and looked at me for a moment. Then, satisfied with something that she saw, she parted her legs and took my hand away, and took my other hand from her breast, and placed them together in my lap, and found her sunglasses and sat back in her seat and brushed at her hair, and looked at her lipstick in the vanity, and she said, off the shoulder, 'I'm not Nickie. I don't fuck in cars.'

My cock went limp.

She said, 'Let's eat.'

Chapter 37

Alix and I sat on her sofa and drank purple cold duck from Welch's grape jelly glasses with cartoons on them. Mine was an orange tyrannosaurus rex, with two smiling baby tyrannosauri riding on its tail, and Alix's was a red Jerry with a football being chased by a blue Tom in a jersey, with *Welch's Welch's Welch's* in a circle around the bottom. The windows of the sun room were open to catch the breeze, but there wasn't any breeze, so we had hooked up an oscillating fan that blew the hot air around us. Its breeze would catch the pages of the TV guide on the coffee table, turning a few at a time as it passed across the room and back, and the bottle and the glasses sweated.

Alix crossed to the stereo and bent to look through her record albums; she looked good in her cutoffs, and I thought about her body, looking at her, I thought about the folds of her skin and the joins of her limbs and her breasts full and loose and her cunt a wet sanctuary, and I saw suddenly Margaret Divine's smart little breasts and heard the way she talked and felt the way she wanted me, and it made me want her back. I sat there with the two women at once, and I liked it, two women at once, I remembered Laura Petty and Deanna Farris from school and I wanted them too, and I felt strong and solitary and secret and limitless in my cock, and Alix gave up on a record and stood up and flipped the stereo selector over to the tuner. The radio came on, radio music came from the speakers, a woman's voice floated across the room while a soft electric guitar teased around her singing, *Never know how much I love you, never know how much I care.* She turned from the console and came back across the room to me and lay down on the sofa with her head in my lap. She said, 'This is good cold duck.'

Her hair was held up with a white ribbon and some combs and I took them out and let it fall down over my bare legs. I ran my hand through it and rested the glass of cold duck on her belly, and she said, 'You like to take my hair down.'

'Yes,' I said.

She ran her hand across my chest and put it to her lips and licked it. She said, 'I like it when you sweat.'

I felt very strong, she knew how to make me feel like a very big man.

The music got blue, the woman sang, *Listen to me, baby,* and the

195

sounds swung gently across the room. Alix said, 'You know what this is about?'

'What?'

'Fucking.'

'Really.'

'Really, honey,' she said. 'That's what they found out in the Sixties.'

I saw Margaret back there in the SDS, with free love for her Weathermen.

'Music is really about fucking,' Alix said.

'Or else it's about God.'

'Same difference.'

I drank some cold duck. 'You know what they'll find out in the Nineties?' I said.

She smiled. 'Fucking is something to sing about.'

'That's right,' I cried.

The woman sang, *Fever in the morning, fever all through the night.*

I got a little hard in my cutoffs, she always made me a little hard, and I felt like she was mine now. I knew she would do anything, and I felt like I could do anything too, and I thought about Margaret and wondered if I could do that, and I wondered whether Alix would go on loving me if she found out, I wanted her to go on loving me, and all the while I watched myself in this sexy game with Alix while I thought about fucking Margaret.

And then I was alone, sitting there with Alix on the sofa and planning to betray her, and sorrow swept over me for her, because she would be betrayed, and then for myself, for the aloneness. I reached suddenly and put my hand against her cheek, and I said, 'Do I satisfy you?'

She said, 'You mean sexually?'

'Start with that, yes.'

'Yes,' she said, and she reached up and brushed at the hair above my forehead.

'Did Stephen?'

Her hand moved to the side of my face and she caressed me, and I knew she would not lie to me. She said, 'Yes.'

I said, 'Did you ever cheat on him?'

She closed her eyes and rolled her head in my lap. Her lips pouted and she said softly, and with a little tiredness, 'Yes.'

And I relaxed, I had the permission of her own history. 'Tell me about it,' I said. 'Please.'

She said, 'I went out after work one Friday with a bunch of people from the office. A bunch of programmers.'

I slipped my hand beneath her neck and massaged it; she murmured and bent her head back into my hand and relaxed into it.

She said, 'His name was Brian.'

'You liked him.'

'I liked him,' she said. 'I still like him. He's cute, and he's a good programmer. And I was tired, and just a little bit drunk, you know, on beer, we drank pitchers of beer at Hemingway's, you know how beer kind of blurs you around the edges and makes everything soft and warm.'

'Did you protect him?'

She opened her eyes. 'I made him get condoms, just like I did you.'

'What was it like?'

'The fucking?'

'No,' I said, 'the cheating.' I wanted her to tell me how I would feel, how it would all turn out.

She said, 'It was just the one time, there, and it just sort of happened. And it was fucking someone new, you know, that's always nervous and hot.'

'A little scary and exciting, too.'

'It's someone you don't know opening themselves to you, and you open to them and let them in.' She said, 'I remember, he fucked me and whispered in my ear.'

'What did he whisper?'

She smiled. 'He was obscene.'

'Did you like that?' I said. 'Would you like me to do that?'

'Sure,' she said quietly, and she lifted her head and drank a little wine.

'Did Stephen find out?'

'Yes.'

'How did he know?'

'I was guilty. I acted guilty, and he knew I'd fucked around on him,' she said. 'I cried and confessed. It wasn't just fucking somebody, you know. Stephen had AIDS. I hurt someone with AIDS.'

'Someone who was dying.'

She said, 'See? I hurt somebody who'd already had the worst thing happen to him.'

'Did he forgive you?'

'Yes,' she said. She held her hands up, empty, supplicating. 'I mean, it wasn't like I fucked around on him all the time or anything,' she said. 'It wasn't like that.' She turned and looked at me again, harder this time.

'What was it like?' I said.

She rolled her head slightly this way and that, thinking, and she said, 'It was like being very thirsty and not taking a drink for a long time even though you could and then drinking something very strong and sharp that clears everything out inside you.' She turned her head away for a moment, and then looked at me steadily. She said, 'It was like being very tired and fighting the tiredness for a long time and then finally lying down to sleep.'

'You rested with Brian.'

She looked thoughtful, like she had not thought this through in a long time. She said, 'I rested from taking care of Stephen.'

'You didn't have to take care of Brian.'

'I put a condom on him,' she said. She lay back. 'Then I let him take care of me.'

'You took care of Stephen with your cunt.'

She said, 'I let Brian take care of me for a little while.'

I said, 'Do I take care of you?'

She did not answer me. Instead, she said, 'AIDS is hard. I know that. Living with someone who's dying is hard.'

I drank all the wine in my glass and set it on the arm of the sofa. I said, 'Do you want me to stay with you when it happens?'

She held her glass of wine in both hands and looked into it, thinking. She said, 'I don't know yet. I'll know when it starts happening.' She said, 'Will you stay with me until it starts happening?'

She was measuring.

I said, 'Yes.'

She said softly, 'You won't regret it, honey.'

'I know,' I said. I reached across her and got the wine and poured myself some more. I drank it, and I looked at her and said, 'You take care of me.'

She lay still, looking at me.

I said, 'You take care of me with your cunt.' I drank all of my wine. I said, 'Would you cheat on me?'

She had a little Confusion in her eyes. She thought a moment, her eyes turned inward, away from me, and I knew again that she would not lie to me, and she said, slowly: 'Probably.' Her eyes rose to mine and she reached up and put her hand around my neck. 'But I'd come back here after I did it.'

'Because I satisfy you?'

'Because taking care of you satisfies me.' She drew my face down to her lips, and they were soft.

For a moment Alix held my face close to hers, looking into my eyes, and then she turned over and sat up on her side and put her hand between my legs and felt my cock. She leaned down and kissed my bare belly, and I took her hair in my hands, and I thought of Margaret's jet black hair around her face, and I lifted Alix's face to mine, and I kissed her, kissed Margaret. Was I tired? was I thirsty? Not yet. But I wanted her anyway, the rest, the strong drink. I ran my hands down Alix's back and undid the clasp of her bikini top and her breasts fell free and I took the top off her, kissing her, kissing Margaret, and I tossed it aside, and she moved her hand to the edge of my cutoffs and unbuttoned me, unzipped me, and my cock was hard, and she got it out of my pants and broke the kiss to look at it, jutting up from my lap, and kiss it on the head, and lift her face to mine and gaze into my eyes, her eyes, clear green burning lights reaching to take care of me. I moved her aside and got up and stripped myself of my cutoffs. She lay on her side on the sofa watching me, and I went to the bedroom and got a condom and tore it open and carried it back to the living room, and now she lay naked on the sofa, face down, away from me, with her head resting on her folded hands, and I turned off the light at the end of the sofa and the room was bathed in a soft blue from the screen of the computer, and I heard the sound of the fan underneath the music from the radio, and I put the condom on and lay down on Alix. She turned her head to see me out of the corner of her eye, and if I closed my eyes in the blue darkness she could be Margaret, couldn't she? she could be anybody, wasn't that right? Confusion could be anybody, enormous surprise of her infinite variety teasing my cock, pleasing it endlessly, I put my arms around her, excited, and laid my hands over her breasts and I thought of Margaret's breasts in my hands that afternoon and I wanted her. Confusion moved beneath me, rising to meet me, and I put my hand down between her legs and felt her wet there and began to massage Margaret and listened to the sounds I made come out of her, and she turned to me and her eyes were green and Margaret's eyes were nothing, and she said, 'I love you, Wiley, I really do.' And I kissed her, kissed Margaret, too, felt her kissing me while the Georgia Tech radio played and the air conditioning ran softly, and the fan made a moving wall of air over our bodies on the sofa and I kissed her down her back and reached into her cunt and felt her there and she arched back and lifted her head and her red hair came down her back and she turned to look at me over her shoulder and she said, 'Oh' reflexively, long and hard, and I could make Margaret sigh, too, I saw. Confusion could be Anne Mathers for me, Confusion could be the Divine Margaret, and I saw Confusion looking at me over her shoulder, watching me make love to her, and I saw how Confusion worked to not be alone, she could be anything I wanted rather than be alone, and we were not alone when we fucked, but I was alone, fucking Margaret in Confusion, I had a secret, Margaret's small tight breasts in my hand and the warmth of her cunt through the cotton and I would fuck Margaret in the flesh, and I was free in my secret, it was a kind of freedom, like that out there on the interstate under my light, where you could change your whole identity with a ballpoint pen, because all you were was a name on credit card, and you bought whatever you needed, you put it into words and dollars and you said to the desk clerk, *Send me a girl, Lee,* and he did, and if you didn't like her you sent her back to Lee and got another, and another, until you had had enough. And I felt my cock hard against Confusion's flesh and there never was enough, and that was why it was only a kind of freedom. I sat up on my knees and lifted her hips to meet me and I went into her, taking her breasts in my hands and leaning and whispering into her ear as she moaned, 'I love your cunt, baby, I want to be a beautiful big cock flowering inside your cunt.'

Chapter 38

That Friday morning, Matt made me his regular screener. The regular screener worked Monday through Friday, and another guy handled the calls on the Saturday show. He said he'd lost his old regular screener a couple of months before to a station in Chicago, and had been making do with fill-ins from the newsroom. He said, 'I want someone who understands how I operate,' and he smiled and patted me on the shoulder.

'That's me,' I said.

We stood in his office, with Patricia Patterson in a beige pants suit and a cigarette going, looking happy. Matt was happy; so was she.

I said, 'I don't know anything about radio.'

'You'll do fine,' said Matt, pleased with himself and his selection. 'You do everything just fine.'

Patricia Patterson took a drag on her cigarette. She said, 'Now don't forget who hired Wiley, Matt.'

He laughed, and she laughed with him.

Patricia left us. Matt sat down at the conference table and motioned for me to sit beside him. I sat in one of the straight-backed chairs, and he said in a whisper, 'Tell me. What is Miss Phone really like?'

I wondered what this had to do with radio. 'She's unique in my experience,' I said. 'She's like some kind of wild animal.'

He put his hands together. 'I myself would tend to shower her with superlatives,' he said.

'She's excellent,' I said.

'I admire excellence,' he said. 'Ours is an essentially mediocre age.' He moved his chair a little closer to me. 'Do you think you could prevail upon her to call me more often?'

'She doesn't call you enough?'

'Enough for what?'

'Enough to satisfy you.'

'Yes, that's it exactly. You have a positive gift for words,' he said. 'I want Miss Phone to satisfy me, and she doesn't.'

'Do you want me to find somebody else?'

'No,' he said quickly, turning to me. 'No, Miss Phone is superlative, when she calls.' He patted my arm gingerly. 'I want her to call more often,' he said at last. 'Do you see?'

'Yes,' I said. 'How often does she call?'

'Sometimes,' he said, 'as much as two weeks go by.'

'I'll tell her,' I said. 'I'm sure she'll understand.'

'Will she?' he said. 'Is she understanding?'

'Very.'

'Does she understand you?'

I thought of Confusion, I saw Alix's smile. I said, 'Yes, she does.'

'A rare thing in a woman.'

'In anyone.'

'And you, Wiley, do you understand Miss Phone?' He reached a hand toward me again.

For once, I saw no harm in telling him the truth. I said, 'I like her.'

'You like her,' he said, weighing the words. 'Do you love her?'

I did not think I wanted talk to Matt about love, but I said it, I said, 'Yes.'

He studied me. He said, 'Truly.'

'I really think so.'

'And you would give her to be saved.'

'By the Gospel?'

'Yes.'

I said, 'Yes,' and I was hacking him, and he was my father then and he did not know me. My father went out whoring and wrote his writing, and I knew it, sitting there, hacking him, and I stayed at home and kept the boyfriends away and I was hacking him, I looked at his white hair and his clean-shaven face, and I saw the map on the wall behind him, and I could fly like Wiley Post, I fucked Alix and flew, and I thought of fucking Alix, and I thought of him fucking Alix, no, he could not fuck Alix, I did not want anyone fucking Alix but me, he could fuck Connie, then, and we would fuck him together, hack him to pieces, and I said, 'Yes, I would.'

Chapter 39

Margaret came by my office when she heard I'd got the screener's job. I was telecommuting again, working on my novel, when she knocked on the door. I looked up, then switched to a blank screen and called out, 'Come in.'

She peered around the edge of the door, smiling. She said, 'Can I talk to Matt, please, mister?'

'Sure,' I said, 'what do you want to talk about?'

'Lunch,' she said. She came in, closed the door behind her and rounded the desk and sat on the corner. She had on a cream-coloured dress that rose up her thigh a bit as she sat down, and I glanced at her legs. She wore white stockings and a small white rose above her right breast and a strand of black beads looped twice around her neck. She looked down at the blank screen and said, 'Writer's block?'

'Subterfuge,' I said, and I switched screens back to the book. She leaned down from the corner of the desk and read the screen, I caught the scent of her musk perfume mixed with the sweet smell of the white rose, it was a love scene, a couple fucked in the back seat of a new car on a hot summer night. The woman was Anne Mathers and the man was me and the factory sticker was still on the rear window, and I had written about the smell of her cunt in all the car's new plastic. We held each other's bodies in the shifting, coloured light from a drive-in movie screen. Margaret said, 'What is this? How to get AIDS?'

'Right,' I said. 'I thought we could publish memoirs.'

She read some more, then sat back on the desk and pointed to the screen. She said, 'Is this what it's like with Nickie?'

'Sure,' I said.

'Really,' she said, and her eyes were as black as her beads, but they shone with interest. 'My car has leather seats,' she said, and I got a little pleasant feeling in my cock, looking at her, thinking about it with her, Alix wasn't here now, Alix was at work with Brian, and I was hacking Margaret Divine. I said, 'But you don't do it there.'

She gestured at the screen. 'But I never knew it could be this good,' she said. 'Will you teach me this some time?'

'Sure,' I said, and the pleasant feeling felt very good.

She looked back at the screen and said, 'What is this, anyway?'

'This is my novel,' I said.

Her mouth opened wide and she looked from me to the console and back again. 'Clever you!' she said. 'You actually do something productive here. I thought I was the only person who did that.' She put her hand lightly on my shoulder, and I liked it there. I liked her getting personal, I liked showing her the writing about fucking, I liked hacking her, she was so responsive to social engineering, and so I laid my fingertips across hers. Her hand turned at my touch and she cradled my fingers in her palm and closed her hand around them. She looked at me and I looked at her, and she said 'Yes' through a smile.

'Yes,' I said, and I freed my hand and placed it carefully on her knee, feeling the nylon wrapped around her legs and looking up at her, watching her face while she looked down at me, smiling with her red lips, and I said again, 'Yes.'

She moved her leg a little to one side and I moved my hand inside her thigh, just above the knee, and I held her there and I felt like she was mine now, she was my toy and I felt strong in my cock, and she smiled and moved towards me a little more and I moved my hand up her leg, inside her dress. I felt the edge of the nylon high up her thigh and the clasp of garter, and I took her flesh there between thumb and fingers, her mouth opened a little and her eyes closed for a moment, and I moved my hand further up her leg and she wore nothing there and I felt with my fingertips along the smile of her cunt, and she leaned back on the desk, her hands held the edge hard, she breathed deep and I slipped my index finger inside her, and she nodded at me slightly, she liked being a toy, and my cock felt huge in my pants and hurting, confined. I rose from the chair and put my hand around her neck and drew her close, her mouth was open, and I kissed her as I felt deep inside her, she was open and soft and wet. I moved my hand down her back and across her hips to the edge of her dress, and I began to move it upward, and her hands were on my hips, between my legs, moving back and forth, and I raised her dress to her waist, and I looked and she held my head in her hands and kissed my hair while I looked. She whispered, 'Do you like it?' and I said 'Yes,' and she said, 'You like it?' and I said 'Yes,' and she said, 'I'm glad you like it,' and I kissed her, and the phone rang, and I saw the comm line lit and a button flashing with a waiting call. I ignored it and kissed Margaret again, and she broke the kiss and whispered, 'If you don't answer it, Marian will bring you the message,' and she squeezed her legs together on my hand and put her hands over it and held

204

me there. I reached across the desk and got the phone and Marian said, 'You've got a call on 79,' and I punched the button and said, 'Hello,' and Sarah said, 'Hey, sweet, what are you up to?'

For a moment I couldn't breathe. Then I said, 'I was just showing some writing to a woman here in the office.' Margaret looked at me with questions in her eyes, she wanted to know who it was.

'A woman?' Sarah had a smile in her voice. 'Is this someone I've already met, or is this somebody new?'

I licked my dry lips and Margaret looked hard into my eyes, deep. I said, 'Someone new.'

'Wiley!' she said.

Margaret leaned towards the phone and I turned it away from her.

Sarah said, 'Cheater.'

I felt myself flush, and Margaret looked at me strangely, concerned, I didn't want to hear that word, though I had known that she would say it, I had felt it coming, with fear building inside me, a truth that I did not want but could not change yet, a truth that I wanted left unspoken, that made me feel crazy, split in two and turned against myself. Sanity was plain and simple, was single-minded fidelity, over there, like Sevrés on a shelf, was something for *my father* to do, but I did not want it. Not now, not yet, now tempted out of control and actually liking the crazy feeling, thrilling afraid to it, crazy fucking feeling, risking everything and not wanting the truth to be true. I could smell Margaret and I wondered what had to change in me before I could change this truth.

'What would you do?' I said. Margaret put her hand over mine, holding the receiver, and turned me back towards her. I moved my hand inside her and she started, then I took my hand away.

Sarah paused, then said, with flat finality, as if revealing the sad secret ending of a story I was reading, 'I cheat, Wiley.'

'Do you?' I said, I tried to see her cheating on my father.

'Every time.'

I felt myself grow older, I felt Margaret's wetness on my hand like blood, and she leaned forward suddenly and caressed my face with both her hands and kissed me lightly on the neck.

I said into the phone, 'What about Alix?' Margaret sighed and turned away.

Sarah asked, 'She doesn't cheat?'

'She did once,' I said. 'She told me about it.'

'On you?'

'Someone else.'

'She would cheat on you, though.'

'She said she would. She said she *probably* would.'

Sarah paused, and I could see her face, meditative, reflective, in a soft light in my mind. She said, 'We're sad, you know?'

I said nothing. Margaret slid off the desk and stood looking at the books on my office shelves with her arms folded before her.

Sarah said, 'People, I mean.'

I said, 'Am I sad?'

'You will be,' she said. '*Probably*, as Alix would say.' She sighed. 'But she's like me, I imagine. Is she like me?'

'There are ways she's like you,' I said. Margaret shook her head.

'Then she'll forgive you,' said Sarah. 'Because she forgives herself.'

I looked at Margaret, her face in profile, her lips were very red.

'Anyway, she thinks she can stop you,' said Sarah. 'She thinks she's the one who can stop the cheating. You always do.'

I turned away from Margaret, I saw Matt's picture on the wall across the office, I lowered my eyes to my desk, the papers scattered there, I didn't want to see Matt or Margaret.

'Now, are we having lunch,' said Sarah, 'or has this new one got all your attention?'

'I was going to call you,' I said.

Sarah laughed, and she said, 'Oh, I love you so much,' and Margaret heard it, she turned and said, 'Who is that?' out loud, and I covered the mouthpiece and said, 'It's Sarah Dresden. She's friend of my father's.'

'What does she want?'

'We're supposed to have lunch.'

'Get rid of her,' she said. It was an order.

I looked at her a moment then lifted the receiver to my mouth and said, 'I was going to call you about this weekend.'

'You don't really love me, do you?' said Sarah, mocking, and I smiled a little. 'I do,' I said.

'You're as bad as nathaniel,' she said.

'That's not true.' And though I said it with a joking tone, I realised that I meant it, and she knew it.

'I'm sorry,' she said. 'This weekend, then?'

'If you have time.'

'I'll see, if you want,' she said.

Margaret drew closer to me, she nuzzled my neck, I said, 'I'll call you,' and I put the phone down and Margaret kissed me hard. She broke the kiss and leaned back, holding me in her hands, and said, 'Let's go to lunch. There's a motel out on Buford Highway,' and I wondered fleetingly if she always used the same place.

Chapter 40

The motel was Mexican, next to a Mexican restaurant. EL AZTECA NUMBER 4 it said in broken neon across the front, and the motel was called La Ventura, the happiness, I remembered from Spanish class, this was the happiness.

The desk clerk must have doubled at the restaurant. He was dressed like a Mexican waiter: white western shirt with black pearl snap buttons and black jeans, with curling black hair, as black as Margaret's, and a suspicious, half-threatened look, as if you were about to speak some sort of English that he wouldn't understand. He stood behind the counter in the office of the happiness with the register open before him, and I said, 'I need a room for two', and he nodded once sharply and turned the register around for me to sign. I wrote *Wiley Jones*, and he spun the register back and looked at my signature and nodded again, once, and looked at me and said, 'No baggage?'

I said, 'No.'

'Then you must pay in advance,' he said.

I didn't have the cash, and I said to him, 'Can you wait a minute?'

'Si, señor.'

I went out to the car and Margaret saw me coming and lowered her window. Cold air poured out of the car and into my face. 'What's the matter?' she said, she had her sunglasses on and she looked curious and annoyed.

I said, 'I'm about $15 short for the room.'

She laughed, while I stood there in the sun, but she got her purse and opened it and got her wallet out. 'Damn it,' she said, 'I don't have it, either.' She looked out the window at me. She said, 'He'll take a credit card', and she handed me a gold VISA. I took it back inside and handed it to him, and he looked at it, saying, 'Ah, la señorita' as if he recognised it, and he smiled at me and Suddenly I felt kept, like Margaret's private stud. I flushed, he ran the card through his machine and I tried to think what I could do to redeem myself, how I could show him I was a man, and I thought of Alix, I saw her bare white body for me, I saw her face wanting me. A short, chubby little woman with long brown unkempt hair came in through the door to the restaurant and began to speak to the clerk in Mexican, very fast, I couldn't follow what she was saying, but something about a *bambino*, she needed him to take a *bambino* somewhere. 'Ah, *si*,' he said tiredly, not looking at her but watching the computer check the charge, and he waved a hand at her, and she frowned at his brushoff and launched into more rapid speech. I wondered again if the clerk knew Margaret, and if he did, I thought, he knew that she would never be fat and unkempt, not unless she went crazy first, and I felt better about the credit card. I said to him, 'Put a pack of Kool One Hundreds on that, too.'

I turned and looked out the front window at Margaret's BMW. She had rolled her window back up and it looked like a question, sitting there in the empty parking lot – what is wrong with this picture?—and I thought about Margaret's smoky eyes behind her black shades and wondered what was behind the glass, the smoke. I wondered if I would find out what was inside Margaret.

The guy gave me the charge slip and I wrote *Margaret Divine* across the bottom of it and took the customer copy. He reached to the top of a rack of keys behind the desk, and I said, 'As far from the highway as possible.' The woman stopped talking and waited on me.

'Si, señor,' he said, and retrieved the key for room 36. He held it up, and I took it. I said, 'I think we can find it ourselves.' The woman began to talk again.

In the car, I said, 'Room 36, near the back. Is that OK with you?'

'You're so discreet,' she smiled, and her shades smiled with her.

Room 36 was all the way at the back, upstairs, and when you parted the curtain you could see the southern end of the airfield. I held it back and watched what I thought was a little yellow Piper Cub rise up and take off into the sky. I said, 'I didn't think they made those planes any more.'

Margaret came up behind me and put her arms around me and moved her hand to mine holding the curtain open and moved it away so that the curtain fell and we stood together in the darkness. She said, 'Did you come here for the view?'

'No,' I said, and I switched on the air conditioning, the the air in the room was close and stale.

'What did you come here for?' she said, and I turned in her arms and put mine around her and I said my line, which was 'You.'

'That's right,' she said, and she kissed me lightly, on the lips. She stepped back and looked at her watch, and she said, 'It's 11.18.' She opened her purse, and reached into it and came out with a box of condoms and a couple of cellophane envelopes and two joints. She laid everything out in a row on the bedside table and set her purse down beside it all. 'We've got until two,' she said, and she turned back to me and loosened my tie and pulled it off.

'You take a long lunch,' I said.

'All my lunches are business lunches,' she said, unbuttoning my shirt.

'What's the business?'

'Divine Intelligence.'

'Is this the recruitment interview?'

'This is the interview for editor-in-chief.' She stopped unbuttoning me and looked into my face. She said, 'Would you like that?'

'I don't know,' I said. 'When will I work on my book?'

'Your book,' she said. 'That impresses me, you know.'

'Does it?'

'Yes. You've got something going for you besides the fucking job. That impresses me.' She went back to the buttons and said, 'So you can work on your book as much as you want, as long as the magazine comes out.'

'What magazine?'

She pulled my shirt out of my pants and finished unbuttoning it. 'The new *Survivor*.' She pushed the shirt back over my shoulders and I finished taking it off and dropped it on the floor behind me. She looked at me for a moment, then she bent and kissed my right nipple. When she rose she put her arms around me and we kissed each other, we kissed each other for a long time, and I got hard.

She felt between my legs, she said, 'Oh, animal', and she tugged at my belt buckle and unzipped me. She pushed the khakis down below my hips, reached into my briefs and took hold of me and said again, 'My animal.' She pumped me up and down and pushed my clothes down my legs. I stepped out of them and stood there, naked for her.

She released me and stepped back towards the bed and looked at me and sat down. She said, 'I like you, animal.' She picked up one of the joints and dug into her purse for a book of matches and lit up. She took a deep draw, then passed the joint to me. I sucked on it, and she said, 'You know what Simon says? Simon English.'

I nodded. 'He says the white man is all used up.'

'That's right,' she said, taking the joint from me. A radio sat on the bedside table, and I turned it on Music came on, a slow guitar strumming low and soft, a song from underground. She handed me the joint and sat looking up at me. She said, 'Do you think he's right?'

'Yes.'

She undid her beads and put them on the table. 'Are you all used up?' she said.

I drew hard on the joint and held the smoke, and my eyes felt big in their sockets and I could feel the blood moving through the vessels in my temples. Standing there naked with her still dressed, I felt like some fantastic animal she had brought to this secret place to breed with. I saw her sitting on the bed looking frankly at my body, and I suddenly wanted to cover myself and run. It was not too late, I could put my clothes back on and leave, I could call a cab, I could remain innocent, innocent with Alix, and Margaret half turned, sitting on the bed, and held a hand up to the back of her dress and said, 'Undo me, would you?'

I looked at the shape of her body through her clothes, and I was all used up, I was all in my cock, half hard now, and I could not move for a moment, and my father lay somewhere imagining me, and there was Sarah, before me, her long dark blonde hair draped gently down her shoulders and across her breasts in a dress of earth colours, and I wanted to fuck her, I wanted to take her from him, and Margaret turned her head and glanced at me over her shoulder to see what was the matter and I wanted to fuck her, too.

Holding the joint between my lips, I reached to her neck and unfastened the clasp. She glanced again over her shoulder at me, and she was smiling, she said, 'Unzip, please'. Her back was bare, she wore no bra, no panties, nothing but the stockings and the garter. I took a deep toke on the joint and passed it to her and she drew on it and laid her head back and held her breath. I put my hands on the skin of her back and parted the dress and moved my hands down to her hips and then forward around her and down between her legs. She sucked hard on the joint again and said 'Animal' in a whisper, and I was very hard. I put my left hand deep between her legs and slipped a finger inside her and she spread her right leg away from the edge of the bed, and the song came softly from the radio, sighing, for a moment, and then it fell silent.

Margaret leaned back and looked at me over her shoulder, then drew one last time on the joint and set it in the ashtray. She put her hand over mine and she reached with her other hand and touched my cock, held it in her hand, and said, 'Don't come, animal, I want that to happen inside me.'

211

I said, 'That's what I want, too', and I kissed her lightly on her neck, and she turned to face me, my hand came out of her, and she lifted the dress off above her head. She opened the box of condoms and pulled one free from the roll and tore the foil open. I smelled mint, and she took it in her hand and looked at me standing beside the bed, and said, 'Let me put it on you.'

She stuck out her tongue and put the rolled condom on it as if it were a piece of candy, then drew her tongue back and closed her mouth, looking at me, smiling red lips, and she bent between my legs and took me by the hips and drew me close and kissed the very tip of my cock and then took me between her lips, sucking, and she moved her lips down it in a long kiss, licking with her tongue, all the way to the root, and I lost my breath, and then she sat back, her hands on my hips, and she looked at me smiling, and I looked down and she had put the condom on me. She smiled, proud of herself. She reached for one of the cellophane envelopes on the table, tore it open along a little red line and shook it empty into her hand, a square of clear latex that she unfolded and, sitting back on the bed with her legs parted, spread over her cunt like a diamond. She lay back and looked up at me and said, 'Kiss me, animal', and I thought of Alix, then, I wanted to have these latex things that Margaret had, and I was hot, the room was suddenly close around me. I turned to the window and cut the air conditioning up to high, and then I turned back to her and knelt beside the bed.

Her legs hung over the edge and I took her feet in my hands and held them, the nylon of her stockings plastic against my skin, and I reached up her legs and undid her garter and rolled the stockings slowly down, one at a time, caressing her legs. I dropped them on the floor beside the bed, and I removed the garter and tossed it aside. I bent and kissed her feet, softly, looking up at her face watching me over the edge of the bed, and I kissed her ankles and the insides of her calves and the hollows inside her knees and the inside of her thighs, and she lay back and sighed. I watched her breasts rise and fall slowly, her nipples hard, and I felt the air conditioning blow cold across my back in the hot room as I bent into her cunt.

I slipped my hands beneath the latex diamond and I felt her, I parted her lips and bent my face into the latex and pushed my tongue through it, it flexed and I pushed my tongue into her and she said, 'My animal', and the words made me very hard and I licked her once with my tongue, through the latex, and it tasted plastic and I could smell her and she smelled like fucking and I wanted to fuck her, I wanted her cunt, to touch and kiss and love, and she rolled a little from side to side and I moved my tongue up and down her cunt and she was excited. I raised my head and she said 'Animal', and I kissed her cunt through the latex. I put my fingers inside her and I made love to her, this was love, I thought, I was loving her, and she came with a cry and a sob, she began to cry, with a long quivering and a sharp tension through the muscles of her legs alongside my face and her hands reaching down her belly to me, her fingertips just brushing through my hair. And I was suddenly frightened: what had I done? I looked up at her, her eyes were closed and tears squeezed out of them and ran down the sides of her face, and I felt very hard, very strong, and embarrassed by my cock, I was about to fuck her and she was weeping. I said, 'What's wrong?'

She opened her eyes wide and shook her head quickly from side to side, crying, and she cried out, 'Nothing', and she said, 'Animal' with a great relief, and 'Make me cry'. I pushed up off the floor and on to her, and I sat above her and took her breasts in my hands and squeezed them and her mouth was open and she was weeping.

I said, 'Talk to me.'

She rolled her head from side to side, her eyes closed through the tears.

I said, 'Talk to your animal.'

Her eyes opened and she nodded quickly and said, 'This is the only way I cry.'

I said, 'Talk to me.'

She said, 'Make me cry again.'

And I was an animal, I was her crying animal, and I wanted her. I held her beneath me and I was an animal strong above her, I said, 'What are you? What do you want me to call you? Are you *Baby*? Are you *Princess*?' and she shook her head, she said, 'What do you want to call me?' and I said, 'What does your father call you?' and the question surprised her, it surprised me, too, and she lay beneath me and said 'Oh', and I said, 'What?' and she looked at me and said 'Girl', and she turned her head to one side and sniffled, and then she said, 'I'm Daddy's Girl', and I sat back, satisfied, and I said 'You be Daddy's Girl, then', and she put the back of her hand to her lips, tears stained her face and her eyes were red, and I leaned down to her and said, 'Does Daddy's Girl like to fuck?'

She looked up at me and her eyes pleaded with me. She nodded her head quickly, desperately, her mouth was open now and she said 'Daddy', and she put her hands on my cock and held it so hard it almost hurt. I said, 'I like to make Daddy's Girl cry.'

She said, 'Oh, Daddy', and she spread her hands flat across my belly and my chest and she said, 'Love me, Daddy', and she was naked beneath me and she took my cock in her hands again, and I said, 'Daddy's Girl likes my cock, doesn't she?'

She raised her head off the bed and put my cock to her lips and kissed me through the condom, and she lay back and said, 'Don't you like it that way, Daddy?'

I said, 'I like Daddy's Girl to kiss me there.'

She said, 'I could eat my Daddy', and I looked at her and she looked open and bare and helpless, lying there with the lines of tears down her cheeks, calling me Daddy. She was more naked than I thought she had wanted to be, and I wondered fleetingly if that were what she wanted, to be that naked, and I felt very strong then and free in my cock, I felt like I had already fucked her.

I said, 'Fuck you', and she lay back, she drew a deep, sharp breath, and I went into her, and she said, 'Let me see', and she lifted her head off the bed and watched me going into her, watched me come out and go into her again, and I kissed her, I pushed her down on to the bed and rocked inside her, and the music started up from the radio again, loud this time, harsh and beating you with sound, a jam of electric noise and drums and human screams, and her legs wrapped around me and wrapped up my legs slowly as she fucked me, and she squeezed her eyes closed and tears came out the corners and she said 'Daddy', and held me and kissed me all around my face and head while I began to come, and I tried not to, I fought it because I wanted to fuck her more, so I could watch her and listen to her crazy talk and hear her moan and cry, but I came, I said 'Now', and I tried not to come, and she nodded her head quickly, and as I came I saw into her wet smoky eyes, and she was watching me, her eyes moved over and over me, and I came hard and cried out, straining against the sound. The radio was full of feedback and drums and cymbals and the air conditioner blew cold air across our bodies and I came for a long time, looking into her eyes watching me and her hands to and fro over my face and chest and back, and she smiled through her tears, and I closed my eyes and lay across her, nestling in her neck and naked with her and smelling her musky smell, her rose gone and nothing sweet about her now but only the smell of our sweat in the cooling room and her cunt and our coming.

The sound died on the radio, and a disc jockey began to talk

214

softly. Margaret caressed me lightly up and down my back and I lay on her with my eyes closed, sleepy with come.

She smiled and sniffled. She said, 'Do you like being my daddy?'

I opened my eyes and looked at her. 'Yes,' I said, 'I do.'

'You're a good daddy,' she said.

'Thank you,' I said.

'You're welcome.' She stretched under me and I rolled to her side. She said, 'You could use this all against me, you know.' She touched me with her fingertips, lightly, unsurely. Would I be her friend, would I tell the others about her daddy after school?

I said, 'I wouldn't know how to.'

She laughed again, she touched my shoulder and lay against me. She said, 'Wiley, you're so innocent.'

I thought of Sarah, I said, 'That's funny. I was just thinking I wasn't innocent any more at all.'

'But you are,' she insisted.

I said, 'Are you really Daddy's Girl?'

She drew nearer and kissed me again.

I said, 'Was Jim Neill your daddy too?'

She rocked her head very slowly on the pillow, she said, 'He didn't have your imagination.' She squeezed my cock gently and smiled again.

'Is that what it is?'

She laughed and said, 'I love the way you let me come first. You just did it. Do you always do it?'

'Yes.'

'I had to teach Jim Neill to do that.'

'What do you have to teach me?'

'I don't know,' she said. 'Maybe nothing.'

I said, 'I expect women to teach me things.'

She laughed along with me. She said, 'What does Alix teach you?'

The question startled me and stopped me and made me think. A pain went through my heart, the twist of my betrayal, and I understood that I had betrayed not only her but something inside myself. I had to answer Margaret, though, I looked into her black eyes and said, 'I think she teaches me love.' Her eyebrows flickered upward, interested, but her eyes betrayed nothing.

I sat up on the edge of the bed, and Margaret moved around behind me. She put her arms loosely around me and laid her head on my shoulder and reached down beneath my cock and

215

fondled my balls. She said, 'You want to fuck me some more, don't you?'

She felt pleasant but I was still thinking about Alix. I was going to get one of those latex squares and eat her cunt tonight, I was going to make her come with my tongue, she would love it, I knew. Margaret had taught me something, then, and I knew I was in this with her, this cheating, this *adultery*, that's what it felt like, it had never felt this way before, adultery pulled thin and tense and bare from lies and lust, myself reduced to the blood filling my cock, I would make Alix cry over it, too, I thought, I would weep over it myself. 'Yes,' I said. 'Yes, I do.' I placed a hand on her leg, beside me. She kissed my back.

'Good,' she said. 'I want you to come back to me again.'

I didn't know I needed the cigarette like I did until I lit one up and started smoking it. The nicotine did its thing on me and I felt, not like I had just been fucked, but like I was working very hard at something, concentrating so hard on it that I had lost all feeling for time or space or hunger, and now, stimulated by the drug, I awoke and I felt myself wound up too tight to be any good. I let go suddenly and felt a tension go out of all my body, my gut, my arms, my legs. I looked at Margaret, and I offered her a hit on the Kool, but she shook her head, and I smoked it, looking at her, naked with me, and I felt loose and high at last and I sat there taking it all in, the last few hours.

I took the condom off, and Margaret got a washcloth from the bathroom and wet it and washed me off and made me hard again. She knelt on the floor beside the bed bathing me and smiled up at me as I got hard, she said, 'I like my daddy, I like to cry for you', and I reached to the condoms on the bedside table and got another and rolled it on, and she climbed up into my lap and sat mussing my hair and kissing me around my face and whispering, 'Make me cry, Daddy.' I lay back on the bed and she lay with me, and with my hands I worked her around the bed and she took the condom off, smiling, and sat above me and lowered herself on to me smiling and said, 'Daddy likes it raw, doesn't he?' And I did, I hadn't had it that way since the very first time, and I remembered it now, real, it was real, the way it was supposed to be, and, strange, lying there beneath her, thrusting up into her, I wanted it real and bare and flesh to flesh with Alix, and I wanted to cry myself. I closed my eyes so Margaret would not see and my eyes burned in the darkness and I heard her say, 'Oh, yes, sweet Daddy', and felt her stroke my chest as I came inside her.

And I gave her come again and she wept, her tears fell on to my bare skin and I felt gone and wasted and used up, and we lay together and she turned on her side and curled up against me and said, 'We'll lie like spoons.' I liked that picture, two spoons nestled together, made for each other into a perfect fit, that was men and women, really, I thought, closing my eyes and wondering how we managed to muddle such perfection, and I curled around her body, my cock against her ass and my hands gently holding her breasts, and I nuzzled the back of her neck, and she placed her hands over mine, and we lay that way together and slowly fell asleep.

Getting dressed afterwards, I said, 'Did I pass the interview?'

She laughed, pulling her stockings up her bare legs. She said, 'You're the editor-in-chief, Daddy.'

'When do we go to press?' I said.

'As soon as I can steal that fucking data base,' she said.

I buttoned my shirt, looking in the mirror at her sitting on the edge of the bed adjusting her stockings. I said, 'Finder?'

'How can I get it?' she said.

I thought about it. 'I might be able to help you with that.' In the mirror, I saw her look up at me, her face suddenly alert and sharp, like some acquisitory predator. 'You can?' she said.

'I know someone who might.'

'Who?'

'Alix,' I said. 'Alix is in computers.'

She got up and came across the room to me, she stood behind me in her stockings, with her hands on my shoulders. She said, 'She wouldn't have to know about us.'

'No,' I said.

She stroked the side of my face. She said, 'I can share you.'

I said, 'Can I share you?'

She smiled lusciously, with her teeth and her lips red. She held me close to her and whispered in my ear, 'Daddy doesn't have to.' She kissed me and placed my hand over her cunt. She said, 'And to think I used to give this away.'

I laughed. I said, 'You mean this isn't free love?'

She smiled without showing her teeth and shook her head decisively, one time.

I crossed to the bedside table and lit a cigarette. I said, 'I give it away.'

'Do you now?' she said, looking at me sideways.

'Yes.'

217

'To me?' she said.

'To you,' I said. 'To Alix.'

'You don't expect anything in return?'

'I guess I expect sex.'

'Is that what you give away, then, sex, or is it love?'

'That's a good question,' I said, and I drew long on the cigarette. I noticed a small mole just below her left nipple; I liked discovering the parts of her body. 'What is love?'

She laughed, her head back on her shoulders and her white teeth smiling, her breasts shook with it, she thought it was really funny. She said, 'What is it your Alix feels for you?'

'Love.'

'What is it you feel for me?' she asked.

I thought about it, looking at her face, looking at her body, which excited and pleased and interested me, the little mole beneath the nipple, I smoked my cigarette, and at last I said, 'I want to possess you.'

She resettled herself on the bed. 'You possess your Alix,' she said, 'don't you?'

I saw the two of us reflected together in the dresser mirror.

She said, 'Her love for you possesses her, and you like that.'

I saw Alix standing in the half-shadows of the bathroom that Saturday with her breasts bare and tears coming down her cheeks, Confusion confessing that she loved me, I had done that to her. I looked back at Margaret. 'Yes.'

'You want me to be the same way,' she said.

'Yes.'

She said, 'And that's how I want you to be, Daddy.' She stood and adjusted her garter, then sat on the edge of the bed and thought for a moment. She hung her head and said, 'Daddy.'

'Yes?'

She lifted her head and spoke very softly, she said, 'Love me.'

So she had asked me, then, and in the cool lightless room with the music playing softly on the radio, *I went to the sun it was too hot, I went to the moon it was too cold*, she sounded suddenly lonely and naked, and I was strong in her nakedness. She wanted Daddy to love her, that would fix all her insides, I would be her Daddy, and I liked it, I liked the way it made me feel, above her and powerful. A man, then, she made me feel like a man, a man who could do anything to her, because she felt like a little girl under me. And how did Alix make me feel?

I sat down and smoked my cigarette and she stood in her

stockings at the foot of the bed, with her hands empty beside her and her face for once uncertain, watching me. Alix sat on the edge of the bed, too. The sheets were yellow and red and the walls were blue like robins' eggs, and she looked at me with her eyes heavy and her mouth open a little and she spread her legs for me to see, her hands inside her thighs stroking herself for me to see, Alix with her killing cunt, and I loved that, I thought, I loved putting my cock into her, danger and wildness all spread on the red and yellow edges of the blue just for me to see and touch and feel, and I could feel my heart beating, seeing her, and I wanted to be bare inside her, to mingle my come with hers, she was so dangerous and I wanted to be dangerous with her, it was no good unless it was dangerous. I looked at Margaret and I could feel her danger: she would cut me, and fucking her made me feel like I had balls, but even if I loved her I would not tell her so, I would not risk surrender with her. I walked to her and stroked her shoulders with my two hands, the cigarette hung from my lips and the smoke came between us. She moved a little towards me, her skin so soft and smooth that I thought she must use some special lotion on it, and I thought it would be good to see her some night in her special lotion, and I said to her, 'It's too dangerous.'

She closed her eyes, she sighed, she said, 'It's not safe sex.' She looked at me again.

I said, 'What do you do when you don't get what you want?'

She laughed. She held her head up high and said out loud, 'I could fix you, Daddy. I could tell your Alix. I could tell her things only a woman would know.'

And she scared me a little. I said quickly, 'Then she wouldn't steal Finder for you.'

She said, just as quickly, 'I'll tell her after I've got it.'

'What can I give you to not tell her?'

She laughed again, short and bitter this time, as if I had asked something stupidly obvious, and she said, 'Your balls.'

I felt them prickling suddenly between my legs, and the room was cold. I said quietly, 'Is that what you got from Jim Neill?'

'Yes,' she said immediately, 'I got his balls.'

I smoked my cigarette and watched her chest rising and falling, she was breathing a little faster.

She said, as an afterthought, 'He was going back to his wife.'

'You could tell?'

'She has money,' she said. 'Jim is such a coward.' He disgusted her.

'So you cut him loose.'

'I cut him loose before he could do it to me,' she said. 'Then he said he loved me. You should have heard him. See? I got his balls.' She looked at me, smiling viciously, proud of herself and what she could do, she smiled with sharp bare white teeth and she drew a deep breath and her nipples swelled, and I got a little hard, looking at her excited by what she had done to Jim Neill.

I turned away, picked up my tie and I went to the mirror and she turned to her dress lying on the bed. I tied my tie, watching her in the mirror: she stretched out tall and held the dress above her head, lowered it on to her shoulders, then shrugged her way into it. It fit snug at the hips. She came over to the mirror and said, 'Zip me, please', and I zipped her up and did the clasp at her neckline. I parted her hair on the back of her neck and kissed her there, and she said, 'You're a sweet animal.'

I walked over to the bedside table and picked up the unused latex dental dam, and said, 'Where do you get these things?'

She came over beside me and picked up her beads from the table. 'There's a dental supply company on 14th Street,' she said. 'You can use Saran Wrap, too, but I feel like the latex is safer.'

'Why are you so concerned about oral sex?'

'I read *Survivor*,' she said, 'and I am one.'

'You don't take any chances.'

She spread her beads out around her neck and clasped the strands together at the back. She said, 'I'm taking a chance with you, Daddy.'

I said, 'You've never been Daddy's Girl with anybody else, have you?'

'No,' she said. She stood looking at me, the predator suddenly wary of the prey. 'I suppose you're special to me,' she said.

'Why?'

'I'm not sure.'

'That makes me risky.'

'What about me?' she said. 'What are you risking?'

And I thought for minute she was stupid. 'Alix,' I said.

Her head rose, she understood. Her eyes had some flicker of light in them at last, like a cat's just before its leap.

I said, 'I don't love you, Margaret.'

And she laughed a little, quietly, as if she had expected this, she

220

knew no one could love her, she was too much a monster, then she sighed and crossed the room to me and stroked my hair and she whispered, 'I'll tell your Alix you don't love me, then.'

On the radio, people cheered they applauded.

Chapter 41

A balding guy in his mid-forties named Ray who smoked Luckies showed me around the control room, where the screener worked. Ray was the show's producer and had been filling in screening the calls for a couple of weeks. He wore blue jeans and a green plaid short-sleeve shirt and he smoked while he talked, with the butt in his mouth, letting the ashes drop wherever they would. 'You never worked in radio at all?' he said, a fresh Lucky hanging down unlit from his lips.

I said, 'Nope.'

He shrugged and lit his cigarette. We sat in two rolling chairs shoved together in a small, glassed-in room next to the sound studio, where Matt sat at a console, adjusting a headset and looking at a yellow legal pad with some notes on it. He was at a round table with three microphones mounted on a metal rod in the centre. One was drawn over towards Matt, the other two hung at odd angles in the air, pushed out of the way. Matt looked up and saw us together and he grinned at me and waved. He touched a button on a board on the console and his voice came out of a speaker above our heads: 'How do you like it, Wiley?'

Ray pointed at a switch on the left-hand side of the control room console. He said, 'That turns on the intercom.' I flipped it and spoke into the microphone. 'Pretty interesting.' But the mike was dead, and Ray shook his head and said, 'Use the mouthpiece on the headset there.' He pointed to a headset lying earpiece down and wrapped around the edge of the control panel. I picked it up and spoke into the little receiver. I said, 'Pretty interesting' again, and Matt said, 'You'll do fine.' He sat back in his chair land stretched and took his jacket off, and I saw it, then, strapped across his back from shoulder to shoulder, the gun. I looked at it closely, I said to Ray, 'Is that his .38?'

Ray looked up from a clipboard in his lap.

'Yeah,' he said. 'You know about that?'

'Yes,' I said, 'but I've never seen it before.'

'Yeah,' he said again, looking out the window at Matt hunched over his notes. 'He shot that guy last year and he still gets threats. Some guy told him just the other day, "Watch your back."' He laughed a small laugh and shrugged. '"Watch your back."'

The holster was warm brown leather against his white shirt and the gun was deep blue. Matt leaned over his notes on the console and I sat forward a little, looking at it, the butt nestled just beneath his left armpit, and I thought of Alix. I wondered what she would say, or do, if she saw it, if she knew. I would have to tell her: I saw her mouth open, I saw her stopped at last.

I was thinking about it when Ray said, 'You political?'

I turned to him. The smoke from his Lucky rose in a thin stream between his face and mine. 'I vote,' I said.

He said, 'I'm not political. I was political in the Sixties, and it didn't work.' He gestured at the counter 'If you put the headset on, you can hear what's on the air.'

I slipped it on and I heard a commercial for a landscaping company, then I realised it was Matt, recorded, talking about his new house and his new lawn from the Phil Cummings Lawn and Turf Company, and there was a big, artificial smile in his voice, he reminded me of Patricia Patterson, or she reminded me of him, the way she smiled without any happiness. I set the headphones down on the counter. Ray said, 'OK.'

The show started with rock and roll, a woman's voice, not a girl's but a woman's, sang out warm and blue and rocking, *Make me come down, Daddy, you make me come down on you*, and I thought of Margaret, I saw her spread across the bed of the La Ventura, and I knew that Matt was going to talk about rock music and sex. The music rose as he fiddled with a toggle on a board to his left, the song rose to climax, *Down, down, down, down, go down, Daddy, make me come down with you*, and then he cut the volume as he leaned into the microphone and he said, 'Down, down, down, down, that's where they want to take us with this so-called music. But just how far down do we have to go with this audio degeneracy?'

Ray nudged me and slid a clipboard across the counter. 'These are today's spots,' he said. 'We need to get the first one ready.'

I glanced down a list of commercials. The first one said *Mario's Italian Rest.*, and I said, 'OK. Where is it?'

'It's in that cart right there.' He pointed to the end of the counter at a stack of tape cartridges. The one on top said *Mario's It. Rest.* on the end.

I picked it up.

Ray said, 'Just put it in the cart machine there under counter.' He pointed at a device with two tape receptacles, and I slid the cart into the top one. Ray said, 'When it's time, cue it on the board there', and he pointed to an array of toggles on a sloping white panel to my left. I touched the first one, and he said, 'That's it', and when I looked up Matt was watching us as he talked, his face questioning. Ray made an OK sign with his fingers, and Matt reached to the board beside him and slid his toggle up again. The music rose into a buzz of feedback and distortion. Matt jerked the toggle sharply downward and the air went silent. Then he said, 'We'll take our first caller after these messages,' and he pointed at me and I slid my toggle up and a woman's voice said, 'Just think.' It came together so smoothly it made me smile.

Ray sat back and drew on his Lucky, then put it out. He plugged a second headest into the control panel, turned to me and said, 'The phones are right there', as he pointed to a switchbox of buttons with a black label that said Control Room Telemix. 'Just punch the blinking button to pick up, and then log them in on the computer.'

He pointed over my shoulder and I turned and saw a system sitting on a shelf above a tape deck, a grey screen and a 101 keyboard. A small baby-blue rectangle window opened in the corner of the screen, with the word **CALLER** flashing in dark blue letters in its upper left-hand corner, and Ray nudged me. When I turned back to him he nodded at the telemix, and I saw that the first button was blinking. I pressed it and said 'Hello.'

'Hello,' said a kid, 'is this the Voice of Reason? Is this Matt?'

I said, 'You want to talk to Matt?'

'Yeah.'

On the computer screen, **CALLER** flashed at me, and I said, 'What's your name?'

'Jeremy.'

I typed in *Jeremy* on the keyboard, and the word **FROM** appeared below it. I said, 'Where're you calling from, Jeremy?'

'Stone Mountain.'

I typed it in, and a **SUBJECT** line opened up. I said, 'You want to talk about music or sex?'

Jeremy said, 'Yeah.'

I typed *sex and music*. 'Hold on,' I said and found the hold button on the telemix. I looked through the window into the sound room and saw a computer on a stand to Matt's left, with a display just like mine, and **Jeremy** flashing at him, on and off. I said to Ray, 'Is that how it works?'

Before he could answer, the telemix started blinking again. I picked it up and said, 'Do you want to talk to Matt?'

'You bet,' said a man's voice, and he breathed with some difficulty, then he said, 'Say, who is this?'

'This is Wiley,' I said, 'I'm new.'

224

'You're new?'

'That's right.'

'Well, New, I'm Fascist Pig, and I call once a week.'

'Like the Sunday paper.'

He laughed, and he breathed heavily, a fat man out of breath. 'That's good, just like a Sunday paper, big and fat. You're quick,' he said.

I heard traffic on his end of the line. I said, 'Are you calling from your car?'

'I always call from my car, New,' said Fascist Pig.

I entered his handle on the **CALLER** line of his window, and typed *traffic* for his **FROM**. I said, 'What kind of car is it?'

He said, 'Well, it's really big and gets really shitty gas mileage.' Then he laughed out loud.

'What do you want to talk about?'

'Don't you listen to the show?'

'I'm usually at work when it's on,' I said.

'Well, I call once a week,' he said, 'like the motherfucking Sunday funnies, and I give Matt an update from all of us fascist pigs.'

I typed *update* on the **SUBJECT** line. 'Hang on,' I said, and I put him on hold.

Inside, Matt talked to Jeremy, his window was red on our computer screens. Matt pulled his tie loose from around his throat and said, 'Why aren't you in school, Jeremy?'

Jeremy laughed. He said, 'I get home schooling.'

Matt said, 'Well, ordinarily, I'd say that's a good thing, given what passes for public education these days, but, tell me, is the Voice of Reason part of your regularly assigned material?'

'I like to listen to you,' said Jeremy. 'You're crazy.'

We worked our way through Fascist Pig. He said, 'Hey, a lot of us fascist pigs like that kind of music!' and we took calls from all over the compass, a prostitute in Midtown and a mother from Chamblee and a male nude dancer in Hapeville. We did the news on the hour and Matt sweated and undid his tie and let it hang down freely on either side of his neck. He would break and make notes on his legal pad and drink Sunkist orange sodas that a woman from Research brought him. Research was a set of *Encyclopedia Americana* and two women at computers across from the control room, and this one took care of Matt, she was professionally solicitous but she handled him like he had a disease, she looked at him with cool brown eyes clinically detached from her surroundings, only here for the money. I bet she voted at least Democrat, she was frosted blonde on brown in her early twenties and thin, but not as thin as Cassandra Brackett or Anna Louis, faded designer jeans and a man's white shirt with a flowered blue velvet vest. She brought him a new legal pad and a heavy black pen and a Sunkist during the four o'clock break while a fat grey guy with a goatee and a red and white Coca-Cola T-shirt read the hourly news about rape and murder from a monitor at the other end of the control room. As she bent across Matt's console with the Sunkist, I whispered to Ray, 'Who's that?'

He was checking off spots on his list and he looked up. 'That's Sexy Sadie,' he said.

'Sexy Sadie?'

'Our lesbian researcher.'

'She's a lesbian?'

'That's right.'

'Does Matt know?'

'So far as I can tell, it's never occurred to him.'

'And nobody tells him.'

'Nobody ever tells Matt anything,' said Ray. He lit up another Lucky, and I said, 'Give me one of those, will you?' Matt switched on again. I blew a smoke ring against the glass.

A local music critic was talking about the sexual content of Christian music. '*He walks with me and He talks with me and He tells me I am His own*,' she said. '*I am His own.* What about that?'

'That's a metaphor,' said Matt. 'That's poetry.'

'So's the blues,' she said.

'Only a liberal would say that,' he snorted. 'This stuff is about unmarried, uninhibited intercourse. This stuff is about making welfare babies.' Bessie Smith sang out suddenly, she had the best jelly roll in town, and Matt said, 'You have been Bracketted.'

So he Bracketted people all afternoon. I turned to Ray and said, 'This is awful.'

Ray said, 'Once a week he has what he calls Enemy Guest Day.'

'*Enemy?*'

'That's right.'

Finally, we had Leon from East Point, he pronounced it East Pirnt', and he talked about Frank Sinatra. 'What about "It was a very Good year", what's that mean? What's a good year?' he said. 'A good year for what?'

'Oh, Leon,' said Matt. 'It was a very good year for *love.* Where's your imagination?'

Sadie came into the sound room with another Sunkist.

'Well,' said Leon, and Matt let the air go dead for just a second, and Leon said, 'Well, look, man. All this new music is about screwing around and rotting the morals and all, and nothing good has come out since Glenn Miller died and nobody will listen to that stuff any more. What you want people to listen to?'

Matt sat back in his chair, his hands flat on the countertop on either side of him and the gun nestled neatly in its holster. He said, 'Talk radio.'

Chapter 42

I found Margaret's dental supply store on 14th Street in Midtown, and I wrote them a checque for a box of dental dams, standing at the counter and watching the hot rush-hour traffic through the front window. I picked up a case of cold beer on the way back to Piedmont and home.

Alix wasn't home yet. I put the beer away and put the box of dental dams in the bedroom and stripped and took a shower. I washed Margaret away, my cock swelling a little as I remembered her, strong and remorseful. I shouldn't have cheated on Alix, Alix cheated on Stephen, but I didn't think she would cheat on me, I was selfish, I realised, I hadn't known how selfish I was. I could still feel her, putting the condom on me with her mouth, and I knew I wanted more of her, I knew it would be a lie to promise I wouldn't fuck her again, but I felt my heart sick, and I promised I wouldn't fuck her long.

Alix came home while I was still bathing, she opened the shower curtain at one end and looked in and said, 'I'll be with you in a minute', and she stripped and got in with me. She stepped under the water and soaked herself, her hair darkening with wetness, and she took me in her arms and kissed me, she reached between my legs and took my cock and played with it until it was hard, and then she said, 'I've been waiting for this all day', and she laughed and took the sponge from me and lathered it full of soap and bathed my chest and between my legs. She rinsed my cock and licked it, kneeling on the floor of the tub, and I wondered if I could come again, it had been about four hours since Margaret, I thought of her, I wondered what she did in the shower and I felt my promise. I took Alix by the shoulders, lifted her to her feet and kissed her a long time under the water, promising her inside myself, and then I said, 'I've got a surprise for you, wait here a minute.' I got out and got the dental dams from the bedroom, got one and zipped it open, took it out and carried it back into the shower.

I held it up for her to see, and she said, 'What's that?' and I said, 'Sit down there on the end of the tub.' She sat, and I stood above her with the water running down my back and shoulders, and I spread the dam out in my hands, and I said, 'Spread your legs.'

She sat on the end of the tub with her hands on her knees and spread her legs open cautiously, watching me. I bent down and put the dam over her cunt and knelt with the water running down my back and I kissed her and began to love her there, and she said 'Oh', and almost slipped into the tub with me, but kept her balance at the last moment and sat very still, her muscles tense through her legs, and she said softly, wanting it and afraid at the same time, 'Be careful, honey.'

She was excited, and then more and more excited, while I loved her with my tongue, and I felt good, on my knees for her, I was better at it the second time. Now it was different, I knew Alix, I knew her secrets, she opened herself to me like a flower opening, beautiful fatal blossom, and I felt out there close to the edge and scared and wild and free, my cock erect between my legs and my hands on her ass pulling her cunt into my face and I was not dying, I was alive and full of come, and I felt the memory of Margaret in my hands, and Alix, at the same time, and I realised that what scared me with Alix was not just the HIV budding silently in her blood but the word, *love*, as she bent over me, running her fingers through my wet hair as I looked up at her, and rocked her head back against the wall, her eyes closed, and said, 'Oh, I love you'. She opened her eyes and looked at me and bent down past my face and took hold of my cock and held it firmly and rubbed it up and down, and her legs spread around my head as I loved her and she let go of my cock and sat back against the wall and slowly lost control a second at a time and at last she came. She cried out, she slid down the back of the tub and under me, she took my head and pulled it to her lips and kissed me, and the water ran down us, we lay in the bottom of the tub holding each other and kissing while the water ran down, and she said, 'Wiley, Wiley, Wiley.' Then she reached and took the dam from between her legs and held it up and said, 'Where did you find out about this?'

I said, 'At work.' She looked at me, startled, and I said, 'The magazine', and she kissed me, and I kissed her back, and she took my cock in her hand again, with the water running over us, and she tugged on it gently, watching me. She took the soap from its dish and worked up a lather in her hands and took my cock again and rubbed it up and down in her hands, and I lay to one side and let her bring me up, and I came in her hands, the come spurting into the running water and washing away down the drain, and she lay back in the tub and laughed.

We dried each other off and got cold beers and lay together naked in bed drinking them and talking. I said, 'Matt wants you to call him more.'

'I thought he'd never ask.'

'You knew he'd ask?'

'Why do you think I haven't been calling him?'

'You're a real bitch, Connie.'

'I'm a ball-buster,' she said matter-of-factly. 'I told you about it, the first time we fucked.'

'You did,' I nodded. 'You said it was very sexual.'

'Isn't it?' She said, smiling.

'I'm sure it is to Matt.'

'What's it like to you?' she said. 'Do you ever think about me fucking him?'

'That's the point of the hack, isn't it?'

'Sure,' she said, 'but how does it make you feel?'

I remembered suddenly. I said, 'Matt carries a gun', and I could see it, nestled beneath his armpit in the shoulder holster.

She sat up and turned to face me, her legs crossed Indian style. Her red hair fell down wet around her face, and she held her bottle of beer by its long neck. She said, 'Does he really?'

'A .38.'

'He carries it with him?'

'He wears it in a shoulder holster.' I drank some beer and I said, 'Ray says he gets threats.'

'Who's Ray?'

'Ray's this guy at the station who tells me how the radio show works. He says some guy told him to watch out for his back just this week.'

'Is it scary?'

'He's scary,' I said. 'He's fucking scary.'

'Are you scared?' she said.

I thought, I said, 'I think Matt is a scary guy. I listen to him talk and I get a feeling that maybe a lot of people think like this, you know?'

She took a long drink of beer and looked at me questioningly.

I said, 'Maybe they're all sitting out there listening, all pissed off and eaten alive with self-pity, and they're all out there with .38s. When you think about that, it's scary.'

She said, 'Do you think he would use the gun?'

'If somebody came after him?' I said. I thought about it. 'Yes. I think he'd use it if somebody came after him.'

'Do you think he'll use it when he finds out Connie Phone is positive?'

'I don't know.'

230

'Do you think he'd ever use it on himself?'

I shook my head. 'He's too insensitive.'

She said, 'Do you think he would kill Connie Phone for giving him HIV?'

I thought of Matt and all his listeners, all the losers out there who had lost out on the dream and had to go to work each day to jobs they didn't want, to earn money that wasn't enough for the things they thought they had to have, and I thought that if you got them all together, like some Roman circus, then they wouldn't be able to stop themselves, and neither would Matt, because he didn't control them, nothing controlled them, but if you could wave a red flag at them suddenly and scare them you could get them to move in the direction that you wanted, and so sap their great energy for yourself. That was what Matt did.

'He's crazy,' I said.

'Yes, he is,' she said.

'I mean, really crazy,' I said. 'He walks around loose and he drives a car and runs a company and votes, and he's really a crazy person with a gun.'

She sat thinking about it. She sipped her beer and said, 'Do you think that would be better than dying of AIDS?'

'I don't know,' I said. 'What does Connie Phone think?'

She laughed. 'Connie says she doesn't want to die any way at all.'

I put my hand on her arm. 'Good,' I said.

She smiled a little. She said, 'You don't want to do it, do you?'

'I don't know any more,' I said. I sat back against the head of the bed and drank some of my beer. I said, 'What if he disgusts you physically? Have you thought about that?'

She laughed again. 'I've seen his picture in your magazine,' she said. 'He's just another dirty old man.'

'Another?' I said, and I smiled. 'You mean, there're more like Matt?'

'Sure,' she said, 'Matt's common. Stupid little self-righteous hateful unfeeling little man. He's ordinary.'

'But you could fuck him?'

She sat up with her eyes closed. She said, 'I could hack him.' She opened her eyes and looked at me.

I said, 'Maybe he won't have to find out that Connie Phone is HIV positive.'

'Then he'd just infect other people.'

'Anyone who'd fuck him deserves to die.'

She looked startled, and I looked at her, surprised. I had startled Confusion, and she said, 'I didn't know you hated him so much.'

I got up and crossed to the chair where I had tossed my clothes when I got undressed and I reached into my shirt pocket for the pack of Kools and the matches. I lit one, and Alix reached for them and I gave them to her and she lit one, too. I stood naked in the centre of the room with her watching me, and I said, 'I didn't know either.'

She said, 'I want him to know. I want the Voice of Reason to know that the Gospel According to Matthew is infected with HIV. I want to hear what it has to say then.'

The room was hot with the summer and she rubbed her forehead with the sweaty beer bottle, then took a long drink and a drag on the cigarette. Her hair was still damp and it curled around her neck and down her breasts. I took a long drag on my Kool and climbed on to the bed beside her. I said, 'You want to kill him with your cunt.'

She said, 'Yes.'

'And you say I hate him.' Her eyes were soft and questioning, she wanted me to understand something. 'You haven't even met him.'

'Stephen met him,' she said.

'Matt?'

'Might as well have been Matt. Stephen's boss.'

'What does he do?'

'He runs a small music company up in Buckhead,' she said. 'When Stephen filed his first insurance claim, and they found out he had AIDS, his boss had the insurance company write in a $5,000 limit on HIV claims.'

I sat back and drank some beer. 'I've read about them doing things like that,' I said.

Her mouth was twisted with bitterness. 'It's not enough that you die,' she said. 'You have to die like a fucking dog.'

She sat in the middle of the bed with the smoke curling upward from her cigarette and her soft red hair around her downcast face.

She said, 'They act as if they never fuck.'

My hand touched her arm.

'They fuck,' she said. 'They do.'

Chapter 43

She called the Gospel the next morning, while we sat at the breakfast table drinking coffee and eating cinnamon rolls. She wore a green kimono with big red and white flowers on it, and her hair shone bright red around her face and I thought that she looked lovely, really lovely.

After she had teased him along a while, her voice sank into whispers and she said, 'Wiley says you want me to call you more often.' She smiled into the portable phone. 'Why is that? Do you like it when I call?' He said something and she laughed, a small quiet laugh, she was enjoying herself.

I went to the stove and poured another cup of coffee. She got up and carried the phone into the living room and I followed her. She sat at her computer and talked softly into the phone and sipped her cup of coffee and started her editor. It loaded a file automatically, the last file she had worked on, and I bent over her shoulder to see what it was. It was something called HIV.ASM and the screen was full of demi-words like **mov** and **aad**. She whispered into the phone to Matt.

'All right then,' she said at last, 'I'll call you three times a week, is that enough?' She smiled and looked at me.

'All right then,' she said again. 'Ciao.' She turned off the phone and put it down.

I gestured at the computer. 'What's HIV.ASM?' I said.

She said, 'It's a virus.'

'For Brackett Data?'

'Yes.'

'What's it do?'

'It infects executables and rewrites their data whenever it's saved.'

'What's that got to do with HIV?'

'It's polymorphic,' she said.

'Polymorphic.'

'It mutates,' she said. 'It makes copies of itself, like a real virus, and it varies the copies with noise instructions. Like HIV.'

'What's a noise instruction?'

She shrugged. 'Say, a NOP instruction.'

'NOP.'

'No operation. NOP. That tells the computer to do nothing for three ticks of the system clock.' 'OK. Why do you want it to do nothing?'

'You don't want it to do nothing. But you want to make each copy a little different.'

'Why?'

'Because at Brackett Data they use an anti-virus software that checks the signature of each file, looking for strings of bytes of code that are found in known viruses.'

'Is HIV.ASM a known virus?'

'It was,' she nodded. 'I got the basic algorithm from this book.' She reached to a shelf above the computer and got down a small blue paperback book and handed it to me. It said, *The Blue Book of Computer Viruses* in a white box.

'OK,' I said, and I handed the book back to her. 'What's HIV.ASM do?'

'It rewrites whatever is written to disk, inserting random garbage into it at irregular intervals, in place of the original data.'

'So Brackett's system fills up with garbage.'

'Right,' she said.

I smiled. 'When are you going to upload this beauty?' I said.

'I'm not sure about the timing,' she said.

'The timing is important,' I nodded.

She said, 'I think it should be Confusion's parting shot.'

I said, 'I've got another job for Confusion, too.'

She turned to me, interested. 'What's that?'

'Margaret Divine wants to steal Finder.' A small, sly, double feeling of guilt and heated excitement crept up from my heart.

'Steal it?'

'Take it from Matt and start her own company with it.'

'What kind of company?'

'She calls it Divine Intelligence,' I said, and I crossed the room to the sofa and sat down with my coffee. I looked at Alix and I felt strong, balancing the two women. 'She's going to put out a new *Survivor*.'

'One that's real?'

'What do you mean?'

'*Survivor* isn't real,' she said. 'You don't think all that is real, do you?'

'It makes real money,' I said.

'Money doesn't make you real,' she said.

I drank some coffee, it was good, hot like the day itself, and black. 'What makes you real?' I said.

234

She sat back at the console and picked up her coffee from beside the keyboard and drank some, thinking. She said, 'Fucking makes you real.'

I laughed. I said, 'Is Matt real, then, saving all these women?'

'Do you really think he has any?' she said. 'Besides me, I mean.'

I saw him, all alone, and the picture surprised and frightened me a little. I said, 'It had never occurred to me.'

'I don't think he has any, besides me,' she said. 'Why would it be so important for me to call, if he had others calling him too?'

She was right, and he was alone, then, on the other end of the phone. I saw him listening in a small, dark room, huddled over the phone in a bathrobe and studiedly masturbating, like some guy in a skin theatre.

'Anyway,' she said, 'no, he's not real, no matter how many he's got calling him, because he doesn't fuck, because he never loses control. When you fuck, you lose control. That's the whole point of fucking, isn't it?'

'What is it he does, then?' I said.

'Rape,' she said. 'He's a rapist. He's never out of control.'

'You're going to let him rape you?'

She shook her head. 'I'm going to rape him,' she said. 'I'll be the one in control.'

'So it won't be real,' I said. 'It won't be fucking.'

'It'll be real,' she said. 'It'll be real hatred. Feeling makes you real, too.'

I thought about it, I said, 'That's what's wrong with *Survivor*, you know. It has no feeling.'

'It has no imagination,' she said. She looked at me. 'Do you think Margaret Divine has feeling?'

'She has imagination,' I said. 'Margaret is a very calculating woman.'

'So am I.'

'When you see inside her, though, she's just a girl,' I said.

'You can see inside her?'

For a moment I tensed inwardly as I wondered if I had said too much. I went ahead. 'Just social engineering. She gives herself away.'

'Will she give Finder away?'

'What do you mean?'

'Information wants to be free, you know.' She got up from the computer and came across the room to me.

'You want her to make Finder a free service?'

'Free for people with AIDS,' she said. 'If she'll guarantee that, I'll steal it for her.'

'Suppose she guarantees it and then goes back on her word?'

Her right eyebrow arched; she said, 'Hell, I can hack Divine Intelligence, too, you know.'

She could, I knew, and I thought of her hacking Margaret, and I knew with certainty that she could beat her. 'How do we do it?' I said.

She cocked her head and thought a moment, sipping her coffee. I sat back on the sofa and watched her, pleased with her performance and smiling. Finally, she said, 'The trick will be to make it useless to Brackett Data after we steal it.'

'Why?'

'What's the point of stealing it if Matt's still able to compete?'

'We want to put him out of business, then.'

'That's right.' She paced across the living room. 'We'll use a TSR.'

'What's a TSR?' I got up and followed her into the sun room. The Saturday morning sun was bright. In the park the grass was green with brown burnt patches, and the trees were still in the heat and people were out.

'Terminate and stay resident,' she said. 'A program that's always in memory, always running.'

'What'll it do?'

'It'll intercept calls to Finder and decrypt the data on the fly.'

'You're way ahead of me.'

She turned to me, excited. 'We copy the data base. Then we encrypt it.'

'OK. Now Matt can't read it.'

'But he has backups of it. He's got three backups of it, they do it that way there. What's the system's manager's name?'

'Stan.'

'That's right, Stan. Stan's maintenance logs list three sets of backup tapes that they use in rotation across a period of three weeks. So we've got to maintain the illusion that everything is OK for three weeks, while Stan backs up the encrypted data base.'

'Then all their copies are bad,' I said.

'Right.'

'And this TSR thing, it does that?'

'It intercepts calls to Finder to read the data, grabs the data, and decrypts it for the user,' she said. 'So everything looks normal.'

'You can do this?' I said. I was impressed.

'I can do it this weekend,' she said. 'I'll need a disassembler. I've got one at the office that produces C code.'

'Is that good?' I said. I had no idea what C code was.

'It's a higher level than assembly language.'

'Oh, that's good then.'

Her eyes closed for a moment, and she turned and pointed at the computer behind us. 'That's assembly language. One line of code, one instruction to the computer. C is easier to read and you can code it quicker. The phone company is written in C.'

'That usually works pretty well.'

'Sure,' she said. 'I'll call Brain and get the key and get the disassembler and we'll do it.'

'*We?*' I said. 'What will I do?'

She smiled at me. 'You'll make the coffee and roll the joints.'

Chapter 44

I called Sarah from my apartment on Sunday morning. She said, 'Well, hi, stud, still have time for old Sarah?' and she laughed at me.

I smiled involuntarily, and I said, 'I like older women.'

'How old is the youngest one?' she said.

'How,' I said,' Alix is thirty-two and Margaret is forty.'

She paused, then she said, quietly, 'What are you going to do about that, Wiley?'

I had known she would ask something like that, and that was why I had called her, to get an answer, but I still rather wished she had asked something else. I said, 'I don't know.'

'Well, what do you want?'

I sighed. I had known she would ask this, too, I said, 'Sarah, that's the absolute worst question.'

'Isn't it?' she said. 'But the answer won't be anywhere near as bad as no answer at all.'

'I don't want much,' I said. 'I just want them both.'

She laughed. She said, 'You're cheating. Do you want to be a cheater?'

I shifted in my chair, I wished I had a cigarette. I said, 'No.' It was too much like my father, and she knew it.

'I didn't think so,' she said. Then she changed the subject. 'What do you think about all these women wanting to give themselves to you?' she said.

The question made me feel very young. I tried to laugh it away, I said, 'I think it's great.'

The answer seemed to please her. She said, 'I remember once when I was in school, it seemed like I could have any man I wanted.'

'Yes?'

'All I had to do was want him, and he'd be mine.'

'Yes.'

'It was wonderful.'

'It is,' I said. 'What happened?'

'It went away.'

'It went away?' I said. 'It just stopped?'

'Yes.'

'You never figured it out?'

'"Figured it out"?'

'You know,' I said, 'figure out what made it all work.'

'Oh,' she said, 'I knew what made it work.'

'What was it?'

'Magic,' she said.

'Magic?'

She said, 'You're an artist, aren't you?'

I hesitated, as if it was a trap, then I said, 'Yes.' I didn't think Sarah would try to trap me.

'What makes that work?'

'I know, teacher, I know,' I said, mocking the drill. 'It's magic.'

'A mere matter of magic,' she said.

'I think I follow you on the art,' I said. 'But this other, I mean, you know what we're talking about, Sarah. We're talking about *fucking*.'

'That's not magic?'

I preferred to be gifted and special, I didn't trust magic, magic was Nigger Jim's hairball and Tarot Cards and the portent of early evening sounds of mourning doves. I said, 'You know what I mean.'

She said, 'You mean that you are young and indestructible and don't believe in anything but yourself.'

'That's not true,' I said, but I knew that it was.

'And the odd thing is,' she went on, 'you don't really believe in yourself.'

I looked at the computer screen on the desk before me. I had just loaded the novel into memory but hadn't started writing, it still said **Chapter One** at the centre top of the screen and the words began, and I knew that she was right, even though I couldn't admit I was so selfish and empty.

She said, 'Not yet anyway.'

I stared at the screen and tried to read the words and could not, and Sarah waited on the other end of the line, and finally I said, 'When is *yet*? When do I believe in myself?'

She said, 'When you believe in the magic.'

I should have expected it. 'That's very neat,' I said.

'It's like a work of art, that way,' she said. 'Your life is.'

'When did you believe it?'

'After Paul died.'

I thought of Alix, and I felt a sharp pain in my heart, all my fears for her and the anticipation of her loss. I wanted a cigarette again, and there was a moment of quiet on the phone. I could hear everything, the birds in the park, the traffic outside Sarah's hotel, and I said softly, curious and afraid, 'What did you do?'

'What could I do?' she said softly. 'I got mad. I made deals with God. I cried and I masturbated and I told myself it was him.'

I shuddered, and at the same time I wanted to see it, I wanted to see her masturbate and suffer, and then I wanted to go to her in the pain. I said, 'You still want him, don't you?'

'Certainly,' she said.

I had never known about this life of hers that might have been, and I realised now, suddenly, that without Paul Coudreau's death I probably never would have known her. And so I was reassured by the death; it was a curious feeling, not gladness or satisfaction or the young outliving the old, but a reassurance that somehow Sarah was supposed to be here.

She spoke again, she said, 'I accepted it.'

I would accept Alix's death, I thought. I did not want to, I was not ready to, God owed me Alix, if there was one, and I wondered suddenly if God owed me Nickie and Margaret and Sarah, too. *All these women*, I thought, and I felt strange, sitting there thinking about them, I felt singled out and special but not for being gifted. I felt blessed to be alive.

'You accept things,' she said suddenly, breaking my thoughts. 'You accept people, anyway.'

'Yes,' I said, and I thought of myself back in the dorm, drinking with the boys, listening quietly and watching while they lied to each other about girls and jocks and cars and money, while I made notes for novels in my head, watching to see what they were really like, to see if their insides slipped out in the loosening of the alcohol or if they remained hidden, tight and alcoholic like my father.

Sarah said, 'You've always accepted me.'

'I like you,' I said.

She laughed a small laugh. 'But you accept people you don't like, too.'

I thought about Matt Brackett. Did I accept that? what did it mean to accept that? I did not know.

She said, 'You accept Nathaniel.'

'No, I don't,' I said. I did not want him.

'Yes, you do,' she insisted. 'You don't like him, but you don't ask him to change.'

'Not any more.'

'Not any more.' I heard a little trace of sadness in her words, at something lost and not any more, and I thought then that something must have changed between them to make her sad in this slight way at the mention of him. I wondered what it was. She said, 'That's very loving.'

I said nothing, I flooded with a slight but conscious embarrassment, feeling special but not gifted, loved for some quality unearned, something prized but unachieved, something I simply possessed, like a gift from God, I supposed. She said, 'That's why I love you. And these other women too, I think.'

I saw the first walker of the morning out in the park, a woman in an exercise outfit. The horse patrol had passed by earlier and broken the day's silence with their hooves, sending the birds into the first flight of morning, and now this solitary woman passed through the gate on the boulevard, her hands swinging at her gently swinging hips, her long brown legs moving with a graceful athletic sensuality as she set out across the sunburnt plain towards the lake.

I said slowly, as I realised it, 'I love you, Sarah. I really do.'

Chapter 45

Margaret came by my office after the Monday morning meeting. 'What time do you want to eat lunch today?' She said.

I looked up at her, she was in blue today, a pale blue silk blouse with a white rosebud pinned to it and a royal blue skirt that covered her legs just enough to interest you. I said, 'I talked to Alix about Finder.'

She came around the desk and leaned against it with her arms folded across her breasts, looking down at me. 'What did you tell her?' she said.

'That you want to steal Finder from Matt.'

'I'm so glad,' she said. 'I was afraid you might be overcome with a fit of honesty or something.'

I said, 'You mean you don't want her to know?'

She smiled at me, a smile that held all the cards. 'Not yet,' she said.

I wondered if she really wanted to hurt Alix, to hurt me. I said, 'You'll have to bankroll a tape drive.'

'What for?'

'We need one big enough to hold the Finder files.'

'All right,' she said. 'How much?'

'Three, four, five hundred dollars.'

'Easy,' she said. 'All right, do it.' Her lower lip thrust out, she looked calculating and cynical, I liked the way she said *do it*, and I felt giddy, I felt light and floating through my chest and wanted and powerful and I wondered if she wore anything beneath her royal blue skirt.

'There's one catch,' I said.

She looked at me, a little bitterly, I thought; it was a little flash of rueful experience, and it made me wonder how many deals she had made since the SDS.

I said, 'You've got to make access to Finder free for people with AIDS, or she won't steal it for you.'

'That's all?'

'That's the catch.'

'OK,' she said, 'but they'll have to pay for the phone call.'

I thought about it. 'I think she'd buy that,' I said.

'All right,' she said again. 'I said do it.' She sat back on the edge of the desk. 'Now, what do you want to eat?'

Chapter 46

Margaret gave me a checque for $500 to cover the tape drive, and I cashed it that afternoon on my way to the radio station and gave the money to Alix when I got home. She scored the drive the next day and was installing it on her machine when I got home from work. I fixed dinner while she worked, some stir-fry in her wok and a bottle of white wine, and afterwards I made a big pot of coffee and we drank it together, side by side on the sofa while the machine downloaded Finder to the tape. The drive whirred lightly as it ran.

'How long will this take?' I asked.

'All night,' she said, 'or most of it, anyway.' She held up her coffee. 'This is good,' she said.

I drank some of mine. 'Are we going to get everything tonight?'

'Yes,' she said, 'we'll get it all, and then we'll run the encryption program on it and load the TSR.'

'You're sure it'll work?'

She sipped her coffee. 'I've tested it. And, anyway, I've used it before.'

After about a half-hour of watching the tape drive I got bored and got a deck of cards and we began to play. We played gin rummy until after midnight, and then Alix wanted to play strip poker and then we made love for a while to the tune of the tape drive and after that I slept a little. Alix stayed up with the machine, and at 5.30 the next morning I awoke and went into the living room to find her sitting at the console, typing. 'What are you doing?' I said.

'Loading the TSR,' she said.

I yawned involuntarily. I said, 'So Finder is encrypted?'

'I just finished running the program.'

I looked out the sun-room windows: there was no light yet outside.

'There,' she said, and sat back from the console. 'Now let's check it out.'

She typed *exit* and we were back inside the bulletin board program. I said, 'We're logged on as Matt?'

She nodded and picked Finder from the menu, then entered a query for *Pneumocystis carinii* pneumonia in a date range of the preceding six months and sat back and waited. In about ten seconds she had scored 139 hits. She smiled and said 'Great', and picked a hit from the list displayed. The screen cleared, then filled with the text of an article from *AIDS*. 'Great,' she said again. 'Oh, I love it when a computer does what I want.'

She stood up and looked at her watch. 'Twelve hours,' she said. 'That's a pretty good hack.'

I smiled at her. 'What now?' I said.

'Stan runs a backup this evening after work All we have to do is wait three weeks, then pull the TSR out of there.'

'What are the odds on getting caught?'

She shrugged. 'Stan doesn't do much in the way of security,' she said. 'He runs that virus software now and then, and that's about it. I'd say we can count on Brackett Data's inherent sloth to see us through.'

'Well,' I said, 'what else can we do today?'

'Call in sick,' she said.

Chapter 47

I woke up with a start about three the next morning and Alix was gone. I rolled over on to her pillow and it was wet and the bed was wet, and I was scared then, and I got up in the dark and called her name and heard no answer, and I saw the bathroom light shining beneath the closed door across the hall and I went inside. My eyes hurt in the light and I shielded them with my hand: she was sitting on the edge of the tub in her white terrycloth bathrobe and her face was wet with sweat and her red hair was wet with it and she shook with fine tremors. She lifted her face to me and she said, 'It's happened.'

'What?' I said.

And she said, 'I've got AIDS.'

I was scared, I said, 'What is it? What have you got?'

She shook her head. 'I don't know,' she said. 'But it's AIDS. It's AIDS.' And she shook with a hard chill.

I sat beside her on the edge of the tub and put my arm around her, and I felt cold and scared and sinking and wanted to cry to someone. I felt trapped inside something big, I felt alone, with Alix, I felt her alone with AIDS on the edge of the tub under the white light of the bathroom, and I wanted to be with her in that aloneness, but it had left me alone too, and I could not reach her, I could not reach anyone. I said. 'Do you want to go to the emergency room?'

She shook her head again. 'What for?' she said. 'It's almost over now.' She rocked back on the edge of the tub and gazed up at the ceiling. 'I called my doctor and left a message with his answering service.'

'Will he call back?'

'In the morning.'

'It's the fourth of July.'

'He'll call.'

I said, 'Maybe it's just the flu or something.'

She looked at me. 'It's AIDS,' she said. She stood up. She said, 'I want some orange juice.'

I jumped on it, it was something to do, I said, 'I'll get it for you.'

She smiled thinly. She said, 'Are you going to wait on me now that I'm sick?'

I stood there naked and my cock was small in the cold night and she pulled her white robe close around her. All in white, her face was pale and framed in her dark wet red red hair, and she smiled at me, she reached and touched my face, and I said, 'I want to take care of you', and I felt stronger, saying the words. I took her in my arms and drew her close and hugged her hard and I kissed her deep, and she kissed me back, and I felt good, I felt all in one piece and strong in my cock, and I could feel AIDS around us, in the room with us, and we were small and clinging to each other for a moment before a long dark silence, about to descend.

I got a robe from the bedroom and we went into the kitchen, and I poured big glasses of orange juice and we sat at the table drinking it. I looked at her across the table, without any makeup. She looked worn out from the sweats and the chills. She drank her juice and sat looking down into the glass. I said, 'How do you feel?'

She lifted her head to me. 'I'm tired,' she said. 'I want to go back to bed, but I'm waiting to get the energy to change the sheets.'

'I'll do it,' I said, and I got up and stepped into the hallway to the linen closet. She watched me from the kitchen as I got fresh sheets and pillowcases and went into the bedroom and stripped the bed. I threw the used sheets out into the hallway, and the mattress pad with them. It was soaked. I stood there a moment, holding it, aware of how much she had sweated, and I was scared. *What is it?* I wanted to know, *What is it?* and then I went on with it, putting the clean sheets on the bare mattress, and I saw her standing in the doorway with her orange juice, watching me, and I wondered if she had seen my fear. I finished with the bed and turned to her and said, 'How do you feel?'

'Fine,' she said, 'I feel tired.'

'Let's go to bed,' I said, and I pulled off my robe and tossed it over the back of the dresser chair.

She turned off the light and we got into bed. We lay together, I held her in my arms, and she shifted uncomfortably and said, 'Now I feel hot.' She sat up and took off her robe and placed it carefully on the edge of the bed then she lay back with me, she turned on her side and curled up with her back against me and I cuddled her body with mine, and we were warm in the dark, and I said, 'We'll lie like spoons', and she moved closer against me. Her bare body felt good against mine and I got a little hard, holding her close, and I felt better, not scared now, there was time, there would be time, to do things, there were things we could do, doing things was the answer, her doctor would call in the morning, he would have something for

246

us to do, and she would not die yet, she would not die yet. I said that to myself over and over, and every now and then a car would go slowly by on the avenue, and if I listened carefully I could hear the sound of the traffic light at the corner cycling through, green and yellow and red, and she slept, tired, and I lay there holding her in the early morning dark.

Chapter 48

We got up around 10.30, when her doctor called. She put on her robe and carried the phone into the kitchen, telling him about her night sweats, and I got up and followed her. She sat at the table talking, and I put some water on the stove for coffee then poured two glasses of orange juice and gave her one. She sat listening to the phone and sipped her juice. I couldn't stand it. I got the cigarettes from the bedroom and lit one, I walked out on the back landing and looked at the sky, it was stunning cloudless and blue and the fourth of July, and Alix had AIDS now, it put a wall of glass between us, and I couldn't get my breath, I threw the cigarette over the railing and gripped it hard, I drew a deep breath that wasn't deep enough, and then I went back inside.

She stood at the stove, pouring the hot water into the coffee pot, and she looked up at me as I came in. I said, 'What did he say?'

'Come in tomorrow for blood work and a check-up,' she said. 'He wants to test me.'

'For what?'

'TB.'

I stood still. Nobody got TB any more. But nobody got pneumonia any more, either.

She reached up into the cabinet above the stove and got two coffee mugs. I said, 'Where the hell would you get TB?'

She shrugged, she poured the coffee. 'I remember when I was first diagnosed,' she said, 'he gave me a TB test then, along with a lot of other stuff.'

'Like what?'

'A bunch of stuff,' she said. 'The mumps, I remember, and tetanus. Stuff we're all exposed to, growing up. He wanted to see if I'd have any positive reactions.'

'He wanted to see if your immune system was working,' I said.

'That's right, he called it an anergy test,' she said. She finished pouring the coffee. 'Anyway, he wants to do that again, and get a sputum sample and a chest X-ray.'

'Tomorrow,' I said.

'Yes.' She handed me my coffee and went to the table and sat down.

I took a few steps after her. 'I'll go with you,' I said.

248

'There's no need,' she said. 'The skin test won't show anything till Monday.'

'I'll go with you anyway,' I said.

'No,' she said. 'I don't want you to.'

I watched her ignoring me across the room. I said, 'You're so damn tough.'

'Yes,' she said, and she looked down into her coffee cup.

I sat down across the table from her. I said, 'All right. So you're the toughest woman I know.'

She smiled at me.

I said, 'The toughest *person* I know. The toughest, meanest, hardest person I know.'

'You could have it, too, you know,' she said. 'You don't have to be HIV positive to get TB.'

'Yes,' I said, leaning forward. 'That's why I should go with you. I should get tested, too.'

'Don't you have your own doctor?'

'No.'

She sighed. 'All right,' she said, 'but if you've got it, you'll have to get your own doctor.'

'What's your doctor's name?'

'Carl Schumacher.' She sipped her coffee. 'He's in an HIV practice with two other guys.'

'All their patients have AIDS?'

'Most of them.'

I drank my coffee and stared down into the cup. I wanted to do something. I said, 'What do you want to do today?'

'Do you have to work?' she said.

'No,' I said, 'Ray's got the radio show this afternoon.'

She sat back in her chair. 'Let's go to Lenox tonight and watch the fireworks. I want to see something explode.' Her eyes looked tired and a little red, she hadn't rested, her hand was tight on the coffee cup, her body was tense with AIDS inside the white robe.

'OK,' I said quickly, but I felt the day spreading empty before us, full of something wrong and undefined. I said, 'What do you want to do till then?'

Her green eyes settled on me above the rim of the coffee cup. She set it down and said, 'This bothers you, doesn't it?'

'What do you expect?'

'I don't expect anything, honey.' She drank some more coffee.

'You can expect things from me,' I said. She cocked her head to

249

one side and looked at me thoughtfully, weighing my words, and I said, 'What are you thinking?'

There was a thin smile on her lips. She said, 'I was just thinking that I sure do love you a lot.'

And guilt spread over me, Margaret spread her legs and called me Daddy and I rutted inside her and Alix had AIDS. I drank my coffee and looked up at her and said, 'What were you really thinking?'

She said quietly, 'Really.'

Chapter 49

We both called in the next morning and took half a day off and went to Carl Schumacher's office for the tests. Alix sat on the examining table, and I paced the little, salmon-coloured room nervously. There were copies of the *New Yorker* and the New York *Native* on the desk against the wall. The air conditioning was on high and it was cold.

Carl Schumacher was in his mid-thirties, in blue jeans, and a pale blue shirt without a tie, and a white coat, and I didn't know what I thought of that. He came in reading Alix's chart in his hand, and looked up and saw me and said, 'Well, hello.'

'Hello,' I said, and I extended my hand to him. 'I'm Wiley Jones.'

'Carl Schumacher,' he said, shaking my hand. He turned to Alix.

She sat with her hands holding the edge of the table. She wore a red T-shirt and a pair of old jeans and sandals. Her hair was tied back. She said, 'Wiley is my lover, Carl.'

He looked from her to me and he said, 'I see.' Then he said, 'Well, we'd better give you some tests, too, Wiley.'

'I thought you might,' I said.

He turned back to Alix. He said, 'How are you feeling?'

'Depressed,' she said.

'I expected,' he said. 'Any more night sweats?'

'No.'

'All right then,' he said, 'I'm going to have Marjorie give you both skin tests and get sputum samples, and then you'll go downstairs for chest X-rays.'

'Me, too?' I said. I hadn't thought about X-rays.

'Yes,' he said. 'Ordinarily I'd wait to see the results of your skin test, but I've a feeling you're going to be positive, and I don't want to take any chances with Alix.'

'All right,' I said, and I was afraid, suddenly. It was like I had discovered one of the warning signs of cancer in my own body. I said, 'TB killed D.H. Lawrence, didn't it?'

'And George Orwell and Stephen Crane,' he said, 'and a lot of people. TB used to kill one-third of the people your age.'

I swallowed fear. I said, 'What do you want us to do?'

'Come back Monday,' he said, 'and we'll see the results of your tests and X-rays.'

Alix said, 'What are the possibilities?'

He said, 'If you're positive, your arms will swell up and turn red at the injection site. That won't mean you have TB, though, only that you've been exposed to the bacterium. The X-ray will show whether you've got active disease.'

'You can be infected and not have it?' I said.

'That's how it works. You get infected, but your immune system handles it. Then, later on in life, as you age and your immune system wears thin, the disease activates. That's why Alix is at risk for it, because her immune system is weakened by the HIV.'

'What if we have it?' she said.

'Then we'll check for drug susceptibility and put you on medication,' he said. 'TB isn't cancer – TB can be cured.'

She said, 'So just how serious is this?

'For you or for Wiley?'

She said, 'For both of us.'

He said, 'For Wiley, I'm not that worried. But any infection in an HIV-infected person is serious.'

'Is it as serious as *Pneumocystis*?' she said. 'Tell me.'

'PCP is the leading cause of death in people with AIDS,' he said. 'Not TB. But TB is serious, especially if it's resistant to the drugs.'

'How will we know that?' she said.

'From the sputum sample,' he said. 'We'll test it for susceptibility at a special lab out in Cobb. Ordinarily that takes six weeks, but at this lab they use PCR, and we should know by Tuesday or Wednesday.'

I knew exactly what lab he was talking about. 'What should I do?' I said.

He said, 'What have you been doing?'

Margaret passed through my mind, she smiled and said, 'I could tell her things only a woman would know', and guilt swept over me, and I did not like the feeling, I wanted to feel different. I said, 'I've been trying to help Alix.'

He smiled. 'How?' he said.

I said, 'I've been trying to do things for her.'

'I'll bet Alix doesn't like that,' he said.

'No,' I said, 'she doesn't.'

'You're not going to have AIDS easily,' he said to her.

'Who does?' she said, her voice tense and prickled with anger.

'You'd be surprised,' he said. 'Some people surrender to it. But I think you're going to fight every minute of it.'

I felt very dark, contemplating the fight, and the three of us were all there together silently in the room for a moment as the war descended. Then she broke it, she said to me, 'Help me fight.'

After the shots and the X-rays, I wanted to take our time and get some lunch, but Alix wanted to go on to work, so I drove back to the apartment and she got out of the car. She didn't kiss me or touch me or speak, she was very far from me and I could feel the space like a disease spreading between us. I got out after her and met her at her car door. She stood there fumbling in her purse for her keys, and I put my hands on her arms and I was afraid and I was alone and I said, 'Kiss me, Alix', and she looked up at me and blinked, and I could see the smallest trace of tears rimming her eyes, and she put her hand to my face and looked into me and leaned close and kissed me lightly, then leaned closer still and kissed me deeper, and I held her close and we were together for a last moment before we left for work.

Chapter 50

Margaret came into my office when she found out I was at work. She closed the door and said, 'We missed lunch.' She did not like it, and a little shade of fear passed through my chest, my cock drew up into itself, and I tried to think of what to do now. I needed things to be smooth with her, I needed everything else to go smoothly today.

I said, 'Alix was sick, I took her to the doctor.'

'How nice of you,' she said. She came around the desk and leaned against the corner. She wore a pink suit with a pale pink blouse and white stockings and she had a red rosebud pinned above her left breast. Her lips and nails were a vivid red. 'I made up special for you today,' She said.

She surprised me, and I felt better, then, my cock stirred faintly, she had done things to please me, and now I saw her anger as interest. She liked the lunches, she looked forward to them, maybe she even cared about them. 'I'm sorry,' I said. 'It couldn't be helped.'

'What's wrong with her?'

'They're not sure,' I said. 'They gave her some tests.'

'Is it serious? Is she dying?'

I looked into her black eyes, looking for her meaning, I wondered if she had almost said *dying at last*. 'I don't think so,' I said. 'It's just something obscure and hard to diagnose.' I didn't want to tell her any more about Alix than I absolutely had to, I wanted to keep the two of them separate, and I realised then, sitting there holding them apart in my mind, in my chest, that I intended somehow to keep them both, two women in two separate worlds, I wanted Alix for a lover and Margaret for a toy, and I hadn't known this about myself, and now I took this step further out and I scared myself, stretching between the two of them this way, I didn't know how far I could go or whether I could get away with it.

She leaned down and kissed me, she took my head in her hands and kissed me hard, and I was drawn into her, my cock swelled and I put my arms around her and I kissed her back. I moved my hands slowly around to her breasts and I held them softly. She broke the kiss and said, 'Lunch on Monday, then?'

'Yes,' I said.

She sat back on the corner of the desk. She said, 'When do I get Finder?'

'After we ruin Matt.'

'Are we ruining Matt?' She looked surprised and pleased by the prospect, and I wondered if she hated him as much as I did.

I told her about the encryption of the data base.

'But the users can still read it,' she said, 'even though it's fucked up?'

'Through the decryption program,' I said. 'It's called a TSR.'

She said, 'Your Alix is cunning. I'd like to meet her.'

I looked at her eyes again, unsure whether she was serious, and I laughed quietly. I said, 'Sure, maybe the three of us could get together some time.'

'For lunch?'

'Sure,' I said again, sitting back in my chair and watching her.

'Alix does women?' Her eyebrows rose with real curiosity.

'I don't know,' I said. 'Do you?'

With a self-satisfied smile she held her hands out, palms up, she was open to anything, and she said softly, 'I do whatever turns me on.'

'Really?'

'Me and my Daddy,' she said. 'Do you know what I found out?' she said. 'I found out my daddy turns on when I talk about cutting off his balls.' She looked pleased with herself, she sat back smugly and crossed her arms.

I thought of the way I had fucked her, I had beaten her then, she could be beaten, and I said, 'You know what I found out? I found out Daddy's little girl turns on when I fuck her like an animal.'

She flushed, and for a second I couldn't believe it. Anger shimmered across her face like a sudden wind moving quickly over water, and I liked her face coloured with emotions she couldn't control, even if only for a second. I liked making her lose control, I understood that I had touched her and realised too that I liked making her angry. I went ahead. 'Would you like me to tie you up some time? Would you like me to punish you for your sins?'

Her jaw was firm and her eyes were deep, I could not see into them, and I was flying, I was diving through space now and I didn't know where I would land, and she said, 'Daddy can be a real son of a bitch.' Her red lips twisted into a sarcastic smile, her teeth were white as snow.

I said, 'I like pissing you off. You're a lot sexier when you lose control.'

255

She liked this, it interested her, and the interest took some of the edge off her anger. She said, 'I can make my daddy lose control, too.'

'You do that,' I said.

She said, 'Did you like it, without the condom?'

My mouth went dry with the memory, and I tried to swallow and could not. I looked up at her and laid my hand softly on her thigh, like a question, can I touch you? and I said quietly, 'Yes.'

She moved her leg a little towards me in answer, touch me, Daddy, and she gazed down at me and her eyes were soft as she said, 'I liked it, too.'

'It was dangerous.'

'It was love, Daddy.'

I looked at her, I felt her in my hand. 'Was it free?' I said.

She shook her head slowly, she said, 'Love is never free, Daddy.'

I moved my hand up and down her thigh, the pink skirt was smooth cotton beneath my hand and I could feel faintly the clasp of her garter, her lips parted and she moved her legs further apart for me to reach inside, and her tongue went around her lips, and she said, 'Do it.'

I said softly, 'Daddy's Girl likes it, doesn't she?'

She whispered, 'Daddy,' and I slipped my hand down to her knee. Her stocking was luscious to the touch, she closed her eyes and spread her legs some more, her skirt pulled tight across her thighs, and I began to reach inside.

There was a sharp knock on the door. I tore my hand away from her and she slipped quickly off the desk and began to smooth her skirt down. The door opened and Matt stepped in. He carried a manuscript in his hand, he was all professional, and he said, 'In conference?'

I stood up, my cock hard and hurting inside my pants, and I started to reply and couldn't, my tongue was thick and I had to clear my throat. Margaret turned to him and said, 'We were just discussing the members' magazine, Matt.'

He said to her, 'An important project. But let me interrupt for just a moment.'

'Certainly,' she said. 'I'll just wait outside.'

'No,' he said, holding up a hand, 'you've been working closely with Wiley a great deal lately, you should hear this too.'

'All right,' she said, and I did not look at her. I looked at Matt and tried to lose my erection.

Matt set his papers down on the desk. They were some of my periodical reviews. I lowered my body into my desk chair slowly. He leaned towards me and said, 'What's the matter, son? Has Margaret here been riding you too hard?' He smiled at her and her face stiffened as she tried to smile back.

'I don't understand, Matt,' I said.

'You're a little off,' he said, and he sat on the corner of the desk and gestured at the manuscript pages. 'You must really put him through his paces, Margaret.'

She was cool now. I admired the quickness with which she adjusted to the situation. 'He's extremely good at everything he does, Matt,' she said.

'That he is,' he said, 'and we all need him.' He turned back to me. 'But your output's down, Wiley, down by half.'

'Really?' I said.

He tapped the manuscript with his finger and said, 'From sixteen pages a week to eight. I can't have that. I won't.'

Margaret took a step forward and said, 'It's my fault, Matt', and she smiled at him, an office diplomat. 'I've been monopolising him.'

He tapped the desk again. 'Use him, Margaret,' he said. 'He's our best writer. Use him.'

'Oh, I do, Matt,' she said.

'Good,' he said, and he studied me a moment, his eyes went to Margaret and back to me and then he smiled and said, 'I think I may know what the problem is.'

I wondered if Margaret's cuteness had given us away, I said, 'Matt?'

'I think I may know what the problem is,' he smiled. He said to Margaret in a stage whisper, 'But it's something I need to talk to Wiley about, man to man. So to speak.'

'Of course.' She crossed to the door and left. He closed the door behind her, and he turned back to me, smirking, and said, 'How is Miss Phone these days?'

I wondered if Margaret could hear. I felt how tensely I had been sitting at the desk, and I tried to relax, and I could not. 'She's fine,' I said.

He sat down in the chair opposite me and he said confidentially, 'You enjoy your fornication, don't you?'

I didn't know what to say. I nodded, I didn't know what he meant.

He laughed, pleased with himself. 'Perhaps you enjoy it too

much,' he said. He held up a finger, making his point. 'Conserve yourself.'

I said again, 'Matt?'

He said quietly and thoughtfully, man to man, 'Women do not give themselves to us freely, Wiley.' His face grew serious and a little dark and his voice became tinged with a very faint bitterness. 'They covet our seed. They consume it in their bellies.'

I couldn't believe what I was hearing, but it was Matt, wasn't it? it was the Gospel According to Matthew. I sat back in my chair and listened.

'Your seed is your strength,' he said, 'and the woman's belly is your weakness. Weakness breeds more weakness. A man who spills his seed in the woman's belly has nothing for his enterprise. Nothing for his real progeny.' His hand rested on the edge of the desk, closed in a tight fist, his real progeny. 'Miss Phone dilutes your strength,' he went on. 'You give your seed to her too freely. Conserve your seed for your true issue.' He opened his fist and spread his hand at the office around us. 'Spend it only as you can afford its loss.' He leaned forward in the chair, and his face was far away, he was deep into it.

I said, 'Do you hate women, Matt?' I could hardly speak.

'I love women,' he said sharply. 'No one loves women more than I do. Why, do you realise, HIV infection is spreading fastest among women. And do you know why? Because they lust after the seed of men, they must have it, no matter how corrupted. So you see, no one loves women more than I, who would deny them for their own sake. Because I see them for what they are, and better than they see themselves. Children, alien children, essentially, incomplete, vessels of our weakness and dis-ease.

'Dis-ease,' he repeated. The words hung between us.

'Women have no creative energy of their own,' he said, brushing their energies aside with his hand. 'That is why they sap ours.' He sat back and folded his hands before him and he sermonised, he had thought out this part of the Gospel in great detail. 'In their weakness and fear, they turn not to us, their true sources, but to Great Serpents, foreign ideas, *isms* – feminism, exoticism, eroticism. And thus armed they seduce us with empty promises of strange wisdom, to such our strength away for their own.' He sat forward and his voice became an intense whisper. 'Eden is now, Wiley, the story is told in the present tense. So we must only use them when we can.'

'When is that?'

'Only once we have already spent our seed for ourselves.'

I understood. 'Write first,' I said.

'Then fornicate,' he said, nodding. 'Conserve yourself. Conserve yourself with Miss Phone. In conservation is your strength. In her belly lies your weakness. Remain full and fertile for your true issue.'

'Research periodicals,' I said.

'Your energy will be restored once you have learned control of the orgasm,' he said, he waved his fingers at me and said it again. 'Control the orgasm.'

'Yes,' I said.

'It's essential!' he said. 'The Tantric masters knew it. Benjamin Franklin knew it.' He spoke in a whisper, 'The Masons know it.' That clinched it. His voice fell into a tense imperative. 'I know it,' he said, and he relaxed a little, sitting back in the chair, 'and now, so do you. The orgasm is the key, the energy you need and already have, if only you knew and wouldn't waste it revelling in feeling for its own sake. For go feeling and you will experience instead the power, Wiley, the power you want, the same power I have, the mastery over things and people that comes to the man who rises above himself.'

I said, 'Above women.'

'Exactly,' he said. He leaned toward the desk again and spoke in a whisper. 'Miss Phone must be a regular sexual acrobat.' He smiled, you could see his gums, and I could only look at him, nodding. 'I can tell,' he said, shaking his head. 'I can always tell.'

I said, 'You must have known a lot of these women.'

He sighed. 'These women,' he said, 'like Miss Phone, they are especially desirable, as you know, and especially vexatious. They must all be tested, of course, but, beyond that, they must be chastened, to receive the seed properly, with the proper attitude. You have not done this with Miss Phone. You do not know how to. I will take care of it. It's for her own good. The Ministry will take care of it.'

'I see.' I felt numb from having to pretend he made sense, I felt nearly overwhelmed by the insanity.

'In the meantime,' he said, holding up a finger, 'no more than once a week, and then, only when you're well rested.'

I said, 'All right.'

He smiled, he tapped the manuscript with his finger. 'Get this up there again,' he said, and then he pounded his fist once on the edge of the desk. 'Get it up!'

'Right!' I cried out. He frightened me.

He rose and threw open the door. Margaret stood outside, I wondered what she had heard. He saw her and he said, 'Get him up again, Margaret!'

'Yes, Matt.' Her face was white, her lips stood out bright red.

And he was gone. She watched his back. Then she came in and closed the door and stood leaning against it, she whispered, 'What the hell did that mean? Does he know about us?' She was urgent and afraid.

I shook my head and she relaxed. She said, 'I hate it when he gets crazy like that.'

I said, 'We need to take shorter lunches, so I'll have more time to write.'

And she liked that, she liked screwing me up. She said, 'Daddy's little girl just drives him to distraction, doesn't she?'

'He might just put us together if he doesn't get his lousy sixteen pages,' I said.

His demands annoyed her, she frowned and said, 'Can't you just write faster or something?'

I laughed at her; she didn't want to cut into our lunches, either. She smiled, she said, 'You enjoy your fornicating, don't you?' She cocked her head and said, 'Who is Miss Phone?'

My laughter faded into a forced smile. I said, 'She's your one true rival.'

'My rival?' she said, intrigued. 'Why haven't I heard about her before?'

'I'll tell you about her some time,' I said.

'Tell me now,' she said. 'I want to know about my rival.'

I said, 'How did you make up special for me today?'

She came slowly around the desk, and took her seat on the corner again and held up her hand for me to see her fingers and she said, 'I painted myself for you. It's called Vermilion Obsession. My lipstick and perfume both match it.'

'That's nice,' I said. 'What else?'

She said, 'I'm wearing a pretty pink camisole. It colours my nipples the prettiest colour. And I've got on a new garter. I know you like them.'

'Tell me about it.'

'It's red with little white roses around the belt.'

'Wear it on Monday,' I said.

'I will,' she said, and she slowly spread her legs wide again. She took the hem of her skirt in her hands and pulled it up her legs a little. 'Now tell me about Miss Phone,' she said. 'But I want you to touch me, like you were about to.'

'She's a girl I met at Rupert's,' I said, and I looked down: I could see just inside her thighs, and my cock felt good, looking at her.

'A girl?' she said. She swung her legs slightly back and forth.

'A good girl.'

'Better than me?' She turned towards me and her skirt spread between her legs a little more.

'She lives up to her name.'

She looked puzzled. 'What's that mean?'

'She gives good phone,' I said.

'You talk to her on the phone?'

'That's right.'

She smiled, she got it. 'And she gets you off.'

'We get each other off.'

'Kinky,' she said, smiling bigger. 'I didn't know you were kinky.' She nodded at her knees. 'Touch me,' she said. 'How does Matt know about her?'

'Matt and I are very close,' I said. I put my hand on her knee.

She laughed. She looked down at me, reached her hand out and caressed my face. 'Daddy,' she said. She bent and kissed me lightly and, holding my face close to hers, she said, hushed and excited, 'Matt calls her too, doesn't he?'

'You can't hide anything from the Divine Margaret, can you?'

She laughed again, her head thrown back. She said, 'Ooh, that obscene old son of a bitch.' She had something on him now, and she wanted to get some more. She said, 'Her name's not really Phone, is it?'

'I don't know her real name,' I said. 'The phone is her idea of safe sex.'

'Matt's, too, I'll bet,' she said. She held my head in her hands and lifted her face upward, she said, 'Oh, what can I do to him with this?' She looked down at me. 'Tell me,' she said.

'What do you want to do with it?'

'Oh, that pious old hypocrite. He'll burn for this, he'll just burn.' She seethed with triumph, she said, 'Touch me. Touch me now.' She leaned forward and made a soft kiss with her lips of Vermilion Obsession, a red round succulent mouth.

I spread my hand across her lap. Her skirt was taut. I closed my hand in a fist, gathering the fabric together, lifting it up; the hem pulled tight against the soft flesh of her thighs.

'Yes,' she said softly and her eyes were a black fire.

I said, 'Monday.'

Chapter 51

But that Monday, we had TB. We were both red and swollen at the sites of the skin tests, and we went into Carl's office and he showed us the X-rays, with the cloudy area in the upper part of our chests where the TB was, and talked about how the tubercles infiltrated the lungs and corroded the tissue.

It scared me, my body out of control again, I remembered the accident and the year in bed, I remembered the tree at my window and the changes of the seasons, and the bedpans and the urine capture bag and the sweet and sour hospital smells, the pasty bad hospital food smothered in pale corn starch gravies, and I felt hot in the air-conditioned office looking at the X-rays, illuminated by bright fluorescent lights through white, flashed opal glass, and I loosened my tie and unbuttoned my shirt collar.

Schumacher stood beside the display of X-rays with both our charts in his hands. He pointed to the red rising on Alix's forearm and said, 'It's a good sign for you, actually. A lot of HIV-positive people can't produce an immune response. You can. Your immune system is still in pretty good shape.'

'That's great,' she said listlessly.

He paused and turned back to the X-rays. He said, 'For now I'm going to put you both on a standard four-drug regimen. I also want to start you on vitamin B^6. We'll get the susceptibility tests from Cobb tomorrow or the next day, and we may have to change your medication if you're resistant. But I'm praying you won't be.'

I said, 'What if we are?'

He turned to me. 'Then we put you on even more drugs,' he said. 'It's a matter of odds. If the odds of developing resistance to one drug are one in a million, then the odds of developing it to two become one in a million million.'

I said, 'So the odds of developing it to four are one a million million million million.' I had read about this in Finder on Friday.

'Exactly,' he said. 'So if you *are* resistant, we really load you up. Of course, there are side effects to consider.'

Alix said, 'What are they?'

'It's strong medicine,' he said, turning to her. 'It can upset your stomach, make your nauseous. You may run a fever. And there's a slight risk of hepatitis with the isoniazid.'

263

'Hepatitis?' I said.

'It's slight. In your age group, on isoniazid, about three cases develop in every thousand patients. We'll monitor you, we'll do up blood work once a month, and you watch for signs of hepatitis: fatigue, weakness, malaise, anorexia, nausea, vomiting,' he ticked them off on his fingers. 'But it's tricky, because all these drugs can cause those effects, too. Do you drink?'

'We both drink,' I said.

'Stop it,' he said. 'Drinking increases the risk of hepatitis, so cut it out. Just watch yourselves, and let me know how you're feeling. The ethambutol can affect your vision, so let me know if you have any problems there. We'll schedule eye exams for both of you, so we'll have an index to measure you against if there's a problem later.'

He turned to me. 'Do you smoke?' he said.

'Now and then,' I said.

'Quit it,' he said.

'Now,' he said, folding his hands over the charts and holding them before him, 'it's very important for both of you to stick to the treatment plan. Otherwise, you can develop resistance to the drugs, and that can kill you fast. It can kill either of you.' He looked from Alix to me. 'Do you understand?'

'Yes,' I said. Alix looked at the floor.

'It's not going to be easy to do,' he said. 'You'll have to take the drugs for at least six months, maybe a year. TB grows slowly and it takes time to treat it.'

Alix said, 'I've got time. I've got lots of time.'

He looked at her, and he said, 'You do have time, Alix. You've still got time, and it can be quality time. And you know that.'

She looked down and sighed, then looked up at him and said, 'All right, Carl, I'll try.' There was something here they had talked about before.

'In fact, I want you to take some quality time,' he said. 'Take some time off, both of you.'

She said, 'I can't. We're doing a major project at work. I mean, major.'

'You've got a major disease,' he said. 'What's more, you're contagious, and you'll remain that way until the medicine takes effect.'

'Well, how long is that?' she said.

'It varies,' he said, 'depending on the extent of the infection.' He turned back to the X-rays. 'In your cases, the lesions are tiny, we

264

caught it early. It might take no more than a week or so. We'll get another sputum sample next Monday and test it for the bacillus.'

'Oh, God,' she said, and she threw up her hands.

He looked at her. 'Time off,' he said, 'or I can hospitalise you, if you want. Both of you. Stay home. I mean it. It's the law. Break it and they can force you into quarantine.' He looked at Alix, and said quietly, 'They did that with an AIDS case in DeKalb County last year. So no contact with anybody.' He looked at me to make sure I agreed.

I said, 'All right.'

He sighed and said, 'Well, at least the drugs are free. The county provides them. I'll write the prescriptions and you can pick them up at the Health Department.' Then he said to me, 'Do you have any idea where you might have been exposed?'

'Me?' I said.

'You,' he said. 'The odds are that you picked it up somewhere and gave it to Alix, not the other way around. TB is hard to catch if your immune system isn't compromised.'

Alix lifted her head at this. She said, 'He gave it to me?'

Carl said, 'Probably.'

She looked at me, and I looked back at her emptily. We had been so careful, hadn't we? With the sex. But it wasn't the sex that did it, it was breathing. I wanted to stop breathing, if I could just stop breathing. I said lamely, 'I don't know where I could've got it.'

She just shook her head, she was rattled.

He said, 'We'll have to notify the public health department, and they'll do some contact tracing, check out the people you work with to see if they're infected, that sort of thing.'

Alix looked at him suddenly and said, 'I don't want to tell anybody.'

'It's the law,' he said to her. 'I've got to report cases of TB to the public health.'

Her voice rose, she said, 'I don't care about the fucking law. I don't want anybody to know I'm positive.'

'I don't either,' said Carl. 'And there's no reason why anyone should find out. As far as everybody else is concerned, you're a case of TB, pure and simple.'

We got the prescriptions from him, and we went to the county Health Department and picked up the drugs: four sets of pills for each of us in large brown bottles, and some brochures about the drugs and about TB. There was paperwork to sign, statements that we understood the gravity of the disease and agreed to abide by the treatment regimen without county oversight. Then we drove around for a while in my car, and Alix sat silently, staring out the side window. I headed towards home but turned into the park instead and drove over to the tennis courts and parked. The sky was overcast, the day was grey and the sun pushed down from above the clouds, and it was hot and still.

Alix looked around us, she said, 'Shitty day.'

'Yes,' I said.

She said, 'Lots of shitty days lately.'

She looked straight ahead, out the window at the tennis courts. A man and a woman in sparkling white tennis outfits sweated at each other over a bright yellow ball, they danced back and forth, right and left across the courts, and I looked at Alix's profile as she watched them. She was incredibly fine, I thought, she was the most beautiful woman I had ever known, far more beautiful than Margaret, white skin so white beside her red red hair and her lower lip curled perfectly down, sad now, and her green eyes shining brightly. I caressed her face with the back of my fingers, and she moved her head against my hand and took it in her own and drew it to her lips and kissed it. She said, 'Are you going to leave me now?' She sounded tired.

I was surprised and hurt, I said, 'Of course not.'

She said, 'You'd better. I'm going to get horribly sick, and I won't be pretty any more.'

'Don't talk like that,' I said.

She went on. 'And you'll do what I did with Brian, and you'll feel terrible.'

'I won't,' I said.

She looked at me. 'You won't do it, or you won't feel terrible?'

I frowned at her. 'I won't do it,' I said.

She kept on looking at me. After a moment she said quietly, 'Then who do you lie with like spoons?' The question exhausted her.

She held on to my hand, and I looked at her, my cock was small and I was very little, but I couldn't hide, and I couldn't get my breath in the heat of the car, I had been caught, and I felt a single drop of sweat course down the side of my face from my temple. I was not who I said I was, I was a phoney and a liar, and I felt the skin of her palm against my fingertips, soft like all of her skin, and I was suddenly tired, too, and I said, 'It doesn't matter now.'

'Yes, it does,' she said. 'Is it Nickie again?' She was very tired.

I couldn't tell her the truth, that I had fucked Margaret and then got Alix to steal Finder for her. So I went further with it and I said 'Yes', and my heart raced suddenly in the close, hot air, and I was afraid, afraid of getting caught again in the deeper lie, and afraid of getting away with it, what would I do if I got away with it?

She let go of my hand and looked out the window and said, 'Is she a better lover than me?'

I looked down at the dashboard and the steering wheel. The odometer read 147,356 miles, a great distance, I needed a new car, I needed money badly. I sighed and thought about Margaret and I said, 'No.'

'Why do you do it, then?'

I wanted to hide and I couldn't, I wanted to take it all back and do it all over, and this time I would never say *We'll lie like spoons*, but I couldn't. I said, 'I don't know.' I heard the tennis ball being hit back and forth quite distinctly, very regularly.

She sighed. 'I do,' she said.

I looked up at her, surprised. She was watching the tennis game idly, covered with a fine film of perspiration. 'Why?' I said.

'Because you want to,' she said.

I couldn't look at her, so I looked at the courts. The man charged hard against the net and returned the ball. I had thought he was going to miss it, and the woman had expected him to miss it, too, so she was a little off guard, but she moved as fast as he did, her skirt flapped up and showed her white pants tight around her firm little ass, and she was good, she countered him, and this time he did miss it, and I thought how easy it would be to just sit there and do nothing but watch them play their tennis game for the rest of the day.

'Because you can,' she said. She turned to me, she looked serious and she looked scared. She said, 'I don't want you to leave me, Wiley.'

I said, 'I don't want to.'

'Especially now,' she said and looked away. Her voice was strained and everything was quiet except for the sounds of the tennis players.

'Yes,' I said.

'I'm scared,' she said. 'I'm sick now and I'm scared. And you do this to me.'

I said, 'I don't want to give you up.'

'What is it you want to do, then?' she said with sudden energy, her hands made into fists and hitting once on her knees. 'Fuck every woman in Rupert's?'

267

Her voice was loud. I watched the man on the tennis court: he bounced sideways on the balls of his feet, and I thought he was looking our way. I said, 'I want to help you.'

She laughed bitterly and shook her head. 'I don't want you to help me. I want you to love me.'

I looked at her steadily, I would not flinch.

'Me,' she said, tapping her breast quickly with her finger. 'Only me. You fuck only me, or you leave me alone, you, you fucking little son of a bitch.' The words rushed out of her mouth and her face flushed and her hand shook with fine, angry tremors.

I turned away and looked out the side window but my eyes wouldn't focus, wouldn't rest on anything, the tennis ball went back and forth now with a steady smacking sound, and the air rose in hot waves off the pavement across the parking lot.

She said, 'What do you think, anyway?' She couldn't believe I had done it. She said, 'I tell you I love you, and I love you, you bastard, I quit fucking around for you, I quit the clubs and the whole fucking scene, and I only fuck you, like your fucking wife, for Christ's sake, I love you so special, I fuck you better than anyone, I do things for you I haven't done with anyone since Stephen, and you son of a bitch turn around and fuck this little girl bitch Nickie. I could fucking kill you. Just how much pussy do you have to have, anyway? Jesus Christ, is your whole life wrapped up in your dick? I do anything for you, anything you want, and that isn't enough for you. What the fuck do you want?' She was shouting.

She looked desperate to know, she really wanted to know, and her eyes were angry and they were hurt, she looked at me a moment and then sighed and turned away. I watched the tennis players and I saw the man glancing our way again between serves. Alix's hands pressed against her thighs in tight hard little fists. She turned to me again and said, 'She does something, doesn't she?'

I shook my head and sighed. I was tired, and I was sad, I felt beaten.

She insisted. She had it figured out. 'She does,' she said. 'Tell me what she does. I can do it better than she does. I know I can. I know it.' She pounded her thighs with her fists, rising and falling, again and again, and she began to speak again, faster and out of control. 'I love you, goddamn it, I fuck you better than her, I know I do, I fuck you better than anybody else has *ever*, and you do this to me. Fuck you, you asshole, oh, I hate you, I hate your guts.'

She put her head in her hands and rubbed her face, she moaned and shook her head and she turned to me, leaning across the space

268

between the car seats, and she spoke into my face, she pleaded: 'Do you know, if I could have your baby I would do that. Do you know that? That's how much I love you, I'd want a piece of your life inside me except for this fucking AIDS, and now I'm dying, fucking dying, goddamn it, and you can't keep your dick out of this fucking little secretary whore Nickie's cunt.' She shook her open hand in the air, she said, 'What's so special about this little bitch's cunt, anyway? Is it because she's safe? Is that it? Do you fuck her without protection? Is that what she does? Is that what you really want? Bare cunt?'

She choked and swallowed hard against tears, but they welled up in her eyes anyway, and I felt the heat very close around me. She was sweating too, and the man on the tennis court was looking over at us, I wondered if he had made out her words, *bare cunt*, I didn't want anyone to know what I had done. He turned quickly back to his partner as she returned the ball to him, and Alix sounded sad and desperate, she said, 'I can't do that. It's not fair, Wiley. You know I can't do that.'

She lay back in the seat and cried, and I felt dark inside and hollow and sad, I had TB and it ate at me, and now this ate at me too, like another disease, and I was ashamed of myself and empty inside, used up and caught in my emptiness. I had unmanned myself. I looked away from her, down at my hands open in my lap, I felt groundless and floating, like a slowly moving target naked there in the park where the tennis players could see us, I didn't want them to see us, and everything she said was true and awful, I was selfish and I was cruel and I didn't care.

Alix's hair was coming undone down around her face in long curls, and her eyes were bright and angry and wet, and her lips were red and parted slightly. I said quietly, because I had nothing left, 'Would you really want to have a baby?'

She looked at me and she sighed once, long, her breasts rose and fell, and I wanted to touch her and was afraid to try, I could no longer touch her freely, and she just looked at me, and her eyes were wet with tears and a veil of softness fell slowly across her face, she looked very tired now. Two drops of sweat ran down the side of her face, one after the other, and her mouth opened and closed and no sound came out. Then she turned and sat back in her seat with her hands in her lap and she looked out the window and said tiredly, slowly, explaining it carefully to me, because I did not understand, 'Nobody ever fit inside me the way you fit inside me. Why don't you just love me, and don't do this.' She covered

269

her face with her hand and she cried. 'Please, please, please. You make me feel crazy when you do this, you make me afraid, and I don't want to be afraid.' She wiped her eyes, and she said, 'I don't want to be sick.' She folded her arms on the dashboard and laid her head down and said again, 'I don't want to be sick', and she moaned suddenly and tore open the car door and leaned out and vomited on the pavement. She held on to the door frame with her right hand and the open door with the other and she hung there, throwing up. The man was running across the court and saw her and slowed and watched and missed the ball altogether; his partner saw him looking and she turned, too, and they both saw us. When her sickness passed I reached across the seats and put my hand on her back, and she quivered and drew a breath and coughed and spit several times and said loudly, 'Don't touch me. You've made me sick.'

I said, 'Please, Alix.'

She sat up, facing out the door of the car for a moment, and then she closed it and turned to me hard. She wiped her mouth with her hand and licked her lips and she leaned out the window and spat, and I heard the tennis ball being struck again. Then she turned and said, 'Why do you want to do this to me?'

'I don't.'

'Then will you stop it?' she said, and she closed her eyes tightly in pain and shook her head. 'This hurts, Wiley. It hurts, it hurts.' The words rushed out from her pain.

I placed my hand on her near thigh, warm and damp with perspiration. She opened her eyes and lifted her face to mine. She said, 'Will you finish it with her?'

'Yes.'

'Today?'

'Yes.'

She turned away from me. 'Nickie,' she sighed, she couldn't believe it was still going on.

I said quietly, 'She really is like Brian, you know.'

She turned back to me. She said, 'You think I haven't thought about that?'

I couldn't excuse myself, there was no excuse for what I had done.

'I've thought about it,' she said. 'I've thought, I did this to Stephen, I'm not getting something I didn't give, he's not doing anything I didn't do. I've thought all that. And you know what? It doesn't make any fucking difference.' Her voice began to rise.

'It doesn't make me feel different, see? You fuck her and it makes all kinds of insane feelings in me. It makes me feel guilty about Brian. It makes me feel sick. It makes me feel like I don't know what's real. It makes me hate you, it makes me want to kill you, it makes me want to fuck you. It makes me want to watch while she fucks you so I can fuck you the same way so you won't do her any more. It makes me want to never fuck you again. It makes me vomit, goddamn it.' She was quite loud now, and I heard the tennis ball hit and bounce once and then nothing. 'And what I did with Brian with Stephen doesn't fucking matter because this is different, because this is me, now, goddamn it, and it shouldn't happen, you shouldn't fucking do this to me. I love you too much. I love you too good for you to do this to me.' She nearly screamed it at me.

The heat was overwhelming. Our clothes were wet with sweat and my shirt stuck to my chest and back. We looked at each other, and I reached to her, and when she didn't stop me, I undid the buttons of her blouse, and she closed her eyes and drew a deep breath, and I slipped my hand inside her blouse and caressed her breasts, she was wet, and she opened her eyes and said softly, 'Just touch me, and you'll feel it', and she began to cry again. Her tears fell on my hand, and I lost my breath, but I could not cry. I wanted my tears to come, too, with hers, but they would not, I could not cry any more, I had lost it somewhere, so I just ached, and I took her in my arms and held her as she wept freely and said, 'You've got to stop it.' I did not hear the tennis ball and I looked and saw the players standing on the green court watching us, with their rackets in their hands.

The man saw me looking, and he wiped his face with the back of his hand, and looked down and bounced the ball once on the turf and caught it on the rebound.

Chapter 52

At home, I told Alix I was going to phone Nickie, and I went upstairs to my place and made a few calls, first to Patricia Patterson and to Grant. And I had to call Margaret, too. I sat in the sun room and looked out over the park as I talked, watching the clouds begin to break up and the sun come through.

Patricia was scared. 'You say they're going to test the whole company?' she said.

'The doctor said they probably would.'

'Matt won't like that,' she said. I heard her light a cigarette, and I wanted one myself. 'He won't like strangers coming in here.'

'I suppose not,' I said. To tease her, I coughed.

She said quickly, 'Are you all right?'

I said, 'No, Patricia, I've got *tuberculosis*.'

'Yes,' she said, she was flustered and I enjoyed it. 'Yes, well, but you'll be back some time next week?'

'The doctor said a week or so.'

'All right,' she said. 'All right. Matt's already left for the station, but I'll call him there.'

'I'll tell Grant,' I said.

'You tell Grant,' she said. 'Who else?'

I said, 'You ought to tell everybody, Patricia. It's not like I've got AIDS.'

'That's right,' she said, flustered but getting it at last. 'That's right. It's not AIDS.'

She transferred the call to Grant. He was shocked. 'You've got TB,' he said slowly, amazed. 'That's hard to get, you know. Takes lots of exposure, takes time.'

'I know,' I said. 'I read up on it when they tested me.' I was careful not to mention Alix. I heard him light a cigarette. The clouds showed pale spots of blue here and there across the sky.

'Shit,' he said suddenly, 'this means I've got to do the fucking periodicals myself.'

I laughed. I said, 'You could upload them to me and I could do them here, then send them back to you.'

'Matt would like that,' he said, laughing.

'I know,' I said, and I thought about his seed talk and I shivered, chilled, but whether from the TB or Matt, I could not tell.

After I hung up on Grant, I sat looking out the sun-room

windows and feeling down. I wasn't ready to call Margaret yet, so I put her off by dialling the Ritz-Carlton in Buckhead and asking to leave a message for Ms Dresden. But when I told the clerk I was Mr Jones, she said, 'Oh, Mr Jones, Ms Dresden left instructions for you to call her at work.'

'Where's that?' I said.

'She's at Colony Square today,' said the girl, and she gave me the number. I dialled it and got a workman, who told me I'd have to wait for Ms Dresden, she was up on a scaffold, he said, with the gesso crew, whatever gesso was, and I said fine and sat looking out the windows again, still wishing I had a cigarette.

When she came on the line she said, 'Nathaniel?'

'Wiley,' I said, and I realised the desk clerk had mixed up her Joneses.

But Sarah didn't miss a step, she said, 'Sweet!' sounding pleased. 'You haven't called in more than a week. Have you been keeping the ladies busy?'

'I've been sick,' I said.

'Oh,' she said. 'Nothing serious, I hope.'

'TB,' I said, and I realised that I was upping Nathaniel, making myself more important than him by being a medical emergency.

'Wiley!' she said. 'You're kidding.'

'Hey—' I remembered the numbers in Finder – 'Atlanta has the highest rate of TB in the United States.'

'You're kidding,' she said again, and then quickly, 'No, you're not. How did you get it?'

'I don't know,' I said, and I told her about the testing.

She said, 'Well, I'll come see you.'

'I'm quarantined,' I said.

'No!' she cried. 'I want to see you. I need to.'

I said, 'What's the matter?'

'Oh, nothing really, nothing specific,' she said. 'I'm just lonesome. I was thinking we could see a film somewhere and have dinner and take a walk together and talk. *Talk.* I have no one to talk to.'

'Call me,' I said.

'You're never home,' she said.

'I'm down at Alix's,' I said. 'Call me there.'

She was quiet a moment, then she said, 'I don't think I want to call you at another woman's apartment.'

And I felt we were sharing something now, we had something together, I didn't want her to call me at Alix's either, suddenly, and

I could see Nathaniel Jones behind us and over us and above us and between us, and I wanted him to suffocate. The desire shocked me, I wanted tuberculosis to eat his lungs alive until he couldn't breathe any more, I wanted him away and dead; no, not dead, I drew back from that, but unmade, never to have been, corrected and reversed and negated, like a premiss in a syllogism or an element misplaced in a truth table. I said quietly to Sarah, 'I'll call you, then.'

'Yes,' she said, and I wondered how long she had been trying to make me understand, I wondered what else she wanted me to understand. She said, 'How sick are you?'

'I don't even have a cough,' I said.

'That's good,' she said.

'It'll be all right,' I said, and I told her about the drugs.

She said, 'I wish there was something I could do.'

I resettled myself in the chair, looking at the sky, the clouds were beginning to break up. 'Maybe there is, I said. 'Can you spare a minute?'

'For you?' she said. 'Certainly.'

'I've got a problem,' I said. 'I mean, not the TB.'

She said, 'It must be a woman, then.'

'Yes.'

'All right ask.'

I began, 'There's this woman, Margaret.'

'She's the oldest one, right?'

'She's forty,' I said.

She said, 'Are you her lover?' The question made my insides twist slowly. I bit the nail on my forefinger, I said, 'Yes.'

'Do you like being her lover?'

I chewed up the bit of fingernail. 'Sometimes I don't think so.'

'Only sometimes.' She was smiling at me, I could hear it in her voice. 'What about the rest of the time?'

I said, 'She—' and I stopped, I couldn't go on.

Sarah said, 'You can tell me,' and her voice was very close.'

I said, 'She's dangerous. I've never known anything like it.'

Sarah said, 'It.'

I felt the sweat under my arms and across my back, I said, 'Yes.' I could hear her breathe as she was waited, there was more and she knew it, finally I said, 'Alix is dangerous, too. Terrifically dangerous. Are all older women like this?'

'I thought you liked older women.'

'I do,' I said. 'That's just it. I like it.'

Her laughter broke over me like cool water, and I thought I might

274

be all right. Sarah said, 'Yes, we're all like that, Wiley. Dangerous and hot.'

'Are you dangerous?'

'Oh, no, not me,' she said. 'Do you know what Benjamin Franklin says about older women? "They are so grateful." That's me.' She laughed again.

'What is it really?' I said, I wanted to know.

'Which?' she said. 'The danger, or your liking it?'

'Both.'

'The danger is that the thread will break.'

'What thread?'

'The thread you're dangling all these women from,' she said.

I saw a big lone blackbird dart down from the eaves of the building and swoop toward the street, then bottom out and climb up high over the trees of the park. Sarah knew everything about me, I did not know how, and I tried to speak and could not, a chocked sound came from the bottom of my throat, and she laughed lightly, a calm and soothing sound, she said, 'It's all right, Wiley.'

'Alix knows,' I said.

'Does she?'

'She thinks she does.'

'She thinks she does? How can she think so and not know so?'

'She knows I'm—' and I stumbled.

'Fucking,' said Sarah. 'You're fucking someone you probably shouldn't be.'

'All right,' I said. 'Alix knows I'm fucking someone, but she thinks it's Nickie.'

'Jesus,' she said. 'Which one is Nickie?'

'Nickie's the one I gave the orgasm to.'

'The young one you almost got sort of pregnant,' she said, sighing, and she was silent a moment. I wondered what she thought, and then she said, 'So Alix thinks you're fucking one you've never fucked, and you're really fucking one that Alix doesn't know anything about.'

'Well,' I said.

'What?' said Sarah. 'She knows about her?'

'Alix knows I work with Margaret,' I said. 'In fact, she's doing a little computer work for her.'

'Oh, Christ, sweet,' she said, 'you're fucking one of your lover's clients?'

I thought about it. 'That's probably about right,' I said.

'So you're guilty,' she said, 'but not guilty as charged.'

'Right.' The room felt very warm and I thought I ought to eat something soon and take some TB medicine.

She sighed. 'So is everybody else,' she said. 'Though your case is a little more involved than most.'

'I don't want to be like everybody else, Sarah.'

'Then quit fucking, Wiley.' From the side window I could see Garcia in the next apartment. He was with some prospects: he stood beside a young blond couple and pointed out the windows from one end of the park to the other, his arm sweeping across the land as if he owned it. The Day-Glo hand downstairs said UP, and the boat with the chandeliers would dock any minute now.

Someone said something to Sarah and she spoke to them over her shoulder. When she came back, she said, 'I have to go now. I've got work to do.'

Garcia turned and led the blonds away and I said flatly, 'Work is a very serious thing.'

'Too serious,' she said. 'No one should ever work. When will you call me again?'

'Soon,' I said.

'Keep me in suspense, then,' she said.

She saw things inside me before I saw them myself, she said them before I was ready. I sat back in the chair, I felt worn out, as if I had just received religious instruction and now I was supposed to meditate on it until I understood the meaning of God. I said, 'Women are treacherous.'

'Especially when men are young,' she said, and she hung up the phone.

I made a final call to Margaret. I wondered what she would teach me today, I wondered if my turn would ever come to teach her something. She was bothered. 'Where the hell are you?' she said. 'We missed lunch again.'

I said slowly and deliberately, 'I've got TB.'

'Tuberculosis?' she said, incredulous.

'Yes.'

'Well, where the hell did you get that?' She was irritated by it and, like Patricia, a little afraid, it was something unplanned and beyond her control.

'I don't know,' I said.

'How could you get TB?' she said, she still couldn't quite believe it. 'TB's hard to get, you know.'

'I know,' I said. 'I read about it in Finder on Friday.'

'Friday,' she said, and she put it together instantly. 'You got it from Alix, didn't you? This is what you took her to the doctor about, isn't it?'

'Yes,' I said.

'You bastard,' she said. 'You got tested for it and didn't even tell me. Why didn't you tell me?'

'I didn't see any point, Friday,' I said. 'I'm telling you now, aren't I? I'm not trying to hide it from you.'

'You bastard,' she said again.

I didn't like that, I wanted her to take it back. I said, 'There's nothing to be upset about. You said yourself, TB is hard to get.'

She paused, and the silence sounded uncertain, she did not know whether to let go of her anger yet or not. She said, 'What did Finder say?'

I told her what I'd read. 'You have to have prolonged exposure in close quarters with someone who's contagious.'

'Are you contagious?' she said.

'Yes,' I said, 'but I got some medicine this morning.'

'Oh, Christ,' she said, 'prolonged exposure in close quarters. Like the La Ventura, I suppose?'

And suddenly I was enjoying myself. I'd never seen Margaret squirm before. 'Probably,' I said.

'Oh, Christ,' she said again. 'I don't need this, Wiley. I really don't need this.'

'You think I do?' I said. 'If you're this upset, why not have your own doctor test you?'

'I will,' she said.

'Good,' I said. 'Anyway, we've got another problem.'

Now I had alarmed her all over again. She said, 'For Christ's sake, what else is there?'

I was not smiling now. I said, 'Alix knows what we're doing.'

She said, 'Well, how the hell did she find out?' her voice full of anger again, all her little webs of plans coming unstrung at once.

I said, 'It doesn't matter. She knows.'

She accused me, 'Did you *tell* her, for God's sake? You told her, didn't you?'

'No, I didn't.' The sun had come out again, but the clouds still cast sharp shadows on the green of the park.

'What about Finder?' she said, suddenly anguished but starting to think straight. 'Have you lost Finder for me, too?'

'She doesn't know it's you,' I said. 'She thinks it's Nickie.'

She stopped. She said slowly, 'You mean you're not fucking Nickie?'

'No,' I said, 'just you.'

'Just me,' she said, surprised, and she fell quiet, thinking about it. She said the words again singly, 'Just me.'

I said, 'We've got to stop.'

She said, 'Did you tell her you'd stop fucking Nickie?' She sounded calmer, she was calculating now.

'Yes.'

'Then you're brilliant,' she said. 'You're not fucking Nickie, are you?'

I said, 'We need to stop, Margaret.'

She paused, and then she said softly, 'Do you want to? Really?'

'We ought to,' I said.

She had been off-balanced by the TB, but now she was back to herself. She said, 'But do you want to?' Her voice was soft and full of sex, full of promises. She said, 'You liked it without the condom, didn't you? You like what you do to me. I like it too, you know. I really do. You're really my daddy. Just the way I want you to be. Do you really want to end all that?'

I swallowed. The sun was very bright, the sky intensely blue. She said, 'Where are your balls, Wiley? Can't you handle this woman?'

I said nothing.

She said, and I could hear her smiling, 'You handled me all right, just now. I liked that. I enjoyed it. I admire it. Why don't you handle Alix the same way?'

I swallowed again. I said, 'You handle me pretty well, too, don't you?'

She said, 'Daddy likes the way his little girl does him', and I could see her smiling. She whispered into my ear. 'You're a man, Wiley,' she said. 'Do what a man does.'

Chapter 53

The sky had cleared completely by the time I went back downstairs, and Alix was sunning on the landing in her red bikini. She looked up at me through her mirror shades and said, 'I saw the sun come out and thought it might do me some good.'

'Good,' I said. 'Sunlight kills *Mycobacterium tuberculosis*. I read that at work Friday.' I bent and kissed her, and she put her hand on the back of my neck and held me there for a moment and I caressed her face with both my hands. My tongue went deep into her mouth: she had brushed her teeth and used mouthwash, and I could taste the mint flavour. She held me tensely, her touch full of nervous questions and hunger, I'd never seen her afraid before, but she was now, she was sick, like she had said in the car, she was dying and afraid, she was out of control, and I was out of control with her, her fear infected me, for myself, for the two of us, and I kissed her with a sudden, panicked passion, as if we could physically dispel the disease and make ourselves whole again.

When I stood up, she followed me inside. I sat at the kitchen table and pulled off my tie. She kept her shades on, and the polished lenses were cool and fearless, but she stood looking at me awkwardly for a moment, waiting for me, her hands together at the fingertips, picking at each other slowly. I did not like to see her so uncomfortable, I was responsible for it and I needed to calm her. I thought, she needs me to tell her I love her, can I say it? and I was afraid of lying to her, I didn't want to lie to her any more, I wanted to tell her the truth, and the truth was, I realised with quiet surprise, that I was very tired – from the phone calls, tired of myself, tired of my games, Margaret and Finder – and I wished, exhausted, that I could be different, I wanted the chance to make myself over inside her, I wanted to fill her with a baby, my baby, myself, and I was sad suddenly because I could not do this, because of the disease, and sad because she wanted it and I could not give it to her.

She turned to the cabinet and got a glass and went to the refrigerator and poured herself some orange juice from a yellow plastic pitcher. Then she turned to me, sipping it, and set it down and got another glass and poured it full of juice as well and handed it to me. I took it and went into the bedroom to change into my cutoffs, and she followed and stood by the dresser drinking and watching me undress. She bit her lip and I saw myself grow naked in her mirrors, and I got a little hard, standing there before her. She set her orange juice down on the dresser and came close to me and bit her lip again and said, 'Well? Did you talk to Nickie?'

'I talked to her.'

'So are you through with it?'

'I'm through with it,' I said, and she relaxed subtly but visibly, the stiffness and fear went out of her. But now I felt empty in my stomach and tense and afraid of her, afraid of what I was doing. *Do what a man does*, Margaret had said, was I doing what a man does? What does a man do?

She put her hand on my neck and leaned close and kissed me deeply. When she broke the kiss she said softly, 'Don't lie to Confusion, Proteus,' and a sudden fear overwhelmed me that Confusion knew all about it and I had trapped myself, she knew it was Margaret and she knew about the La Ventura and the dental dams and Daddy and his little girl and all of it.

I said, 'What will she do?'

She said, 'Confusion will get you, honey.'

I was too tired to do anything. If she knew the truth, I was doomed, and I felt doomed anyway. The doomed man pushed back at last, he said, a little sarcastically, 'Does Confusion want to have my baby, too?'

That got her. A little shock went across her face, and she reached slowly to her sunglasses and took them off. Her green eyes were hurt, and I was out on the edge of things, I wanted to fuck her, I wanted to sleep, but I wanted to make her all right and I only knew one way to do that, I was tired and I wanted a rest, and, finally, I wanted to rest with her, Alix, I just wanted to sleep alongside her.

'Yes, she does,' she said, and she waited.

I looked into her eyes and I said, 'Do you know how that makes me feel?'

'Yes.'

'Is this a hack, then?' I said, thinking suddenly. 'Are you hacking me?'

'No.'

I picked up my orange juice and drank it all and set the glass back down. I turned to her and said, 'I would like to give you a baby, you know.'

Her mouth opened a little and closed, and then she said, 'I can't do that. I can't fuck you the way she can.' She lowered her head and looked at her hands.

It made me a little hard, to hear her say that, to see her baffled and defeated at last; it made me feel sad for her and it made me feel better, she was human after all, she had a limit, she reached a point where she had to stop, and at the same time I felt guilty for my reaction to her weakness, I felt her ruin and I wanted to reach to her and make it all right to be ruined, I wanted to love her, I did love her. She stood there looking down, disconcerted, confused, and I reached and touched her arm, and her eyes touched mine, and I said, 'Don't do that to yourself.'

She said, 'I know how it feels. I know the difference.' Her voice was faint and distant and bitter, and she looked away again.

I said, 'That's not what makes it love.'

She dropped the sunglasses to the floor and looked at me again. Her eyes shone with tears and she said, 'I know that. I know what makes it love.'

'I know you do,' I said, moving my hand slowly up and down her arm and drawing her nearer to me, 'I really believe you do.'

She put her arms around me and we kissed, softly and deeply, for a long time, and I got harder, and she took me in her hand and stroked me gently while we kissed, and I undid her bikini, and we were naked together.

We made love. I had never seen her so excited, she trembled with life now that she was dying. I knelt between her legs and spread the lips of her cunt apart and gazed into her wet pink life and she closed her eyes and sighed, yearning, and I felt life heavy and sweet and miraculous between my legs, through my flesh, bigger than me. Like a strong force of living water moving through a deep stone channel, the water washed over me warm and clear and sparkling with light and left me new, and I wanted to live inside her and I was not alone, she wanted me there, and I wanted to die with her so we would not be alone again, I was so tired of being alone, and I lay back on the water flowing around us and she bent her body between my legs and took me living in her mouth and the water could wash everything away, and I flowed into her, and she swallowed me and I was living, I was flying with her through the water, and I took her and held her to me like a little child, and she dressed my cock, and when I went inside her, she lay on top of me and flowed down my legs and gripped my flesh and she moaned terribly, the most beautiful sound, and afterwards we lay together in the sunlight with damp soft sponges and a basin and bathed each other clean.

And then we slept. We rested.

Chapter 54

We grilled a couple of steaks and took our TB medicine, three big white tablets and a red and gold capsule for each of us, with glasses of orange juice. 'Too bad about the alcohol,' she said, pushing her plate away from her. 'Some wine would have been good with this, wouldn't it?'

'I guess,' I said. I had made coffee and now we sat drinking it. We were in our bathrobes and the last of the sun was dying outside.

She drank her coffee and looked serious and said, 'I've got to fuck Matt before I get too sick to do it.'

'You're not going to get sick,' I said. 'We've got these meds.'

She looked at the pill bottles, sitting in the middle of the table with the salt and pepper. She said, 'There'll be something else, though, later.'

My heart tightened with dread, and I couldn't get my breath. I didn't like this, I wanted a way out, I had never been any place where there was no way out. She sat looking down at her empty plate and thinking, thinking about AIDS, I guessed, her face calm and her eyes far-seeing. I could be anything with her, she let me, she let me be whatever it was I was and she loved it, what I was, any way at all, and I loved her, she was important to me, and the time was important and I didn't want to spend it hacking Matt, it was a waste of the hours left us. And I felt too a prick of possession, she was my lover, she was mine and she was going away from me, I knew that, and I didn't want to share her now, I didn't want him to touch her, I thought of his dishonest flesh and his mean spirit, I saw all of it closing around her like a shadow on its prey, and I didn't want her to do this. But I tried to hide my feelings, I tried to be a hacker. 'You still want to do it?' I said.

'Of course.' she gave me a curious look: something was wrong with me that I would ask such a question. 'It's the point of the whole hack.'

The hacking mattered to her, it was real, fucking him was only part of a hack, like cracking the bulletin board system or copying Finder and screwing it up. I drank some coffee and I let it go for the time being. 'All right,' I said. 'Have you called him lately?'

She smiled. 'I thought I'd give him a ring tonight. Want to listen in?'

I went along with her. I thought about Matt and his seed, I

thought maybe he wouldn't be so easy to get into bed. I sipped some more coffee and I said, 'Sure.'

She picked up the portable from the table, and I went into the living room and got on the extension.

'Hey, there,' she smiled at him when he answered the phone.

'Connie,' he said. He was surprised, he was eager.

'That's right.'

'I've been waiting for you to call.'

His weakness disgusted me.

'Oh,' she said in mock dismay, 'I'm sorry to keep you waiting.'

'It's all right,' he said quickly.

She smiled again. 'Am I worth the wait?' she said.

He said, 'Well worth it. What have you been doing?'

'Oh,' she said again, 'Wiley's sick.'

'I know.'

'I can't see him for at least a week.'

'What will you do?'

She paused to let him think about it. Then she said, 'Do you really want to know?'

He cleared his throat. He said, 'Of course.'

'I'll confess, then,' she said. 'I'll confess what I do when Wiley's not here.'

He said, 'What is it?' I wanted to hear this too. I leaned forward, sitting on the sofa, and listened closely.

She said, 'I look at sexy pictures.'

'Of what?' he said.

She said, 'I look at pictures of women sucking men's—' and she stopped.

'Men?' he said.

She said, 'No, men's —'

He caught his breath. 'Men's what?' he said.

She paused a moment, then said quickly, blurting it out, 'Dicks. I look at pictures of women sucking dicks.'

There was a long quiet while he imagined her looking at these pictures, and I imagined it too, and when he spoke again his voice was tight and a little strained. 'Where do you get such pictures?' he asked.

'Off computer bulletin boards around town,' she said. 'They're graphics files, I've got them on my computer.'

'Does Wiley know about them?'

'I got some for him, too. Pictures of women. I gave them to him so he could tell me how much better I look than they do.'

She laughed, and then became serious again. 'But he doesn't know about these other pictures.'

There was a long silence, and then Matt said, 'It's good that you confess this.'

'I thought it would be,' she said. 'I've been thinking I ought to tell you about it.'

'This is just the sort of thing the Ministry exists to address,' he said. 'Do you do anything in particular while you look at these pictures?'

'Yes,' she said, and she waited.

'You must tell me,' he said.

'Well,' she said slowly, 'I get them on the computer screen and I sit in front of it and I pull up my dress and take down my panties and I imagine Wiley's cock in my mouth and I —'

'Yes?' he said quickly.

'Can I tell you?'

'You must tell me everything, child,' he said. 'You must.'

She said, quietly, 'I look at the pictures and I think about Wiley and I play with myself.'

'You abuse yourself,' he corrected her.

'I masturbate,' she said.

He sighed. I was a little hard, and I wondered if it were true.

She said, 'Am I bad?'

'You must be saved,' he said.

She said, 'Can you save me?'

'You must be saved from yourself.' You could see him shaking his head gravely.

'Save me,' she cried, and she began to cry real tears. I was astonished at the social engineering: she sobbed on the other end of the line, she begged, 'You must save me.'

'I don't know if I can,' he said. 'You are so far gone in carnality.'

'Carnality,' she cried.

He said, 'You covet the man's seed. You must learn that it may be received only in a state of grace.'

She said thickly, through tears, 'How can I get grace?'

'It can be granted to you,' he said. 'The Ministry provides.'

We'll all come when Matt says so, I thought, like mother-may-I.

'Please,' she said, 'grant me grace.'

'I will, child,' he said softly.

'How?' she said. 'What do I have to do?'

'We must meet,' he said.

And then she made her move, she said very softly, like a little girl, 'Oh, I've always wanted to meet you. From the very first I've wanted to, you know, be with you.'

'Be with me?' he said.

'I want to show you all my appreciation,' she said. 'All of it. In person. In the flesh. You know?'

I imagined his flesh, old and discoloured with age, and his mind and what it had done to him, loathsome, husbanding his seed for the magazine, the radio, the money. I shivered.

He said, 'We must be together for me to grant you grace.'

'Oh, good,' she said. 'That's exactly what I've always dreamed about.'

And then he said softly, slowly, preying on her words, 'Tell me about your dreams, child.'

She began to speak, tentatively, like the child he called her. 'Well, you know, I dream about you sometimes. In the night. And when I do, I wake up, and then I go into the computer and I look at pictures and I think.'

'You think,' he said, and her thinking was full of delight and made me harder. I knew her thinking, I knew what it did to me, I loved what it did to me, and I did not want to give it to him, not for the hack, not for anything.

She said slowly, 'I look at the pictures, and I pull up my nightgown, and I think.' She measured the words out for him, one at a time, her voice was tense, she was working hard, hacking him, hacking me. 'I think about you.' She said the word long and luxuriously. She said, 'I put my fingers all the way inside me, and I move them all around, and I think about you.' *You*, like soft music, like a silk scarf winding between her legs, and I knew that she was talking to me, that was why she had me listen, so she could say these things to him, and I wanted to stop her, I wanted to hang up, and I wanted to hear her, too, I wanted to hear her say these things to me.

She said, like a little girl asking for Christmas, 'Please tell me we can be together soon. I love you,' she said hungrily, her voice raw with feeling. 'I love you bad.'

'You should love the Ministry,' he said. 'The Ministry is the grace and the life.'

I was very hard. I put the receiver down on the sofa carefully, quietly, and I lay down and I felt my cock hard for her between the folds of my robe and I wanted to die.

Later, I heard her cry out, 'Ciao!' and in a moment she came into the living room carrying the coffee pot. She sat down on the sofa with me. 'Got him,' she said, smiling. 'Colony Square Hotel on the twentieth. A week from Saturday.'

I poured myself a fresh cup and sat looking at her. Her face was flushed and triumphant, she was hacking and winning, she smiled bigger and said, 'Did you hear him when I told him I couldn't see him this Saturday?' She laughed.

I said, 'What if we're still contagious?'

She shrugged. 'I'll tease him along,' she said. 'I'll have to hack it.'

I smiled in spite of myself, impressed, and then I said, 'You really do that, don't you?'

'Do what?'

'Masturbate over me.'

She smiled proudly, and she looked lovely, vibrant with life. 'I really do that, honey,' she said. 'Would you like to watch me some time?'

'Yes,' I said immediately, and I lifted my coffee to my lips, it was hot and sweetly black, 'I'd like to see you come that way.' I wanted to fuck her again, a feeling for her hard and soft all at once.

'All right,' she said softly. 'I'll show you.'

But I thought of Matt again, feeding on her, and I said, 'Are you going to show him, too?'

'Don't think about him, honey,' she smiled. 'He's just a hack.'

I drank the coffee and set the cup down and I tried to hack her, I turned to her and said, as softly as I could, 'I don't want you to let him fuck you.'

'He's not going to fuck me,' she said. 'I'm going to fuck him. You know: *Fuck you, Matt Brackett!*'

Her fine distinctions annoyed me, but I tried to stay smooth, I pleaded with her gently. 'I don't want you to do it,' I said.

She stared at me, she couldn't believe I was serious. She said, 'It's the whole point of the hack.'

I said, 'But I don't want you fucking him.'

'Why do you think I've done all this?' she said, losing patience with me, her hand spread open in the air before me, holding the hack there in her palm.

'Look,' I said, reasoning, reaching for something that might stop her, 'You could catch something.'

She laughed out loud, her head rocked back and her breasts shook through the bathrobe.

'You could,' I said. 'You've got AIDS now. Your immune system is down.'

She said, 'You heard Carl say it was strong.'

I said again firmly, 'I don't want you to fuck him.'

She studied me a moment. 'You're jealous,' she said, finally. 'You want me all to yourself.'

I sat on the sofa and looked across the room at the computer screen, little windows opened across it, her pictures were there, I wanted to see her masturbate to her pictures, I wanted to fuck her, I wanted anything but this. I said, 'That's not it.'

'Yes, it is.'

I turned to her. 'What if it is?'

She smiled, she knew she was right, and she was pleased to be right, and pleased that I was jealous. She said, 'You're sweet, that's what it is', and she reached and touched my cheek.

I covered her hand with my own and rubbed my face against her flesh. I tried another tack. 'Do you realise what the odds are on your giving him HIV?' I said.

She shrugged.

'It's one chance in a hundred per sexual exposure,' I said. 'I read that in Finder. And it's seventeen times harder for a woman to give HIV to a man than it is for a man to give it to her.'

'Women always get the shitty end of things,' she said.

I said, 'That's got nothing to do with it.'

'It doesn't matter,' she said and she drank her coffee. 'I'm going to give it to him. I know it. And even if I don't infect him, I'm going to scare the piss out of him. I'm going to show him his ass is up for grabs just like everybody else's.'

'You can actually do it?' I said. 'You can actually fuck this dirty old man?'

She looked determined. 'Confusion can do it,' she said. 'Confusion is a number one hacker.'

'Christ,' I said, and I looked at her with quiet astonishment, overmastered by Confusion, out-hacked.

'Look,' she said, laying her hand on my knee, 'it'll all be over a week from Saturday night.'

I sighed. I said, 'Saturday.'

'Well,' she said, 'Sunday morning.'

I turned to her, I said, 'If you get there and he's got that gun with him, you get out of there.'

She smiled.

'I mean it,' I said.

'I know you do.'

'Don't fuck with that gun.'

'I never fuck with guns, honey,' she said, still smiling and squeezing my knee. 'I always fuck with my cunt.'

Chapter 55

I was in my sun room working on my manuscript early Wednesday morning when Margaret called. I was deep into a love scene and I didn't want to stop working, but she was upset, she sounded like she had been crying, and I turned from the computer and listened to her talk. I sipped my coffee and tried to imagine her crying, and I couldn't.

'I've got your fucking tuberculosis,' she said, her voice thick with hurt accusation. 'I've got this fucking red lump on my forearm and my lungs are *scarred*, my doctor said. *Lesions*, she said, she used that word, *lesions*.'

'Where are you?' I said. 'Are you at the office?'

'No, I'm not at the office,' she said, annoyed by the question. 'I'm at home. I'm fucking contagious.'

'I'm sorry, Margaret,' I said. 'Did your doctor give you some meds?'

'I started taking them yesterday,' she said. 'They make me sick and I can't eat.'

'I'm sorry,' I said again, but as I said it I realised it wasn't true, I was glad to see her in a situation she couldn't control.

'Oh, you're sorry,' she said, thoroughly irritated with me. 'Why did you have to give me this fucking disease?'

'Well, hell, Margaret,' I said, a little irritated myself, 'somebody gave it to me, too, you know?'

'Oh, fuck it,' she said, tired of it all.

'That's the best attitude to take,' I said, 'believe me.'

'How can you be so calm about this?'

'I've been through this kind of thing before.'

'You've had TB before?' She was shocked.

'No,' I said, 'I broke my back once and was in the hospital for a year.'

'A whole year?' she said. She was impressed.

I told her about it.

'What did you do for a whole year?'

'I read a lot of books and watched old movies.'

'I can't do that,' she said, bitter. 'I can't just wait it out.'

I knew she couldn't do that, and I felt strong, possessing knowledge of her. I said, 'You crave action, Margaret.'

I startled her; she said, 'You think this is funny.'

I smiled, I felt good, fucking with her head, I said, 'I like to see you out of control.'

'You think this is fucking funny,' she said again. 'You don't know. This is fucking scary, Wiley. What if this stuff resists the drugs?'

'I know,' I said. 'I read about it in Finder.'

She said quickly, 'Did you read about this Strain W they've found?'

'I just read the historical summary,' I said. 'It used to kill a lot of people, back before antibiotics.'

'It still kills a lot of people,' she said. 'This Strain W is resistant to all of the drugs.'

Her words went straight through me. She had been trying to touch me and now she had, I felt a little coil of uncertainty curl up in my heart and the coffee sat light and sickly on my empty stomach. I thought of Alix, I saw her face, white, green eyes, red lips, soft, without any protection.

'So the only way to treat it,' she went on, 'is to give you all the fucking drugs at the same time.'

'Christ,' I said, worried now and wanting a cigarette, a drink. 'That could really make you sick.'

'Right,' she said, 'and even then, it still kills half the people who get it.'

The uncertainty turned to dread, and I sat back in the chair and held the phone tightly. 'What's this called again?' I could not let this happen to Alix. I could not stop it.

'Strain W,' she said. 'They've got it in New York.'

'Well, has it turned up here?'

'No,' she said, 'not yet.'

'Not yet,' I repeated the words. 'Do they think it will? What does the CDC say?'

'Fuck, Wiley,' she said, 'you know doctors. They have to have answers for everything, and they don't even know why aspirin works. Of course it'll turn up here. Just give it time.'

Time, Alix had said, we've got lots of time. And it could be quality time. Maybe it would be agony time. TB patients coughed up blood, didn't they? rich, red arterial blood, and the sky was white above me with clouds outside the sun-room window. Schumacher had said on Monday that we'd know about the strain's resistance by today, and I got a red pen from the desk and wrote a note across one of the pages of the printed manuscript to call him. I said to Margaret, 'When do you find out about your susceptibility?'

'Friday,' she said.

That was quick, I thought. 'Don't tell me,' I said. 'Your doctor sent the sputum sample to this fast lab out in Cobb County.'

'That's right. They use PCR there. It's expensive. How did you know?'

'We should all buy some stock in that lab,' I said. 'It's a coming thing.'

She was silent a moment, and then she said insistently, 'Are you scared now?'

'Yes, Margaret,' I said, and she pissed me off, 'I'm scared. Are you glad I'm scared?'

'Well, you ought to be fucking scared,' she said, angry with me, angry with TB.

I still wanted a cigarette, and there wasn't one. I picked at the nail of my little finger with my thumb. I said, 'Well, I'm fucking scared.'

'Good,' she said, she sounded angry and glad, all at once. 'Have you heard from your Miss Phone lately?'

The question made me apprehensive, her knowing about Connie had brought her closer to the truth about Alix and me and Matt, and I knew she wanted something and I was afraid of what it could be. 'Monday night,' I said.

'Was it good?' she said.

'She's always good,' I said, making up Margaret's version of Miss Phone as I went along.

'As good as me?' She had to be first, she had to be on top, and I felt hard and strong when she called herself that, but I was still afraid of what she wanted. I said, 'You're good in a different way.'

'I really get you off, don't I?' she smiled.

'Yes,' I said, I admitted it to her.

'You really get me off, too, Daddy,' she said, her voice very soft and vulnerable, and it fell even softer as she said, 'Has she talked to Matt lately?'

I shifted uncomfortably in the desk chair; we were getting closer to what she wanted. 'I think she called him Monday night,' I said. 'Yeah, she said she did.'

'I'd like to meet her,' she said.

I shook my head quickly at the whole idea. 'She won't meet you,' I said. 'She's not into women.'

'How do you know?' she said, and she sounded open and ready and sexy.

'I just don't think she is,' I said weakly.

291

'Well, I don't want her to turn me on,' she laughed. 'I just want to do some business.'

'What sort of business?' It was getting deeper and deeper and I didn't want it.

'Matt's sort of business,' she said, and I felt a little nauseated at the mention of his name. 'I want to cut a deal for a little information.'

I tried to think. I glanced at the computer screen and thought of how simple my life had been before the accident, before AIDS. I longed for it, I wanted to be somewhere with Alix far away, like Robert Louis Stevenson gone off to Samoa, South Pacific breezes blowing through South Pacific palms, 'Tusitala,' the Story Teller. But I had to tell Margaret something, I said, 'I'll see if she'll call you.'

She thought it over. 'All right,' she said at last, and then, slowly, 'What are you wearing?'

My cock stirred beneath the folds of my robe, and I heard the back door open, I turned and looked at the doorway into the kitchen, and I said, 'I can't talk right now. Someone's here.'

'Is it Alix?' she said, her voice suddenly edged with a tense displeasure. 'Has she been listening?' Deep suspicion coloured her voice.

I said, 'I'll have to call you back.'

'Get rid of her,' she said, angry again.

I said, 'I'll call you,' and I hung up the phone just before Alix stepped into the living room behind me. She saw me watching the doorway and she smiled and raised a hand and waved. She wore faded cutoffs and a plain white, sleeveless boxer's T, and she carried a cup of coffee and brushed a hand through her long red hair.

She came into the sun room and said, 'Are you writing?'

'Yes,' I said. I looked up at her; her nipples were dark sweet circles through the white cotton.

'I won't disturb you, then,' she said. 'But I want a good-morning kiss.' She bent and put her hand on my shoulder and I lifted my face to her and we kissed, and I was still hard. I kissed her deeply, she tasted of coffee, and she murmured and reached between my legs and felt me and broke the kiss and smiled and glanced at the computer screen and said, 'What are you writing, anyway?'

Chapter 56

Eating tuna salad sandwiches in the kitchen at lunch, Alix looked at me curiously and said, 'Lift your arm.'

'What?' I said, in the middle of biting into the sandwich.

'Your armpit is orange,' she said.

I had on a white shirt, and I glanced down into my armpit, and she was right, there was a sweat stain encircled by a ring of bright orange. 'That's weird,' I said.

'TB,' she said, and looked grim, sitting there with her sandwich in her hands and her elbows on the table, looking at me.

I shrugged and bit into the sandwich. 'If it's TB, then it'll go away,' I said, and I chewed the sandwich and said between bites, as casually as I could, 'Margaret Divine wants to talk to Connie Phone.'

'She does?' she said, eating now. 'How does she know Connie?'

Good question, I thought, and I hoped my answer was as good. 'She overheard Matt ask me about her.'

'And?'

I shrugged. 'And I told her.'

She set her sandwich down and leaned forward. She said, 'What did you tell her?'

I said, 'Matt's into phone sex.'

She couldn't believe I'd told Margaret; she said, 'You told her about the Ministry?'

'No, no,' I said, shaking my head. 'I embroidered it. I said I met this woman, Connie Phone, who was into phone sex.'

She listened carefully. 'And?'

'And Margaret said she liked kinky people.' I broke out in a sudden sweat and I couldn't think. I bit quickly into the sandwich and chewed it, it was dry in my mouth and I wanted to gag. Alix waited impatiently for the rest of the story, she prompted me: 'So Margaret likes you.'

'Margaret's kinky, I think,' I said, picking up my glass of milk and trying to wash down the sandwich. 'So I told her, hey, Matt's into it too.'

She smiled slightly, amused that the employees were seeing the boss with no clothes on. 'What did she say?'

'At first she didn't believe it, but I said Connie had told me so herself.'

She smiled bigger, her eyebrows arched, and she picked up her sandwich again. 'Then what did she say?'

'Then she said she wanted to meet you.'

'Not good.'

'No, I told her you only did business by phone.'

'Good,' she said. 'What's she want?'

'She says she wants to cut a deal for a little information.'

'Oh, shit,' she said, and she rolled her eyes upward. 'That's what that private detective said that got me arrested five years ago.'

'You don't have to call her,' I said, and I had an excited hope that she wouldn't.

She said, 'She wants tapes, I'll bet. She wants to blackmail him.'

I had thought about this, and I didn't like it. 'That wouldn't surprise me,' I said. I set the rest of the sandwich down, I had lost my appetite.

'We'll call her,' she said.

My stomach twisted. 'Are you sure you want to?'

'Sure,' she said. 'You'll both talk to her, you and Connie.'

'Why both of us?' I didn't want to talk to her with Connie listening.

'You talk to her about Finder, and Connie'll talk to her about Matt.'

I didn't want this, my stomach was sick. I asked, 'What for?'

She put her elbows on the table, rested her face in her hands and looked directly at me, her eyebrows raised. 'You'll tape her,' she said.

Chapter 57

'How are you going to do it?' I said.

We sat on the sofa in the living room with her tape deck between us. The afternoon was warm and we were damp with sweat; the fan oscillated on her desk. She wore a boxer's T-shirt and her breasts showed teasingly. The phone lay in her lap and she held up a small cylindrical microphone with a suction cup at one end of it. 'This sticks on the phone,' she said, and she licked the suction cup and attached it behind the earpiece of the handset. 'No wires to the equipment, so there's nothing to pick up.' She plugged the other end into the tape deck, set it to record, then picked up the handset and dialled a number. I heard the phone ringing through the earpiece, then somebody picked up and talked for a moment. She hung up, turned off the tape deck, rewound it, and played it back for me. 'Lonely?' said a male Southern voice. 'Confused? Visit Briarlake Baptist Church this Sunday. Services at eleven, Sunday school at nine.' The voice changed to a professional announcer's. 'The time is 1.34 p.m.,' he said. 'The temperature is 94 degrees.' She punched the stop button and rewound the tape again.

'It's called a pick-up mike,' she said, and she punched the record button again, hitting pause along with it. She was ready. 'Now, is Margaret at work?'

I shook my head. 'She's at home.'

'She's not working?'

'She's taking a day off.' I didn't want her to know Margaret had TB, too, I didn't want her to put us together, but my stomach flopped when I lied to her.

'You dial her and talk a while. Talk about Finder,' she said.

'What if she doesn't want to talk about it?'

'She'll talk about it when you tell her the delivery may be screwed up because we're sick.'

'OK,' I said, thinking about it, 'that sounds plausible.'

'It is plausible,' she said. She held the handset out for me to see, I could hear the dial tone, and she pointed to a small button marked CONF just beneath the dial. 'This is for conference calling. After you get her on the tape talking about Finder, tell her you're going to call Connie. Then punch this button. She's made conference calls before for sure, and she'll recognise it and think you're dialling Connie. After I pick up the extension,

295

punch it again, and we'll all be on the line together. Then we'll nail her.'

She impressed me, as usual. I sat back on the sofa and said, 'You know, you're a lot like Margaret.'

She glanced at me and set the phone down. 'Hey,' she said, smiling, 'I'm a real bitch.' She hit the pause button and the tape started running. She sat back and handed me the phone. 'Dial her up,' she said.

Chapter 58

Margaret picked up on the fourth ring. 'Hello,' I said, 'how are you?' I shouldn't have said that, I thought, she might say something about TB. My stomach was uneasy and I wondered if it were all the tension, or if the TB medicine were affecting me, too.

Margaret ignored my formality. 'I thought you'd never call,' she said impatiently.

'Yeah, well, I'm sorry about that,' I said, and I rushed to get into Finder before she could say anything about Alix and the call that morning. 'I called as soon as I could. I talked to Alix about Finder this morning.'

'Finder?' she said, suddenly alert. 'What about it?'

'Well, we're both sick, you know,' I said.

'Yeah, so?' She didn't get it.

'So that might screw up the timetable for delivery to you.'

'Oh, shit,' she said, her voice sinking. 'Christ, I hate this fucking tuberculosis.'

'Me, too,' I said. 'So does Alix.'

'Well, when can I get it?' She was exasperated.

'That's just it,' I said. 'We don't know when we won't be quarantined any more. You'll have to wait until we're not contagious.'

'Oh, fuck,' she said. 'I wanted it sooner than that. I really wanted to get Divine Intelligence going this month.'

'I know.'

'I want to get the fuck away from that old son of a bitch.'

Alix sat back against some pillows in the corner of the sofa, listening on the portable. She raised her head to me quickly and mouthed the word, *Who?*

I said, 'You mean Matt?'

'Who the hell else would I mean?'

'That's who I thought you meant,' I said. I felt inept, a second-rank hacker. I was sweating, and when I swallowed, my stomach seemed to feel better. I said, 'What are you going to give Alix for this, anyway?'

'What does she want?' she said, annoyed with the question.

'Money,' I said immediately, thinking about AIDS, about doctors and hospitals and drugs and bills. Alix looked at me and nodded thoughtfully.

'I'll give her some money, then,' she said.

Alix nodded again. 'Lots of money,' I said. 'Finder's worth lots of money. A piece of the company.'

'A piece of the company?' She didn't like it.

'Unless you can front lots of money right now,' I said. 'Otherwise, she'll take it over time.'

'When did you become her agent?'

I didn't like the question, Margaret knew about me and Alix. I said, 'I look out for Alix.' Alix smiled at me, and I felt a little better, taking care of her.

'All right,' Margaret said, shaking me off. 'A piece of the company. I'll have to see what I can do. Is this why you called?' She was annoyed: TB was screwing up her plans, and she wanted the other, too, I knew, she wanted Daddy to get her off. My stomach turned again at the thought, and I tore nervously at the cuticle of my thumb with the nail of my index finger.

I said, 'You wanted to talk to Miss Phone, didn't you?'

'You've got her?' she said, suddenly excited again. 'She's there?'

'I've got a conference line,' I said. 'She's waiting on it.'

'All right,' she said, eager for it. 'Have you been talking with her?'

Alix grinned.

I sweated and tore at my thumbnail. I said, 'Do you want to talk to Connie?' I turned to Alix. She sat in the corner of the sofa holding the portable phone and listening closely, her face concentrated on the call.

Margaret said, 'Let's have her.'

'Wait just a minute,' I said, and I pressed the conference call button. Alix held up a finger to wait for a moment, then nodded, and I pressed the button again and put the handset to my ear.

Alix held the portable to her ear and said in Connie's voice, innocent but sexy, like a teenage girl with a filthy mind, like, I thought, Anne Mathers, 'Miss Divine? Can you hear me?'

'Yes, dear,' said Margaret.

'I'm here, too,' I said.

'Hey,' said Connie, warming to the conference call, 'we could maybe get into some neat group stuff here.'

I felt sick and I shook my head at her quickly, and she laughed and sat back against the pillows in the corner of the sofa.

Margaret said, 'Wiley tells me you're a friend of Mr Brackett's.'

'Mr Brackett's just a wonderful man,' said Connie.

'You don't have to tell me,' said Margaret. 'I know.'

'Of course, I've only talked with him on the phone,' said Connie.

Margaret said, 'It's safer that way.'

Connie laughed again. 'Hey,' she said, 'you pick up on me pretty fast.'

'Yes,' Margaret said.

'Wiley said you were smart that way.'

'Thank you, Wiley,' said Margaret. 'He said you were quick, too, Miss Phone.'

'Call me Connie.'

'Connie.'

'That's short for Constance. I'm constant,' she said.

Margaret said, 'You're dependable, then?'

Connie thought a moment. I picked at my fingernails. She sat in the corner of the sofa with her legs crossed and her head down, concentrating on the hack, and she said, soft and sincere, 'You can trust me, Miss Divine.'

'Margaret.'

'Sure,' she smiled. 'Everyone I talk to trusts me. Isn't that so, Wiley?'

'You can trust Connie with your life, Margaret,' I said quickly, and I realised that, in fact, I did.

'That's good,' said Margaret, she was calculating, she was weighing things. 'I wouldn't be interested in you if I couldn't trust you.'

'You're interested in me?' What an idea. I felt feverish now, sweating and feverish, I had torn some flesh free from the edge of my thumbnail, and I bit it and pulled the skin away.

'Very,' said Margaret, emphasising the word.

'Really?' said Connie. 'What for?'

'Wiley's told me about your little preoccupation with the telephone.'

Connie laughed. 'Hey,' she said, 'I just really dig telephones.'

'Oh, I like them, too,' said Margaret happily. 'How do you feel about tape recorders?'

The tape turned silently in the deck on the sofa between us. Connie spoke like a child, 'You know what, Margaret?' she said. 'You must be positively psychic. Because I've thought about that before, you know?'

'You have?' said Margaret. 'What did you think about it?'

Connie laughed again, softly, cautious. She said, 'Well . . .' she drew the word out long before she went on, 'I've thought a girl in my position, so to speak, could really do a lot for herself with a little tape recording now and then.'

Margaret said, 'You've no idea how true that is.'

'But there's a side to it that's always scared me, too,' said Connie.

'I understand,' said Margaret.

'You do?'

'Certainly. You're a sensitive person.'

'That's right,' said Connie; someone had recognised it at last.

'What you need is some insensitive person to handle the scary part,' said Margaret. 'That's where I would come in.'

'Oh,' said Connie, a big, unbelieving *oh*, 'I think you're very sensitive.'

'Well, thank you,' said Margaret, 'but I know how to be, shall we say, firm.'

Connie said, 'I'm not very firm, that's true.'

Margaret went ahead. 'I want you to handle the sensitive parts,' she said. 'Wiley tells me you're very good at the sensitive parts.'

Connie laughed, her green eyes laughed, she said, 'Well, he has very sensitive parts, you know?'

Margaret laughed, too. 'Yes, I do,' she said.

Connie paused. 'You do?' she said, a little curious.

I said quickly, 'What about the tape? Do you know how to work it, Connie?' I looked down at my fingers and saw blood all over my thumb.

Connie looked at me curiously, but she answered, 'No. Do you?' Her eyes fell to my hand, and she pointed at the bloody thumbnail and backed away from me into the pillows in the corner of the sofa.

'I don't,' I said. I sucked the blood off my thumb, it was warm and salty. 'I don't know anything about that technology.'

'I have a man who can show you all about it,' said Margaret, everything under control. 'A private detective who's worked for me before.'

Connie spoke up quickly. 'What's his name?' she said. She reached to a box of Kleenex on the end table, got one and passed it to me. I wrapped my thumb in it.

'Darrell Manes,' said Margaret. 'Why?'

'Oh, I knew a private detective once,' said Connie. 'I thought maybe it was the same guy.'

'Is it?'

'No,' she said, 'and that's good. Mine was a real motherfucker.'

'Darrell is a professional,' said Margaret.

Connie said, 'I like professionals.'

'So do I,' Margaret smiled.

'Wiley is a professional, you know,' said Connie.

'Yes, I know,' said Margaret. 'Wiley is quite adept at everything he does.'

Connie said, '*Adept*. What's that mean?'

Margaret save a small laugh. 'That means he has a natural talent and he refines it a lot.'

'Oh,' said Connie, 'I like refinements.'

'That's my favourite part too,' said Margaret, and she was smiling, but I couldn't tell who she was smiling at.

I smiled weakly, I felt everything sinking around me, inside me, I looked at the bright red bloodstain on the Kleenex and I said, 'Practice makes perfect', ever the incompetent hacker. I closed my eyes and thought, I said, 'What's this Manes' phone number? So Connie can call him.'

Margaret said, 'Well, Connie, don't you want me to send him around, to set everything up for you?'

I looked at her. Connie had TB too, and Margaret couldn't know it. She was quick, she said, 'I prefer to do everything over the phone, Margaret.'

Margaret paused, she hadn't expected this.

'I told you that,' I said to her.

Connie said, 'I'll call him and get the directions. I'm good with directions. Wiley can tell you that.'

'Well, all right,' said Margaret, and she gave her Manes' phone number. Connie picked up a ballpoint from the coffee table but had no paper so she wrote the number across the inside of her thigh, the blue ink smeared a little in the sweat, the numbers large and pale across her smooth white skin. Margaret said, 'You're going to call me tomorrow, Wiley?'

I thought it was almost over, there was only a little more lying to be done. 'That's right,' I said.

'You promise?' she said.

'Scout's honour.'

She said, 'All right. I'm really looking forward to it, you know. So pleasant to meet you, Connie. I'm sure we're going to get alone famously.' She hung up.

'Call her?' said Alix. She sat cross-legged in the corner of the sofa, holding the portable in her hand. 'Why do you have to call her?'

'The members' magazine,' I said. I wanted a cigarette badly. 'We've been working on it, and this TB has screwed up the roll-out.'

'Oh,' she said. 'You're the editor? She said you're an editor.'

'Of the members' magazine,' I said, and I was grateful for the AIDS Research Council. 'Christ,' I said, 'I'd give anything to have a beer.'

She pointed at my bandaged thumb. 'You better watch that biting your fingernails,' she said. 'You shouldn't bleed around me.'

'I'll get a Band-Aid.'

'Gloves,' she said. 'I've got some latex gloves. You'll have to wear one.'

'A glove?' I said. 'Really?'

She said, 'You could die from that, honey. You really could.'

Chapter 59

We were resistant to the rifampin, but Carl said it didn't matter, the other three drugs would kill the infection, given enough time.

'And my sweat's staining my shirts orange,' I said. I sat on one side of the kitchen table and Alix sat on the other, listening on the portable. I wore the thumb, cut from a yellow latex glove, over my left thumb.

'That's the isoniazid,' he said. 'I forgot to mention that.'

'What can I do about it?' I said.

'You got any tank tops?' he said. 'Wear tank tops. Wear sleeveless shirts.'

'We sweat fucking orange?' said Alix, annoyed that there was nothing to be done.

'You're sick, you've got TB,' said Carl. 'You want to get well? You sweat fucking orange. You just have to accept it.'

She said, 'That's fine for you to say, Carl.'

'Alix,' I said, and I shook my head at her.

'Fucking orange,' she said. 'What the fuck are we supposed to do? Body paint? This shit ruined a Calvin Klein blouse, Carl. Calvin Klein.'

'I'm sorry,' he said. 'I just forgot, when I was going over the side effects.'

'It doesn't wash out.'

'I'm sorry,' he said again. 'Wear your bathing suits. It's hot enough, and you don't have to go out.'

'Can't,' she corrected him. 'Can't go out.'

'Alix,' he said, and there was a firmness in his voice that had been there when he talked to her about time, 'You'll just have to live with it, and the keyword is *live*. Do you understand me?'

'Live,' she said.

'That's right,' he said.

'Well,' she said, 'I'm taking the price of a Calvin Klein off your next bill.'

Chapter 60

I sat in my sun room watching the evening sun go down and drinking a sweating glass of iced herb tea and wishing it were a drink and wishing, too, that I had a cigarette, staring at my computer. The novel was onscreen and I did not feel anything like a writer. Alix was soaking in the tub downstairs and reading a James M. Cain thriller, the blurb on the cover actually said *thriller*. I picked up the phone from the desk and dialled the Ritz-Carlton and asked to speak to Ms Dresden.

The girl said, 'Ms Dresden checked out this morning, sir.'

I sat up. I couldn't believe she would leave without telling me. 'Where did she go?' I said. 'Did she leave a forwarding notice?'

'Oh, yes, sir,' said the clerk. 'She's just moved to the Colony Square Hotel, to be closer to her work.'

She was in room 814 at Colony Square. 'You're two blocks from where I live,' I told her.

'Fantastic,' she said. 'Are you still contagious?'

'As far as I know.'

'Too bad,' she said. 'When you're over it, we'll go for walks in that big park down the street.'

'That's right across from my apartment.'

'Good,' she said, she was looking forward to it. 'I've got some more to teach you about older women, don't I?'

'I guess so.'

And she laughed and said, 'Older women are so grateful.'

'Margaret talks about gratitude.'

'She's like me.'

I said immediately, 'No she's not.'

My objection caught her interest. She said, 'Why do you say that?'

'Margaret's an absolute whore.'

You don't think I'm a whore.'

'Of course not.'

'You know, 'she said,' your mother thinks I'm a whore.'

'She's on Valium all the time.' And it occurred to me, it bothered me, so I asked about it. 'Has Nathaniel ever called you that?'

She paused, she was weighing something, and I waited. At First I couldn't believe he would call her that, and then I could. 'Once,' she said finally, 'when he was very upset.'

Drunk, you mean,' I said. 'Jesus.'

'No,' she said, 'Jesus likes whores.' And she laughed.

'You're not a whore, Sarah.'

She sighed. 'No, I'm not,' she said. There was a moment of silence, and then she said quietly, 'I love you, you know.'

I felt warm and uncomfortable and pleased and exultant, all at the same time. I felt like I could take her away from him, and I wanted to, and it scared me to want it.

She went on, quietly and calmly, 'If you're not careful, I'll come after you.' Her voice was steady and even.

I laughed, a little nervously.

She said, 'I'd get you too. You couldn't get away from me if I wanted you.'

'You're right,' I said, I meant it. And at that moment I realised Sarah could save me from Margaret and from AIDS, if not from death itself: she could paint and I could write and we could be poor beautiful lovers together in a dream of art far away, in a long hot summer night, perpetually cooling into welcome darkness. I said, 'I wouldn't want to.'

'Oh, sweet,' she said, and her voice was full of a soft ache that I thought I understood. I thought I felt it too.

I said, 'Let's give the TB a week to get better and go ahead and make a date.'

'Yes,' she said. 'What about next Saturday?'

'All right,' I said, without thinking, and then realised that was when Connie was meeting Matt, but she was already saying, 'Wonderful!' and I let it go. The TB would still be active, I thought, and it would all become academic, and then she said, 'And if the TB is still around, I'll just have to risk it, that's all,' and I wondered how I would explain my date to Alix, or to the Public Health, whoever asked first.

'I'll rescue you,' she said. 'I've always wanted to rescue you.'

I laughed. 'From TB?'

'From Nathaniel.'

'That's who I want to rescue you from.'

'Maybe we should rescue each other, then,' she smiled. 'How can we do it?'

305

Chapter 61

Alix spent the evenings as Connie, taping Matt for Margaret, while I played Doom endlessly on her computer. The violence of the game suited my sickness and my boredom, I slaughtered the enemy wildly and I died with abandon, because I could die over and over.

Margaret was the tricky part. She wanted me to call her every day, so I would go upstairs in the mornings to write and finish the sessions by calling her up and getting her off. 'You're wonderful,' she said one morning when we were done. 'I want to read your book. You have such a fabulous imagination.'

I usually felt like fucking after I talked Margaret off, and I would go back downstairs and approach Alix. She smiled at me one morning as I took her in my arms, and she said, 'What is it about writing that gets you so hot, honey?' and she fondled me through the folds of my robe. 'I like it,' she said.

But everything ages rapidly when it is compulsory, and all our actions were compelled by our isolated waiting for the antibiotics to work. I wanted things. I wanted cigarettes and alcohol, and I wanted movies and walks in the park and trips to the grocery store and rides in the car. I wanted to go to a book store and open a book of poems and smell the new ink and fresh paper. I felt like somebody's sick dog that couldn't go outside till he was better. I would step out on the landing behind the apartment and look at the city across the roofs of Midtown, holding on to the railing hard and full of yearning, and Alix would lie for hours in the sun on her recliner beside the back door.

She handled it better than I did. She looked up at me from her chair on the porch, her body almost bare in her little red bikini and my figure reflecting back at me in her mirrored shades, and she said, 'It's like debugging a computer program. It just takes for ever to do it, that's all.' At night, we went to sleep to the sound of the little two-piece rattling around in the drier after she had washed it out.

And I handled it better than Margaret, because I'd spent that year in the hospital, so I did know a little, after all, about things that took for ever, like the mass death of bacteria.

A male nurse named Victor Polanski who wore ill-fitting suits from off the rack at Sears and Roebuck came from the Health Department once a week and took sputum samples from us and asked how we were doing. Once he came with another nurse in tow, a little blonde who made me hot her tits were so big and I was so bored. She said she had done the testing at Brackett Data the Friday before, and I asked her how it went. She said she didn't know yet, they were heading out there that afternoon to read the results.

I called Grant about 4.30 to get the news about the testing, but Marian said he had been taken to the hospital.

'The Public Health people said he might be the *index case*,' she said, and she sounded tearfully afraid. 'What's an index case?'

I saw his smiling face and his bottle of Day Care I saw the smoke rising sensually from one of his little cigars. I said, 'That's the probable source of the infection.'

'Oh, God,' she said. 'You mean Mr Cummings made every-one sick?'

'Everyone?' I said.

'Almost,' she said. 'We've got twenty-nine people working here, and they said twenty-one of them were positive, counting you and Miss Divine.'

'How's Mr Brackett?' I said.

'Oh, he's fine,' she said, and you could tell she did not think it was fair. 'Nothing ever happens to him, does it?'

'I suppose not,' I said.

She worried. 'Poor Mr Cummings,' she said. 'I just can't believe he gave this horrible disease to everyone.'

'It's OK, Marian,' I said. 'It's not like he did it on purpose.'

Chapter 62

We got the news on Friday afternoon from Victor Polanski and his little nurse with the big tits that we were no longer contagious, and we went out immediately. We walked for an hour in the park, the sun was hot and the sky was a blue dome that rang like a bell above us and we were free, we were rich Americans.

We went back to the apartment and took a shower together and went out to eat, then took in a movie about a man who couldn't come, and went to a club in Midtown. We sat drinking Virgin Marys while punk rock alternated with blues on the sound system. Alix wore her bikini top and blue jeans and long spangle earrings and some bead necklaces and her mirror shades, and I watched the other men look at her, and the women too, and I felt sexy being with her, I wanted everyone to know I fucked her.

'Tomorrow night's the night,' she said above the music. 'The Gospel gets the good news.' She sipped her drink.

'You're going to do it?'

'Wouldn't miss it for the fucking world.'

I leaned forward on the table. 'What would you miss it for?' I shouted, and the rock ended with a sudden blast of sound, and blues started up, *You better come on in my kitchen, it's goin to be rainin outdoors,* I saw myself in the lenses of her shades, along with the lights of the club and the other people moving through the room behind us.

She shook her head at me determinedly. 'No way, honey,' she said. 'I'm going to take that son of a bitch down.'

Some cigarette smoke drifted my way, and I breathed it in deeply, I wanted it, and I wanted a real drink, too.

'I'll make it up to you,' she said, looking at me with her eyes very warm and sexy and drinking her tomato juice.

We were in her car, and we drove fast out on to the interstate with the radio playing rock and roll loud and the air conditioning going full blast into our faces, and we drove around the perimeter highway, and at midnight we checked into a motel in East Point and made love on the clean sheets like a fucking machine, full of pure energy and in a water rhythm together, joined cunt and cock, in love, really in it, in love each with the other's body, the other's mind, the minds working through the sex, thinking, do this to her, do this to him, we were alive, *Mycobacterium tuberculosis* quelled within our chests, and we breathed deep and heavy and the air was sweet and clean, and we sweated tenderly over each other while the radio played the Friday night news from Georgia Tech, music that soothed us, the music of truth, *Jesus didn't want us, Jesus wanted money, Jesus wanted brass, and we didn't have any, all we had was life, and that was not good enough.*

Chapter 63

Sarah called after Alix had gone to Colony Square. I was sitting in my sun room, waiting for the call and trying without much success to concentrate on the computer, looking at the sharp little amber letters of my manuscript, so orderly across the screen, and thinking instead of Alix up the street with Matt, imagining the room and the lighting, black walls with big mirrors and a red bed with white sheets, and the covers torn up, imagining what she would do with him, hacking him with her body while he prepared her to receive his seed. I caught myself biting my nails, and I wanted to smoke and could not, and I wanted a hard drink and did not have one, and I kept imagining Matt with her and I shivered in the slowly cooling evening. I picked up the phone on the first ring, thinking it might be Alix, hoping that it would be her calling me to call it all off, and I said quickly, 'Hello?'

'Hello, sweet,' said Sarah. 'How dangerous is it to be around you now?' She was teasing and I felt good for the first time since Alix had gone to the hotel. I liked making a woman smile, I was good at it.

'Not contagious,' I said, with a sense of relief. 'Found out yesterday.'

'What did you do to celebrate?'

'Went out, of course.'

'Does that mean you don't want to celebrate with me?'

I smiled. 'Sure.'

'Oh, Wiley,' she said, 'we're going to have such a good time the rest of the summer.'

'I'm finishing the novel,' I said.

'Oh, yes? Hey, we can be artists together,' she said, 'like you always talked about.'

I used to tell her in the hospital that we would run away to Paris and create art. I had no idea then what *create art* meant. Now I laughed and I said, 'Where do you want to eat?'

'You choose,' she said. 'It's your date, and my expense account.'

'All right,' I said. 'You're at Colony Square, right?'

'Right here in Midtown,' she said. A coldness moved across me. I saw Alix with Matt, and he was old and obsessed with a gun and a fear of death, but I moved ahead with Sarah.

'You're just a couple of blocks from where I live,' I said.

'Why don't I meet you in the lobby, and we'll take it from there.'

'All right,' she said. 'Can you give me half an hour?'

'Sure.'

I took a shower and put on my khakis and a tie and a blue blazer, and walked up to Colony Square. The evening was mild, cooling off and pleasant, and I walked briskly, trying to concentrate on Sarah and not think about Alix. I went by the automatic banker in front of the building and got $100 which left me with $12 till payday, twelve days away. I went inside and walked around the lobby for a while, then sat where I could wait for Sarah and watch the staircase and the elevators, looking through an *Esquire* without reading it. I crossed and recrossed my legs and I kept thinking of Alix fucking Matt. I wanted a cigarette and didn't have one, I was surprised again at how addicted I had become to them, and I saw Alix's body in motion above his, her hips rocking, and I could see her mouth, red and round, and I tried to think instead of Sarah, she was pleasant to think about, but after a while I set the magazine aside and went to the desk. The clerk smiled at me and his eyebrows rose into a question, and I said, 'Do you have a Mr Matthew Brackett registered here?'

'Brackett?' he said.

'B-r-a-c-k-e-t-t, yes.'

He turned to a console on the desk counter and typed in the name, hunting the letters across the keyboard, and I felt someone watching me, and I looked around the lobby, seized by the sudden fear that Alix or Matt might be there, and I saw a man in a grey suit looking at me, and I wanted to know why he was watching me, and then he looked away and walked out of the lobby and I wondered whether I had imagined it, and I began to fabricate stories. Why had I come here? I could tell Matt I was meeting a woman, but what could I tell Alix? I would tell her I had come to stop her, and I began to rehearse the speeches in my head as I turned back to the clerk, who looked at his screen and said, 'No, sir, no Mr Brackett here tonight.'

And I tried to think why Alix would come down to the lobby. 'How about a Matthew?' I said. 'A Mr Matthew?'

He typed again and looked and said, 'We have a Mr G. Matthew in room 1503.'

That would be G for *Gospel*, I thought, in room 1503, trying to commit the number to memory. I was one, and Alix and Matt and Sarah and my father and I were five, and everything was adding up to zero, and Margaret and Alix and I made three, and I said to the clerk, 'G. I don't think it's a G. Thanks, anyway,' and I went back to my easy chair. I picked up my magazine again and looked at a spread of Varga girls and I thought about Alix and Matt in the room, I looked at my watch, she had been with him a couple of hours, and I wondered what she was doing, I wondered if she would do him the way she did me, and then wondered uncomfortably how much alike we were, and then I could not help but wonder if she liked it, if it felt good, even with him, or if she felt like a whore, and how a whore must feel, indifferent to her own sensations, rising above them like a good Christian lady, and whether a whore ever felt good *against her will*, and I looked up from the magazine and wondered what a whore's *will* was, and all the unanswered questions left me full of vague fears. And it occured to me, with a light and sudden relaxing of tension through my shoulders, that if anyone saw me in the lobby I could actually tell them the truth, of all things, I could tell them I was here to take my father's girlfriend out to dinner.

Then I heard Sarah call out, 'Wiley!' from across the lobby, and I looked up and saw her at the foot of the stairs. She wore a burgundy red knit top, cut low in the front, my mother dressed the same way, my father liked women with large breasts who showed them off, and a faded pair of torn blue jeans and sandals. Rings shone on her fingers, and she wore her long blonde hair pulled back tight with big golden hoops dangling from her ears, and she smiled and called my name again happily and came across the lobby with her right hand held out for me. I rose from the chair and took it, smiling back at her, and said, 'You look great, Sarah.'

'Thank you.'

'You always look great.'

'You're full of compliments tonight,' she said. 'Are you trying to turn my head?'

'Yes,' I said quickly.

She laughed, her breasts shook slightly. 'You'll probably succeed, then,' she said. 'I'm getting easier in my forties.'

'Good,' I said. 'You know I prefer older women.'

'Oh, you're marvellous,' she said, and she leaned forward and kissed me on the cheek, lingering just long enough for me to feel the warmth of her body and smell her scent, the sharp, pungent essence of oil of drakar, and I thought of Vermilion Obsession and I said, 'You've changed your perfume.'

She said, 'You noticed! You really *are* marvellous.' I wondered

312

if the change in scent meant a change in things between her and my father. Above us, Connie was sitting on the stool of the dresser: now the room was red and the bedspread was royal blue with sparkling white sheets, and she wore only a pure white bra, and she spread her legs for Matt to see and began to masturbate while he watched. Sarah looked at me, smiling, then kissed me again on the cheek. 'You're just the sweetest,' she said.

And I risked it, I said, quietly and privately, 'I like your kisses', asking her for another.

Her face lit up, her pale blue eyes shone, and she said softly, 'I like kissing you – Wiley.' She said the new name carefully, savouring it, and she kissed me again, on the lips this time, lightly, fleeting, but lingering at the same time, like she wanted more, and she drew back a bit and looked into my face and said, 'There you are.'

She had never kissed me on the mouth before. Her lips were soft and I stood a little off balance for a moment, looking into her eyes, they looked glad, she knew what she was doing, but I wasn't sure. I recovered enough to say, 'What would you like for dinner?'

She looked up at the ceiling, in a pose of thinking. 'Something expensive,' she said, 'and full of blood.'

I laughed. 'All right,' I said. 'Let's walk up to my apartment and get my car.'

I took her deeper into Midtown, to a continental place I knew on West Peachtree, and we ate *filet mignon* with escargot and she drank a split of red wine. I drank water, and she said, 'This wine is a great one. You don't want any?'

'The TB medicine doesn't mix with alcohol,' I said.

'Oh, no,' she said. 'You're still taking it?' She leaned forward a little and my eyes went to her breasts: in the air conditioning her nipples showed hard through the fabric, and her skin was deeply tanned and I knew there was no tan line.

'Six months to a year,' I said.

'That's really too bad,' she said, sipping the wine.

'It's OK,' I said, eating some steak. Her breasts came together slightly as she breathed, and Matt petted Connie, he caressed her hard nipples with his thumbs, I thought of his dark hands moving over her white body, and I hated my thinking. I lifted my water to my lips and looked down through the glass table top. Sarah's legs showed tanned through the tears in her jeans and I thought of her long smooth legs and drank some more water. Handel played on the restaurant stereo and I named the piece, *Alexander's Feast*, and slowly came back to myself.

313

She ate a piece of steak and a snail and took another long drink of wine. I watched her lips move while she savoured the food and drink. She set the glass down and said, 'I've thought about it and I much prefer Wiley to Willie.'

G. Matthew met Connie Phone at the door of room 1503. He wore a blue suit and smiled at her, and she liked his snow-white hair. She smiled back and said, 'Hi, there', and ran her right hand through it and leaned into the room and kissed him lightly on the lips. 'No,' he said, surprised at her eagerness and pulling away from her, but at the same time drawing her into the room after him. 'Not yet,' he said. He took her inside, holding her lightly by the forearm, and he closed the door behind her. 'You must prepare,' he said.

'All right,' she said. 'What do we do?'

He took off his coat and tossed it on to the back of an easy chair, and she saw the narrow holster straps of brown leather across his back and under his arm, and her stomach was empty, she had never seen a gun this close before. She nodded at it as he turned to her and said, 'What do you need that for?'

'Protection,' he said.

She looked at it. She held out her right hand and said, 'Can I touch it?'

He took it out and passed it to her. 'Don't be afraid,' he said, 'the safety's on.' She held it between her thumb and forefinger, she didn't know how to hold a gun, and she looked at it and said, 'It's smaller than I thought', as she handed it back to him, and she thought of what I had said to her: Don't fuck with the gun, she thought, and she didn't like it, but she wasn't going to leave because of it, she could handle it, she could hack it.

He had her bathe, he sent her into the bathroom alone, where she found arrayed on the counter special soaps and oils. She took off her clothes and ran the water and bathed. She took her time, she let him wait on her, she enjoyed the bath, the soaps, the oils, she lay in the water and smiled at him outside, she dried herself slowly, tenderly, and she powdered and perfumed herself. She slipped into the blue shift he had given her to wear and she looked at herself in the wall mirror. The shift ended just above her thighs and zipped down the front, she pulled the zipper up to her breasts, leaving the collar open for him to see her. She stepped out of the bathroom, and he stood there outside the door in his shirt and tie and trousers with the gun and his hands on his hips, and he went into a kind of trance, watching her. His eyes were alive, dancing nervously across the bare flesh of her collarbone and upper breast, she

*stepped back and let him look at her, and he reached and took her by
the hand, and said, 'We can begin.'*

*She followed him across the living room of the suite and into the
bedroom. He pointed at the floor near the foot of the bed, he said, 'Kneel
here, please', and she got down on her knees for him. He stood before her
with his hands on his hips and his legs a little apart, and she looked up
at him. 'Now,' he said, 'I will show you the nature of grace.'*

*He turned away from her to the bed, he rounded the corner and pulled
the spread down and tore the slip off a pillow. It was red and he drew it
taut between his hands and walked back to her holding it before him,
and she lifted her head to him and he placed it over her eyes, he said,
'Don't look at me', and the world closed down around her, he tied the
blindfold behind her head, and she lost her breath in a sudden rushing,
suffocating fear of the dark.*

*She heard him underssing, then, through the darkness, the sounds
of the gun being examined and laid down and, later, picked up again,
and then there was a silence so long that she wondered where he had
gone, and he slapped his hands together before her face and she cried
out and her hands went automatically to her eyes, and he grabbed
them and pulled her forward, saying, 'No, you mustn't look at me',
and he dragged her to the head of the bed, her knees skinned across
the carpet, and he held her two hands in one of his and she heard the
bedclothes being moved and then he drew her hands behind her back
and twined them together with the other pillowcase, and she knew it
was all going to be different from what she had expected, crazier and
beyond her control, perhaps beyond his, and she bit her lip and tensed
and tried not to think about the gun, and her stomach sank and her
heart emptied and she wanted out, and he said 'Yes' and he said, 'Now,
yes.' Everything was working for him the way it was supposed to, and
she shivered uncontrollably in the cool of the room.*

'So do I,' I said.

She took a smaller bite of steak and said, 'It's sharp and
enticing.' She smiled, her eyes bright, and said, 'Can I outsmart
the wily one?'

I laughed. 'Probably,' I said. 'Most women seem to be able to.'

She laughed with me. 'Oh, no,' she said, 'I was right – you're
not anyone's boy any more.'

'And how did you know?' I said, curious to see where this
was going.

'Well, you have Alix,' she said. 'I don't think boys have Alix,
do they?' My breath came suddenly short, I hid behind a drink of

315

water, and I realised that I hadn't wanted her to talk about Alix, I had wanted her to consider me alone, and I knew then that I really meant to fuck her, I meant to fuck my father's mistress. She drank some wine. 'Of course,' she said, looking directly at me, 'I had noticed before I knew about Alix.'

And it occurred to me that Sarah wanted to fuck her lover's son. Connie lay between Matt's legs and caressed him, and he groaned with pleasure, and I hated him coolly and wanted him to die. I breathed deep, gratified by the certainty that I would outlive him, and I wanted Sarah and I entertained the thought that she might want me, and my heart beat fast and I looked at her with new interest.

She said, 'She's beautiful, isn't she, Alix?' and she drank some more wine and cut more of the *filet*.

'Yes,' I said, glancing at the soft shadows between her breasts and recalling the time I had seen her fuck my father.

'Is she very beautiful?'

I looked into her eyes, they asked another question, *As beautiful as I am?* and I said, 'Yes' and watched her eyes: they widened slightly, interested in this other beauty. My mother had been in California at her mother's, and he had brought her home late on a Friday night in the middle of the summer. I was fourteen, and he was drunk, as usual past six, and I heard their laughter and left my bed and stepped out on the landing at the head of the stairs and looked down from the shadows to the pit sofa in the living room below and saw he had been fighting again, he had met another son of a bitch in some bar, and he had to de-son-of-a-bitch him, and now he had a nick on his cheek where a small bruise had spread, and I watched him strip her, standing above them in the dark, my heart beating fast and my stomach hollow, afraid that he might catch me looking but fascinated by her slowly revealed flesh. I had never seen a real woman naked before, only pictures, and Sarah was so beautiful to me.

'You deserve someone very beautiful,' she said. She ate the steak.

'Thank you, Sarah,' I said.

She said, 'I want all the beautiful things for you.' She had worn jeans that night, too, and a blue checked blouse, they had been bar-hopping in the District, I guessed, but she never drank as much as he did, I'd never seen her drunk. I'd seen him drunk a lot, and his hands were drunken and clumsy now, skinned and raw across the knuckles from his fighting, her breasts fell free and he took them in his hands and drew her to him and kissed her hard.

She swallowed the steak and drank some wine and said, 'And Alix isn't your only lover. That's another sign you're not a boy.'

I asked her again, 'Are you going to tell Nathaniel this?' careful to call him by his name and not to use the words *my father*. She had not moved to undress him that night, he had taken his cock out of his pants and put it between her breasts and moved it back and forth, groaning, and I leaned forward to see it: it hung down limp from his groin, and he said, 'Touch it, baby', and she took it and stroked it, looking up into his face for some sign of approval and love as it grew hard and big in her hands. I watched it, I recalled him teaching me how to piss standing up when I was a little boy, standing beside him at the toilet and looking up at the huge thing hanging down between his legs, held between his fingers as he aimed the heavy yellow stream into the water. Now it was no bigger than my own grown hard, and his body was soft and pale and white as a fish's belly beside her deep tan, he leaned over her and sighed deeply as she sucked him, but that was not enough, he wanted to fuck her, and watching, I wondered if he had ever fucked her at our house before, it must make him feel particularly strong to have her there. I looked at her across the table and I felt his strength fading, and I felt my own.

'Of course not,' she said and she picked up her fork and took another bite of steak. 'You know that you and I have always had our own relationship. We still do.'

I said, 'Margaret is exciting, in a morbid kind of way.'

Sarah's eyes were alight again, she said, 'I didn't realise you were into things like that.'

I drank some water and said, 'I like dangerous things.'

'I'll remember that,' she said. 'And Margaret is dangerous?'

'She's a dangerous person.'

'What about Alix?'

I started inwardly, and I covered it with another drink of water. I saw her on our bed at home, I saw her fucking Matt. I said, 'Alix is dangerous in a different way.'

'What about me?'

I was suddenly pleased with her, her intelligence and quickness. I said, 'You could be dangerous too.'

'How so?'

'You're my father's mistress.'

'That makes him dangerous,' she said, 'not me.'

317

Can you handle him? she said, and I looked at her, I wondered if he would come after me, and suddenly, inside, I let him come.

She picked up a snail shell with the tongs and probed into it with the escargot fork. She said, 'But Alix knows about Margaret? I know how that feels.'

Is Alix like your mother? she meant.

'She knows there's someone,' I said, 'but she doesn't know who it is.'

She laughed, a small laugh, quiet. She said, 'So how does she feel about your little arrangement?'

'She thinks I've stopped it.'

She ate the snail, and said, 'But you haven't, of course.'

Of course. I flushed hotly.

She laughed again. 'Wiley—' she drew the name out long – 'you're embarrassed.' At last she had taken off her jeans and panties, they were black, I remembered how that had excited me, and she lay across the sofa for him and he had taken her drunkenly and uncaring, the way he took everything, the way, I thought, watching them through the banister uprights, the very way he must have taken my mother the night that I was conceived. And that was when I saw she tanned naked, her body bare for him and warm brown all over with no lines anywhere, her nipples small and hard and pink against the tan. I grew hard beneath my bathrobe as she spoke to him, she said, 'Fuck me now. You're ten times the man he was', and I thrilled to hear her ask for it, *fuck me*, she said, and I took my cock in my hand and began to masturbate for her while he came very quickly, drunk, and then passed out on top of her, and she lay there for a moment and finally said softly, 'Nathaniel?' but he had left her alone, and she sighed tiredly and moved him off her, grunting under his weight, and stood up and looked down at him a moment, shaking her head. She drew a deep breath, and slowly wiped at her eye with her hand and sighed again, and then she began to dress.

'Why are you embarrassed?' she smiled at me over a sip of wine.

She impressed me. I said, 'Shouldn't I be?'

She had seen me that night. She had leaned down to pick up her panties from the floor and I made a small, desperate sound at the sight of her bent from and her big breasts hanging down, I couldn't help myself, and she looked up as I slid back along the floor of the landing and tried to hide in the shadows. I was terrified she would see me, she would be angry and tell the old man when he came to, but I could not look away from her, from her body, and I lay coming and her eyes shone with tears and we saw each other and she wiped her eyes again and looked straight into me, I felt her seeing my insides, naked, we were both naked, and she stood there, looking up at me, and her face changed: her eyes softened and a bittersweet smile stole across her lips and she stepped towards me and stood still and naked and glorious for me to see, and I fell in love with her. I thought she was magnificent, and I came then, flooding the inside of my bathrobe, and she watched me come for her, she nodded slightly, with just the faintest trace of eagerness, and I loved her, and my head fell forward on to the carpet and I closed my eyes and concentrated all my feeling in my cock, coming for her, and I felt her watching me and loving it, and I felt this was what it was all about, giving this part of yourself to a woman, giving your insides away to her.

I crawled back along the floor into the deeper shadows against the wall and I did not watch her any more, but I listened to the sounds of her dressing and fixing herself one last drink and leaving. I lay in my bed later, after she had gone, wondering what she was like, who could make the two of us come, I wondered how many other men there were.

I liked her seeing me desiring her. I sat back from the table and let her see me.

'Two women at once, that makes you interesting,' she said. She stopped eating and looked at me, interested.

I said, 'Is that what interests you about Nathaniel?'

'Of course it is,' she said, leaning towards me. 'And I'm the Other Woman, remember? That makes me more interesting, too, don't you think?'

'Yes, it does,' I said, and she gave me a look of understanding and drank her wine, and I felt my cock like something very fine, I wanted to see her naked again and touch her this time, I wanted to fuck her and I knew that I could and that I would. Alix would never know, it had nothing to do with Alix, it was between me and Nathaniel, who was the better man? I was, I knew it, and I wanted Sarah to know it, too, I wanted to hear her say it.

'We're different,' she said, looking at me. 'We're artists.' Her lips were pleasant, red and wet with wine and smiling.

'Of what?' I said.

'Sensation.' She held up her glass and said, 'Are you sure you can't have even a little of this? It's exquisite.'

319

Her eyes invited me to the wine and more than the wine. I picked up my glass and held it out for her to fill.

'Sweetest,' she said, smiling and pouring, and I smelled the wine and drank it, the alcohol went through me like water through a sandcastle and I held the glass out to her for more. She poured and sat back and said, 'So there's nothing to be ashamed of. That's for other people.' I thought of Matt, I thought of Margaret's tapes playing for him in his empty office.

'You are a weakling,' his words came to her in the darkness. 'But discipline can make you strong. As I am. I am strong in the Lord.'

'Yes,' she said. She said what she thought he wanted to hear.

'Yes, sir,' he corrected.

'Yes, sir,' she said.

'You are the slave of your desires,' he said, 'the slave of your own appetites and flesh.'

'Yes, sir,' she said.

'I am not a slave.'

'No, sir.' She lifted her head, she tried to find his voice in the darkness, his face, and she was lost in the dark and shuddered inwardly at the sound of his absolute certainty.

He said, 'Are you the master of your passion? I am your master.'

'Yes, sir.' She nodded, she knew he was crazy, she knew she had to get out of here.

'A master disciplines,' he said.

She trembled, against her will, afraid, afraid to show her fear, afraid to be afraid, she bowed her head and said, 'Yes.'

'The Master disciplines me,' he said, 'and I shall discipline you.'

'Yes.'

His voice quivered for a moment, his voice filled with theatre, she thought of Cecil B. De Mille movies, talking bushes burning and Charlton Heston. 'I will punish the world for their evil, and the wicked for their iniquity; and I will cause the arrogancy of the proud to cease, and will lay low the haughtiness of the terrible.'

She whispered, 'Yes.'

He calmed, explaining it to her. 'It is a matter of the law. Do you see?'

'I see.'

'The law is of the spirit, and disciplines the carnal.'

'Yes.'

'I shall sow into you discipline. A spiritual thing.'

'Yes, sir.'

320

'Then, I can reap from you the carnal thing.'

'Yes, sir.' What would he reap? How?

'Then, we shall both deserve eternal life.'

She lifted her head. 'I understand,' she said.

'The discipline may seem like punishment,' he said.

'Yes?'

'Sometimes, it will be punishment.'

'Yes, sir.' She tested the pillowcase binding her wrists, it was tight and chafed her skin.

'Punishment benefits the wicked,' he said.

She said meekly, 'I am wicked.'

'Confess and accept the discipline,' he said.

'I want it,' she said.

He talked like a schoolteacher calling for lessons, he said, 'Tell me first about the passions you cannot control.'

She lifted her face, she was afraid of him, physically afraid, he was insane and he was on the radio, wasn't he? he did things to people and he got away with them. She smelled him, smelled his flesh near to hers, and she thought of me, she whispered, 'Wiley.'

He sighed, satisfied with this answer. 'Tell me about Wiley,' he said.

'I love Wiley,' she said. 'I can't help it.'

'You can't help it,' he sneered. He caressed her face with just the tips of his fingers, and she flinched involuntarily, her body was tensed against her will and her stomach fluttered sickeningly, he was hacking her, too.

'He's the best,' she said quickly.

'What makes him the best?'

'He makes me feel the best.'

'Feel?' he said. 'How does he make you feel?'

She bowed her head and hacked him. 'It makes me wet to think about Wiley,' she said softly. 'Do you want to make me wet?'

'Slut,' he said, his voice thick and heavy as he luxuriated in her sexuality. 'You're such a slut.'

She wanted him to free her hands, she lifted her head to him and said, 'Do you want me to touch you, master?'

'He slapped her suddenly and sharply with the back of his hand across the left side of her face. His fingernails stung hard and cut her cheek, and she cried out in hurt and anger and rocked away from him and felt thin lines of blood burning out of the wounds into the open air, and the fear washed over her like cold water, her flesh prickled with it and she shook as he cried 'Ah!' long and satisfied and full of

321

pleasure and fear. 'Touch me!' he dared her. 'Do you think I'd let you touch me?'

She almost ran, but she could not see, she turned her head from side to side in the darkness and she tried to pull her tied hands apart, and then she sat still, and a wet heat filled the room between them, full of blood and fear, and her breath came quick and heavy and her nipples hurt and her neck ached with the tension, and a panicked hatred burgeoned slowly and sweetly in her heart, like a black orchid flooding open, rich in the heat. She caught herself, wanting to run, she bore down inside herself, and she lowered her head and concentrated and she hacked him, she clenched her teeth and shivered once in the air conditioning and tried not to imagine what he might do, and she felt her hatred for him instead and she said, 'No.'

'No,' he said through his teeth.

She bowed her head and a brief wave of vertigo swept over her. The blood trickled slowly down her cheek, it cooled on her skin.

'You must be prepared before you can touch me,' he said, calming, explaining, and he reassured her. 'Don't be afraid—' he put his hand gently to the unhurt side of her face – 'you will touch me.'

She lifted her face to him, her cheek stung and she gathered herself to save herself, she swallowed and stiffened, and then went limp and said softly, 'Prepare me, please.'

She hacked him.

I paid for the dinner with my own money, not her expense account or the American Express card, and Sarah watched me count out the tab and tip, and I felt rich as she watched me. I knew my father would have told her about his card, and I wanted her to know that I could afford her without him, even as I added the change to the money I had left in my cheque account and divided the result by the twelve days till payday.

I drove back to my place. Sarah stumbled going up the back steps, and I caught her and she turned in my arms and went limp. I held her, my forearm crossed her breasts: they were full and soft and excited me, and her body was warm in my hands, and she threw her hands around my neck and pulled herself up, smiling, and said, 'Now I'm drunk, I can take advantage of you', and we both laughed.

We went into the sun room and I lit candles. She stopped me after I had set fire to two of them and she drew my hand to her lips and blew out the burning match. 'Three on a match, that's terrible luck,' she said. 'We need all the luck we can get.' I struck

322

another match and lit two more candles then got a bottle of Perrier from the refrigerator along with two glasses from the cabinet, and we watched the last of the sunset across the big park. 'I walked around the lake out there last weekend.' She nodded at the park out the window, and I stood beside her and said, 'We'll have a fabulous summer.' A horse patrolman slowly crossed the park at a trot, elegant and beautiful with his white helmet crowning his blue-black uniform, and I looked at my watch.

Sarah saw me checking the time. 'Where's Alix?' she said.

I turned to her. 'She's out with a friend tonight.'

'That's good,' she said. 'Will she be late?'

'I don't know.'

'Well, that makes it more interesting.'

'You like it interesting, don't you?'

'Yes.'

'That's something else that makes you dangerous.'

She laughed hard, and the faintest breeze blew through the room and the candle flames flickered slightly. I gave Sarah the rocker, and I sat beside her on the desk chair and tuned in the radio on the bookcase, a blues sang, out, a woman hid in the cold, cold dark, and I smelled her oil of drakar, the old fucking, teasing smell of Anne Mathers, the Nickie smell, and everything everywhere was still and waiting for a moment, waiting for us.

'Tell me,' he said. 'Do you want me to touch you?'

She raised her head eagerly, she said, 'Oh, please.'

He unzipped the front of the shift. The cool air spread across her bosom and belly, and he reached inside, cuddling her left breast, he lifted her chin with his other hand and then squeezed her hard suddenly, and she cried out in the pain, and he said, 'The wicked are weak and tender.'

She said 'Yes', straining to get the word out, and she hoped he would like her begging, she said, 'Please don't hurt me any more.'

He closed his hand into a fist on her breast and she groaned in agony, she closed her eyes and tears came against her will and she hated him as she strained to breathe, she would kill him for this, she would kill him with her weak and tender parts. He said, 'This is a great blessing for you, Connie. You might have continued endlessly in your carnality otherwise. You must thank Jesus', and he squeezed her breat hard, kneading her flesh.

She cried out involuntarily, 'Oh, Christ.'

'Exactly,' he said. 'Say "Thank you, Jesus."'

323

She gasped for air, the pain spread out from her breast through her whole chest and down into her gut. She whispered thinly, 'Thank you, Jesus.'

He released her, she collapsed and breathed deep.

She felt him rise above her. She lifted her head, following him. He said, 'You have come for Jesus.'

She said 'Yes', and a wild fear seized her and she wanted to run.

'You are spared by the hand of a God you can only anger.'

She bowed her head. 'Yes, sir.'

'Such is God's love,' he said, 'that He has delivered you into the hands of a master who can correct your ways and make them acceptable.'

'Please accept me,' she said.

'Not yet,' he said. 'You must surrender, to rid yourself of a wilfulness that offends God.'

'I surrender.'

He stood above her, he said, 'Whatever brings you to Jesus is right for you.' His voice was tight and hard and rising out of control, and she shivered with fear and he cried out, 'Oh', and his voice was gone, he took her other breast in his hand and pinched the nipple, slowly at first and then with increasing pressure, and he said, 'do you see?' and she closed her lips and bit them hard to keep silent, she bit them until she tasted blood and she swallowed it and it ran down a corner of her mouth.

'Whatever,' he said, releasing her breast, and he raised the hem of her shift up off her buttocks, she felt the air across her. 'Jesus,' he said, and he stroked her backside softly. She said tentatively, 'Do you like it?' She hoped he liked it. But he groaned, the sound was of him being torn in two, and he paced away from her, groaning, she followed the sound, and he was moving a lamp: through her blindfold she sensed a haze of light rise and rock from side to side, then die as he pulled the plug from the wall. She heard something tear, and he groaned, and she heard him strike himself, he was whipping himself with the cord from the lamp, and she tensed, afraid, and he groaned and struck his flesh again and again and the sound moved back across the room towards her. He said, 'We must come before Jesus', and he whipped the cord across the bare skin of her buttocks sharp and hard, and she squirmed in a circle on the floor, trying to escape him, and she stung and burned and bled in the darkness as he lashed her again and again, his voice strained and pitched high. 'Do you see? It brings us before Jesus. It is right.'

She lay on the floor and she bled, he began to pace the room around her, she tried to work her hands free but the pillowcase was too tight,

324

it chafed her skin raw around her wrists, and he began to talk about his seed and the grace she needed.

'I have the grace now,' he said, his voice moving around her in the darkness as she turned on the floor trying to follow him. 'I am in a state of grace. The grace that can save you from the punishment you deserve. Do you want it?'

She had to concentrate hard to go on with it. 'Yes,' she said.

He said, 'I have it in my seed. Do you still want it?'

She sat up and turned her head, trying to locate him. He cried out in her face, a sound of frustration and sadness, he cried, 'You make me punish you!' and his hand closed on her breast again and squeezed, and she groaned. He said slowly, 'I asked you a question.'

'I want it,' she breathed.

'You want it, you slut,' he said, 'but do you understand it?' crying once more and drawing her up by the collar of her shift and hitting her with his closed fist, her right eye burned and watered and began to swell shut. He dropped her to the floor and paced away from her, she heard him breathing heavily and moaning, an almost tearful sound, she shook and licked her lips, they were split and her nose was bleeding and her throat was parched. He cried out and struck himself with his whipcord, and he turned back to her and began to talk again. He said, 'You only want the seed in your belly.'

She said nothing.

'Bitch,' he said, and then he said it again, 'bitch', turning the word over and over in his mind like a small boy exciting himself with forbidden words. He said, 'No woman may have my seed in her belly.'

He waited for her to reply, and she sensed him waiting and she said, 'Yes.'

He said quietly, reflecting on his words, 'I am the master. I have the grace you need.'

'Yes.'

'I will give it to you.'

'Thank you.'

'Sit up.'

She pulled herself up on her knees and felt him step near her: he stood before her and took her chin between his fingers and drew her face close to his crotch, she smelled him, and she felt the warmth of his body.

'Take the grace into your mouth,' he said.

She couldn't see anything.

'Your mouth,' he said again.

She opened her mouth and laid her head back, and he put himself into her, and she closed her lips on him, he was limp, and she suffocated, her nostrils full of blood, she opened her mouth wide and drew breath around his organ, and he said, 'Receive the grace', and he was limp and she was supposed to make him hard, she tongued him and sucked and nothing happened. Her face hurt, her dry lips split and she bled around him, and her wrists rubbed against the binding cotton, and her breasts were sore and tender: she could feel the bruises spreading across them, and she sucked hard on his cock but it refused to grow, and she heard him sigh tiredly in the darkness, and he said, 'You are no different from the others. I thought you would be different. You were so different on the phone.'

She ached through her head and body, her arms and wrists, and she held him in her mouth and waited in the dark.

He said, 'You haven't the power I thought you had. How do you expect to receive grace without any power?'

She waited. She shook her head a little from side to side, she was confused and sick to her stomach and cold and naked and bleeding, and he was insane, inside her, and she was too exhausted to hack, she could not think what to do.

She heard metallic sounds, and she knew that he had the gun, and she drew away from him, she shrank with cold and sudden fear creeping up her back to her neck, and she felt the circle of the muzzle round and cold against the side of her head, just above her ear, as he swelled huge in her mouth and said, 'The power.'

She sucked.

He came quickly, a little slick salty stuff spurting into her. She sat back very still and received it as he said, 'Yes, yes', over and over, the mouth of the gun growing warm against her flesh.

He said, 'Swallow my seed', and she flushed hot with hatred and would not, she sat still and waited.

He cocked the gun, the sound was huge in her ear, and he said, 'What happens to women who will not receive grace?'

And she thought of letting him do it. She thought of dying here in the hotel, fast and painless, she thought of dying because she would not eat this used-up old man, she thought of the sound the gun would make and of the police and the ambulance and the ruin of his life, but she thought he would only run away from it deeper into his madness, into his ministry of illusion, where it could not touch him, and so he would not feel any of it, and that would not work. She wanted him to feel it, she wanted him to feel. She swallowed.

He breathed softly, satisfied, and he removed the pillowcase from her eyes. Her right eye was swollen shut, and she sat back and watched him through the other as he stood before her and lifted the gun to his head and placed it against his temple. She stiffened, watching him with clenched teeth, scared and braced for the explosion, and he squeezed the trigger and the gun clicked and nothing happened, and he squeezed it again and again and it clicked emptily over and over, and he smiled slightly and said, 'I am your master.'

She sat back, and her arms, drawn behind her back, ached at the elbows and shoulders, and she looked up at him through her single open eye.

He had hacked her.

He tossed the gun on to the bed and knelt and reached down between her legs and touched the lips of her cunt with the tips of his fingers. 'You're not wet,' he said, and he stood again. He said, 'I have saved you.'

She sank inside herself, she had been beaten, her head fell and she stared down sullenly and beaten into the intricate Persian pattern of the blue carpet that she noticed now for the first time, and she whispered, 'You.'

'Me,' he said.

Sarah looked out the windows at the sun setting among the clouds, purple and orange and red above the black rim of trees across the park, and I looked at the shadows between her breasts and at her face in profile lighted by the candles, and in the light I noticed a few white hairs in all the blonde. I felt the time between us then, ten years she had been sleeping with him, and we would walk through the leaves of Lafayette Park in the autumn and she would talk me into staying in school when I wanted to quit, and we would talk about writing and art, and she had come to see me in the hospital: she sat beside the bed and drew my picture while I read poetry to her, the *Four Quartets*, she watercoloured 'Burnt Norton' and hung it on my wall: *Go, go, go, said the bird: human kind cannot bear very much reality.*

She took her glass of Perrier, got up and crossed the room to my pallet and lay down on it. I sat in the desk chair looking down at her, and she said, 'Is this where you sleep?'

'Yes.'

'When you sleep alone.'

'Touché.'

'Do you ever sleep alone, Wiley?' she said. She undid her hair and shook it out and put her hands through it and lay back on the pallet. Her breasts looked beautiful that way and I gazed down at her as she went on. 'You have all these women. Do you want every woman you see?' She smiled brightly at the idea.

I said, 'Sometimes I think so.'

'I'll bet you're good to women,' she said.

I said, 'Thank you.'

'Good,' she said, 'but not true.'

I drew up and looked away. I felt a hot flush creep across my face, and she laughed softly. 'Come here,' she said, and I looked at her, she moved to one side of the pallet and smoothed a place for me beside her. 'It's all right,' she said. 'I'm good, too, you know. And I can't be true, either.'

She stroked her hand across the empty space beside her. I moved down on to the pallet beside her, I lay on my side facing her, and she leaned back, resting her head on her hand and looking at me with a pleased and pleasing smile.

'You can't stop it, can you,' she said, 'with Margaret?'

I looked at her: she was my father's own Margaret, his toy, his divine thing. I said, 'I don't think so.'

She smiled very slightly to herself, she knew a secret. 'Do you want to?' she said.

'I need to.'

'For Alix.'

'Yes.'

'But do you want to?' She was the other woman, asking about the other woman.

'No,' I said, and I knew that I had just affirmed her place in all our lives.

'I didn't think so,' she said. Her eyes were blue inside soft grey shadows, and at last she said, 'Cheaters are so attractive.'

I looked at her steadily, I felt myself tensed, and I said, 'Yes, they are.'

Her eyes fell. She said, 'Do you think you might be the one to make the cheater stop?'

'I might be right,' I said.

Her eyes came up again. 'That's what Alix thinks, anyway,' she said. 'Is she right?'

I leaned back and looked up through the window above us at the dying sunlight. I said, 'Probably.'

'You love her, don't you?' she said. 'You love Alix.' She rolled a little towards me, her breasts shifted lusciously inside her top. 'I mean,' she said, 'you play with Margaret, but you *love* Alix.'

And I looked at Sarah's eyes and I thought of Alix, of Confusion, Connie, the bitch, all of her. 'She loves me,' I said.

'That's not what I asked,' said Sarah.

I had not wanted it to interfere with us, but now I said it. 'Yes, I love her.'

Her eyes flickered with interest, the same look I had seen there when she had asked if Alix were very beautiful. 'You talk about giving up Margaret *for* her,' she said. 'Men do things *for* the women they love.'

'Yes,' I said.

'But you love me, too, don't you?' she said, and she looked directly into my eyes and smiled ever so slightly, amused by my dilemma.

She sat on the floor, she looked up at him now: a thin line of blood traced diagonally across his chest where he had cut himself with the lamp cord, and somehow she was going to kill him for this beating, he would die by his closed fist and his gun and his whip and his radio, since he could not be fucked any other way. She looked at him and said, 'I love you, and you do this to me.'

He sneered, and she hung her head and said softly, 'Master.' She lifted her face again and looked at him, he was going away into it, half aroused. Her arms ached, her wrists burned against the pillowcase that bound her. She whispered, 'Fuck you.'

He said, 'You wish.'

And she laughed with him, and she told the truth. She sat back and said, 'I'd like to, master, I really would.'

'Whore,' he said.

She said softly, 'Whore.'

'Slut,' he said. His voice was weaker, strained and sounding a little unsure of himself before her unselfconscious sexuality.

'You like sluts, don't you?' she said. 'You like whores.'

'No,' he said, 'I have saved you. You may now receive grace continually.'

She lifted her face to him and made a kiss with her bloody lips, she said, 'Bless me.'

'Blasphemy,' he said tensely, and he slapped her hard, and she rocked to her side, she fell to the floor and lay there a moment, face down, and she said, 'Grace hurts.'

And he sobbed. 'Yes,' he said.

She lifted her face to him. 'It hurts you, too,' she said.

'Yes,' he said. 'Do you understand?'

'I understand,' she said. She lifted herself from the floor. 'It shouldn't.'

He looked down at her helplessly. He said, 'What would you know of it?'

'It should be all right,' she said.

'What is all right?' he said.

'Grace is all right,' she said.

He lashed himself with the cord, hard and suddenly over his shoulder and across his back.

She said, 'Now you can be the master.'

His breath came heavily through his open mouth.

'Be the master,' she said. She leaned towards him, she whispered, 'Make me wet.'

He breathed deeply; his breathing became even longer and heavier.

'Make me wet,' she said.

'Oh!' he cried and closed his eyes tight and struck himself again.

She said, 'Wiley can do it.'

His eyes opened wide on her. He said, 'I am your master.' And he was a slave.

'Wiley goes crazy,' she said. 'It's all right to go crazy.'

'Harlot!' he whispered.

She said, 'Do it.'

'Strumpet!'

She raised her face to him, she said, 'I love you.'

He shrank away from her as from a snake and he held his hands out in fists before him; the lamp cord hung down from his closed right fist. She sat up and said, 'You love to hurt me.'

He shook his head, he cried out, 'It is God's work!' but his voice was full of fear.

She smiled, and a drop of blood fell from her lips on to her breast, and she wondered how she looked to him. She nodded at his limp cock and she said, 'Your God wants you big and hard.'

He looked down at it. He said, 'God wants me to save you!'

'For yourself,' she said.

'But the seed is sacred,' he said.

'Give it to me,' she urged him. 'Give me your grace.'

'I can do anything with God,' he said.

'Wiley can.'

'Sacrilege!'

'Wiley does it the way he wants it,' she said. 'I like that. Do it the way you want it.'

330

And he stopped and looked at her, his face softened, hurt, himself discovered, and tears formed in his eyes.

'Wiley wants what I want,' she said.

He said softly, curious, 'What do you want?'

'What everybody wants,' she said. She shook her hair back out of her face. 'To fuck. To come. To love.'

He looked very tired, very old. He said, 'Everybody.'

She nodded: Yes, everybody. 'What you want,' she said.

He said, 'What I want.'

'It's all right,' she said, 'to want what you want.'

He said softly, he couldn't believe it, 'No.'

'Yes,' she said, soft and insistent, even loving. 'What do you want?'

He said quietly, 'No one knows,' and he looked at her, and he was a boy, and the tears fell from his eyes, but his face was flat and dead and his hands were fists, and she said, 'You can have it', and he drew back from her and he whispered 'Yes' and she breathed deep through her open mouth, relaxing to receive the blow, what he wanted, and he struck her hard, square in her uplifted face, and her lips split open and she bled and his knuckles tore across her bared teeth and he bled with her, their blood ran together down his fingers, she saw it and collapsed backwards, pain shot through her arms to her shoulders and across her back, and she coughed and spit blood and began to pass out, everything in the room cast over with orange and pink, and it all turned black as he loomed above her, naked but for his gun and erect now, reaching down with his bleeding hand to touch her between her legs, and she had hacked him, she had done it, he had AIDS.

'What would you do for *me*?' she said.

Her scent mixed with that of the candles, and I said, 'Just about anything you want, Sarah.'

She rolled on to her stomach and looked at me sideways. 'Would you give up Margaret for me?' she said.

'Yes,' I said quickly.

She smiled, she knew secrets. 'Only because I would take her place,' she said softly. 'What about Alix? Give up Alix for me.' She moved back on to her side and her breasts fell together for me to see and she put her hand alongside my face and drew near to me and filled me with her scent.

I breathed her in, and I put my hand on her side, and she moved even closer, she murmured and lifted her leg and laid it over mine, opening herself to me, and I felt huge, I felt drunk on her smell and her breasts and her willingness. I felt her hand on my belt, tugging gently, and I looked into her face and desire crept across it slowly as she freed the buckle and undid the clasp of my khakis and unzipped me and reached inside, I filled her hand and she whispered quickly, eagerly, 'I just love you, Wiley, I've loved you since you were a boy, since you came for me that night, don't you remember? Don't you love me? tell me that you love me.' She laid her other hand alongside my cheek and kissed me deeply and I kissed her back, my hands held her breasts and pulled her top away and they fell free. I bent and kissed them, her nipples swelled hard into my mouth and I bit her and sucked on her and she cried out tenderly and stroked my hair, she liked it, she sat up and tore the top off over her head and unsnapped her jeans and pulled them open on her black lace panties and lay back down with me, kissing me and taking me again into her hand, she said, 'Love me now, sweetest, you're ten times the man he is.'

And I wanted to fuck her, I wanted her to suck me, I wanted to use her like my own private human woman thing all covered with roundnesses and soft silken warm wet holes in her for my exclusive use, and I knew that she wanted these same kinds of things from me, a young heaviness fitting snug and vital inside her, wanting her and hurting Alix for her, she wanted me to do things *for* her, and I would have, I was ready to, but through it all I could feel him winning, high over me and drunk for ever, despite me, despite everything I had ever wanted. Sarah and I lay there on the pallet hot and moist and swollen with blood, and Nathaniel was right again, the world was made in his dull, shabby, drunken image, or we were, at any rate, or I was, and I was hollow then, neither living nor dead, and I went little in her hand and soft, and she said, 'What's the matter?' and I looked into her eyes, full of sex and water and softness, and I said, 'Did he tell you she has AIDS?'

There was a still beat of about a second between us, and then she slowly moved away from me across the pallet and lay looking at me, her hands outstretched to me before her.

'AIDS,' I said quietly. 'Alix has AIDS.'

Her face looked pale in the candlelight, her eyes bright within the shadows. She said, 'Well, do you have sex with her?'

I said, 'She's better than anybody.'

She stared at me, she whispered, 'Christ.'

'He didn't tell you,' I said.

She said nothing.

'What did he tell you?' I said. 'That Wiley is infatuated

with some woman who'll take advantage of his father's con-
nections?'

She said nothing, she opened her mouth to speak, then closed
it. At last she said again, 'Oh, Christ.' She closed her eyes and laid
her head sadly down. She bit her lower lip.

I got up and adjusted my clothes and crossed the room and sat
down again. I drank some Perrier and looked at the candles burning.
The radio played, I heard it again, electric guitars like silver bells
and voices singing sadly, *I was the one who let you know, I was your
sorry-ever-after*. I reached for my wallet and got out my HIV-free
card and tossed it on to the floor beside the pallet. She picked it
up and read it, holding it up to the candlelight, she covered her
breasts with one hand now, curiously modest before the disease,
and she read the card. She lifted her head to look at me, and her
mouth opened and a tear rolled down her cheek from her left eye,
and she said, 'He's throwing me away.'

I said, 'What?'

'Nathaniel,' she said. 'He's got another girl.'

I looked out the window. The sky was starless above the lights
of the city. I said, quietly, 'Is she younger?'

She sobbed, and her head nodded sadly up and down, her yellow
hair glowing softly in the candlelight. She dropped the card to the
floor, and she hung her head in her hands in the darkness and said
through tears, 'Please. Please, Willie.'

And I felt her loneliness and fear, felt him abandoning her to
me, and the *Constitution* too, the whole package, without Alix,
without AIDS, deathless and unreal, and we had moved together
inside his dream, Sarah and I, and now I wanted to make her OK
and could not, I did not know what would make her all right she
wanted to be fucked, but I knew now that I could not do it, blood
rushed through my heart and to my temples and I knew I needed
to find Alix. I didn't know what to do for Sarah, I said softly, sad,
'I don't know what to do.'

She lifted her head. She said, 'He did it on purpose.'

'What?'

'He set me up for this.' Her voice was flat, her hands rested in
her lap, her breasts were bare but sexless now.

I sighed at him. I said, 'You were supposed to break us up, Alix
and me. Maybe he thought she'd catch us.'

She looked down at the floor, she folded her hands together in
her lap. She said, 'I'm going to get him.'

'How?'

'I've got letters,' she said, defiant and defensive at the same time. 'He's a public figure. I've got letters. I've got some pictures too.'

'Good,' I said. I couldn't tell how serious she was, I couldn't imagine anyone getting him, finally; all you could do was get away from him.

'He can't get away with this,' she said.

'No,' I said.

'He can't.' She looked up at me, questioning.

'He shouldn't,' I said. 'You shouldn't let him.' I sat back in the chair and rocked, once. I said, 'I'll walk you back to the hotel.'

As walked back up the street, she walked beside me and a little away, with her arms crossed before her breasts, hugging herself in the evening chill and looking at me from time to time and saying nothing. In the lobby, at the elevators, she turned to me and said, 'I won't ask you to take me to my room.' She looked drained, she looked lost, she hadn't taken it all in yet, just what he had done to her. Her eyes would flash momentarily, I suppose she was thinking about the letters and the pictures then, and then she would go flat and old, thrown away, she had said, for a younger girl. I took her hand and looked into her eyes and said, 'I wanted you.'

She lifted my hand and looked at it, and I looked at the rings on her fingers and I saw that the stones were real, there was some small thing real about Sarah, still, and I said, 'You're better off without him.' I drew her hand to my lips and kissed her. She squeezed my hand and released it. She looked sad, she looked beat and tired, and I wondered if she felt beaten, and by what, exactly, or if she could feel free, the way I did. She turned silently and caught the elevator. I watched the numbers light up above the doors as the car rose, and I thought about room 1503, and I wanted Alix to know that I had at last been true to her, and the desire made me smile. I turned away from the shining chrome doors of the elevators and left the long hotel.

Walking back towards the park, the air was cool around me and full of the sharp smells of the city streets, asphalt and the clear scent of water from a street sweeper heading up towards the corner of Peachtree, and I felt old at last in a luminous city and the night was dark, and I stopped on the sidewalk and looked up at the irregular pattern of lighted windows in the big hotel. I wondered which one was room 1503, and I felt sad, and suddenly I missed Sarah, I still wanted her, with a kind of nostalgia for my corrupt desire, I wanted to see her big breasts held out for me in her ringed fingers and my hands taking away her black panties and then myself inside her, I wanted to see her face when I was inside her, and I felt doomed, then, doomed to be Wiley flying high in terrifying freedom in the wide open sunlight and air above the clouds, and I felt something different for the first time in my life.

I felt Nathaniel Jones was gone.

I stood still and looked up at the sky. I could see just a few of the brightest stars through the haze of the streetlights, and I shivered in the cool and put my hands in my pockets and was lonely and thought of Alix and wanted her, wanted to see her and talk with her, and I wasn't so lonely then, with that desire, it felt good to want her, and I walked on down the street to the corner.

Chapter 64

She had stitches in her lips, and they sealed the wounds on her cheek and buttocks with something like butterfly closures, the red-stained wings spread out from the lines of the lacerations like the petals of a flower blossoming across her flesh. She said to Carl, 'Can you fix this with plastic?' and she pointed to her mouth.

'A surgeon can,' he said.

I had called him, and he surprised me. He had come down to the emergency room at Piedmont, and I supposed to myself that maybe AIDS doctors were different. The nurse in charge wanted to call the police, but Alix insisted she had fallen down a flight of utility stairs at the hotel and that no one else was involved. The security cop on duty in the parking lot helped me bring her inside and stood by and said, 'Somebody did this to you, lady. You'd be better off if you told who', but she had only said, 'No, I did this to myself.' She had tried to smile at the cop through her torn lips while I filled out the paperwork at the admissions desk, and a nurse called to her from behind us. 'It's what I get for going where I don't belong,' she said. It was some social engineering. She was hacking, I realised, she was covering Connie Phone's trail through a haze of shock and fear and anger.

The nurse held a blood-pressure cuff and waved it at Alix, gesturing for her to join her, and she left me. The admissions clerk asked me how I was going to pay. In the car, coming down, Alix had said not to use her insurance. 'I'm not ready for them to know about the AIDS yet,' she said, and now I had $12 in the bank and about $6 between my wallet and change, and I sat there stunned by the question and couldn't think for a moment and, in a flash of feeling bursting through the numbness, I hated fucking with money. I looked up at the clerk's face: she was in her fifties, with hard grey hair and clear plastic horn-rimmed glasses that had yellowed with time. I said, 'Do you take American Express?'

Chapter 65

It was hard to listen to Matt during the Monday morning meeting, knowing what I knew and thinking about Alix. He welcomed me back to work, and announced that Grant Cummings was in isolation at Piedmont Hospital. Margaret sat next to me. She had come back to work in the middle of the week before, and during the meeting, while Simon English explained that the sociological content of rap music was identical to that of blues singing of the 1940s, as part of a presentation on modern American black culture, just to bug Matt and Patricia, she rubbed her calf against mine under the table. I looked at her casually and she returned the glance. I could tell she wanted to see me, and I wanted to see her, too.

So as the meeting broke up, I said to her, 'Coffee?' and she said, 'In my office.' I met her there, carrying two black coffees and, in my shirt pocket, a single tape of Connie Phone talking with Matt. She closed the door behind me and I crossed the room to her desk and set the coffees down, and she was right behind me. She caressed my buttocks and put her arms around me and buried her face in the back of my neck and kissed me repeatedly and reached down between my legs and petted my swelling cock.

She said, 'I've really missed you, Daddy.'

'I've missed you too,' I said, truthfully.

'But you are good on the phone,' she smiled.

'I had a good teacher.'

'Connie?'

'That's right.'

She squeezed my cock gently and said, 'Can we go to lunch today?'

'We'll see.'

She released me and said, 'What's the matter?'

I tapped my shirt pocket. 'I've got something for you to listen to,' I said.

Her eyebrows rose. 'Connie and Matt?'

'Yes.'

She pointed to a tape deck on a side table, and I crossed to it, loaded it and set it running. She sat down before her desk, and I handed her her cup of coffee and sat with her while the two of them talked softly, telephone voices disembodied through the little speaker on the deck.

I like to masturbate men, said Connie. *I like to see the jism come out.*

Matt said, *I need you to tell me all about that for the Ministry to work.*

'She's good,' Margaret said when it ended. She smiled, the same way she had when she first learned about Matt and Connie, a bitch's smile, holding a pair of balls in her hand. 'This is exactly what I needed.'

'There's more,' I said. 'He's been talking to her a lot, up until the last couple of days.'

'When do I get it?' she said.

I got up and retrieved the tape from the deck. I put it back in my pocket and sat down again. I said to her, 'Let's talk about Alix.'

She fell silent, suspecting something, and I wondered if she were at all jealous. 'All right,' she said at last.

I said, 'I want Alix to be the chief information officer of Divine Intelligence.'

'You don't ask much, do you?' she smiled a little, manoeuvring.

'CIO and a cut of the profits, shares in the company,' I said. 'For her contribution to the enterprise, which, I'm sure you'll agree, is substantial and essential.'

'How much of a share?' she said, and I watched her calculating.

'Fifty per cent.'

'What?'

'Fifty per cent, or no Finder and I'll queer the deal with Connie Phone.'

She paused, looking at me steadily and thinking. 'You son of a bitch,' she said at last, flatly. 'You motherfucker.'

'Margaret,' I said, 'I'd do the same for you, if I were in love with you.'

'*If* you were in love with me?' she said. She laughed, and the laugh had real bitterness in it.

I went ahead, I said, 'Is Divine Intelligence incorporated yet?'

'Of course,' she said. 'Everything's been ready for months.'

'Not everything,' I said. 'The company still needs a CIO. Have your attorney draw up the contract and Fedex it to us.' And I said *us* on purpose, I wanted suddenly to fuck with her head, I wanted to keep her off balance.

'You'll do this, won't you?' she said, a slight, dawning astonishment in her voice. 'You'll really do this.'

338

'Really.'

'What if I tell Alix about us?'

'Tell her,' I said, and I was breaking inside, I despaired of what to say or do, I didn't know if this would work or what I would do if Margaret should actually tell Alix. 'Everything's ruined anyway.'

'What?' she said, alarmed. 'What do you mean?'

'Alix is sick now, Margaret, Alix is dying.' And then she was dying, she was really dying, she would be alone, and I would be alone as well, the two of us alone and apart, and tears swelled into my eyes and I tried to blink them back but they broke free and traced their way down my face and my throat closed for a moment and I opened my mouth wide and drew a deep, desperate breath, and then I plunged ahead, I said, 'She has bills, you know? Dying doctor bills, do you get it?' and I was breathless and mad, I wanted to take Margaret and shake her little world of tapes and data bases.

She was silent a moment, watching me. I wiped my eyes. She spoke softly, 'I get it,' she said.

'So you go ahead and tell her,' I said. I sat back in the chair, tired and relieved at the same time. 'You tell her anything you want to. See? It's all different when she's dying.'

There was another pause, as she thought about something, I couldn't guess what, I didn't care any more, and then she said, 'What about us?'

I sighed, tired. I looked at my watch, it was tediously early yet and I wanted the day to be over. 'What about us?' I said.

She said, 'Will you still see me?'

I looked at her, then. I had got her, I had hacked her, she was in love, she had called it love, and now I did not want it. I took a deep breath. I said, 'Do you want me to?'

'Of course,' she said immediately.

I shook my head, tired. I said, 'I can't cheat on Alix any more. I can't do that to her while she dies.'

'What about after?' she said.

I rested my head in my hands, covering my face, I said, 'I don't want to think about after.'

'You'll need someone,' she said. 'I'll be there for you. I will.'

And I looked at her. She looked back at me, she looked earnest and sexual, this was Margaret in love, and I wondered if I could ever escape her. I wondered how Jim Neill had done it.

Chapter 66

Margaret came into my office that afternoon, just before I had to leave for the radio show. She looked out into the production offices, then closed the door and sat across from me. She said, 'I think we may have a problem.'

'What's the matter now?' I said.

'I just heard Stan talking to one of the other programmers.'

'And?'

'And he's taking part of Finder home with him tonight, to work on some piece of code or something. Something he doesn't have time to work on here at the office.'

'So?' I said. 'Stan works at home. All the programmers are crazy.'

'But won't he find out it's screwed up when he tries to read it on his own machine?'

I realised she was right. He wouldn't have the decryption program on his home machine. I thought about it while my stomach growled, empty and angry, I had missed lunch. 'We're screwed,' I said, and I didn't know what we could do about it.

'Yes,' she said.

'I'll call Alix.'

'She'll think of something.'

I picked up the phone and dialled Alix at her office. I had wanted her to stay home and heal after the beating, but she had spent two weeks there with the TB and so she had gone to work instead. But now she was in a meeting.

'Shit,' said Margaret.

I left a message for her to call me, and I hung up. I wanted a cigarette, and I wondered if I could find any in Grant's desk.

'She's smart,' Margaret said. 'She's clever. She'll know what to do.'

'Don't worry,' I said.

'I've got to have that data base.'

'You'll get it.'

She sat and looked at me. 'You'll get what you need,' I said.

Chapter 67

Alix logged on to the office system as Matt. She said she had to get to the files on Stan's machine, and I couldn't figure out how she could do it. I said, 'You're logged on to the server, aren't you?'

'Yes,' she said.

'So how can you get to one of the nodes of the network?'

'They've got an old piece of software on the server that Stan installed a couple of years ago,' she said. 'It checks software usage on all the nodes, and can limit use to licensed copies only.'

'Matt has something like that?'

She laughed. 'He doesn't use it. But Stan put it on there and never took it off.'

'What's it do?'

'You load it, and it runs the network peer-to-peer.'

'What the hell does that mean?'

'That means every station acts as a server, and I can access the local drives.'

'And get to Stan's.'

'Right.'

She loaded the program, and gave it a series of commands I couldn't understand. Then she was reading a directory. 'This is Stan's drive,' she said.

'What are you going to do?' I asked.

'I've got to find a couple of files,' she said. 'The program he wrote to extract the data sample from Finder, and the data sample itself.'

'How can you do that?'

'By looking at the dates of the files,' she said, and she entered

```
dir | sort /+25 > file.lst
```

'What'll that do?' I said.

'That'll display the files sorted by date,' she said, 'and save the listing to a file called FILE.LST.'

After she captured the file listing, she entered

```
type file.lst | more
```

and the file was displayed twenty-four lines at a time. She went through more than a dozen directories, reading them, creating her FILE.LST, checking it, then deleting it and changing directories and starting the process over again. I wanted a cigarette badly, I said, 'Do you have any dope?' I didn't want to get high, I just wanted something to smoke.

'It's not good for your TB,' she said. 'Look!' and she pointed at the screen. 'There!'

I followed her pointing finger into the listing on the screen and saw five files with today's date. I said, 'Is that them?'

'That's them,' she said, and she hit the Print Screen key and in a moment a page hummed out of her printer.

'Now what do you do?' I said.

'Now I look at his code, to see what records he pulled from the data base, and then I write a routine to pull the same records into the same file, decrypted.'

'What good will that do?' I said. 'Stan's at home right now, with the fucked-up files.'

She nodded. 'But why are they fucked up?'

'We fucked them up,' I said. 'You did.'

'No,' she said. 'There's something wrong with Stan's floppy disk drive.'

'There is?'

'It writes bad copies of files.'

'It does?' I said. 'How do you know?'

'Because tomorrow, when Stan comes into work and checks out his sample file, he's going to find nothing wrong with it.'

I followed her, and I smiled. 'Because you'll have created a good one.'

'Right,' she said. 'So something must be wrong with his hard-ware.'

'But what if he finds out there's nothing wrong with it?'

She shrugged. 'I bet he won't find it out in time,' she said. 'We've only got to stall him through tomorrow night. That's when he makes the final backup on the encrypted copy of Finder. Then we're home. We pull the decryption module.'

'What about the date and time on the sample file?' I said, pointing at her printout. 'Won't it be different?'

'I'll touch it.'

'What do you mean?'

'Touch is a program that changes files without really changing them. It just resets their date and time. I'll set the time to that of the original file here—' she pointed at the sample file on the printout –' then touch the new file so it'll have the same attribute. Then I'll reset the time correctly. Then we log back on to the server, unload the peer-to-peer program, and log out.'

'Then what?'

She looked up at me and smiled. 'Then I fuck you,' she said. 'To celebrate my genius.'

Chapter 68

I went by the systems office early and found Stan frowning at his terminal and tinkering with his A: drive, locking it and unlocking it, popping a disk in and out of it. He said softly, to himself, 'This is really fucked.'

'Problem?' I said.

He looked up at me. 'Oh, hi, Wiley,' he said, and he gestured at the drive. 'I just replaced this disk drive in May, and the new one here is apparently defective.'

I smiled slightly. I had my hands in my pockets. 'How can you tell?' I said.

Chapter 69

Alix got up early with me on Wednesday morning and removed the decryption program from the Brackett Data computers. Then she rebooted the server. The screen of the communications program seemed to change subtly: you could tell things had died at the other end, even though the user menu was still displayed. Then the words **NO CARRIER** appeared at the bottom of the menu. She sat back at her computer and sipped a cup of black coffee. She said, 'He's fucked.'

'We did it?' I said, standing behind her in my robe with a cup of coffee. 'We really did it?'

She smiled and said, 'Really, honey.' She leaned back in her chair and I bent over her shoulder and kissed her.

She gave me the Finder tapes for Margaret, and I put them in my briefcase along with the recordings of Matt and Connie Phone. Then she gave me a sealed manila envelope and said, 'Give this to Margaret, too.'

I took it from her and held it in my hands. 'What is it?' I said.

'It's something from Connie to Margaret,' she said. 'It's personal.'

'It's a tape,' I said, feeling it.

'It's a tape and it's a letter.'

'A letter?'

'A thank-you letter.'

'What's Connie thanking Margaret for?'

She smiled. 'For all the things she's taught me about being firm.'

I shrugged and tossed it into the briefcase with the others.

She said, 'Are you going to write now?'

'I don't know,' I said.

She said, 'You haven't been very hot in the mornings lately, like you were when we were quarantined. What are you writing?'

'I'm finishing it,' I said.

'What's that like?'

'I don't think I want to finish it.'

'You like writing it.'

'I'm comfortable with it.'

'You'll be comfortable with something else later.' She drank the coffee and poured another cup. She wiped her mouth carefully after she dran, she dribbled a little where the stitches crossed her lips. 'How are you going to sell it?'

'I thought I'd call my father's agent.'

'Yes?'

'Yes. She's good. She'll tell me what to do with it.'

'She's honest?'

'Yes.'

'Then why is she your father's agent?' She smiled.

I smiled back at her. 'Because she has big tits and only charges 10 per cent,' I said.

Chapter 70

They had received the first calls about Finder before anyone got to the office, and everyone was crowded into the systems office to see the ruin. Matt was trying to run things, but he didn't know enough about his own system to do it. I stood in the doorway and watched, I thought it was too bad Grant was in the hospital and had to miss all this excellent chaos. Stan sat at his terminal, patient and methodical, a system man, scrolling through a display of what I assumed were data base records, saying again and again, 'This has all been encrypted.'

'Encrypted?' said Matt, leaning over Stan's shoulder and staring without understanding into the display. 'What do you mean, *encrypted*?'

'Somebody's encoded the data,' he explained, as if he were explaining a technical term.

'I know what it means,' said Matt. 'How the hell could they do it?'

'I don't know,' said Stan. 'They'd need access to the system for an extended period of time.'

'What about the backups?' said Matt.

'We're restoring them now,' said Stan.

I went to my office and dialled up Margaret. 'It's happened,' I said.

She laughed a long time, she enjoyed it as much as sex, I could hear it in her voice.

'I've got some tapes for you,' I said. 'Do you want to come get them?'

She came back to my office carrying a banker's box full of hard copy and disks for the first issue of the members' magazine. I put all the tapes in it, and she put the lid back on it and set it on the floor. She sat down in the chair across from me and said, 'I want to go to lunch.' She had on a purple dress, cut snugly to show her figure, and a small white rosebud; she smelled of roses and Vermilion Obsession.

I looked at her, and she looked good to me, and I handed her the manila envelope and said, 'This is something personal, from Connie Phone.'

She took it, looked at it a moment, and tore it open. The tape fell out into her lap, and she reached inside and got a piece of paper

347

with one line written across it. She held it up and read it, and I wondered what it was. I watched her eyes moving over the paper, and they changed from sexy, confident Margaret Divine eyes to disturbed, then alarmed, then angered ones. She put the paper down and looked at me and said, 'Did you know about this?'

I said, 'I haven't seen it, Margaret. What is it?'

She tossed the paper on to my desk and I picked it up and read

screw my Wiley again and you're sunk, bitch

Connie was scrawled across the bottom of the page in huge, round, happy, blue cursive.

Margaret held up the tape. 'What's on this?' she said.

I looked at her and shook my head. I took it from her, slipped it into my tape deck and played it back. Margaret and Connie and I talked about taping Matt to blackmail him.

She sat stiffly, and she looked magnificent, being beaten, and she said, 'Turn it off.'

I turned it off.

She said, 'Fuck her. Little cunt.' I could hear the hurt in her voice. She said again, 'Fuck her. I want to go to lunch anyway.'

'We can't, Margaret,' I said.

'Why can't we?'

'She'll know.'

'How will she know?'

I sat back in my chair. 'I'll tell her,' I said.

Margaret looked at me, her mouth twisted, she was hurt even more and trying not to cry. She said softly, pleading, 'I love you.'

I shook my head at her, at the two of us. I said, 'We love things and use people. Both of us. It's supposed to be the other way around.'

She twined her hands together in her lap. She said, 'It's not fair.' She sobbed, she hid her face in her hands and I watched her cry and I thought of Sarah, and I wanted to go to her and I did not, I sat still and did not touch her. I did not touch anything. I looked at the paper with Connie's words on it, and I thought of Confusion, and I wondered when and how she had put it together. Probably during those morning phone calls when we were quarantined, I thought, and I shrugged then, it did not matter, it was some piece of social engineering, and I was glad of it. She had saved me from myself, for herself, and there was only a little ways left to go now, anyway.

Chapter 71

After lunch, I wrote a letter of resignation and put it in Patricia Patterson's in-box, and then went back to my office and started cleaning things out. There wasn't much to do, but I removed Carbon Copy from my system, wiping the directory clean and removing it, so no one could put that together with my novel. I stepped over to the systems office and looked in. I rather wanted to say goodbye to Stan, but they were all too busy working on the Finder disaster. Patricia Patterson stood in the centre of the room with her back to the door and said, 'Can't we try to figure out the encryption algorithm?' Stan looked at her with a pained expression on his face, and I left them alone with her.

I went back into my office and sat at my terminal and thought about everything I'd learned at Brackett Data. It was just one thing, and I decided to let them know it, to let them know I had learned it. I sat up and started the word processor, centred the text on the page and on the line, selected a sans serif, 12-point font, and I wrote
Ronald Reagan didn't care.
I sent it to the printer then got my coat and carried the page to Nickie's desk. She was going through the mail, reading it and tossing it into the trash a piece at a time. She looked up at me with a smile, and she said, 'How many hours do you think we'll be in business without Finder?'

I smiled back at her, I said, 'I'm leaving early today,' and handed her the paper. 'See that Matt gets this, and knows who it's from.'

She read it, still smiling slightly, and she looked at me quizzically. She leaned forward a little and said softly, 'Are you quitting?'

I said, 'You're the wily one.'

She laughed. She said, 'Will you call me?'

'Sure,' I said, and I left the office.

Chapter 72

I sat in the control room and watched Matt try to do his show. Stan had called about the Finder backups, they were all bad, business was bad, the day was bad. It was a black day for Brackett Data, the company had been bracketted, and Matt had to be right now, he had to be on top of everything and have all the answers for the radio, when everything was coming undone.

So he talked about gay people. He refused to call them *gay*, they were all *homosexuals*. 'Diversity?' he asked. 'Perversity,' he answered, and he talked a lot about 'special' rights.

He was mad, and he let it all go, and he got calls from all the mad losers in radioland who had ever been bested at anything in their lives, and for a while it looked like he was going to be all right. He would recover if he could just blame someone enough for something.

Then he got a call from Connie Phone.

'Hey,' she said, smiling.

'Hi, there, Connie,' he said.

'I think you're kind of hard on these gay people,' she said.

'You mean, the homosexuals?'

'You know who I mean,' she said.

'They carry a plague, you know,' he said.

'Oh,' she said, 'you talk like people get AIDS because they're bad.'

'Don't they?' he said. 'How do you get AIDS, Connie?'

She said, 'I think people get AIDS because they're weak.'

He laughed at her.

'That's what I think,' she insisted.

'Some weakness is inexcusable,' he said.

She said, 'But we're all weak, some way or another, don't you think?'

'Any "weakness" that exposes other people to harm should not be tolerated in this society. We're way past old liberal ideas like that. That's why testing should be compulsory.'

'AIDS testing?'

'Of course.'

'Have you been tested?'

'I don't need it,' he said. 'I'm not in a risk group.'

'Oh.'

'But all people who are in risk groups should be tested every three months.'

'And that's gay people?'

'Homosexuals,' he said. 'And IV drug users and medical care providers and the homeless.'

'You test the weak,' she said.

He laughed. 'I knew you'd get some of your liberalism in, Connie. You're sharp, I'll give you that much.'

'Hey, guess what,' she said suddenly.

'What's that?' he smiled.

'I finally met that minister fellow I've told you about.'

'Did you now?' I sat forward, looking at him closely, but he wasn't afraid, he was mad, he was coolly insane with righteous anger and hurt pride, and he wanted to hear from a saved woman.

'Yeah. In person,' she said.

'What's he like?' he said.

'He's wild.'

'Why don't you tell us about it?'

'Hey, he got physical,' she said. 'I mean, he got real physical.'

'Did you like it?' he said. He smiled like a shark. He leaned forward over the console, and his eyes were alight, he thought she had liked it, and he wanted to hear her say so, he wanted to hear about her weakness.

She paused. 'I thought I did,' she said, 'but now I'm not so sure.'

'Well, do you want talk about it?' he said, he wanted to know about it.

'Well,' she said, 'I'd like some help finding this minister guy again.'

'So you want some more,' he said. He sat back, pleased.

'I want to find him again,' she said. 'I need to.'

'You want me to help you?'

'Would you?'

'Hey, I'd do anything for you, Connie.'

'Well, I need to find him,' she said.

'Do you now? Do you have a need? Is that like a weakness?' He was smiling hugely now, the radio would save him.

'Well, yeah,' she said, 'because, see, I'm HIV positive now.'

Matt said nothing. He looked at the console and I watched him. I looked at the smooth, thin brown lines of the holster straps cutting around the shoulders of his clean white shirt, I looked at the blue

351

gun metal and the red striped tie and the sudden bloodlessness of his face beneath his golfer's tan.

She said, 'Since I met with him. See?'

He said nothing. He looked at his hands flat on the console before him.

She said softly, 'Are you there, Matt?'

'Yes,' he said, and his head snapped up at the clock and down again to the console as he remembered he was on the radio.

'Yeah,' she said. 'We made a mistake. We exchanged bodily fluids. And now I've got it. I've got AIDS.'

He said, slowly, softly, 'Are you sure?' It sounded like a prayer.

'I'm weak,' she said simply. There were no tones in her voice, no edges to it, no hidden meanings. Everything was open now, you could see everything. 'He said so, that minister did.'

Matt swallowed once. His right hand closed in a fist, then opened again and lay still.

'I'm just weak,' she said, 'that's all.'

Chapter 73

He found the apartment that evening. Alix met him at the back door, and I heard his voice, sitting in the living room, as he forced his way inside. I walked into the kitchen and saw him standing in the open doorway with his gun in his hand and sweat pouring down his face, and I went dreamy on him, I knew we were going to be killed, and it was all a sudden dream. I stood behind Alix and a little beside her, and she stood before him with her hands resting casually on her hips, and he said, 'You did it on purpose.'

We said nothing. The air was still and hot and humid.

He looked over her shoulder at me, he said, 'What about you? Are you infected too?'

I hated him, and I refused to help him, I wouldn't tell him anything. I said, 'What do you think?' I would let his own thinking take him wherever it would.

He cried out, something between laughter and a sob. He said, 'I'm going to kill you both.'

Alix's hands moved to her sides. She said, 'Sure. Do us a favour.'

And he stopped, and he looked into her face. I wanted to see her face, I could see it in my mind, firm jaw and strong green eyes shining and lips set in a thin red line, unafraid of Matt and his quick and ordinary death, and I saw his face as the realisation of his powerlessness crept across his soul, and I saw then that he had a soul, at last, and that maybe he could attend to it now, now that we had given it back to him.

The gun was very small in his hand, and he folded up like a paper cup and began to cry, and we let him.

Chapter 74

She sat in the corner of the sofa and said, 'Did you give Margaret Divine Connie's envelope?'

I sat at her computer, playing Doom. I let a demon kill me and I quit the game and turned to her. She wore her red bikini, and I was in my cutoffs. The sun was still up, the sky was a deep royal blue and many reds, like one of Margaret's colour schemes, and the streetlights had come on, clear white stars floating in the air, and the light had that special evening quality for me. 'Yes,' I said to her.

She said, 'Did she read it?'

'She read it.'

'Did you read it?'

'I read it, too,' I said.

'Then you must have listened to the tape.'

'We heard enough of it to get the message.'

She sighed, and she put her hands together in her lap, between her crossed legs, and she shrugged. She reached up and undid her hair and shook it out around her shoulders. She said, 'You can go to her if that's what you want.'

I said, 'I want you.'

She looked up at me. She smiled ever so slightly; her lips were torn by the stitches. She said, 'I'm not going away any time soon.'

'You're going to be around a long time,' I said.

'It'll get bad,' she said.

'It'll be hard,' I said. And I shook my head at myself. I said, 'It'll be love.'

She looked at me steadily. She said, 'You really don't want her?'

I said again, 'I want you.'

'You'll be Confused,' she said.

I laughed. 'I like being Confused.'

She smiled, and I liked making her smile. She said, 'Fuck her again and I'll kill you.'

'That's no idle threat, is it?' I said.

'Ask Matt Brackett.' Her chin was up, her face was traced with defiance.

'I don't have to,' I said.

'You know –' she sat back against the arm of the sofa, she stretched her body out long and said – 'you're going to miss me when I'm gone.'

I got up and crossed the room and stroked her cheek, and her hand rose and touched mine. The two of us were in the evening light together, and I leaned down and kissed her, and she kissed me back. I said, 'Life goes on.'